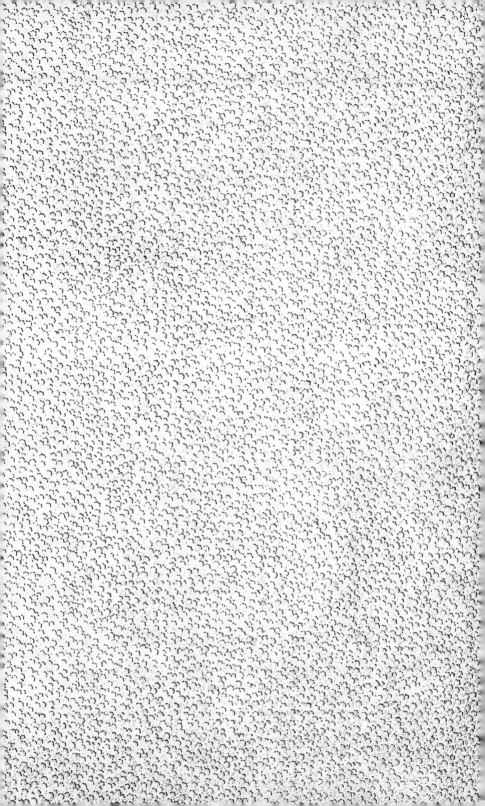

THE
VIPER TREE

Joseph Monninger

SIMON AND SCHUSTER

New York London Toronto Sydney

Tokyo Singapore

SIMON AND SCHUSTER
Simon & Schuster Building
Rockefeller Center
1230 Avenue of the Americas
New York, New York 10020

SIMON AND SCHUSTER and colophon are registered
trademarks of Simon & Schuster

Designed by Laurie Jewell
Manufactured in the United States of America

1   3   5   7   9   10   8   6   4   2

Library of Congress Cataloging-in-Publication Data
Monninger, Joseph.
The viper tree / Joseph Monninger
p.   cm.
I. Title.
PS3563.0526V56   1991
813'.54—dc20   90-10182
CIP
ISBN 0-671-70085-5

To
Bob Harvey
and
Tom Polman

My gratitude to the
National Endowment for the Arts,
whose generous support
helped me with this novel

This is the sorrowful story
  Told as the twilight fails
And the monkeys walk together
  Holding their neighbors' tails.

—RUDYARD KIPLING
The Legends of Evil

THE
VIPER
TREE

January 1991
Ouagodougou, Burkina Faso

Holy Father,

    I write to inform Your Excellency of the results of my investigation into the merits for possible Beatification of Frederich Loebus.

    You will find enclosed three documents. The first is a record of Loebus's arrival to this continent, preserved by Mother Superior Marie DuChamp. The account was pieced together from parts of a journal she found among his effects. Regrettably, she destroyed the original document. As a result—though I didn't tell her this—she severely undermined the admissibility of this record.

    Her own account is also included. Since it has a bearing on her petition for the Beatification of Frederich Loebus, I should say I found the Mother Superior to be not at all senile. She is approximately seventy years old and has worked the last fifty years in West Africa. The Beatification of Frederich Loebus has become an *idée fixe* with her. She assured me she encased the body in cement—this would be roughly twenty years ago—so that we might exhume the body and see if it has degenerated. When I declined to issue the order to have it exhumed, she was incensed. I don't doubt her conviction; I only feel she has been too close to this particular situation for too long, and now lacks perspective.

    The final account, told to me by a young American named Hawley, is a curious one. I recorded his story on tape, edited it to give it continuity, then had it transcribed. Hawley himself is hardly reliable. He is one of those expatriated Americans who seems frightened to go home. It's possible he's an alcoholic; certainly he talked willingly as long as I bought drinks for him. The

Mother Superior as much as told me she despises him; however, she was anxious to add his testimony to her petition.

I make no judgment on any of this, Holy Father. I will remain in Ouagadougou until you advise me what to do next.

Finally, and because you requested it, I should point out that the political climate of this country is doubtful at best. The population is fiercely nationalistic; the Church is under scrutiny. Archbishop Boniface, a man raised in a small nearby village, has talked to me at length concerning the Church's position in this region. Although he did not try to sway me or influence my investigation, he did suggest that this was not a particularly politic time to raise the prospect of a white saint when so little has been done to mark African participation in the Church. I report his words as he spoke them.

I will inform Mother Superior DuChamp of your findings regarding this matter. I doubt she will cease petitioning you regardless of your final decision. She is convinced she once knew a holy man named Frederich Loebus; she calls him, at every turn, a possible saint.

As always, I am

Your Humble Servant,
Father John A. Nodrah, S.J.

THE GOAT

1941

THE *MEDUSA* LEFT MARSEILLES on the full tide shortly after midnight. It was a disgusting vessel. It stank of rancid food and oil. Everything about the ship was in a state of disrepair and, had my circumstances been different, I wouldn't have considered boarding it.

But, in truth, I saw little of the ship. Shortly after I concluded my arrangements with Terboven—a man who purchased passage for German soldiers from that French port—I was ushered into one of the lower holds, not gently, by a gruff seaman of Portuguese extraction. He didn't attempt to hide the hate he felt for me as an escaping soldier of the German army.

My impression of the ship as we went down through its bowels didn't improve. The smell of oil increased. Combined with it was the stench of human bodies and, even more pronounced, the odor of urine. The walls on either side of me were damp. Each passage produced its own sweat and in many places rags had been left scattered on the deck to collect the drips and drainage of a thousand fissures.

I followed the Portuguese seaman as well as I could, but it didn't placate him. He swore at me. He cursed me. He waved his arm emphatically, as if to tell me he had no time to spare. Several times, when he ducked under some new hideous bulkhead, his body blocking the dim light thrown from the lantern he held, I came near to punching him in the back. It would have been a pleasure, though I was aware I could afford nothing of the kind.

At last we came to a large pile of rope and sail canvas lodged midway through a passage. The seaman stopped and spoke to me in Portuguese. I didn't understand him. I shrugged my shoulders and raised my eyebrows in the idiocy of such situations, to which he muttered a loud curse and began tearing at the ropes.

I understood and helped him as much as I could, but I had begun to feel seasick and the heat and exertion only compounded it. He waited for me, however, to lift the last shank of canvas free and I collected myself sufficiently to help him. The canvas sagged in the center and we were forced to drag it awkwardly to one side, the Portuguese cursing me the entire time.

We had uncovered a door. I didn't see it at first so tightly was it fitted into the bulkhead. Narrow, rounded, with a small circular valve control at its lowest border, it appeared to open directly into the sea. The seaman twisted the valve and the door swung open.

The chamber—I couldn't see inside it—smelled of sawdust and ammonia and vomit. I was reluctant to enter, and, I confess, had the absurd notion that some misunderstanding had occurred. Terboven had assured me the accommodations, while not luxurious by any means, would be adequate.

I was a fool, of course. Terboven had my money. Yet ridiculously I held onto the idea of fair value, fair exchange. I pointed to the door of the chamber and wagged my finger "no." Then, in gross pantomime, I enacted a charade of withdrawing my wallet, paying a phantom Terboven, and ended by pointing to the door once more and wagging "no." I raised my finger and pointed to the decks above me, then pretended to put my head on a pillow. I would sleep up there, I motioned.

The Portuguese laughed. He nodded and pointed up with me, then switched fingers and waved his middle finger at me.

"Fuck you, too," I said in German. "Take me upstairs where I belong."

I was answered not by the seaman, but by a voice replying in perfect German from the dark chamber.

"They'll throw you overboard, you ass," the voice said. "Do you think they give a damn about you? Get in here while they'll still permit it."

I was stunned by the voice. It had never occurred to me that others might be in the same predicament as myself. Certainly Terboven had said nothing about it. I tried to think quickly—there would be some way out of this—but nothing came to mind. Even then, however, I believed matters would be set right later.

I stepped into the chamber. I caught a glimpse of a few faces below me at knee level, but then the door slammed shut. I didn't move. Behind me I heard the Portuguese twist the valve lock. Then there was the thud of the canvas hitting against the door, the lighter patter of the ropes being tossed against the bulwark. Finally the Portuguese moved off.

I didn't move. I held my hands in front of my face, not to explore, but to protect myself. I listened to the breathing, but the chamber echoed, and it was impossible to determine direction.

"Heil Hitler!" a man's voice said and laughed.

Another voice laughed with it. Someone else whispered something and I moved my hands to fend the voice away. But then, in a firm tone, a man spoke to me.

"You are in a chamber that is approximately two meters high and seven meters long . . . it is a compartment that can be flooded, I think, without damage to the ship . . . a containment compartment in case we take on water. If we are boarded, they may lie and say the chamber is already sealed, or they may open the valves and drown us. That's my understanding, in any case."

"Who are you?" I asked.

"My name is Gustav Stresemann. We are five, counting yourself. I am not sure of everyone's location, but somewhere to my right is Charles Tansill, a German officer two weeks ago, now a man . . . well, a man like yourself. We also have a married couple with us . . . Stefanie and Lieutenant Julius Raeder. The lieutenant is on leave from the German Army, and Stefanie has agreed to follow him. Would you care to introduce yourself?"

"Frederich Loebus, twenty-two years old, an infantryman."

"A German soldier?"

"Austrian."

"Welcome . . . if the word can be used in such circumstances. You'll find us sitting on the floor . . . the deck, rather. The wall slopes up following the shape of the ship, and it is comfortable, at least for the first quarter hour, if you can wedge yourself in properly. There is a bucket in case you feel seasick . . . Herr Tansill has already succumbed, I'm afraid. There is only one bucket for all of us, so if you can control yourself . . . you get my meaning. We also have a bucket of water, which we must use sparingly. The bucket is to last a day . . . they can't be troubled to open and shut the hatch more than once a day. Food is brought at the same time, so you see, there is one great event every twenty-four hours."

"Have we left Marseilles?" the woman, Stefanie, asked as soon as Stresemann finished. Her voice was high-pitched and nervous.

"I came on board as they cast off," I told her. "How long have you been down here?"

"Two days," she answered.

"We were told they were to cast off as soon as we came aboard, but they only lay off the coast and wait for more supplies."

This voice, I was fairly certain, belonged to her husband. He, too, sounded unnerved. His voice contained a strident element which seemed to accuse anyone who listened to it. I didn't like his voice and instinctively felt I couldn't trust it.

"Did Terboven arrange your passage?" I asked them.

"Terboven!" Gustav laughed. "Terboven, the devil. We booked our own passage, didn't you know? A pledge with Satan is more like it. Terboven handled the arrangements, but you must admit there is something Faustian in the bargain. Payment for sin, and all that."

"Shut up, you jackass." This from Tansill. His voice was watery, though I attributed its tenor to seasickness.

"Well, isn't it true?" Gustav asked. "The goals of the Third Reich are realized in our group . . . you wouldn't happen to be blond, would you, Frederich?"

"Oh, shut up," Tansill said again. "I'm tired of your cheap philosophy."

"It isn't cheap . . . look how I'm paying for it. Now, Frederich, would you care to sit down? We have worked out a system for movement . . . we extend our hands and you use them to guide yourself. Reach in front of you . . . I think Stefanie's is the first hand you'll touch."

I did as I was told. It took me a moment to locate her hand. The heat of her flesh was reassuring and, earning my eternal gratitude, she squeezed my fingers. I placed my free hand on top of hers, patted it, then let go and reached for a second hand. It was a man's hand, just to my left. I took a careful step in the same direction and placed the toe of my boot on someone's leg. "Easy," a man said. Slowly I managed to squeeze my foot onto the deck and shift my balance.

Stefanie had been given the place nearest the door. I was led by different hands to the left, which was, from what I could tell, to the rear of the compartment. It was dark, dark as I had ever known anything to be, yet I continued under the mistaken belief that light would eventually penetrate the chamber.

At last I reached the farthest wall, a fact I only realized when my outreached hand struck metal. Someone moved beneath me, as if scuttling out of the way, and I understood I had arrived in my place. I wasn't displeased to have the wall beside me. Two walls joined in a corner, I felt, would at least allow me a comfortable niche in which to sleep.

I was mistaken, naturally. The others had already considered this, but from experience realized that the farthest corners were also the most damp. Two walls sweat instead of one; whenever the ship rose or fell, as it did continually, the liquid that gathered in the bottom of the compartment lapped back and forth, splashing as it came into contact with the side walls.

There was nothing to be done. I lowered myself against the wall. Tansill, who must have had possession of the bucket, retched weakly as I slid into position.

"Frederich, was it day or night when they brought you aboard?" Gustav asked.

"Just past midnight," I answered.

He sighed. I closed my eyes and crossed my arms in front of

me. Water—or whatever the liquid might have been—lapped against my legs.

I can't detail the emotions I felt during my first hours in that hold. Terror, certainly. Terror of the darkness and the thin shield of metal that protected us from the sea. I had never—not even during the worst of the war—been in such a place of complete desolation. I despised Terboven and formed many splendid vows of revenge, but these vows lost strength even as I conceived them. I knew, as Terboven assuredly foresaw, that I was bound for destinations from which one didn't easily return.

My companions in the hold slept, save Tansill, who frequently made use of the bucket. I wanted a drink of water, but felt too awkward to wake anyone for it. My back, lodged as it was between the deck and the sloping wall, ached terribly.

Sound took on great importance. Once I believed I heard a bombardment, but the noise turned out to be something rattling in the engine. Another time I heard an object striking the hull of the ship, bouncing slowly down its entire length. A log? A mine? I closed my eyes and waited, but nothing happened.

It was much later when Stefanie woke.

"The engines are still going," she said. "We're not laying off."

"Don't get your hopes up," her husband, Julius, cautioned.

"But they haven't stopped and you can feel the ship is in deeper water. Feel? It's not the same at all."

I felt it as well. The ship rolled more solidly now. The water at my feet splashed with greater force. I was glad to have even this small omen.

"How many days to Argentina?" I asked her.

"Argentina?" Gustav laughed, his voice coming from a surrounding yawn. "We'll be put off in Africa if we're still alive."

"I paid through to Argentina," I said.

"Take it up with the purser when you see him. Tell him I'd like a bottle of schnapps and a sausage while you're at it. It's a credit to you, Frederich, that you haven't lost your Germanic sense of proportion and duty. For all of that, we're bound for Africa."

"Where in Africa?"

"That's up to the captain. Tangiers? Unlikely because of the French and Americans. My bet is Mauritania or Dakar . . . maybe the Ivory Coast. Someplace secluded, where five white Germans won't be quite so obvious an addition to the local population."

"You don't know anything more than the rest of us," Tansill said. "Quit acting as if you do."

"Think it through. I doubt this ship is seaworthy. Besides, they're not rigged out for Argentina. They have nothing on board worth trading as far as I can tell. No, this is a short run, a sort of modern-day pirate run."

"You're frightening Stefanie," Julius said.

"Pardon me, Stefanie. In any case, we shouldn't waste our breath trying to figure out where we're going. Destiny will take care of that. I think we should play a game . . . Chaucer's invention of having each of his party tell a story. But we'll add a twist, won't we? I think it would be interesting to hear from each of us why we've ended up in a place like this."

"Gustav, be quiet," Tansill said softly.

"Frederich? Frederich, do you see the merits of such a game? Do you think there was a moment—I don't mean with Terboven—when you made the first of a series of choices that led you here? Was it induction into the army? Your first mesmerizing speech by our Führer? What I'm after is whether you believe you deserve to be here."

"We agreed not to say anything of our pasts," Julius said. "If we're interrogated it won't help to turn witness on each other."

"You're as bad as he is, Julius," Tansill said. "Interrogated? Who will give a good goddamn what we're doing in this ship? I doubt the outcome of the war depends on any of the secrets we carry."

"Then I take it you're for playing the game, Tansill?" asked Gustav.

"You can fuck yourself with your game, Gustav. I know your type. You've developed a greater distance from your life than the rest of us, but you're a bloody vampire about it. You won't care at all about anything you tell us, yet you'll probe and wheedle confessions out of the rest of us."

"Please, both of you stop it," Stefanie pleaded.

Despite my fear and discomfort, I was fascinated by the accuracy of this exchange. It seemed like dialogue in a play, constructed to reveal the characters.

We were quiet after this. The ship rode more heavily into the swells. I tried to summon my childhood lessons of geography. The Mediterranean wasn't wide. From Málaga to Tangiers was a day's ferry ride. Of course, there was no way to determine what our route might be. It was conceivable we would head east, toward Libya, but that direction would be dangerous. Gustav's assessment was the most reasonable. Two days to strike the African coast . . . after that, who could say?

I feel asleep for a short time, but was awakened by the sound of the valve twisting. Then the hatch opened and a light appeared. I blinked at the light and shielded my eyes. A guard stood outside, but from my position I couldn't fully see him. He said something rapidly in Portuguese. When no one answered, he repeated it.

After this, confusion. I saw an arm reach through the hatch and pull Stefanie to her feet. Julius rose up as well. A club flashed in the dim light, crashing against Julius's shoulder. He spun to one side as another club banged against the edge of the hatch.

I describe this with the accuracy of recollection. The actual events happened so quickly I barely had time to make sense of them. The light was intolerable. Even Stefanie, whom I saw pulled through the hatch, was only a wave of skirt and long hair.

The hatch shut with Stefanie still outside. I understood the implication immediately. To my shame, I also experienced the prisoner's relief at seeing the guards appeased by someone other than himself.

Julius heaved his shoulder against the hatch. He screamed and ranted. The futility of his actions was nothing when weighed against the necessity of performing them. Gladly, I'm sure, he would have suffered a beating. Instead, he was forced to throw himself against an unyielding door, one that couldn't possibly shatter. It was devastating to hear.

He didn't stop, however, and soon I detected darker forms above me. Gustav or Tansill or perhaps both were wrestling with him. Grunts and shoves, and a few curses. Gustav said, "You can't do anything about it . . . easy . . . you can't . . ." But this was followed by more cries from Julius.

"Move him away from the door," Tansill said. "Do you have him, Gustav? Frederich, see if you can help."

I moved forward blindly. A body slammed into me and I barely remained on my feet. The ship continued to rock, and in a strange dance I felt the mass of arms and legs drift away from me, only to return on the next tilt in my direction. An elbow hit my chin; a finger clawed at my ear. I circled my arms around someone's head and leaned backward.

A body lurched into me and I hugged it closer. I sensed the deep shudders of breath in the body I held and suspected from this that it was Julius.

"Are you all right, Frederich?" Gustav called.

"Where are you?"

"I'm here . . . Tansill?"

"Yes, right here."

"Don't let Julius near the door, whatever happens. He'll want a beating and there's no point to it," Gustav said.

I was left with Julius in my arms. At some point I realized that he no longer struggled. He sobbed quietly against my chest. I sat with him against the sloping wall. A mixture of compassion and revulsion stirred in me. How had he expected anything else? Why had he allowed his wife to join him? It was a weakness, and I had seen too much of weakness in myself as well as others.

. . .

Stefanie was gone for some time. Julius continued to sob. Gustav tried to talk to him but it was no use. After a while his sobs became babyish and blubbery. I had to control myself not to order him to be quiet. His cries, amplified as they were in the metal chamber, were horribly grating.

I was not indifferent to him or to Stefanie's plight, but my actions in the war had changed me. I no longer believed in my own morality. What the seamen did to Stefanie was reprehensible, yet I couldn't help weighing it against the atrocities I had witnessed during the last year.

To his credit, Gustav spoke soothingly to Julius. The cynicism Tansill had identified in Gustav before was absent. He didn't force responses from Julius, but spoke quietly, asking Julius to go along with him in his remembrance of better days. Sun again, warm days, beer taken on a shady porch.

Stefanie was returned several hours later. The door opened. Julius flinched beside me but made no move to stand. The guard banged his club against the brackets of the hatch, much like a zoo keeper hitting the bars of a cage to mark a feeding. It was unnecessary; we were entirely under the guard's power.

The guard set a bucket of food by the door, then removed our bucket of slops. He placed a water bucket beside the food. Then Stefanie stepped inside, without aid from the guard, and the hatch was sealed.

All of this was accomplished without a word. As soon as the hatch was tight, Julius climbed over the men toward his wife. Since I was on the other side of him, I followed this by the grunts of protest coming from Tansill and Gustav. They yelled at him to be careful of the food and water buckets.

I don't know what the couple's reunion was like. Some crying followed, but whether it was from Julius or Stefanie I couldn't tell. My mind—insensitive as this sounds—was already focused on the food and water.

Gustav apparently felt the same way because he began to pass food down the row of hands to me. I couldn't see what I ate; something of meat and something of bread. The food tasted exquisite and after the first few gulps, I slowed to savor the taste. I believed Gustav had fairly proportioned the food. Tansill, I noted, made no objection on receiving his share.

We were more suspect of each other concerning the water. What size swallow did he take? How long did the man hold the bucket to his lips?

When the bucket came to me it was half empty. I drank silently, carefully closing my throat over each swallow. I wanted my share, and, perhaps, a little more. I rationalized that I had been in the hold for almost a day with nothing to drink. Whether this was fair or not, I hardly cared.

As I finished drinking I heard Gustav speaking to Stefanie. She should eat, he said. Try a little bread at least. She replied in a voice so empty of emotion that it chilled me.

"Give the others my share. I'm not hungry."

Julius began to entreat her, though his voice didn't carry conviction. Gustav gave up. Julius went on speaking, doubtless trying to mitigate his guilt. But Stefanie would have none of it. After a time, Julius's voice changed to a cuddling, infantile drone that revolted me.

"Leave her alone," Tansill said eventually. "She's made her position clear enough."

"This is no concern of yours," answered Julius.

"Just let it go."

"Let it go?" Julius said, his voice becoming tight. "Don't you understand what they've done? They're animals, all of them. I'll kill them. I swear on my mother's grave I'll kill them before this is through."

"Oh, for God's sake," Tansill said.

I would have respected Julius somewhat more if he had attacked Tansill, but he was too timid even for that. Gustav intervened and told them both to be quiet.

I dozed. I dreamed, as I often did, of bodies falling in an open pit. Three bodies, spies, sagging at the knees before they fell. The puncture of bullets, the ridiculous splotches of red blood on garments. Myself lowering a rifle, staring down at the empty cartridge chamber, the scent of cordite sickening in my nose.

This dream repeated itself, showing different facets each time. I woke frequently, relieved to be away from it, yet oddly drawn to resume it. Never did I witness my own bullet striking the slumping bodies. It was always the snap of gunfire, the sergeant shouting, the privates moving forward with spades. I had been there, but I couldn't remember pulling the trigger.

I woke at Gustav's request for more water. The bucket was beside me. I took a solid swallow and passed it on. The chamber had become hotter. We were moving south. After drinking, Gustav began to speculate aloud.

"We've traveled a full day from all signs. If we're bound for any port directly south of Marseilles, we should strike it soon. Then customs, or whatever papers they must fill out if they bother with that sort of thing. Then unloading, loading . . . I figure at least three or four days in port before moving on."

"South again?" I asked, interested because Gustav's thoughts followed my own.

"I suppose."

"Do you think the Spanish Sahara?" Tansill asked. He seemed to be over his seasickness. The food had given his voice more authority; he seemed less irritable.

"The men said they are going to Dakar," Stefanie said. "Something about fish meal."

Her voice was frightening in its blandness.

"Well, Dakar it is then," Gustav said. "We won't receive much of a welcome from the French authorities, pompous little bureaucrats that they are. How do you guess they'll put us ashore?"

"We'll swim," Tansill said.

"Equatorial waters, sharks, I should think."

"They won't chance the authorities, that's certain," I said. "Tansill's right. If we get close enough to a shore, they'll send us overboard."

"I can't swim," Gustav said, seeming perfectly calm about this fact.

The engines continued to run through another feeding. The heat inside the chamber increased. Dehydration was a constant worry. Tansill tested the moisture on the wall with his tongue but reported that it was brackish. Stefanie removed a petticoat and ripped it into rough squares. We used the rags to bathe ourselves with the water collected at the bottom of the chamber. It was little comfort, doubtless hygienically unsound, but the listlessness that gradually came on us made any fastidiousness seem a luxury.

Other worries surfaced. From the poor diet and constant friction against the walls, we each developed sores that wouldn't heal. We stood when we could, but the heat collected at the top of the chamber was formidable. Gustav suggested we massage each other's back, and for a day or two we practiced this. I massaged Tansill's heavy shoulders and he mine, but each day I noted the pressure of his hands became weaker. During the long, silent period when we lay in port, our resolve crumbled and we abandoned the massages.

During the same period, Gustav spoke to us frequently in French, interrogating us with questions he imagined a French soldier might ask. Absurdly, this became our dream. We would pass for French citizens. It wasn't something we actually believed, but it was a hope. Gustav alone among us was fluent in French. The rest, myself included, spoke schoolboy phrases without content or understanding. I could ask, for instance, whether it looked like rain on Sunday, but I couldn't answer my own name with proper fluency.

Julius and Stefanie would not join in the lessons. They became more withdrawn. Stefanie was pulled from the chamber one other time. She returned doused by water, since the men apparently found her stench revolting. Again a moment of reunion with Julius, a few cries, then silence. It was a labor to get them to speak at all.

Sometime during our fourth week the hatch opened and we were told to step out. The light, even from the dim lanterns held by three guards, was excruciating. I covered my eyes. The sores on my legs and waist, pushed to stretch in unaccustomed ways, began to bleed and sting.

The guards complained about our smell and prodded us with the tips of their clubs to keep us away from them. My eyes, slowly dilating, began to take in the features of my companions. Tansill, I saw, was blond and muscular. His face was somewhat pinched and sullen and even after weeks of not shaving, his beard was sparse. He possessed mechanic's hands. Short, swollen fingers, with nails thickly guarding his fingertips. Oddly, I imagined him as being the type of boy who could walk on his hands or balance on logs thrown across a brook.

Gustav was the opposite. Short and probably round in better days, his belt rode too high over his hips. He was fifty, perhaps fifty-five. He wore suspenders in addition to the belt. In the pocket of his shirt he carried an elegant fountain pen. His beard was gray, his eyes green.

Stefanie and Julius were both thin and drawn, both dark with wide eyes. They clung together. The guards were merciless with Julius. They poked him with their clubs, taking care to goad his rear and private parts. He was a cuckold, a weak one, and the guards couldn't forgive him either fault.

We were herded into a rough file and marched up through the decks of the ship. The ship was in the same state of squalor it had been in when I boarded, but now it seemed an inviting place to me. We passed stacks of bananas on one deck, their smell sickeningly ripe. On another deck we passed sheaves of dried fish, their tails stapled together so that they could be hung over an exposed pipe. The fish had begun to curl and flies boiled over them.

At last I saw sunlight above us. A patch of blue sky squared by the final gangway. I began to cry in a sodden way I couldn't prevent. Gustav cried as well—I could see just his profile—but Tansill only climbed the gangway nimbly, his muscles more resilient than mine. Behind me, Julius helped Stefanie up the stairs. The guards taunted her by lifting the trailing edge of her skirt with their clubs. They whistled and laughed, while Julius kicked at them ineffectually.

My first glimpse of Africa was overpowering. I had no idea of our exact location, of course, but it was unmistakably Africa. The light told me this, and the heat.

Someone yelled, "Heil Hitler!" The cry was taken up on all sides by seamen gathered to watch us. "Heil Hitler!" from a dark devil; "Heil Hitler!" from a grinning black man, his teeth rotted. An officer—I assumed this from his hat, which was similar to the type worn by yachtsmen—clicked his heels, though he wore no shoes.

We were given no time to orient ourselves. The guards pushed us forward. The other sailors made a funnel which we were obliged to pass down. One or two spat at us, but it is evidence of our terrible condition that not more did so.

The *Medusa* moved slowly parallel to the beach. It was exactly as Tansill had predicted: we were to be shoved over the edge. If we made it to shore we might survive, but I saw large breakers casting against the white sand. Even had we been in excellent condition, the swim would have been a feat. Exhausted as we were, the sailors were condemning us to death.

A large seaman came toward us and demanded our wallets. I gave over mine, as did Tansill and Gustav. Julius, in an act of defiance, threw his wallet overboard. It grew silent while we listened for the report of leather striking the sea.

"Nazi pigs!" someone said in French.

I used the distraction to speak to Gustav.

"Let me hold your belt when we jump. Don't fight me. I can swim well enough. Don't panic, whatever you do, or I'll let you sink. The moment after we've struck the water, spread your arms and legs so that we don't go straight to the bottom. If I can get you onto your back, you can float. I may have to pull you by the hair."

He nodded. He appeared close to collapse. I glanced at the breakers and knew it was unlikely I could swim with him through the roughest water.

The men closed around us, pushing us to the gunwale. It was pointless to delay, but instinct kept us in check. As I neared the edge I looked over and saw, to my astonishment, a small African fishing fleet hanging off the ship. They rode in dugouts on a green sea, their skins beautifully black. They waved when they saw us looking over the edge and began to shout.

Confused, I grabbed Gustav's belt at the rear and held it tightly. Tansill jumped. His arms did pinwheels as he fought for balance, then he struck the water. The sailors cheered. In the same moment, Stefanie stepped out of her dress, facing the sailors in her slip.

More cheers. Julius tried to hide her body, but she pushed him aside and raised her hand. She screamed at them. Her neck strained and saliva sprayed from her lips. She cursed their ship and every member of the crew. She promised them they would drown. They didn't understand anything she said, but the intent of the message was clear enough.

Then she jumped. She took no care to leave the gunwale properly and as she disappeared from sight I saw her leaning too far forward. Julius hurried after her. He jumped like a startled creature, his face shocked and stiff, his eyes terrified.

We went last. I had misgivings as we stepped closer. How could we leave together without throwing off each other's balance? The ship rode high off the water. It was a drop of twenty meters, if not more, and I wondered if my arm could stand the strain.

Gustav watched me. He was frightened, but listened attentively for any orders I might give. I told him to put his arm around my waist. We should step off the ship, only pushing ourselves forward the slightest bit. He nodded vigorously. Finally, when we could delay no longer, we jumped.

The fall went on for a long time. We maintained our balance. Gustav, I realized as we fell, had taken a large breath far too soon.

Then the water slapped my feet and we were down beneath the surface. We continued down in a great wave of bubbles. I spread my arm out to the side, while my other arm, the one on Gustav's belt, strained at the shoulder socket. Though it was difficult to tell, I felt Gustav hadn't spread his legs. He continued straight down, slowing finally with his body well beneath me.

I saw him through the perfect water. His cheeks were puffed in ridiculous mounds. His eyes were wide with panic. I yanked at the back of his trousers and opened my hand to tell him to calm down. He flapped with his arms. I began to kick and pull him up, but it was more difficult than I had imagined. Trying to help, he fought against me. His air was giving out and he began to dog paddle wildly, his head tilted back to see the sunlight on the surface.

I kicked steadily. I was conscious of the sores on my body stinging from the salt. My muscles held no reserves. For an instant I considered letting him go. It was a waste of energy to help him; one should survive where two will drown.

But then the surface was just above us. We broke through it and Gustav coughed out his air and tried to take more in. I yelled at him to lie on his back, but he wouldn't listen. He began to sink again. I could only lift him to the surface by allowing myself to go under.

He turned at last and began to cling to me. He attempted to climb me—I can put it no other way—his legs clamping around my ribs, his arms reaching around my shoulders.

I let go of his belt, hoping that would terrify him into submission, but it only increased his desire to cling to me. He hugged me. He ceased kicking and paddling altogether, and was now only a solid weight. We were drowning; my thoughts became peaceful.

In the next moment hands grabbed me under the arms and began to lift. The Africans. I was pulled backward into a dugout, my back sustaining a terrible scrape on the gunwale.

Gustav fell on top of me, but I no longer cared. There was air around us and sky above. Two Africans stood near us, grinning. Their physiques were perfect. We lay on a mound of fish at the rear of the canoe, gasping for air. It was only later that I discovered Julius and Stefanie had not been saved. They had swum for open water and fought the Africans who offered help.

I TRIED TO DETERMINE what manner of Africans I had fallen among. I watched patiently to get a glimpse of their teeth, suspecting I should know from this if they were cannibals. I expected, I admit, to see their teeth sharpened to points, but instead they were perfectly ordinary. Indeed, the African men were extremely handsome. Their bodies were slim and firm, their skins, when wet, actually stunning. They laughed easily among themselves. If they understood we were Nazi scum thrown to them from a ship of scoundrels, they showed no indication of it.

The Africans began to chant when the *Medusa* had steamed out of range. It was a song of rowing which was quite haunting. They bent to their oars and pulled with great heaves. Gustav had recovered to some degree by this time, and he sat up long enough to renew a bout of coughing. When he had cleared his lungs at last, he asked my opinion of the Africans.

"Do you think they are friendly?" he asked.

"I don't know."

"I feel . . . I can't say how I feel. We haven't a thing in the world."

I hardly paid attention to him. My eyes were on the beach. The cove we were bound for was beautiful. The beach was a crescent bordered by palms. I saw more fishing boats drawn up on shore, their bottoms reflecting light where the barnacles were heaviest. Drying racks for the catch were erected everywhere and most were loaded with fish. Nets had been spread out on the other racks, hung like bunting to air. Children ran back and forth, waving at us, at times even dodging into the surf. I saw a line of women approaching the village from the hillside behind it. They carried wood on their heads; many of them were all but naked.

We passed over a long bar of coral that was remarkably alive with fish. We approached the surf, which broke in long runners to the beach. It was not calm, and I imagined in a storm the waves grew to monstrous proportions. The boats pulled up short of the first waves, just where the water bulged and began to break as it cleared the reef. A slender man in the rear stood and watched over his shoulder at the water as it rose and promised a wave. He talked quickly, obviously in command, but he did not seem concerned. The boat beside us, containing Tansill, stood off in the same manner, waiting on the waves. It took me a moment to realize the boats were competing to catch the first wave.

The necessary wave came after three had passed. The water began to swell, then the man at the rear shouted something. His oarsmen—there were four—pulled with all their strength. They smiled as they did so, grinning at the members of Tansill's boat who rowed beside us.

The wave lifted us, dangerously I thought, but then we began to slide along its crest. The men shipped their oars. The man in back yelled something and turned to taunt the other boats that still waited for a proper wave. In the next instant we were on a long glide over pure sand. A wave broke around us, then another, and finally the oarsmen leaped overboard and ran us up to the beach. More men waited there. Using our momentum, they jammed the boat onto the beach, then dashed back into the water to receive the second boat.

We were instantly the object of attention. The children ran around the boat, shouting and leaping. The women trilled their tongues—a sound unlike any I had ever heard—while a few older men hobbled forward to inspect us. I wanted to be out of the boat,

but the people were on both sides of us. An old man yelled something and made motions for the people to step back, yet their
excitement was too great.

In the meantime, Tansill's boat slid in beside us. The crowd
divided. Tansill was blond, and all the more remarkable for being
so. At the same moment I heard one of the men begin describing
something. The crowd became quiet. I listened closely, and in time
I deciphered that he told the story of Julius and Stefanie. I understood they hadn't survived. He made motions with his hands and
shouted his words. When he finished, the crowd stepped away from
both our boats and made room for us to come ashore.

I climbed out first, then helped Gustav down. Immediately the
Africans began to bow. It occurred so quickly that I couldn't un-
derstand it at first. Tansill looked at me and shook his head. Only
Gustav had the presence of mind to ask if anyone spoke French.

His words were whispered throughout the crowd, and soon a
man of about thirty stepped forward. His expression was bland.
He appeared neither reluctant nor anxious to speak, although the
crowd clearly marveled at this ability to communicate with us. The
calf of his right leg had been bitten, probably by a shark, because
the wound was in a perfect half circle. He hobbled slightly, though
the rest of him was perfectly formed. He introduced himself as
Paul and said he spoke a little French. Around him, men and women
pressed close to hear the exchange.

Gustav asked a series of simple questions that even I understood.

Where was the village located?

North of St. Louis.

In Senegal?

Yes, well north of Dakar.

Were there French officials about?

In Dakar, also a small outpost in St. Louis. Sometimes they
came north, but not often.

As I listened, children snuck up behind me and touched my
arms and hands, then ran off shouting and jumping. It became a

contest, and soon even the smallest children worked their way behind me. "*Nassarra*," they said, a word I began to understand as meaning stranger or white man. At one point a mother lifted a child in her arms and held him out to me. The child screamed. It should not have been humorous, but the child was so obviously terrified that the other children began to laugh and spring about more wildly.

Finally, Gustav told Tansill and me that the village had cleaned out a hut for our use. We were to stay as long as we liked. Paul bowed and stretched out his hand to show us the way.

The villagers formed a procession. I couldn't distinguish rank, though I suspected, except for his command of French, Paul was not a citizen of great importance. He walked beside us, stopping every few seconds to make sure we understood we were to follow.

We passed through the first huts and I was disgusted by what I saw. They were filthy, constructed of mud brick. There were no windows. The sand around the huts was soiled by dung and fish entrails. Flies moved about everywhere, collecting in roiling masses which jumped into the air at the touch of a shadow. The dogs— and there were many—all suffered from mange. They were thin, ravenous creatures, whose appetite for food was surpassed only by their constant urge to bite at their flea-bitten coats.

But there was beauty as well. The palm trees were wide and graceful. Many of them bore coconuts. Grasses grew at the highest level of the beach. A herd of goats grazed there, occasionally pulling at saplings and bushes.

Eventually, we arrived at a hut which had been quickly readied for us. It was set well back from the sea, but still gathered stiff breezes that were refreshing and cool. The roof was made of palm leaves, linked in a rough weave. Primitive designs were drawn in charcoal on the walls. Here was a lion dancing; near the door, an antelope with its head craned to feed on leaves, its hooves notched on the ring of a palm trunk.

There were questions of protocol we could not hope to understand and this caused some awkwardness. Paul offered to send us food, but Gustav, after consulting with us, asked if we might be allowed to sleep for a time. We were exhausted, he told them. Paul nodded, smiled, then turned to the crowd. He spoke in a loud voice. At once the crowd began to disperse.

"Do you think they'll come back and slit our throats when we're asleep?" Tansill asked.

"They could have done that already," Gustav replied.

"I don't trust them for all their smiling."

"We don't have much choice, do we?" I asked.

We entered the hut when the last people had trailed away. I intended to sleep outside on the beach, but the floor of our hut was pounded flat and sweetened with sand. Three straw mats had been spread on the ground to serve as beds. A calabash of water had been placed in one corner, with a long-handled gourd tucked inside as a ladle.

We each chose a mat and set up individual camps. I folded my clothes and placed them by the water calabash, then carefully laid out my belongings on the straw mat. My wallet was gone, but I still retained a few French francs. A gold pocket watch, a tin of peppermints, a ruined pack of cigarettes, a metal lighter, and a sewing kit—these comprised my earthly possessions. I examined my boots carefully and saw that they had been badly bloated by the water at the bottom of the hold. The sole leather was cracked and mushy; the stitches, where the top of the shoe was joined to the sole, had burst.

This was a blow I took out of all proportion to my circumstances. "My boots are ruined," I said, surprised to find myself suddenly near to crying.

"Go without them," Tansill said without looking up. "You'll be better off if you can build up your calluses."

I rearranged my pile of belongings several times before I finally gave up. To one side, Tansill bound his valuables in a tattered handkerchief and buried them beneath his mat. That done, he lay down and covered his eyes in the crook of his elbow. Gustav stripped to his underwear and lay down on his mat. He left his possessions in full view near his feet.

It isn't surprising our initial conversation was filled with our own concerns. Should we leave at once? Should we continue inland, or make for St. Louis? How long would it be before the French officials were alerted to our presence? We talked nervously and reached no conclusions. We were ignorant, laughably ignorant, though we didn't know it at the time. We had no knowledge of the terrain surrounding us, nor did we know our exact location. We spoke to reassure one another.

It was Gustav who asked first about Stefanie and Julius. Tansill told us he had seen them leave the ship. Neither of them had jumped well. Julius had leaned too far backward, Stefanie too far forward. He saw them land, then lost sight of them.

Tansill himself had fared well. He had landed within a few meters of a fishing boat and they had scooped him out of the water quickly. It was he who had directed the men to fish us out—not that the Africans ignored us. They found our flailing humorous, however, and I learned several boats had been around us the entire time, ready to rescue us. Tansill had pleaded with them. The Africans, exhibiting a strange sense of humor, laughed and nodded. When they finally pulled us up, they pointed to the fish at the rear of the boat and then to us. It was apparently a great joke with the others, because they laughed for some time whenever a man pointed at the gaping fish beneath us.

Tansill didn't see Julius and Stefanie after their leap. Apparently they had survived the jump but mistakenly made their way toward the open sea.

When Tansill finished reciting his story, no one spoke. Shortly afterward, I heard Gustav drawing long breaths. Tansill turned several times, but then he also slept. I couldn't immediately let go of Julius and Stefanie. It was no accident that they had headed out to sea, and I pictured them swimming one after another out toward the horizon, their strokes becoming weaker and weaker until their bodies glided down into the quiet waves.

I WOKE IN EARLY EVENING. The light had turned softer and a land breeze blew from the west. I was aware of children standing somewhere nearby, though I couldn't see them. I heard them talking quietly when the sea was momentarily silent.

I sat up and saw Gustav propped against one of the walls, reading. It was such an uncanny sight that I began to laugh. He looked up from his book with surprise. He had bathed. His hair was wet against his head. Tansill, who was still asleep, only turned on the mat. His cheek was sugared with white sand.

"You've caught me with my addiction," Gustav said, holding up his book, a copy of *The Odyssey*. "I don't require cigarettes or alcohol, but I fear for my sanity if there's nothing to read on this continent."

"Can you make out the pages?" I asked. The book was water-logged.

"I know most of it by heart."

"What did you do in the war, Gustav?" I asked. I couldn't conceive of him in a uniform.

"Ordnance . . . supplies. It was a joke in our office that the war ran on paper, not gasoline. I was particularly handy with train schedules. It was the kind of detail work that fit my talents. Unfortunately, at some point I began to wonder where all the trains were going and that was my undoing. I didn't demand to know anything, because knowledge brings its own obligations, doesn't it?"

"You were sending the Jews off to the camps?"

"Oh, I suppose. Yes, of course. But almost as bad in my own mind was the idea of sending soldiers to their deaths. German soldiers, Russian soldiers . . . what did it matter? Once you realize you're helping to pull the oars, it's difficult to pretend the ship isn't moving. Eventually, I made a few scheduling mistakes, important ones judging from the resulting clamor, and I'm not sure to this day if I did it deliberately. I was suspected of treason. There was talk of prison, or even a trip to the front, so I left."

He carefully closed his book and placed it on his mat. We exchanged a look that I broke off with difficulty. I stood and went to the water calabash. The water was tepid and tasted heavily of clay, but I drank three ladles dry. While I drank, Tansill began to stir. Hearing our voices, the children outside had become more bold. Two or three ran past our open door to glance inside.

"Have they come to check on us?" I asked Gustav.

"I don't think so."

Tansill finally woke completely and sat up. His hand went beneath his mat to check on his valuables. Satisfied they were where he had left them, he wiped the sand from his cheek.

"Well, we're still alive," he said. "Maybe they want to fatten us up before they make a meal of us."

"Your optimism is encouraging," said Gustav.

Tansill stood and took my place at the calabash. He drank several ladles of water, then splashed more over his head and shoulders. His body was dense; his muscles seemed purposeful like the shoulders of a good dray horse. His movements were economical, and directed solely to his own welfare.

We took a few moments to dress and organize our affairs. The children apparently sensed our preparations and ran to tell the village, because Paul appeared a few moments later. Gustav stepped outside and shook Paul's hand. Tansill and I followed.

The beach had grown more beautiful in the evening light. The sea was calm. Close to the water, the first cook fires had been started. I was anxious to find something to eat, but Paul spoke to

Gustav in French that was too rapid for me to follow. Gustav nodded repeatedly, then turned to us.

"I gather we're to be received by the chief and elders. This afternoon was something of a breach of protocol. They were embarrassed that they weren't more prepared for us."

Before much longer a small ceremonial party approached from the huts below. The party was formed of five men, all dressed in elaborate costume—white skull caps, beautifully embroidered gowns that came down to their ankles. Packs of children ran beside them, though they were wary of the elders and didn't venture too near. As the men came closer, I saw they were quite old. The sand impeded their walking; two of the men carried staves which were richly carved with all manner of birds and reptiles.

They stopped short of us and looked at Paul. He stepped to a position halfway between our parties. Gustav, responding to social instinct, bowed deeply to the elders. Tansill and I did the same. The elders bowed in return, then stepped forward and shook our hands. All of this was done in silence.

Finally Paul introduced the tribesmen. Their names were foreign to me and difficult to grasp regardless of how I concentrated. Paul introduced the *chef de village* last. His name was Indrissa. His lineage was recited by one of the men at his side. He was tall and thin, but his eyes were powerful. Two ritual scars slanting down in brackets from his nose gave his mouth and lips the appearance of a muzzle.

He offered a short speech, translated slowly by Paul. He welcomed us to the village; we were his guests; if we required anything, please demand it.

Indrissa then turned to the group of children collected behind him and clapped his hands. Three children stepped forward, each carrying a while rooster. The roosters hung upside down, their wings trussed. Nervously the children handed us each a bird, then stepped back quickly.

"A present from the people of Batie," Paul told us.

We held the fowls only a moment before the children, at another command from Indrissa, stepped forward again to take the chickens from us. Paul told us the children would watch over the poultry for us. We thanked Indrissa and the men beside him. Finally they led us down the beach, toward the cook fires.

The village members swarmed around us when we neared the fires. For the first time I began to suspect that we were not merely guests, but harbingers of luck or fortune. Certainly we represented something spiritual, because the women went to great lengths to touch our hands or arms. One old woman fell on her knees before Tansill and would not stand until he lifted her. "Nassarra," she said several times.

It was confusing and exhilarating. The fires burned to shoulder height. A large shark lay roasting across a bed of coals, its center split and pregnant with rice and smaller fish. The sand around the fire had been carefully groomed; straw mats were placed in a circle a comfortable distance from the heat. Above us, the stars had begun to appear.

We were escorted to the mats and asked to sit. While we took our places two women advanced with drink. The drinks were given to us in calabashes; the liquid smelled old and rancid, but we couldn't refuse them. We waited for the others to be served, then raised our drinks in a toast. The Africans seemed pleased by our desire to toast them and apparently understood the gesture.

The liquid was a type of beer which tasted of charcoal and roots. The first sip was horrible, but I decided not to judge it too quickly. As famished as I was, the alcohol went quickly through my blood.

Paul sat beside Gustav to make translation easier. I sat beside Indrissa, with Tansill to my left. For a time I pointed to different objects and asked for the word in the native tongue. It was tiresome, I'm sure, but the Africans were willing teachers. When I repeated the word in their language, then in German, I was greeted by surprised laughter.

Tansill made no effort to communicate with the Africans. He

was wary of their smallest kindness; when he saw me drinking the beer, he nudged my side with his elbow.

"Don't drink it. It will make you sick," he whispered.

"We'll have to get used to it."

"Maybe you will," he said, then looked off to the fire.

The food was served in large calabashes and eaten communally. Eating with our right hands—a courtesy Gustav luckily pointed out to us—we scooped rice and fish into our fingers, then dunked the whole mass in a green sauce. The food was not succulent, but it was warm and fresh, and I ate greedily. Indrissa ate from my bowl and matched my appetite.

We ate steadily for a half hour. The night grew darker; the sea became only a sound. A drum began beating and soon I became aware of a group of men poised near the edge of the sea. The fire limited my vision, but I felt anticipation growing in the Africans around me. They looked frequently at us, as if trying to gauge our reaction. Gustav asked Paul what was happening, but he shook his head and pointed to the fire.

A moment later the first young man leaped through the flames. His appearance was so sudden that I actually leaned backward. He wore a magnificent mask, cut from a large coconut shell, the face a demon's frown. He cleared the bed of coals easily, but the higher flames broke into sparks as his body soared through the fire. He was followed by another, this one in a mask formed of a tortoise, with white cowrie shells set in bands around his wrists and ankles.

It was a splendid sight. Three men jumped through the fire at once, the man in the center nearly clearing the flames altogether. One of the men at my side rolled a large log onto the fire, and the flames, after withering for a moment, rose even higher.

Women and children had collected behind us, circling the fire completely. The dancers began appearing from different directions, jumping the heads of the men who sat in the circle, then bounding across the fire. Sparks followed them everywhere, sometimes catching in their hair or on the faces of their masks. I feared for a collision, because the dancers came at no set intervals, but this too seemed part of the spectacle.

The drumming increased until the tempo was irresistible. Each dancer tried to outdo the last, and some managed to make full spins in the air before landing on the far side of the fire. One dancer dropped a live fish in the coals as he crashed through the flames, and for a few long moments the fish thrashed and struggled, sending a thousand sparks into the air.

A wind came up and stirred the flames, broadening them until even the best leapers came down through orange licks of heat. Nevertheless, they showed no sign of pain. I had become indifferent to the dance by the time I witnessed the strangest spectacle of all.

A large man wearing a mask cut to resemble a dog's snout walked slowly to the fire. He was powerfully built, slightly fat through the gut. His body was coated with some form of grease which made his skin glisten, but also, I suspected, protected him from the heat. He moved around the fire in a counterclockwise direction, his arms slowly lifting to his sides. He danced solemnly, apparently in a trance. The people around the fire moved back. The women began trilling their tongues. Watching him, I was surprisingly apprehensive. My emotion was not quite fear; it was distrust mingled with sharp curiosity.

He danced a full circle around the fire, then paused when he was directly opposite us. He placed the fire between us, and I leaned to the side to watch him better. In one short move he reached into the coals of the fire; his fingers pawed through the charred logs without hurry. As he straightened, the oil on his skin casting reflections, a fish wriggled in his hands. He lifted it above his head.

It was a trick. I was sure of that. But the man held the fish with difficulty. It was alive, vibrantly alive, and his arms trembled with the effort of restraining it. I squinted through the light, hoping to see if the fish was of the same species that had been dropped in the fire, but I couldn't be certain.

I looked at Gustav. He watched intently, but I couldn't tell from his expression what he made of the magic—for magic it was clearly intended to be. By the time I turned back, the young dancers were again plunging through the flames. The man holding the fish moved slowly backward, finally disappearing in the darkness beyond the fire.

How were we to take this? Was it a warning or simply a demonstration of power? I glanced at Indrissa, who only nodded at the disappearing figure, a bowl of beer to his lips. The women trilled until the man was gone.

"Ask Paul where the magician has gone," I said to Gustav.

"Not right now," he answered, his expression conveying that it was not appropriate. Then he said it was time to go.

We spent several minutes thanking the elders and shaking hands all around. Three children were elected to walk us back to the hut. They were nervous to be with us and stayed well ahead. I turned to look at the fire and was struck by the illusion that it had been built on the surface of sea. The tide had risen while we sat eating, and now the flames and sparks reflected off the flat calm of the ocean. At any moment I expected the waves to douse the fire, but instead the fire seemed to drift across the water, the smoke and sparks wavering as if lifted by swells.

TANSILL WAS GONE the next morning. Gustav woke me at dawn and pointed to the empty mat.

"He's taken everything," he said.

"Our things?" I asked.

"Everything."

It wasn't quite true. Tansill had left behind those items he considered worthless. My boots, Gustav's book, a few odds and ends. He had left us each a pair of pants and a shirt. Gustav said more than once—nearly driving me to distraction—that it was fortunate he had slept with his fountain pen clamped in his pocket. Otherwise that too would be gone.

"Do you think we should go after him?" I asked.

"For what? To bring him back? We're better off without him."

"But what if he stumbles into the French guard?"

"Don't worry. Tansill left because he sees an advantage in being the first to reach Dakar. He's clever and selfish, and I suspect he'll survive. First to table, first finished, that's his motto."

I could not let it go so easily. Although I hated Tansill for stealing our few possessions, it was the fact of his departure that concerned me more. I wondered if he had perceived something the night before that I had missed. Was I naive to trust the Africans? Tansill's pragmatism made me doubt my faith in the village's hospitality.

Gustav drank water from the calabash, then turned to me.

"What do you think the villagers will make of it?" he asked. "It isn't much of a reply to their hospitality."

"We might make up a story around it. Tell them we felt Tansill was an evil man and we drove him from the village."

"Enhance our position in the bargain? It isn't a bad idea. You don't suppose Tansill went on a sort of scouting mission, do you? That he might come back?"

It was such an innocent question that I realized Tansill had also left me Gustav. Drinking from the ladle in the soft morning light, he appeared weak and uncertain. True, he spoke French and possessed a diplomatic flair, yet I could not imagine him standing up to the rigors of such a primitive life. His flesh was soft, his arms flabby. He did not have the cruelty necessary for survival in these circumstances. Despite this, I felt fondly toward him—a fact Tansill had doubtless figured into his equation.

I told Gustav that Tansill wouldn't return, then set about dreaming up a story to cover ourselves. We would tell the villagers that Tansill was a thief; he had stolen things on the ship and we had been ill-treated because of it. We couldn't allow him to steal from the people of Batie, so we had placed a curse on him that drove him away. I thought up the idea of the curse—Gustav had been all for an old-fashioned drubbing. I sensed, however, that the spiritual approach would be more effective.

Our plans concluded, we decided to bathe in the sea. It was early enough that not even the fishermen were awake as we walked down the beach toward the sea. A few dogs barked, but it was morning and their hearts weren't in it.

At the waterline we stripped. Gustav entered only to his knees, then sat in the sand, rubbing his body clean. I swam out a little farther, but the surf was strong. A sharp undertow cut against my legs whenever I stood. I rubbed my scalp and face repeatedly in the water. The sores on my back and legs stung from the salt, but they were healing. Despite Tansill's treachery, I felt better than I had in months.

"Frederich, you didn't tell me why you left the war," Gustav said when I swam back. We sat beside each other, only our heads and shoulders above the water.

"I don't mean to pry," he went on, "but you strike me as a man who might be skilled as a soldier. You have an air of command . . . does that embarrass you?"

"I was a good soldier, I suppose," I said.

"But you left the war?"

"There was an incident in one of the camps," I began carefully, surprised to find myself speaking so frankly. "Three civilians were accused of spying. I don't know the truth of it even to this day. I had seen them about, but our position was hardly a matter of secrecy. In any case, they were eventually apprehended—that was the official word, though they never tried to escape to my knowledge. One of them was a woman who granted sexual favors to the officers in exchange for information—at least that was the charge. A trial followed, and all three were given a sentence of death. They were Jews. A lottery was held the next day to determine who would act as executioners. I was the fifth chosen out of six. There was the usual ploy of handing out a blank cartridge so that no one would know for certain that he was a murderer, but that's a convention of the cinema. You know if you shoot a man . . . there is no mistaking that."

"And you were given bullets? Real ones?"

"I don't know."

"But you just said there was no mistaking live ammunition."

"True, but psychology also bears on the situation. We can delude ourselves into believing anything—that's the real use of the blank cartridge. I closed my eyes when it came time to fire so that I could preserve the doubt."

"Couldn't you have deliberately missed?"

"Our bullets were rationed. We couldn't spare four or five rounds for six men to finish off three spies. The spies were to be shot into the graves they themselves had dug, and I was certain the sergeant would order them buried whether they still breathed or not. Strange to think that an accurate shot is an act of mercy, but that was our understanding."

"It sounds to me like you had no alternative but to shoot. That, or be thrown in jail for insubordination."

"Or turn the gun on myself, or shoot the sergeant. You're being kind. I should have put the gun down and walked away, but I clung to the belief that by closing my eyes, I wouldn't know the difference between the blank cartridge and a real one. And besides, I'm an excellent marksman and that was a consideration. What if I succeeded in putting one of the spies out of misery more efficiently than the rest? That's an obligation as well."

"I'm fascinated by this, I must tell you," Gustav said. "Go on if it isn't too painful."

"No, actually I'm finding some relief in telling this. I won't describe all the details, but eventually there came a moment when I was called on to shoot. The first spy was placed in front of his grave, given a handkerchief to cover his eyes, then told to stand at attention. He slumped horribly, I'm afraid . . . a sullen dog ready to be put down. The sergeant called out the command, and we fired. My rifle kicked, the shell exploded, and the man snapped back into his grave, dead before he touched the earth."

"And your eyes were closed?"

"Yes, but the fellow next to me complimented me on my shooting. Stupid not to think of that. Of course, he might have only done so to rid himself of guilt, but he was a dumb German—excuse me, but you know the type—who saw absolutely nothing wrong in what we were doing. I am sure he was sincere. Another spy was led forward and again we followed the same drill. This time, however, I deliberately shot high, and again the soldier beside me whistled at my accuracy. A tricky fellow, perhaps; or perhaps he believed what he told me. Perhaps it was necessary for him to believe what he told me. Maybe he wasn't so dumb after all."

"He sounds sinister."

"Actually, Tansill reminded me of him. Tremendous self-interest, but in such an open, frank way you can hardly find fault. And who knows whether I shot the first spy? When the woman was brought forward I resolved to shoot with my eyes open, as precisely as I could. I reasoned that she was dead anyway and the best I could do for her would be to put her out mercifully. When the sergeant commanded us to shoot, however, I lost my nerve and simply pretended to fire. This time I saw the woman fall, her legs slumping horribly, her face surprised and somehow relieved. Then the privates were sent forward to bury them. The sergeant patted us on the back and sent us to a tent for brandy."

"Did you check the rifle afterward to see if you had drawn a blank?"

"Yes, eventually. I was alone when I did it. I opened the breech and found no bullet at all inside. I'm fairly certain I fired it."

"But you said . . ."

"I don't know, you see. I have no recollection of firing the gun, but the bullet was gone. I've had moments since where I seem to remember pulling the trigger. Certainly I recall the smell of gunpowder, but that might have been from the other rifles. I spoke to a priest about it once and he said that it was a common reaction.

It is called a buried sin, one which is too painful for the sinner to recall. There is a provision for it in the Catholic Church. From what he told me, I'm forgiven the sin unless I remember pulling the trigger."

I waited when I finished, as attentive to my own reaction as to Gustav's. He bobbed in the water beside me, his white belly sometimes poking through the surface.

"I think you behaved as well as anyone might under the circumstances. It was a war. You weren't free to choose," he said after a time.

"I worry that someday I'll remember."

"If you do, you'll seek confession or some penance. I'm not a religious man myself, so I can't speak with any authority. But if the day comes when you remember, you must forgive yourself."

We stayed in the water awhile longer. The village had begun to wake behind us. Gustav finally patted my shoulder, and we stood and waded to shore. A few early fishermen were now at their boats, loading them for the day's work. We slid into our undershorts and waited for the sun to dry us.

We dressed a little later. It was disheartening to wear the same soiled clothes we had worn before. Gustav, putting on his shirt, tapped his fountain pen.

"I asked Paul last night if there were any documents that needed an official stamp . . . that sort of thing," he said. "I've never tried it, but I think I might have some ability as a forger. Paul seemed excited by the prospect. It might lead us to some income."

"I can't imagine there would be much income here," I said, buttoning my shirt. The shirt was so filthy, however, that I removed it and carried it in my hand.

"It's relative, I'm sure, but their hospitality won't last forever. It will go easier if we can earn our keep. Paul promised me he would ask around. The French probably demand papers on trains. They can't just let the Africans wander about without any documentation. I thought it wouldn't hurt if we had a look at a few official papers ourselves."

I coaxed Gustav into walking with me to inspect the fishing boats. The boats were pulled high on the beach. Logs were set on either side of the keels to keep the boats from listing. I was attracted to the boats. They were designed simply, each one apparently cut from a single tree bole. The bows were carved into intricate bowsprits—a horse head, an elephant, even a mermaid.

Three fishermen worked to fold yellow nets into the center of the boats. Evenly spaced about the rim of the nets were hollow coconut shells, used to keep the nets afloat. The mesh of the net was fine; nothing larger than a trout might pass safely through the squares.

The fishermen spoke no French, but I was able to manage a few words in their local language. My phrases were a jumble, naturally, but they pleased the fishermen immensely and encouraged them to show us all aspects of the boats.

One of the men—Karamadji—pointed to the interior of the boat, then pointed to me. Did I want to go along? I hesitated; he began to smile and I told him yes, I wanted to fish.

This brought a large laugh from the other two fishermen. They pointed out to sea and waved, gesturing to indicate that the boat would go out to the horizon. I nodded, agreeing, but they weren't convinced. Gustav tapped my shoulder.

"Think what you're doing," he said. "Rest is the thing for you."

"No," I said, "I want to go. Besides, we may need one of these boats before we're through." I was trying to think like Tansill. I had resolved to keep my wits about me and watch for opportunities of escape.

I remained beside Karamadji and followed him at his work. Initially the Africans were reluctant to give me any duties, but I made a nuisance of myself until they gave me instructions. When the men lifted the nets, I rushed to help them.

Gustav came beside me as we finished loading the boats.

"I'll see what I can do about the documents," he said.

"Yes, do that."

"You'll be careful, won't you? This would be desolate without you."

He seemed so frightened that I wrapped my arm around his shoulders. I pointed to the interior of the boat and asked Karamadji if Gustav could go along. Karamadji said *"nye,"* which meant yes, but Gustav backed away, bringing more laughter from the Africans.

The sun was up and it was time to go. Gustav helped us pull back the logs that propped up the boat. Karamadji gave a signal and the men began to run beside the boat, pushing it like a sled through snow. The boat gradually picked up speed, the sound of its keel on the wet beach a song.

WE WERE HARDLY LAUNCHED when I feared Gustav had been right. I should have rested on shore and regained my strength. The waves that had been so delightful to glide in on now turned against us. They came with shocking strength and regularity. Several times the boat was slapped until it stood almost on end; it was questionable whether we would make it over the crest of the wave or simply tumble backward. I pulled at the starboard rear oar, but I caused more trouble than I was worth. Karamadji didn't raise his voice to me, though I'm sure the impulse crossed his mind. On one particularly strong wave I lost my grip on the oar altogether. I was positive it had been washed overboard, but fortunately it was lashed down in a crude oarlock. Nevertheless, my mistake had thrown the boat off line, so that the port side had gained on us. We began to turn broadside to the waves, and would have taken the waves full on if Karamadji had not yelled to the port rowers to ease off.

I was exhausted by the time we had cleared the last of the

breakers. We had dropped well behind the other boats. I felt I couldn't continue, but the rest of the crew seemed to find nothing wrong with being the last boat to clear the waves. Indeed, they appeared quite pleased with my performance. As I rowed, I thought very hard and finally came out with an awkward sentence.

"Nassarra no fish man."

This set them to laughing. They repeated it over and over. Karamadji, standing at the rear of the boat, reached over and slapped my shoulder. My gratitude on feeling his hand on my shoulder was surprisingly sharp. I pulled my oar with a new heart. I wasn't a match for any of the rowers, but at least I didn't fall behind in cadence. Several times the port side overpowered us and began to shove us to the north, but I was no longer embarrassed. When this occurred Karamadji simply yelled, "Nassarra no fish man," and the port side knew to let up on its rowing.

Fortunately, we weren't going out to the horizon, as Karamadji had indicated, but only a little beyond the reef. When we finally stopped rowing we were perhaps a kilometer off shore. The sunlight hit the coral at a more acute angle than the day before, which made the colors less vibrant but no less beautiful. The sand between the fans of coral was pure white. Fish swam everywhere; I had never seen so many species of fish.

The fleet had dispersed along the seaward edge of the reef, and already some of the boats were putting out their nets. In my boat I was paired with a young man named Coulibaly. He sat across from me, on the port side; the other pair, Diaba and Ahmadu, sat directly in front of us. Karamadji instructed Diaba and Ahmadu to take the first turn.

The manner of fishing was primitive, but efficient nonetheless. Diaba dropped over the edge of the boat and treaded water while we paid out the net. It was Coulibaly's and my job to slowly row the boat in a direct line northward along the face of the reef. Diaba remained in the water to make sure the nets dropped properly. He ducked his head frequently into the water to see that the lowest

portion of the net, weighted with stones and a rope that would
serve to close the bottom when the time came, fell in the correct
position against the sand below.

We gradually arched away from the reef and began to complete
our circle. When we were directly across from Diaba, Ahmadu
dropped into the water to perform the same tasks as Diaba had
done earlier. The nets were well manufactured and sank, for the
most part, without problem. Yet once Ahmadu called us to halt
when the net dropped over a corner of the reef, and he dove below
to free the net.

It took perhaps ten minutes to form a circle, finally closed at
Diaba's station. I looked repeatedly in the center of the net, but it
was difficult to determine what our catch might be. Many of the
fish were camouflaged; others lay close to the bottom where the
refraction of light made it all but impossible to see them.

Karamadji told Coulibaly and me to ship our oars. Coulibaly
did so at once and stood. It is not a simple thing to stand in a small
boat unless one is accustomed to it, and when I rose to my feet I
had to prop my knee against the side of the boat to keep myself
steady. Diaba, still in the water, handed us the last edge of the net,
and together Coulibaly and I began to hoist it into the boat.

I wasn't prepared for the weight of the net. Empty, it must
have weighed a great deal. Now, dragged through water and containing fish, it was almost more than I could pull. Coulibaly struck
a rhythm immediately and swung backward from the net, using
his back and legs to advantage.

Karamadji stood behind us and folded the net as it came in.
When the net had tightened to half its diameter, I began to get
some estimate of the catch. It wasn't great—approximately twenty
fish of various sizes. A few fish rushed at the net and actually jumped
to clear the top edge. Diaba and Ahmadu lifted the top sections
whenever this occurred to discourage more fish from escaping.

The net became heavier as the fish sensed their peril. They
surged back and forth. My palms began to blister as the coarse
hemp of the net jerked in my hands; my back felt as if it would

split down the middle. I was aware, too, that I had neglected to take the strength of the sun into account. I wore no hat or shirt, and the skin across my shoulders was already burned.

Minutes later we had the net tight. The fish beat against the side of the boat; the surface teemed with their tails and fins. While we held the net steady, Ahmadu and Diaba climbed back into the boat. I wondered how we would load the fish over the gunwale. The fish would scatter and slip overboard. Karamadji, however, didn't seem concerned. He pulled beside me just as Ahmadu pulled with Coulibaly. The net began to lift and swell, exactly like a wave, while the topmost sections began to spill fish into the boat.

Diaba stood between us with a killing club and struck the fish as they flopped onto the deck. He was remarkably accurate. No fish escaped him, nor did many require more than one blow. The net became lighter as we pulled it higher. The fish poured toward us in a quivering jet. Smelt, tuna, perhaps cod. Diaba stepped forward and back, raking the fish toward him one instant, smashing them to stillness in the next.

By the time we finished, several boats had rowed over and tied up with us to form a small flotilla. It was mealtime. I didn't feel particularly hungry, but when Karamadji placed a bowl of rice and fish in the center of the boat, I ate with surprising appetite. The meal was taken with a great deal of laughter and jokes. At one point Karamadji pointed to me and said in a loud voice, "Nassarra no fish man." The other boats repeated the phrase, finding it more hilarious each time it was spoken.

I would have liked to sleep when the meal ended, but the other boats began pushing off to return to work. The morning freshness had been replaced by a growing torpor. The sea appeared to be caught by sleep; the surface became calm and the sun spread on the water until we could see nothing beneath us. The gulls that had followed us all morning quieted and rode the easy swells without appearing to move at all. No wind came from the land. Except for the distant wash of the breakers, everything was silent.

I watched my companions to see if such stillness was normal

given the time of day. They appeared nervous; I suspected we were due a profound change in the weather. Karamadji looked often at the horizon, his eyes tracing an arc overhead to check the clouds, but there had been no change that I could see. The sun was brilliant; the clouds were white. Still, the silence continued. Each knock of the oars on the side of the boat resounded with remarkable volume. Occasionally we heard shouts from the shore—children playing, a woman scolding—and they were a full kilometer away.

When we finally came to the first station, I slipped overboard. The water was tepid. I immediately began pulling the net from the boat—not waiting for it to be paid out—and Karamadji made a joke and motioned for me to go slowly. I wanted the net in the water, however, thinking foolishly that it would at least give me some protection from a shark—the thought of my legs dangling in such placid water above a quiet reef unnerved me. It required an act of will for me to place my face in the water and check the net's descent to the reef.

The boat had not even reached the second station, where Coulibaly would be dropped, when I heard a shout from the fleet to my left. Immediately, in my ridiculous fear, I assumed they had spotted a large shark, for the cry was insistent and clearly meant to draw attention. I kicked as high in the water as possible and looked down the row of fishing boats. In each boat a man stood at the bow or stern, pointing to the open water. I looked in the same direction but saw nothing. When I glanced at Karamadji he had turned to the other members of my crew and shouted instructions at them. Suddenly the torpor was gone. The gulls lifted and wheeled in sunlight. It was then that I saw the fin.

I yelled when I saw it, but to my amazement Karamadji simply raised his hand and waved at me. I kicked high in the water once more and wrapped the net around my legs as much as possible. But then, in front of me, the water exploded with a thousand fish—no, more than a thousand. Everywhere there were fish and I felt them whipping around my legs, their bodies passing with incredible speed. Even more fish slammed into the net. I felt it begin to vibrate, then sag. The coconut floats were pulled under the water by the sheer weight of the fish passing into the net.

Karamadji yelled at the men to row in order to close the net. The men pulled frantically, yet with a certain joy across their features. In the same instant I saw three dolphins glide past me. I knew their shapes only from pictures, but now, seeing them pass not more than a meter from my chest, I couldn't mistake them. Their silver sides flashed and I saw one make a lunge at a fish just darting ahead of it. Obviously, they had driven the school of fish toward us, and now took advantage of the nets which had stopped the school's flight.

The net grew increasingly heavy. Gulls dove at the fish and caused more confusion from above. I saw more dolphins around me. Some were deep underwater; some swam near the surface, their dorsal fins tall and sharp. Periodically I felt a large heave as one of the dolphins struck the net.

I lost sight of the boat in the mad splashing all around me. I was startled, therefore, when Karamadji suddenly appeared behind me, bending from the bow to receive my end of the net. I handed it to him, then was assisted out of the water by Coulibaly and Ahmadu.

The dolphins were beautiful. At our first tug against the net, they jumped over the closing top and hurried out to sea. Then, apparently sensing the school had been left behind, they returned and hurtled the net once more and gorged on fish until again they felt the net's confinement. Up and over again, and so on, until the net became too small for them to enter. Even then they lingered just on the outside of the webbing and plucked fish from within the bulge.

We did what we could to get the fish into the boat. The catch was so great it became almost comical. Ahmadu actually lost his footing on fish; Coulibaly, once the net was half depleted, made himself a stool of fish and sat down as he pulled in the rest. Our boat was quickly filled from bow to stern with gleaming mullet. Larger fish lingered near the bottom of the net, and these Karamadji picked through, taking only the choicest and returning the rest to the sea.

The dolphins moved off once the net was pulled onto the boat. They didn't leave altogether; they moved cautiously around us, sometimes rolling onto their sides to inspect our movements. I was enchanted by them. I threw several fish to them and watched them rush forward. Karamadji laughed when I did this. He made no protest that I wasted the fish.

We stored the net over the mounds of fish as neatly as we could. As soon as we finished, Karamadji urged us to row. He seemed nervous about the weather, which appeared to be darkening on the horizon. We pulled hard and I was gratified to see we beat some of the other boats back across the reef.

Karamadji watched the waves intently as they rolled toward us. At last he gave a command and we pulled as hard as we could. My hands burned and my back ached, but I felt wonderful. Ahmadu began a chant—a quick, melodic string of voice that was followed by a deep refrain from Coulibaly and Diaba. I didn't know the words but I couldn't keep from joining in on the refrains, a fact which none of them found humorous. We pulled and chanted until the last wave lifted us and we began our long glide to the beach.

"THEY THINK YOU CALLED the dolphins, Frederich. I half believe it myself. You weren't on shore so you couldn't know how the village reacted. They screamed and shouted—you could see the fish being driven for some time before they reached you. It's happened before, I gather, but it's rare."

"Who said I called the dolphins?"

"Paul—but it's safe to assume he's translating for the others. He told me the dolphins actually drove the fish up onto the beach some years back. Then they disappeared and haven't returned for a decade. They haven't hunted here until today."

Gustav sat on a small milking stool in our hut. He wore a pair of shorts given to him by Paul. The shorts were baggy; he held them up with suspenders. He wore his old shirt, though it was badly tattered. Across his lap he held a plain wooden board as a writing desk. Paul had fulfilled his promise. Documents had been produced, ink provided. Now, as he spoke to me in the early afternoon, Gustav idly practiced forging the necessary stamps for a travel pass.

I lay on the mat, near to dozing. I was tired and sore from rowing, but I also felt content. The idea that I actually called the dolphins was absurd, of course. Nevertheless, the wonder of the moment had remained with me and I couldn't close my eyes without conjuring images of the dolphins leaping to escape the net.

I slept. When I woke it was evening and I smelled rain. I stepped outside. The storm that had rested on the horizon when we returned at noon was now moving over the beach. The air had become cool. On the hillside above me the grass moved and the palm trees creaked in the first rushes of wind.

As I watched the clouds darkening, Gustav appeared from one of the huts on the southern rim of the village. He laughed and backed out, his hands filled. He paused a few paces from the doorway, much like a man thanking his hosts one last time before taking his leave, then turned and began walking rapidly toward me.

He carried two large fish, each one laid out on its own palm frond in place of plates. At his side dangled a goat skin filled with some kind of liquid.

"Roasted," he said, handing me one of the fish. "I had to show them how—it isn't easy over charcoal, but I worked it out with an old woman."

Inside the hut, we sat near to the doorway to get the full benefit of the fresher air. The rain came before we began our meal. Gustav passed me the goat skin, which was filled with millet beer. I drank a good dose, though the taste was even worse than the night before. The goat skin lent the liquid a gamey smell that made it nearly impossible to drink.

We hadn't made much headway with the meal when Gustav excused himself and stepped outside. The rain was heavy and he was drenched in a moment. He looked around, then moved off, disappearing up the incline to the field of grass above us. He stayed ten minutes, and when he returned his face was white.

"Are you all right?" I asked. He sat on his mat, but didn't take up his food.

"A touch of dysentery, I think," he said. "I suppose it's to be expected. It started earlier."

He lay back on his mat. I didn't grant much importance to his condition at the time. During the war, dysentery and constipation were constant problems. When Gustav continued to lie on the mat without sitting up, I asked for his portion of food and he waved at it, telling me to take it. He had no appetite.

The dysentery worsened as the night progressed. No sooner did Gustav lie on his mat than he was forced up. I offered to dig him a trench nearby so that he would not have to make the long march to the beach grasses, but he refused to hear of it.

It was an unsettled night. Gustav was up and down, and the rain drew out countless insects. The mosquitoes were dense, ridiculously so, and I slept only when I managed to wrap some clothing around my ears and eyes, sacrificing the rest of my body to indiscriminate bites. We waited for a wind to chase away the insects, but nothing came. I was happy to see the sunrise, and was up for my morning bath long before full light.

I swam and washed, then sat in the sunlight until I felt warm. When I returned to our hut Gustav was awake. He didn't look well. His flesh was white and chalky; his eyes were red from exhaustion. His copy of *The Odyssey* was open beside him, though I doubted he had the strength to read.

"You know," he said quietly as I sat on my mat, "I was just

lying here wondering if Tansill wasn't right after all. Make a clean break, keep moving. We can't stay here forever."

"You don't feel well right now. We should at least stay until you have your strength back."

"It's different for you. You like it here, Frederich. This life appeals to you. You jumped in the fishing boat at the first opportunity. Don't laugh, and don't apologize. Perhaps you'd like to stay longer? Make a home here?"

"No, I just think we should try to figure out what our next move should be. It makes no sense to jump from one place to the next until we have a plan. Maybe we shouldn't even go to Dakar. Maybe we should move north."

I was lying of course. I did like village life; I craved its simplicity in a way I could never have anticipated. I had felt many things since arriving in the fishing boats, but not a trace of homesickness. Europe was engaged in a war, a very dubious one, and I felt myself well out of it. The logic of Gustav's position escaped me—leave to go where? To risk imprisonment? It seemed much wiser to remain until we determined where we stood.

But these were only brief thoughts. Gustav's condition was more central to my thinking. He was drained; his forehead was covered with sweat. His eyes didn't quite follow my movement around the hut. They were a count behind, as if he couldn't focus quickly enough to take me in entirely. I moved closer and put my palm on his forehead. He was frighteningly warm.

"Are you chilled?" I asked him.

"It comes and goes."

"I'll find a blanket. Maybe we should put you in the sun for a while."

"I'll be all right."

"Do you have an appetite? I could get one of the women to make broth or soup."

"No, nothing."

He lay back on the mat, his chest glassy and wet from the effort of sitting up.

I searched out Karamadji down by the fishing boats. Using a few phrases and pretending to shiver, I managed to convey to him that I wanted a blanket. Paul arrived just as a woman from Karamadji's compound gave me a blanket. He asked if Gustav's condition was serious—already the news had spread. I told him no, just a touch of fever. Paul, speaking slowly so that I could understand, told me that he could get a man of some learning to pay a visit to Gustav. I thanked him, but told him no.

Gustav was worse by the time I arrived with the blanket. He didn't wake when I ducked into the hut. His brow was wrinkled as if wrestling with a problem; his eyes moved beneath their closed lids, much like a person having a painful dream.

I bathed him with water from the calabash, then covered him. I touched my hand to his forehead once more, but it was futile. He was hot—that was all too evident. I stripped the tail of his shirt into a long bandage and made a compress out of it which I placed on his forehead. The water dried rapidly in the open air.

It was not much later when Paul arrived with Indrissa and three old women. They clapped at the door but didn't enter; behind them, a group of young girls carried household goods. One child had a pot, another a stack of wood, and so on. Clearly, they had come to work a cure.

"These women can help, Nassarra," Paul said when I stepped outside.

"He will be all right," I answered.

"Dream fevers," he said, shaking his head to indicate I didn't understand the severity of the situation. I took him to mean delirium.

I relented eventually. It was possible, after all, that they understood this type of fever.

The women were old and quite ugly. They smiled as they passed me, though they had perhaps ten teeth among them. The children hurried into the hut behind them, each one carrying some practical implement. In no time the women had built a small fire in the center of the hut. A boy was sent onto the roof to cut a hole in the apex with a machete. I should have thought that the child would break through the thatch, but he stayed on the wooden understructure and cut the hole in minutes. The other children then handed the boy buckets of seawater with which he doused the grass matting. This way, no errant spark could prove a problem, and, as important, the weave of the roof tightened and kept the smoke inside the hut.

The women arranged themselves around Gustav and fanned smoke at him. They didn't actually push the smoke onto his face and eyes, but instead managed to make the smoke curl above his body before the draft carried it up. The hut quickly became heated; Gustav's sweat increased. Whether this was good for him I could hardly say.

He didn't wake for the rest of the day. At sunset his fever took an alarming jump and he began to hallucinate. He spoke in German, recalling names that drifted through his visions. Gerta was one name, Sylvia another. Once, for a dreadful half hour, he recited train schedules. The times and stations didn't come all at once. Instead, his mind seemed to follow a single train as it moved from Berlin to Munich and finally to the front.

I stayed with him and eventually convinced the women to relent somewhat on their fanning. As a result, only one woman continued to fan while the fire was allowed to burn lower. Nevertheless the air was intensely hot. I had to remain close to the ground in order to breathe without discomfort. The remaining old woman didn't appear to notice the heat. She rocked on the stool and let the fan droop and rise, wafting the smoke in wreaths above Gustav's chest.

As it became darker, Gustav's fever cooled a few degrees. I bathed his forehead with the compress. I wanted light, but there were no lanterns in the village. I made do with the firelight, although it wasn't trustworthy. At times Gustav sank into darkness and I almost believed he was gone. Then, with a coil of wind from the old woman's fan, the fire burned red once more and I might see his profile, stiff and white in the dimness.

I slept eventually. When I woke near dawn, I discovered that his fever was broken. He wasn't nearly as warm as he had been before; the sweat on his forehead was less angry. His breathing was easier and his sleeping appeared to be restful. His blanket smelled of smoke.

I fell asleep beside him and woke only when the sun cut through the doorway and lay across my legs. I went to the calabash and drank. I drank a great deal, then dampened the compress on Gustav's forehead and washed his face and hands. At the touch of water he came awake. It took him awhile to pull back to consciousness, and once or twice he seemed to regret returning. But then his eyes stuttered open and finally he tried to speak.

I gave him water—just a little—and held his head up to make it easier to swallow. His body trembled. His neck was too weak to lift the weight of his skull. When he brought a hand up to steady the ladle at this lips, it shook so badly he eventually gave up the notion of assisting me and allowed himself to be fed.

"How long?" he asked in a whisper.

"You've been under all night. How are you feeling?"

"Terrible."

"The fever has broken. You're lucky. Are you hungry?"

"No. I'd like to sleep."

"Sleep a little longer, then we'll get some broth. You should eat something," I told him.

He nodded. I made him as comfortable as I could.

By the afternoon Gustav was much improved. He sat up and ate a decent meal. We had a nervous hour waiting to see if he could keep it down, but when he settled back and smiled, I knew the worst of his illness was over.

Later, Gustav slept while I read his copy of *The Odyssey*. When he woke he demanded that we bathe. I accompanied him to the beach, occasionally giving him my elbow to lean on until he felt steady. We were stopped several times by villagers who obviously wanted to say they were happy to see him back on his feet.

Each time this was conveyed by a series of hand gestures and phrases repeated over and over.

At last we came to the sea and Gustav stripped his clothes and went cautiously into the surf. He went in only to mid-thigh and then sank down, relieved to have a chance to clean himself. He knelt for a long time and scrubbed himself with sand. I debated about going in myself, but finally contented myself with sitting on the beach and watching the evening sun.

It was a peaceful moment, made more poignantly so by the contrast of what came next. As Gustav waded to shore a sudden scream rose from behind us. I turned to see a child running down to the beach from the hillside behind us. The child screamed repeatedly, his running spastic with fear. Two more children, who had apparently been playing on the hillside to the north, also screamed at the same moment. They too came hurtling down the hillside, their cries warbling and vibrating with their jarring run.

Just as they reached the bottom of the hill I saw the first horseman, an African. He appeared on the horizon, his outline black and definite, as if sunlight avoided him. Without pausing he kicked his horse forward and began down the long incline. He was followed by twenty men, all mounted. Had the children not screamed so violently, it might have been a beautiful sight. The horses turned and pranced, ears back, eyes wild, their front legs stiff to take the shock of their descent. They whinnied and nickered while a tremendous cloud of dust filled the air above them.

My attention alternated between the horsemen and the villagers of Batie. The children had raised an alarm. Now the cry was taken up by men and women up and down the beach. Here a woman came running out of her hut; there a man, caught by the fishing boats, dashed back to his hut to be with his family. The attack occurred too quickly to form any defense.

When the first horseman reached level ground he whipped his horse into the center of the village. He was a magnificent looking man, a blend of Arabic and black African, who rode with exquisite posture. His face was badly scarred across the cheeks and forehead, and it looked, at that distance, that perhaps the side of his face had been staved in by a horse's hoof.

He rode into the village followed by the rest of the horsemen. They were dressed similarly, though their clothes didn't comprise a uniform. Most wore conical hats; others wore the white burnoose of the desert wrapped around their heads and over their faces. Their horses were elaborately decorated, with long skirts of rawhide across their chests to protect them from arrows. At least ten carried rifles, but the remainder carried scimitars, the long curved sword of the nomad.

I hadn't moved. Gustav stepped free of the surf and pulled on his shorts. "In the name of heaven," he said beneath his breath, but I didn't respond. Together we watched the leader pull his horse to a halt and order his men to circle the village.

When the village was surrounded, the leader rode past the huts, yelling for those hidden in each to step outside. He appeared to fear no resistance since he turned his back on the people as they came outside. It took him only a moment to have the villagers collected in a loose group in the center market. At his signal, three men dismounted and began going through the huts one by one. More than once they found a child hidden in a hut and chased him out. Occasionally the men reappeared with some treasure—an old musket-loading rifle or an especially fine knife—but otherwise the search turned up little.

As they concluded their search, one man finally saw us. He was in the process of swinging his leg over the rump of his horse, when he lifted his hand and pointed at us, clearly astonished. He had to bounce once more on the ground, then swing again into the saddle. By that time two other guards rode toward us.

The horsemen made a splashy show of charging through the surf, shouting and kicking at their horses as they approached. Gustav and I remained stationary, waiting docilely for them to invite us to speak. But they continued to charge until one of the riders came close enough to whip me across the shoulders with a thick crop of rawhide.

The force of the blow was shocking. Shocking that a black man could raise a whip to a white man. Shocking that they failed to see we had no interest in the minor skirmish of two African tribes. Shocking that the man didn't satisfy himself with one blow, but lifted his arm and whipped me again, this one no less violent, across the bare flesh of my forearm.

During the same rush Gustav was knocked down into a tidal pool. I took a third lash across my shoulder and tried to grab the disappearing leather. Another lash hit me on the back, just as the neck and chest of a horse suddenly pushed me forward. I was being herded down the beach toward the rest of the villagers. It was impossible to resist and reluctantly I began trotting to the village center, calling to Gustav at the same time to do as he was told. I looked around quickly and saw him struggling to his feet. One of the horsemen whipped him and this started him running. He could barely move due to the residue of fever, but the guards took no notice. They whipped him until his pace satisfied them.

The men cut into the crowd and selected people at random. It was done rapidly, as if they were aware the villagers might eventually recognize they outnumbered the horsemen and attack. I had no idea why they wanted captives, or what they hoped to do with us, but the method was clear. The men cut this way and that through the crowd, signaling to different people to form a smaller group away from the center. The men chose three young girls. They also cut Gustav and me from the larger group.

Then it was over. Three horsemen headed us toward the beach grass at the top of the hill. The girls screamed; a few women in the village called back to them. Yet no one made any attempt to stop the men from running off with the girls. We were jarred on all sides by the horses, and the whips came down from every side. I looked once and saw Gustav, barely able to breathe, already dropping behind. The men hovered over him mercilessly, whipping him to make him run faster.

They also whipped the girls. My memory of that first afternoon of running was locked to the scarlet flash of blood trailing after a whip. We staggered up the hill, scrambling to keep away from the surging horses. At the top we were herded into a pack and set to run across the sahel. We headed east toward the desert.

I COULD DO NOTHING for Gustav, though I knew he suffered. The men whipped us if we slowed, shouting at us if we veered too far to avoid a bush or particularly uneven stretch of ground. I had no doubt that the men might shoot us if we stalled or pretended an injury.

We ran several kilometers without a word or command except the advice of the whip. The sea air left us. We entered desert, dry barren land that supported little but thorny bushes as far as I could see. It was remarkable to think this land existed not more than three kilometers from the ocean, but it spread in front of me, brown and pure and more powerful than any land I had ever seen. It was a sea itself—a trite comparison but true nonetheless. No mountain or hillside ruined our view of the horizon. We could see for hundreds of kilometers to the east, far enough so that we might see the edge of nightfall before it swept over us.

At last a halt was called. I immediately turned to find Gustav. He had already fallen to the ground not far from where the girls squatted together. Gustav's back and shoulders were severely cut by the whips. It was only when I saw his feet were badly bleeding that I realized mine were as well. I felt dizzy and empty. I sat beside him and put my head between my knees. Bright spots of light cracked inside my head.

"I can't keep up," Gustav said, barely able to speak. He didn't open his eyes.

"They'll whip you if you don't," I panted.

"Then they'll whip me. They can kill me right here. I don't care anymore."

I looked around, trying to assess our position. The horsemen had dismounted; many moved about smoking cigarettes or talking quietly. The women, perhaps ten meters from us, had not stopped crying.

We were not given water. In no time a call was given to start again. The orders were spoken with such authority that I got to my feet at once. The men made no pretense of caring for our welfare as European captors are schooled to do. They would slaughter us if it came to it. We were simply an element of their troop, not unlike a horse or a dog.

Gustav could not get to his feet. Two men rode by on horses and shouted at him. Gustav shook his head. When one raised his whip to strike Gustav, I stepped in between. It was a stupid act—I knew it was stupid as I did it—but I couldn't stand to let them whip him.

Both men set on me. The whips I could endure; I was more concerned with avoiding their horses, which spun and side-stepped dangerously. I covered my head with my hands and accepted the lashes on my arms. They whipped me repeatedly, screaming at both of us to move. Yet Gustav couldn't stand. He tried once to struggle to his feet, then fell on his side and moved no more.

The leader, a man the others called Zinda, eventually rode back to find out the cause of the delay. It was the same man who had led the charge into the village. I hadn't seen him since we had climbed the hillside, but now he rode calmly toward us, his posture erect, his eyes shaded by the round sweep of his conical hat. My initial impression of him had been correct—his right cheek had indeed been staved in by a horse's hoof. The injury had apparently paralyzed the right side of his face, so that his every look was somehow duplicitous. He was a Janus.

He rode close to me and stopped. With great deliberation—the deliberation of a leader who is called on to straighten out the mess made by a subordinate—he bent across his horse and motioned for me to approach. When I took a step nearer he suddenly brought his whip up from behind the flank of his horse and struck me squarely across the face. In one quick lash he had severed the flesh of my cheek, splitting it nearly in two so that I felt air directly against my teeth. I spun back, my hand to my mouth. It wasn't only the pain that made me recoil, but also the certain knowledge that he had aimed at my eyes. He had meant to blind me, to take out my eye, but had missed by a few centimeters.

He showed no remorse, no emotion at all. He wiped the bloody end of his crop against the neck of the horse.

"Get him up," he said to me in perfect French. "Get him up or we'll kill him here."

"He's been sick."

"Get him up."

I bent close to Gustav and spoke into his ear. He couldn't hear me. I slapped his cheek softly at first, then with more force. Gustav came around slowly. His eyes were filmy, his breathing short and labored. He was a fifty-year-old man suffering from fever. I couldn't imagine what they wanted of him, or how they expected him to survive such treatment.

With difficulty, I got him to his feet. I put his arm around my neck. His hand came into contact with my open cheek and I felt my head turn light. The rest of the troop had begun to move and I limped with Gustav after them. Each time I turned, gripping Gustav's arm tightly around my neck, I saw Zinda riding behind us, sometimes his dead right profile turned to us, other times his left.

The terrain did not change except that the dryness around us became more of an established fact. The air was hot and dry and the scrub bushes appeared hollow with heat. We saw no water, nor any clouds. Now and then, on the horizon, we glimpsed herds of antelope. Yet beneath us, near our footsteps, the world was restricted to lizards and ants, a predatory exchange carried off in near perfect dryness.

Zinda rode to the front of the procession after following us for half an hour. Gustav had recovered somewhat by this time. His legs frequently buckled, but he was now conscious and willing to make an effort. He walked to please me; he walked to forestall my guilt. But I had no illusions about his appetite for living. If I lifted his arm from my neck, he would gladly fall and die—that I knew without question.

It was near nightfall when we mounted a small rise and at last saw the caravan. It stretched for two kilometers at least, and was half that distance in breadth. Dust followed it everywhere. It was difficult to distinguish the animals through the haze and fading light, but in my first glance I saw cattle and horses flocked around a center spine composed of camels. Goats weaved everywhere; a solid pack of mongrel dogs barked at our arrival.

The sound of the caravan struck me more forcefully than any other aspect about it. Besides the dogs barking, there was the loll of cattle. Strained through that bucolic note was the trident chafing of the camels, the quickening bleats of goats, the occasional crow of chickens as they rode in baskets strapped to the humps of the camels. Beneath everything was the purr of pigeons which rode in wide wicker sleeves hung from the spur of the camels' saddles. All of this combined to give the caravan a recognizable voice.

Despite my fear and the weight of Gustav's arm around my shoulder, my eyes remained fixed on the camels. Each camel carried a tremendous load strapped by ingenious lashings around its girth. Many of the loads appeared to be simple salt; other camels carried tents and bedding and the provender for the entire caravan. Dirt clung to their coats, turning them a cinnamon color. They wore bells around their right forelegs so that every step produced a jingle, a light, airy sound like a silver knife touched inadvertently to a crystal goblet.

"Nomads," Gustav said when we drew close. "It's an entire village . . . a moving village."

"Shhh."

At no signal that I could detect, the caravan ceased to move. Or, rather, the forward momentum suddenly halted. The caravan always moved—a fact I would gradually learn—and all around us animals continued to circle and walk, though they put no distance behind them. Immediately, women and men began setting up camp. A camel was made to kneel by a driver who hit him on the neck. The pack was removed by a pair of women, then the camel was hobbled and allowed to wander where he would. This was repeated over and over throughout the caravan. In a short time the women raised tents demarcating family groups.

Remarkably, we were left alone. The guards, including Zinda, had ridden ahead of us, leaving Gustav and me to fend for ourselves. In my naïveté, I thought this a perfect opportunity to escape—it would grow dark, the guards would be occupied with domestic matters, and we could slip off unobserved. Yet I soon realized no guard was needed. Water was here, and food. In its barrenness, the land around us was a perfect prison.

"Let me sit," Gustav said when we were safely within the confines of the shifting caravan.

Gustav dropped off to sleep in an instant. His brow was covered with sweat; he twitched and shivered in his sleep. His feet were the color of rust from dried blood. His shoulders and arms were marked with red lashes.

I left him and found an old crone who offered me water. She was blind in her left eye and badly crippled. She gave me a calabash of water and pointed toward Gustav, then indicated that I was to bring back the empty calabash.

He was unconscious when I returned. I moistened his lips and tried to force water down his throat. Nothing worked; the water burbled back up. I continued to wedge the calabash between his lips. Each time he refused to drink, I was goaded to try harder. If he could drink, he would live—that was my reasoning. But the water only curled out from his lips, lingering on the dusky gray of his beard.

I don't remember a great deal more of that first night. I recall holding Gustav in my arms for a time. I was ashamed that I could do nothing more for him—he would perish on the bare earth with not so much as a blanket to cover him.

It became cold, terribly cold, and the sand blew in stinging waves. I dragged Gustav by the feet until I found several camels lying in the sand. One camel shied at our approach, but it soon settled and allowed me to pull Gustav near. I placed him as close to the camel's side as I could, then pressed my body against his. It was possible he was dead at that point. Yet his body was warm for some time longer, and near him, through this chest and arms that were around me, I heard the beat of a gigantic heart—the camel's, the earth's, the sky's.

GUSTAV WAS DEAD. At first light I dragged him away from the camels to a small copse of stunted trees and buried him, not deeply, among the knotted roots. His copy of *The Odyssey* had fallen out of his pocket. I picked it up and put it in my own pocket.

I couldn't make a wooden cross for him, since I had no ax or machete. Instead, I drew a cross in the sand, then recited a brief prayer.

When I finished the prayer, I went to kill Zinda. I had no formed plan, nor did I even know where Zinda had spent the night. It didn't matter. He had killed Gustav and I now intended to kill him. It was justice, and I approached my decision—if it can be called a decision—with complete detachment.

The caravan was just waking, and the noise and maddening

screech from the camels was confusing. No pattern or design governed the campsites. The odors were horrible. Several times I had to stop and turn my face to a different wind to remove the stench of urine or defecation. Everything within a square kilometer smelled of rancid oil and wet fur. Nothing was clean; nothing was ordered. The tents I had seen the night before now proved to be the worst sort of hovels. They were loaded with mats and food for entire families, while, among the bundles, any number of people slept nearly on top of one another.

I walked the length of the camp before I found Zinda. He had just stepped out of his tent. He rubbed his eyes and looked toward the east, perhaps judging the weather. He hadn't slept alone. One woman was already seated before a cook fire in front of the tent, feeding it twigs and branches to warm the morning tea. Another woman, in the deeper recesses of the tent, was busy knotting her pagna tightly around her waist.

I only dimly recall what happened next. I know I made a sound, a deep, guttural whine that turned his head toward me just as I left my feet to tackle him. I didn't scream or cry out. Instead, as my shoulder struck him in the chest, I discovered that I was crying.

What I remember next was dirt and sand and stinging sweat. We locked together. His arms came around and tried to roll me over. At the same time the woman by the fire began to shout, her voice gradually lifting into a terrible scream. Immediately, more voices joined hers. The sounds were like strange warbles—trains heard at a distance—as I punched at Zinda, careful to keep my weight on top of him. I ripped at his eyes and ears, and bit his arm when he tried to push his elbow in my face. He kicked at me and tried to knee my testicles. But I had him—I had him down.

Men pulled me off him. Their arms came under mine and, despite the rage I felt, I couldn't keep from remembering the Africans lifting Gustav and me into the fishing boat. Nevertheless, I kicked at Zinda as they pulled me away and landed one last shot on his upper thigh. I cried strangely, on the edge of hysteria. Added to this was the very real pain I began to feel from the cuts that had reopened across my shoulders and back.

Zinda took his time getting up. The paralyzed side of his face was turned to me and this was more unsettling than if I had been able to actually witness his anger. The ugly hole stamped in his cheek was flecked with sand and blood—mine or his, I couldn't say. Very deliberately, he brushed himself free of sand and dirt.

"Your friend is dead?" he asked finally. Still he hadn't turned to face me. The men behind me held my arms.

I didn't answer. I didn't want to give him the satisfaction of an answer, though I was aware how foolish that was—how falsely heroic it seemed. My composure was lost in any case. My chest pumped up and down trying to capture air, while my hands and arms twitched at my sides. My nose was wet with mucus and blood; my eyes stung with sweat and sand.

Zinda turned, his eyes calm. He was bleeding from the ear— a cut I must have administered, although I had no recollection of doing so. He dabbed at the cut with his finger, then held his hand out to examine the blood. He appeared surprised that anyone could conceive of attacking him.

He said something to the men and their arms became tighter around me. Zinda took two steps closer and looked very carefully at me. He looked at me for a protracted period—not for a minute, but perhaps for two. His eyes—the weight of his vision—became increasingly heavy. Try as I might not to look away, his stare was more penetrating than mine. I averted my eyes several times, and each time the crowd tittered appreciatively.

Finally he spoke rapidly to two of the men. They pushed me to the ground and tied my hands behind my back. Three other men sped away to return within ten minutes, carrying something that made the crowd laugh. The men holding my arms wouldn't allow me to look. They pressed my forehead into the ground, forcing my eyes closed.

A moment later something damp touched the flesh at my back.

I started and arched against the hands that restrained me, which again caused the crowd to laugh. But the dampness was frightening. It wrapped around my shoulders and neck, sliding down to my ribs. The rawhide thong around my wrists was tightened and reinforced with a stouter strap. All of this occurred behind me, my face pressed into the sand.

It did not take long for them to finish. They passed several rawhide strings beneath my chest and over my stomach; something was knotted around my throat. I was given a cap, and at last I began to have some inkling of what had transpired. They had made me into a figure of mockery, but I couldn't guess what that might be. Whenever I tried to twist my head to see, it was pressed harder into the sand. Obviously, I was to be surprised by whatever was on my back—it was part of the entertainment for the villagers.

The last thing to occur before I was released was more frightening than anything that had gone before. Zinda lay on the ground exactly opposite me, so that our foreheads nearly touched. He said something to the men. They let me lift my head enough to look directly at Zinda. His pretense of calm was gone now; he hated me and made no effort to mask it.

Zinda touched his finger to the blood on his ear, then rubbed his finger across my forehead. The crowd suddenly became silent.

"I have made you an animal,' he whispered. "You are no longer human."

As soon as he said this, he stood. He told the men to let me up. I got to my knees awkwardly. The crowd found this tremendously amusing. They laughed—the stillness from a moment before diffused. Even Zinda smiled. Ridiculously, I smiled in return.

The crowd laughed harder at seeing my confusion. They pointed at my back, and I foolishly obliged them by turning to see what was attached there. They laughed again. A few small boys, showing off, ran by laughing and pointing at me and touching me with sticks.

At last I gained my feet. By now I was becoming nervous about the object attached to my back. I looked down and was horrified to see blood dripping on my thighs and legs.

I turned rapidly, trying to see what was on my back. The Africans retreated whenever I came near them. I forced myself to be calm. The crowd watched expectantly, as if the joke had already been made but the unraveling of the story remained unfinished.

Slowly, I walked through the village with the people following. I found a calabash of water near a weathered tent. It was positioned in the shade, yet enough sun found it to give me back my reflection. Protruding from the top of my head were two long ears.

It was an illusion, naturally, but a disturbing one just the same. I was confused and dazed, and for an instant the illusion looked quite real. When I moved a little to the side, however, I discovered the source of the ears. A goat skin had been attached to my back. Rawhide straps kept it pressed close to my ribs. The cap I had felt was nothing more than the empty goat's head, its long ears sticking up ludicrously from the top of my skull.

The people found each of my minute discoveries extremely rewarding. They laughed and pointed repeatedly. For my own part, I felt relief. It was gory to have the skin attached to my back, but it wasn't painful. And with my hands tied I would not be forced to work. I looked around for Zinda, but he was gone.

The crowd dispersed finally when I refused to play the fool for it any longer. The children remained and continued to rush in toward me, brandishing sticks as if they herded me. It was a game to them; I would have kicked them if I could have been sure of my timing. But they were quick and nimble and I knew if I missed them I would become the center of even more attention.

I wanted sleep; I wanted food. I moved to a spot of shade thrown by a dwarf tree, and sat. It was awkward to do so, my hands tied behind my back as they were, but I needed rest. As soon as I was down, I slumped to one side and felt near to vomiting. The blood on my arms and legs had begun to dry, matting the hairs and pulling against my skin. A few early flies found me. The children sometimes ran close, but their feet were nothing more than tremors in the soil.

The flies woke me. It was late morning and the sun was directly on me. I was conscious immediately that the goat skin on my back was becoming rigid. It was tightening as well, but it was difficult to determine by how much. It was an odd phenomenon: The skin felt attached to my muscles, so that each movement on my part brought a corresponding flex from the goat skin. If it was Zinda's plan, or curse, that I should begin to perceive the goat skin as my own, it was not without a certain genius.

But the flies were more impressive. To say they were everywhere is to understate the case. They moved in the ridges of my ribs and on my knees and neck. I felt their fine, endless feet lighting and lifting in a thousand variations. The sound of my own breathing was accompanied by the buzz of flies as they reacted each time my chest swelled. I couldn't lift a hand without scattering them with my shadows. I stood simply to have them less dense on my skin.

Once on my feet, however, I did not know where to go. The caravan was all around me, hot in the midday sun. I began to walk slowly through the caravan. I did not know what reaction my appearance might invite, so I kept to the side of any path or opening between tents. The ridiculous goat's head remained squarely atop my crown. It did not flop back against my spine, as I had at first hoped it might, but rode in position, giving me a shadow that struck me as comical, but also sinister. I wondered, in those first minutes of full consciousness, how many times I could look down at the shadow without accepting it as my own—I possessed the shadow of an animal, therefore I was a beast myself. Doubtless, that was Zinda's intention, but I was shocked to find it more subtly powerful than I had anticipated.

Someone must have alerted Zinda that I was up and about, because I had not gone much farther before he appeared. He was dressed in a white robe and wore leather sandals on his feet. As he approached me, I tried to compose myself. I feared him. He did not appear to move so much as undulate. His movements were smooth; even the smallest motion of his hand or neck carried through to the rest of his body.

He brought me carrots—or at least the African equivalent of carrots. Walking toward me, he extracted a bunch of tuberous plants from his pocket and shook them softly toward me. The gesture wasn't lost on me. I was a goat and this was my food.

"You are hungry, I suppose?" he asked. "Thirsty as well."

"What do you want with me?"

He ignored my question and shook the carrots again. I tried not to look at them, despite the churning in my stomach.

"I believe you are a goat. Perhaps you will become one for me."

"Please untie my hands."

He smiled and shook the carrots again.

It was a remarkably intimate act, almost sexual, to take food from his hand. He held the carrot steady while I slowly chewed it into pulp. Once or twice he moved the carrot and, to my astonishment, I felt my mouth and body following it in a gesture uncomfortably similar to a goat or cow.

The root had no taste to speak of, but the fiber felt extraordinary in my mouth and stomach. This was my rationalization for demeaning myself—I was famished and near to death; to eat was my only chance. And yet, as I pulled at the carrots and took them from his hand, I was aware of my back teeth grinding the tubers, my cheeks filling with pulp. I had seen horses consume hay in just this manner. As I chewed I stared straight down at the ground, watching the pair of ears wag above my head while my jaws ground sideways.

THROUGHOUT THE MORNING and afternoon I remained in the sun as much as possible. I prayed the heat would dry the hide on my back so that the flies would find little to attract them. Nothing worked; the flies plagued me. They found my cuts and the open sore on my cheek; there was no escape from them. By early evening they had become almost more than I could bear.

As night approached, I fell asleep from pure exhaustion. I slept near a tree, hoping it would give me shelter. I slept fitfully. Once I woke and maneuvered around the tree in order to be out of the wind. I tried to bury my legs in sand and earth, thinking to insulate myself, but the soil was chilled and hinted of the grave.

It was during one of these abbreviated spells of sleep that Kama found me. Kama was a village fool. I had glimpsed him once during the day. He had been intent on attaching what looked like a bicycle spoke to a long lock of his matted hair. The bicycle spoke was only one of hundreds of metallic odds and ends attached to Kama's body. On his belt were coils of springs, more bicycle spokes, rusted watches, the triangular tips of fountain pens; in his hair, dangling in every direction, were iron nails and curtain hooks, the neck of a metal hanger and paper clips. He wore two bandoleers of metal scraps crossed loosely over his chest.

He was filthy; his hair was disgustingly matted. For clothing he wore only a belt around his waist, which served to anchor the brown loincloth he pulled over his groin and up between the hemispheres of his buttocks. His feet were horny with calluses, and his eyes were almost yellow with ancient maps of fever.

I saw all of this in one ghastly instant as he crouched over me. I lay still, pretending to sleep, afraid at any moment he might smash out my brains with a rock. He crouched and looked at me curiously, as if he would place me in his memory if given a moment. He smelled horribly, and, after opening my eyes, I sat up to be away from his odor. Still he squatted in front of me, idly watching my discomfort at having him so near.

"What do you want? I don't have anything. Leave me alone," I said in French.

"Nassarra no fish man," he answered in the language of Batie, then smiled broadly, all the while maintaining his position.

I could not imagine how he had heard the phrase. It was uncanny. Then, when I had a moment to consider, I realized he must have talked to the three women who had been captured along with Gustav and myself.

I smiled at the memory. Kama smiled in return. His teeth were clean and white, in complete contrast with the rest of him. He repeated the phrase, then repeated it until I no longer smiled at it.

When he saw I was tired of the game, he stood suddenly and reached into his crotch. I thought he was about to engage in some confused masturbatory display, but instead he removed a plain black rock. He took a step backward so that I might see him better. Then, composing himself, he began to slowly move the rock around his body, passing it from one hand to the other and then behind his back.

It was a magnet. As he passed the rock from one side to the other, the various pieces of junk first lifted from his body, then patted back against his skin. Slowly, he raised his hands and passed the rock in a halo around his head. His hair lifted. It was extraordinary to see, not only for the effect, which was stunning against the sky flushed with stars, but because his belief and pleasure at performing for me were so evident.

This was his one glorious trick; I could break him easily by laughing. His eyes, expectant, waited to see if I would ridicule him. At the same time, his expression tried to convey the wonder he felt in what he was showing me. Never did his hands stop; never did his metal objects cease lifting and following the invisible currents of attraction.

Once he appeared convinced I believed in his powers, he slid the magnet back into the crotch of his loincloth. The magic over, he pointed into the maze of tents and motioned for me to stand. This was too much. I had no intention of following him.

"You go ahead," I told him.

In reply he said, "*Waca*" . . . come.

"No, I'm all right here. I have the tree."

"*Waca.*"

He was emphatic. I allowed him to help me to my feet. He walked quickly into the tents. Almost at once it was warmer out of the wind. I looked around for a suitable place to rest, thinking I had been mistaken in not realizing I could do better than a tree in the middle of the flat plain. I even slowed once, ready to sit down, but Kama touched my shoulder and waved for me to continue.

We weren't far into the caravan when Kama finally stopped beside a cook fire which still panted red in the late winds. He crouched and buried the coals beneath a thin layer of dirt. I thought he was putting the fire out, and I started to speak, but then I realized he was covering the coals to form a bed. He worked quickly, impervious to the heat. When he had the dirt spread smoothly over the coals, he lay down and tested his handiwork. Satisfied, he jumped up, pointed to me and then the bed.

I wanted to lie down, but hesitated, afraid he would take this as permission to sleep beside me. He grabbed my elbow and pushed me down. I didn't resist. When I lay down, the sand was warm. I wasn't completely comfortable—far from it—but the wind didn't find me so easily among the tents. The coals sent up enough heat to keep one side of my body warm; the scent of smoke turned back at least some of the insects. I knew I would be cold long before dawn, but at least temporarily I could rest. It was a thousand times more comfortable than my bed by the tree.

I waited for Kama to lie beside me, but he only squatted again in front of me. Whether by luck or manners on his part, he squatted down wind so that I wouldn't have to contend with his smell. I smiled at him, then closed my eyes, hoping he would wander away. But he remained where he was, watching over me and staring into the night beyond.

. . .

When I woke it was dawn and Kama was gone. The flies were with me as soon as I got to my feet. My shoulders were numb; I feared the rawhide bands had cut off my circulation completely. I wouldn't have been surprised to find my hands were blue or even black. My fingers had very little sensation.

I found a calabash of water and drank from it. I knelt and put my face near to the surface. It would have been easy to actually submerge my lips and suck in the water, but my head was too large—it was blocked by the rim of the calabash. As a result I had to lick at the water with my tongue, which was an extremely tedious process. It was also humiliating. I frequently lifted my head from the water to look around me, pained when a man going off to tend the cattle saw me and was confirmed in his conviction that I was changing into a goat. I had little doubt that the news would spread—Nassarra was seen in first light, drinking as an animal.

I looked for Kama, but couldn't find him. I was surprised by the sharpness of my disappointment that he had abandoned me, even temporarily. I was hungry and cold, and the condition of my arms and hands worried me. I didn't know what Kama could do about any of these things, but I felt that he might have some advice.

I waited in the sun until the caravan began to move. The noise started softly, then increased as the caravan surged forward. The sound swelled into a wide harmony: the snore of cattle and the bleat of goats; the cawing of chickens and throaty warble of pigeons from their wicker sleeves. Everywhere there were bells and shouts, and slobbered heaves from animals dreading the day in front of them. The children chased after any wayward animal, while the women walked with huge burdens on their heads. The men smoked; some rode horses. A few old people sat high atop a camel's load, entirely useless, their gray heads like hoary pendulums on the swaying packs. The dust rose at once. A camel inadvertently rammed its shoulder against a termite hill and cracked the mound in two. A flock of birds drifted over the fractured cone and hung above it, diving to take insects from the brittle mound meat.

We moved south by southeast. I followed without thought. If

it was my goat's heart that called for movement, it at least called forcibly. I couldn't resist the momentum building around me. No one told me to advance; no one forced me to fall in behind the forward wave of cattle. In motion there were fewer flies, and that alone was sufficient blessing.

THE DAY PASSED in a painful dream. Everything was reduced to motion. I had no thoughts. I followed whatever was in front of me.

Kama appeared once or twice in the morning, but he didn't pay me any special attention. The metal objects dangling from his body glinted in the sunlight. When he turned, the objects spun away from his body and the sun was thrown out in white paddles of light. He looked, in these moments, as fluid as water or wavering gas.

At noon one of Zinda's men rode to my side, leaned over his saddle, and cut the rawhide straps on my hands. It was done so simply, with neither compassion nor interest, that I mistrusted my freedom. The man said nothing. He spurred his horse and trotted back to a pack of women and children some fifty meters ahead.

The sudden jolt of blood into my shoulders staggered me. In one pulse my head grew dizzy; my fingers felt hot. The pain grew until I found it almost comfortable. In the war I had seen men lose a leg and claim to feel no pain. What they felt instead, I now understood, was nothing but pain. Without contrast, the pain was everything.

I wanted to see the condition of my hands, but the deltoid muscles in my shoulders had spasmed; I couldn't unlock them sufficiently to bring my hands in front of me. When I attempted to straighten my shoulders, the pain pushed me back down immediately—I remained hunched over. I saw that by lashing my hands together higher and higher on my back over the course of several weeks, Zinda could gradually deform my muscles until I could no longer stand upright. In a month, my back parallel to the ground, I would be a goat.

When the caravan halted well into the afternoon, I set about begging a meal. I didn't work very long at finding food, because after eating three mouthfuls I rushed into the bush to vomit. No sooner was I finished vomiting, than my bowels suffered a severe grinding. At first I told myself it was the heat and the exhaustion from walking. I drank from an unguarded calabash, hoping the water would calm my stomach, but it came up again in a matter of minutes. Along my neck and shoulders an odd tingling prickled my skin. Whatever it was that possessed me was in the process of traveling down my spine. I felt it touch each portion of my back as it descended.

The fever grew more pronounced as the sun set. It swelled and crept through my blood. I felt it take control of my body and almost welcomed the sensation. Sickness isolates us, and I felt the privacy of my own feverish hallucinations growing deeper. I was too ill to worry about my own death. I lay still and listened to the caravan. None of the activity concerned me; nothing they did interested me any longer.

The night passed in a terrible, sweaty haze. I was often in the bushes with dysentery; I vomited until I choked on my own bile. The fever roared in my ears and a headache made any movement painful.

In the early light I learned a trick from two goats who wandered near. Standing with near perfect balance on their hind legs, they licked the tent to steal the morning dew. The dew wasn't dense—far from it—but at least it was moisture. I crawled near them and licked as well. I was aware I acted exactly as the goats, but I didn't care. I found a gutter of water where the tent sagged, and I kept my lips against the canvas for some time, tasting in the fiber remnants of sunlight and mud and rivers.

Afterward, I fell back to the ground and slept well into the morning. I slept solidly; I heard nothing for several hours. When I woke, the caravan had moved on—it drifted peacefully on the eastern horizon, at least three kilometers away. It was not far off, but in my condition, it was an impossible distance.

Four dogs stood near me, their tongues out, their eyes watching me intently. They were savage looking, their muzzles blockish and heavy, their coats rippling with muscles underneath. I knew they waited to rip me apart, yet were not quite brave enough to dodge in before my breathing stopped.

Despite my feebleness, I forced myself to throw sand at the dog nearest me. The suddenness of my movement scattered the dogs temporarily. They trotted away twenty meters or so and took up their watch.

It was only the viciousness of a death administered by the dogs that eventually pushed me to my feet. I stood carefully, worried that if I fell it could bring on an attack. Even without falling, my slow climb to my feet brought a deep, chilling growl from one dog. I looked in his eyes and maintained my stare until he finally pretended interest in a small ant hill nearby.

I began to walk. My legs nearly gave out several times before I gained a rhythm. I avoided looking to the horizon to see the caravan. To do so would have been too discouraging. I rested my eyes on the ground and followed the caravan's tracks.

My life depended on catching the caravan before night settled over the countryside. A night sleeping in the open bush was unthinkable. The dogs would be on me; even as I walked they tagged along at my flanks, ready to rush in if I faltered, their pursuit as calm and as inevitable as a wake wedged carefully behind a boat.

In the afternoon the land began to grow softer. The vegetation increased. Near noon I passed over a large field covered with minute wildflowers, tiny bluebells quivering in the bright sunlight. The air actually became purple; my skin turned blue; my toes, dragged through the flowers, pulled up nosegays of buds that remained trapped between my toes.

The dogs abandoned me at this point—a hopeful sign. They ran directly east. The desert was gone. Instead, I entered a marshland, the type that generally signals a river or a major lake. An entire field of plum grass spread before me. Much of the grass had been trampled by the caravan, but it was resilient. Already the grass had partially mended its position with its instinctual groping for sunlight.

My strength was gone by the time I finally pushed through the last ten meters of tall weeds. I was covered with mud and slime. Bugs had bitten me to such a degree that I could actually feel the skin near my eyes drawing tight. My toes and feet had been cut in several places by grass and stones. The goat hide attached to my back was damp from my falls, and the moisture released its hideous odors.

But when I stepped clear of the grasses at last, it was like opening a curtain on Africa. I had arrived at a river, a brown, sluggish river. The main body flowed gradually from the north to the southeast. It wasn't continuous—at least not in the way one usually envisions a river. It was nearly pinched to extinction in several sections; sandbars stretched across the flat surface of the water like the backs of so many whales sounding into the desert.

I lay in the sand and slept.

FOR TWO WEEKS I did nothing but eat what I could find and sleep as much as possible. Had the caravan pushed on the day after our arrival, I couldn't have remained with it. But the river was too gentle, the food too plentiful to consider moving. In a matter of days the animals actually took on weight and became less skittish; the children, dry and pale looking during normal days of travel, appeared healthy and clean. Even the women, who were generally so taxed by their daily labors that they were often harsh and short-tempered, gradually relaxed enough to sing as they did their chores.

The men hunted. The plains on either side of the river were rich with herds and birds of all descriptions. Each morning the men saddled their horses—Zinda among them—and rode off with their rifles and bows. Each evening without fail they returned with an antelope over their saddles or a larger buffalo stretched over a green pole.

My health returned, and for the first time since my capture I began to appraise my situation in a clinical fashion. Several times I hiked the river to the south, looking to see if I could determine where it led. I suspected that I could follow it to some settlement. Twice I made a lunch of birds' eggs to test my ability to find food. The eggs were somewhat rancid, but I forced myself to eat them anyway. There were no ill effects; my options became less limited. I wondered why I hadn't thought of escape before.

I also began to steal in order to have on hand what I required for my escape. For the most part, the thefts were accomplished easily. Since I had no identity as a human, I was ignored. In a week's time I collected a short hatchet, an awl, a knife, and three separate calabashes to serve as canteens. I even stole a square of cloth to use on a hobo's bindle stick.

I still required a flint and steel—a fire was a necessary precaution against the threat of dogs or predators attacking me at night. I also wanted a fishing line. I couldn't count on finding birds' eggs; it was out of the question to believe I would kill my own game. The children caught fish from the river—capitaine and catfish, and small, sluggish fish no larger than a sparrow. The fishing line was essential if I intended to follow the river for more than a week.

I waited. In the meantime I cached these items a kilometer

away, well to the south of the cattle herd. The cache itself was nothing but a hollow among the roots of an oil palm tree. An animal had burrowed there, leaving behind a hole half a meter in diameter. Using the cloth to wrap the items, I managed to make the hollow disappear. The bulge of the bundle was large enough to fill the hole, and by spreading leaves and sticks across the cloth, the texture of the surrounding soil was uninterrupted. When I left the oil palm tree after visiting it, I made certain my tracks were obscured.

My resolve to escape became more firm one night when rain moved in from the south. Never before had I seen such cloud formations. They built for several hours just at sundown and the air became heavy and hot. The animals sensed the coming storm and walked in nervous bursts, jumping away as a bush or branch was moved by gusts of wind. Lightning flashed in wild flourishes for hours before the storm finally hit. I wouldn't have been surprised to see grass fires kindled out on the southern plains. Instead, the rain broke in a wide funnel several kilometers away, and from a distance it was impossible to tell if the rain fell or the wind merely sucked up water from the river.

When at last the rain arrived, it produced a sodden, soaking dampness that seemed somehow even wetter than the river. Everything was washed within minutes of the first drops. The animals faced north to keep their eyes out of the rain, but otherwise they did nothing but suffer silently. I was no better off than they. The coals which normally formed my bed were doused; the tents were tied up tightly against the wind. I stood in the lee of a tree and in that way at least escaped the wind, but sleep was impossible.

I worried about the fever returning. I worried about lightning striking the tree above me. The goat skin, which had protected me initially, began to sag and pull with its dead weight around my throat.

Kama found me near midnight. He was wet; his matted hair was pushed hard against his scalp. The metal objects draped around his chest and ribs glistened with moisture. He squatted in front of

me, apparently oblivious to the rain. Nevertheless, he looked
chilled. Occasionally he slapped his arms and legs as if the sting
of the blow could warm his skin.

I held out my hand, opened it to the rain, then, in pantomime,
pointed around the camp. It was a question, a ludicrous one, since
he obviously had no shelter. Ridiculously, he mimicked me; he held
out his hand and looked around him. There was no shelter, he
seemed to say. Afterward, he lowered his hand and continued to
squat, watching me as if I might suggest another game.

I sat against the tree and waited for morning. Eventually I
dozed. I woke several times to the crash of lightning. The storm
was directly above us, and with each beat of lightning I saw the
tents outlined against the flat horizon. They looked ghostly, disappearing as soon as the light failed. The animals, too, were caught
in the flash of light so that I could look up and see a cow standing a few meters off, frozen in the brilliance, until the darkness released it.

Much later, close to dawn, I woke to find Kama standing
perhaps fifty meters away, staring up at the sky. A sudden crack
of lightning had just faded, but the electricity clung to him long
after the illumination was gone. He held his arms up in wonder,
turning slowly to keep the metal objects surrounding his body
pouring about him in a metallic swirl. He intentionally called the
electricity, his face fixed with the same wonder that it held when
he used his magnet. I didn't care in that moment if the lightning
killed us both. I spoke to him, but he didn't answer. He turned in
a tight circle, chanting something unintelligible, while the lightning
continued to crackle around him. The light was blue and gold;
Kama, the wick of a candle.

I spent the morning calculating when I should depart. It seemed I
should leave as early as possible some morning—perhaps the next
day—so that an entire twenty-four hours could elapse before I was
missed. Of course more time might pass before I was discovered
missing, but I reasoned that twenty-four hours would be an ade-

quate start. I couldn't outrun dedicated pursuers in any case. I hoped only to put enough distance between us to make a search too difficult to undertake easily.

The thought that I might leave the next day made me nervous. I roamed the campfires incessantly, taking careful note of the women who possessed flints. My mind was so active, however, that I interpreted the slightest glance from a woman as an indication that she understood my motives. It was my own guilt eating at me. After moving away clumsily on one or two occasions, I decided to avoid the women until later in the evening.

I had worked my way around the campsites and was almost to the edge of the river when I heard shouts. Because of the weather and the proximity to the water, the shouts echoed and carried. Yet they confused me as well—I couldn't immediately determine their source. There was no trilling; the voices were masculine.

I didn't move at once to join them. My habits were too firmly ingrained—I looked first to the tents to see if they would be abandoned and the food left unguarded. But the women didn't seem to hear the shouts; they continued working and I realized I had only heard the noise because of my position near the river.

I walked toward the noise, and eventually spotted a group of older men standing in a circle at the edge of the river. They were staring down at something on the bank. I guessed they had landed a fish, or the storm had carried something onto the bank, except the men appeared inordinately excited. Their arms were raised to their sides to prevent jostling; they pushed back and forth, as if each man was intent on keeping the others from rushing into the center. They shouted, but it was all confusion.

I didn't want to attract their attention when they were in such a state and I started away. But then, down by their legs, I saw a small boy apparently dead from drowning. He rested in the center of the circle, flat on his back, one arm raised above his head. He was no more than twelve years old, perhaps eleven, and I knew him only vaguely by sight. He was a shepherd; I recalled seeing him as he slept in the midday sun, his left leg wrapped around a shepherd's staff, his sleep perfect and complete as he balanced there. Now, however, his body was flaccid. His face was turned to one side. His skin was shiny and black, though it was rubbed with pink abrasions around the hips. Wet grass clung to his hair and pubic region.

Even then I wouldn't have moved forward if the jostling hadn't continued. But the men appeared so ignorant, so ridiculously helpless, that I felt rage at them more than compassion for the boy.

I shouted something in German and pushed against the men, trying to get to the boy. My sudden appearance startled them. They let me by and I quickly knelt beside the child. I cleared his mouth; I bent back his head and pinched his nose shut. I breathed into his mouth, tasting mud against his gums. His lungs received the air but didn't hold it. I turned my head, keeping count as I had been trained to do in the military, resting my cheek and ear next to the boy's lips in order to hear him breathe.

I am not sure how long I worked on the boy. The men, at one point, reached forward to touch my shoulder. I slapped them away, not convinced the boy was truly gone. I pushed back the boy's eyelid—though what I hoped to diagnose I can't say—and saw only white. It didn't deter me. I continued to breathe for the boy, despite the unnerving sensation that I had lost count and was administering the technique too rapidly.

Eventually the boy coughed. It was so feeble that I barely detected it. I breathed into his mouth again and this time was met by an exhalation and a strangled cough. I turned the boy's head just in time to allow him to vomit up water. Above me the men stepped back for the first time.

The silence that accompanied the boy's coughing was distinct. It was a comment. I leaned back on my haunches and pinned the boy's lower jaw between my first two fingers. The boy continued to cough, now with increased force. His arm lifted from above his head, pawed once at the air, then fell back into its place. I rolled him onto his left shoulder and held him carefully while he continued to cough up water.

THE BOY'S MOTHER brought me food. I had gone down river a quarter kilometer to wait for nightfall, but she followed me. I ate until my stomach swelled. Afterward, I went to the river and drank from my cupped hands.

Despite the woman's gratitude, I didn't dwell on the boy. Instead, I concentrated on my plans for escape. Specifically, I wondered if I hadn't ruined whatever hope I had of leaving the caravan.

I weighed the possibility of leaving immediately. I didn't have a flint or a fishing line, but I thought I might survive without them. To escape predators, I could climb a tree at night, perhaps sleep a portion of the day on the ground.

A pack of children found me before I came to any decision. I counted ten boys, all naked, who peeked at me from around the bushes lining the river. They carried throwing sticks over their shoulders; two or three had slingshots dangling around their necks. They were uniformly thin, their stomachs swollen with malnutrition, and they possessed a collective identity that made it difficult to distinguish among them. They reminded me of animals—wild animals unused to direct attention. If my eyes locked on any one individual in particular, the individual faded back, blocking my stare with the forms and shapes of his fellows.

I did not want to be watched. I moved toward them a few steps and they scattered. When I stopped, they formed again into a wary pack watching me from a safe distance.

They didn't leave me throughout the afternoon, and since I decided I could do nothing before nightfall in any event, I attempted to sleep. It was a peculiar sleep because of the children watching me. They were silent, remarkably so, but that only made me more aware of them. After dozing for an hour, though never attaining full sleep, I bathed in the river. The water was cold but I didn't care. I washed my hair and my legs; I washed my torso and arms, but stopped short of my back where the goat skin still clung around my neck.

It wasn't much later when the hunting party returned. I saw them first as a speck on the southern plain—seven men, all mounted, all advancing at an unhurried canter. The sky was already dark behind them.

My impulse to leave was never stronger than at the moment they forded the river. I wasn't far from them. I watched the first horse enter the water, feeling with its front legs for the sand beneath the current, the rider's heels slamming into its sides. Another horse entered, then a third. Zinda was the last to ford, and it struck me that he was in greater command of his mount than any of the others. His horse didn't pause or test its footing. It plunged through the river at a steady pace, while Zinda raised his legs to keep them dry.

The arrival of the horses drew the children away. They ran toward the ford, shouting and leaping, showing off for the returning men. They yelled greetings to the first riders—the word *nassarra* occasionally rising up from the middle of a sentence. What the riders thought of the children's stories I couldn't tell. They continued to ride toward the tents, though now the horses walked quietly in the last sunlight. A springbok was draped across the saddle horn of one rider's horse.

Within an hour the boys returned, this time approaching close enough to shout and wave for me to follow them. I knew Zinda had sent them to find me.

I walked behind the boys. They remained at least ten meters ahead of me, frequently running forward to announce our approach. That much was different—I was recognized by everyone we passed. Indeed, the people appeared to regard me as a man. They demonstrated no special reverence, but at least they observed my passing with forthright glances and honest appraisals. Several of the people—an old woman stirring a pot, a young man of sixteen mending a harness—seemed sightly frightened of me. As I passed, they didn't move. Only their necks turned so that their eyes could follow my progress.

I was led to a tent in the center of the camp. It wasn't Zinda's tent. The boys danced to one side and pointed for me to enter. I pushed into the tent and was immediately met by the smell of cooking food. The smell was so solid it nauseated me. Smoke was everywhere and I couldn't see my surroundings clearly. I was no longer habituated to meat, and the odor of cooking fat was overpowering. I turned to get a breath of fresh air. At the same time Zinda spoke to me from the far corner of the tent.

"Sit down," he said.

His voice was neither kind nor menacing. When I turned back, he waved me to a small stool not far from him. To my surprise, we weren't alone. A second man sat beside Zinda on the ground. He was older; his neck was abnormally thin. In compensation he held his head perfectly still, as if a lean to one side or another would cause him to topple. I knew his name—Klima—but nothing else about him.

The boy who had nearly drowned was behind the men, stretched out on a mat. He pushed himself to one elbow as I took my seat. He looked recovered, if weak. He smiled at me, but said nothing, then lay back down, effectively disappearing behind the men's bodies.

"This is the boy's father," Zinda said in French. "His name is Klima. He is worried that you gave the boy a soul from his ancestors."

It took me a moment to grasp the words. I hadn't been spoken to in over a month.

"I don't understand," I answered.

"The boy was dead. Now he's older," Zinda said plainly.

"How is he older?" I asked.

Zinda conferred with Klima. Klima, for the first time, became excited. He talked rapidly, occasionally reaching behind him to find the boy's knee. He gestured fiercely, but I couldn't tell if he was genuinely angry.

"His soul was gone—and you brought it back. The father wants to know how you are sure it is the boy's soul," Zinda translated for Klima.

"It is the boy's."

Zinda shook his head. "The boy is older," he said again.

"I breathed for the boy," I said, trying to form the phrases in my inadequate French. "I did not touch his soul."

"The boy was drowned in the water—his father thinks you gave him a different soul. The boy is not the same."

I hadn't expected this. The entire concept struck me as abysmally primitive.

"I don't know why the boy is older. I gave him back his own soul," I said.

"The boy died last night. He told us himself."

"That's impossible."

Calmly, to show me it wasn't merely his opinion, Zinda bent to the boy, the dead side of his face turned to me. He pulled the boy to a sitting position and put several questions to him. Yes, the boy answered while Zinda translated, the boy had gone for water. A spirit had risen from the water and invited him to swim. The boy had refused and backed away. The spirit, composed of water and sand but manifesting a human form, had stepped closer. It was dark and the boy couldn't see clearly. The spirit confused him; in no time he was turned around and backing to the water, the spirit slowly blocking his retreat.

I watched the boys' face, hoping to detect a lie, but his manner was inscrutable. Klima, listening, nodded on his frail neck. What most disconcerted me was the notion that the boy had drowned the previous night. That was impossible. At the same time, I dared not refute him.

"The boy needs time to recover," I said eventually.

Zinda shook his head. Klima, impatient with all of us, called loudly to someone outside the tent. Immediately a woman, the boy's mother, pushed meekly through the tent flaps. She seemed disoriented. She genuflected and placed the tips of her fingers to her chest. "*Naba,*" she said, then moved forward, her face ready to break with emotion.

She stopped in front of Zinda. I expected her to give her

testimony, but at that moment the tent flap was pushed aside again and a man jumped through. He was painted white; he wore leggings of braided grasses which fit the contours of his legs precisely. His energy was enormous; it filled the tent instantly. In his right hand he carried a rattle which he brandished continually. He shook it over the mother. He shook it over me. Then he danced in a tight circle, chanting unintelligible words.

At the same time Zinda stood. Klima, apparently satisfied that some ritual was about to be performed, pushed back out of the way. I looked quickly to the boy, but he was curled in a fetal position. He didn't move or respond to the noise. The magic man danced near him, shaking his rattle.

Zinda removed the goat skin from my back. The pain as he pulled it free was acute. Zinda flinched at the odor; my back was infected. The magic man danced near me and touched my back with the rattle. Zinda folded the goat skin in a rough square and handed it to Klima.

Zinda turned back to me. He placed his hand on my bicep and pulled me off the stool. Then, without speaking, he pushed me onto my knees. He didn't employ force. He bent with me slowly, continuing down until I had to put out my hands to prevent myself from falling on my face. I was on all fours; I was a goat again.

I was fascinated by this; I was also frightened. Zinda, however, did nothing cruel. He looked at me closely, staring into my eyes. His look, remarkably, asked for my cooperation. I regarded him closely to make sure I interpreted this correctly. His eyes deliberately softened, and I saw I was not mistaken.

The magic man, during these few minutes, became clumsy. He lurched around the tent in what would have been, under different circumstances, a parody of himself. He staggered back and forth, twice hitting the walls of the tent, once nearly upsetting the vat of cooking broth that still simmered on a low fire. His chanting increased. His rattle flicked in infrequent bursts. The chants became mixed with painful moans.

The woman in front of me entered a trance—I don't know

what else to call it. She leaned forward clutching her stomach. Zinda, seeing this, rushed forward and pulled her to her feet. She sank down and almost fell on the ground, but Zinda supported her. To my amazement, he led her to me and placed her in a sitting position squarely on my back.

It should have been ludicrous. The chants, the moans, the noxious cooking, the sight of Klima and his thin neck pressed back against the tent wall—all of it was absurd. Nevertheless, I could not ignore the heightened tension in the tent. The air was dark and hot and I felt my mind slipping, or rather pulling to enter the performance.

Zinda moved to the boy and began to push him forward. He remained curled on his side. I turned my head back and forth— now to see the witch man dancing and moaning, now to watch the boy being shoved toward me. The woman on top of me began to moan as well. She rocked back and forth, her round buttocks rolling against my spine. She screamed once in a sharp, startled burst. Her breathing began to quicken.

In the next moment I understood: it was a birth. An hysterical pregnancy—quite real nonetheless. The witch man twisted and turned, pressing at his stomach as if he too were in labor. The woman, in time to the witch man's writhing, pushed and pulled at her own stomach, pressing into me with her full weight.

But it was the boy who unnerved me. I watched him as he came toward me—he was to pass under me and through the legs, symbolically, of his mother—his face as smooth and untroubled as a newborn's. This was no illusion. Whatever it is that ages us was gone from him. The hollows on either side of his skull were without wrinkles; his face was drawn with the wonderful expectancy of a fetus. He was unconscious. He was not breathing.

When he began to slide beneath me, his mother's shouts became more extreme. The witch man squatted and pretended to bear down. For a long moment the woman held her breath, squeezing her buttocks tight, until at last the boy's head appeared between her legs. She screamed at this sight, letting out such a gasp of air that she nearly slid off my back. With two more shoves the boy was through his mother's legs. He lay silently for a moment before a mewing cry broke from his lips.

It was unmistakably the cry of a newborn. His hands groped before him, his fingers still tucked into solid fists. His eyes were closed. His breathing, begun the instant his head appeared, shuddered and convulsed. He couldn't have been taught this. His actions were a perfect imitation of a newborn's first sensations in the world.

The mother stood and knelt next to the boy. Klima smiled. Zinda, still calm, lifted me to my feet and led me to the tent flaps. I was no longer needed.

I WAS A MAN AGAIN.

The boy's birth, the sight of him as he waited to breathe, his untroubled face in that first instant as he passed between his mother's legs—were more than I could contemplate. A moment outside the tent and it no longer seemed real. And yet I didn't doubt that I had witnessed something extraordinary.

Outside the tent, I was immediately aware of people collected nearby. The women particularly watched me. I was anxious to be alone, but for a moment I remained outside the tent, too stunned to move.

It was the pain in my back that finally forced me to walk forward, straight toward the river. Inside the tent my back had been numb. Now it began to sting mercilessly; the scabs had been pulled loose. Mosquitoes came at me, making it even more difficult to organize my thoughts. I walked stiffly to the water.

I ladled handfuls over my shoulders and back. The coolness was soothing. The clouds had finally broken and the stars reflected in the surface of the stream. Dipping my hand caused the sky to shake and shimmer; the illusion created a sense of vertigo which made me dizzy. I moved back from the water and sat on the bank. My legs and arms began to shake. I was cold.

I sat until a few people collected behind me. They didn't come forward. They remained well up on the bank, close to the tents, but their attention was palpable. Except for an occasional complaint by a baby, they were silent. Now and then the young boys ran off and returned with a report from the center of the camp. The family was still inside, the tent lashed shut—the report remained unaltered. The villagers continued to watch me.

I ignored them. My back had started to throb, and my attention was absorbed by that. Naturally I couldn't see the cuts, but I touched them with my fingers and tried to determine their severity. It occurred to me that I had given away my hide—that the pain would not subside until the hide was again in place. I couldn't rid myself of the notion, illogical though I knew it was, that I had abandoned a critical part of my identity.

That wasn't all. A short time later a woman advanced and came to stand beside me. Her face was old and faded, the skin sunk back to the bone, her brows two pursed underlips petulant over her sockets. She bowed, struck her chest with her fingers, and addressed me as "Nassarra." Then, almost in a continuation of her bow, she suddenly sat beside me and held out her foot for me to examine.

I recoiled, but the woman held out her foot, nodding to insist I inspect her injury. Though I couldn't see the foot clearly in the darkness, it was evident that her toes were infected. They were swollen to spatulate oars connected by a brooding rash which climbed her instep. It was remarkable she could walk; a thick rope of gangrene wove higher up her ankle.

I was nauseated at the sight—nauseated, too, at the ignorance such a condition symbolized. And still her foot was held out to me, her ridiculous eyes consciously turning soft so that I might have pity. We couldn't speak; regardless, she attempted to manipulate me in a strange, feminine manner. She was coy, despite her age, and could apparently think of no way to convince me of her need except by a sickening coquettishness.

"Nassarra," she said again—this time a statement and question combined. Her strength gave out and she lowered her leg, only to raise it again higher. For several seconds the air became still and I noted the people behind us were watching closely.

I touched her ankle; I didn't know what else to do. Then I dropped my hand and stood. I nearly fell from dizziness. I walked toward the river, feeling my coordination giving way, hearing behind me her cry of "Nassarra" repeated several times.

A pig, somewhere deep in the bushes, grunted and moved away at my approach. A dog lapping at the water looked at me. I was too exhausted to think. At the edge of the river I ducked under the bushes, unmindful of the snakes and scorpions I had learned to fear, and lay against the heavy roots. The smell of earth and mud was all around me. I wrapped myself closer to the roots and lay listening to the village.

What had happened? As fatigued as I felt, my brain was active. I did not for a moment believe I had brought the boy back to life after a full twelve hours. A mistake had been made; there was some error in calculation. Thinking back, I was fairly certain the boy had lied. No, I was positive. I recalled his confident look, his innocent air, and would have wagered he had rehearsed his story. Perhaps his father, Klima, had put him up to it. Or perhaps he had invented the story to increase his importance among the villagers. Zinda clearly didn't believe the story himself, but had been forced to go along with it. For my compliance he had made me a man once more.

I fell asleep curled around the bushes. When I woke it was the middle of the night. I knew the camp's sounds; I had several hours before daylight. I climbed to my feet and climbed out of the bushes. I knew at once what I was going to do. I made my way south along the river, cutting up onto solid ground only when I saw the oil palm that marked my cache.

I found the items undisturbed, still wrapped in cloth. I dug out the bundle, then began to walk. The night was black—no stars, no moon. I couldn't see more than ten or twenty meters in any direction. Twice I heard animals sprint away from the water as I approached.

I walked steadily until dawn. I tried to estimate how far I had traveled. At best guess it was something like ten kilometers. My arms were tired from carrying the bundle; my back, still raw from the scabs, ached constantly.

Dawn made me more optimistic. Light advanced from the east—or rather, night tilted on the eastern horizon and began to slide to the west. With the improved visibility, I walked more quickly. The river ran placidly on my left, its waters remaining darker than the surrounding land as the sun gained height.

I rested for a time, then drank from the river until my thirst was quenched. Water, at least, wasn't a problem. I untied my bundle and checked its contents. I owned an awl, a knife, and a short hatchet; in my rush, I had left behind the calabashes.

For some time I sat and considered my next move. My impulse was to continue south as rapidly as possible, but the sun was already warming my skin and I knew I risked exhaustion and heat prostration. The alternative—to rest now and travel at night—was unthinkable. Lions and hyenas were in this vicinity and I suspected their stalking improved at night with their superior eyesight. I resolved to travel through the morning, sleep until early evening, then find a resting spot for night. Whether this plan was wise I could hardly guess; nevertheless, I felt better for having a plan, even a tentative one. I took one last drink of water, then set out due south.

I traveled throughout the morning. The sun was merciless. It penetrated my skin and seemed to heat my bones. Only my back benefited by the harsh light. The scabs pulled tight and ceased to bleed at the slightest movement.

I ate when I found food, which wasn't often. I consumed three birds' eggs, then, in the afternoon, slaughtered a lizard which basked against a tree. I passed by the tree, saw the lizard didn't move off, then returned on tiptoe to crush the lizard with one stroke of the hatchet. The lizard was pressed to the tree by the force of the blow. This sight sickened me, and I stood beside the tree for a full minute before I could bring myself to touch the reptile. No amount of rationalization could convince me that to eat it was a pure act of survival.

I closed my eyes and pulled the animal from the tree bark. Moving quickly for fear of losing courage, I carried it to the water, washed it, then sliced it into small morsels with my knife.

I ate it with large mouthfuls of water. I didn't chew. I was aware, as I stood knee-deep in the river, of how sad a spectacle I presented. I was no longer a goat, but also no longer a man I might recognize. Glancing at the reflection of myself in the water, I couldn't believe I had come to this. Eating, I resembled a bird, or a thick-necked crocodile shifting its jaws to gulp a fish. The taste of the lizard remained in my mouth; water did nothing to remove it.

The afternoon became calm. Whatever winds had circled now faded. The river spread, seeping into the earth at its edges and trickling off into minute tributaries that culminated in flat pools interrupted by hummocks of grass. Here were hundreds of birds' nests tucked away among the grasses, with only downy heads occasionally rising up above the wall of a nest to shout for food. I worked my way around the dampest sections, afraid to go into the water above my knees. Even so, I spotted two snakes in a five-minute interval. Both lay on a wide hummock sunning themselves, or perhaps waiting to invade a nest of fledglings. The sight made me worry about my footing. I moved farther west, spending at least an hour circumventing the swampy area.

Afterward, I sought out shade and lay on the ground, too tired to search for a protective hollow. I slept with my head on the bundle, my hand tensed on the shaft of the hatchet. Twice I woke to the sound of bird song, but fell asleep again instantly. My sleep was heavy and dreamless. When I woke the sun was on me, but I saw immediately darkness would not be long in coming.

I traveled another seven kilometers or so before evening was established. In the quiet light I began to search for a place to spend the night. My choices were limited. The trees beside the river attained no great height; I couldn't persuade myself that I would be safe from animals by climbing one. This tree was too low, that one afforded easy access, but what I could climb other animals could climb. I examined the few outcroppings of rock carefully, hoping to find a hollow which might provide shelter. But the rocks were smooth. The land was flat as far as I could see.

In last light I climbed a thin tree, hoping the suppleness of the branches would dissuade larger predators from climbing. Once in the tree, however, I realized how exhausting it would be to cling there throughout the night. I tried to arrange myself comfortably in several notches, but each time I settled in a new place the branches dug into my back ten minutes later.

I slept as the sun went down. My limbs became stiff and woke me often. I moved cautiously in these moments, frightened that movement in the tree would make a predator curious. Several times I came close to climbing out of the branches. Each time, however, the stillness of the plain kept me where I was.

I WOKE STIFF AND SORE from the night in the tree. Climbing to the ground, my legs were painfully cramped. When I recovered sufficiently to walk, I went to the river and drank from my cupped hands. I felt unsteady as I stood. I tried to walk, but must have blacked out. The next thing I knew I was on the bank, my right ankle still in the river. I felt dazed and exhausted.

I sat for most of the morning. I didn't move to escape the sun. Distantly I heard bird song around me. Once, some thirty paces downstream, I saw a springbok come to water. Plans formed in my mind—now I will have to get up, now I will have to find food— but I couldn't muster the strength to stand.

At last there was nothing to do but continue walking. I walked steadily until late afternoon and only stopped when I felt ready to fall over. I ate nothing; I drank only a little. Several times I contemplated altering my tack. Perhaps, I thought, I should attempt to make my way back to the sea. Then, ten meters beyond, I changed my mind. I tried to persuade myself that matters would grow clearer if I simply continued on, but I no longer believed in my own salvation.

I prepared for death in those last hours of sunlight. It was not a conscious thought; it didn't alarm me. I knew by this time I wouldn't escape. The trek was too long. Such adventures, I reasoned, didn't have happy endings. A man slows, becomes confused, makes incorrect choices, then perishes without a visible trace to mark him.

This dwindling concern for life, if it can be called that, was insidious. My walking slowed, then stopped altogether. I needed food, but took no steps to find it. I had entered a sort of rapture.

I spent the night against a tree, sitting calmly. Sleep no longer separated the world for me. Awake I was no different than at rest. I felt the dirt around me, the coiled hardness of the tree trunk behind me, but the impressions passed to me by these solid objects did not enter my mind.

It was not mere lassitude—far from it. I was active in my abandonment of life. I forfeited my life willingly, though I didn't rush to death. There is a difference, one which I clung to even in the emptiness of my senses. I had done enough; I had struggled. I accepted the loss as inevitable.

In the morning a hunting party—not from the caravan—found

me. Four men, all carrying spears, surrounded me. The men were unadorned and nearly naked. They approached quietly and waited for me to speak. I saw them, but I was barely conscious. They didn't brandish their spears, nor did they lay them aside. I tried to take some interest in their activities, but it was too late for that. They might have been examining the tree behind me for all I knew. I was not there; I was gone.

The fact I was Caucasian saved me. I was white, a novelty, potentially a troubling affair with the authorities. They could have passed on to pursue their game and no one would have been the wiser, but they stopped instead. They argued for a time. One man even picked up a stone and lobbed it at me, the party tensing to await my reaction. When I did nothing, they returned to their discussion.

In the plainest terms I was a tactical problem. How did they plan to lift me, to carry me—and then what were they to do with me?

It was arranged with economy, but not before two of the men advanced sufficiently to prod me with the blunt end of their spears. As soon as their spears touched me, they jumped back and stood ready, bracing to fend me off if I moved. Satisfied I was incapable of harming them, they began to speak again. They talked loudly to bolster their courage. One of the men was told to cut branches; another was sent to look for vines with which they could lash me to their litter.

I don't know how long I was carried. We left the edge of the water at one point and went, I think, east. The men were apparently accustomed to long marches. They stopped only once to rest in the shade. One of the men offered me water, but when I showed no inclination to accept it, he poured it in my mouth. He watered me much as a woman might water a plant. They had decided to keep me alive.

They camped that night on a slight rise overlooking the river. My hands and legs had been bound to the litter to keep me steady or because they feared me. In either case, they didn't untie me at night. In fact, before they slept they checked the vines to make sure I was still secure. They had a fire and a well-supplied stock of wood and dung. Two of the men smoked. In a last act they placed fish hooks on my chest, the barbs pointing up toward my head. In this way they anchored my soul, setting a trap for it in case it chose to wander.

They broke camp while it was still dark, then halted not long before sunrise. They moved off several paces and argued again. One man in particular, whose voice was high-pitched and decidedly nasal, expounded for a long time without interruption from the others. When his voice stopped I heard, unexpectedly, the bleat of a goat crying.

We were near a village. The men apparently argued over their next step. Eventually I heard one of them run off, only to return a half hour later out of breath. More shouting, more recriminations. Then, when that was done, the vines binding me to the litter were severed.

They dressed me. Manipulating my arms and legs, they worked at me from both ends. One slipped on a shirt; another, grunting and swearing, pulled a pair of pants over my legs. The cloth scraped me. The shirt stuck to my back.

Afterward, they hoisted me again. Two men carried me while the other two walked ahead. In no time I heard dogs barking. The steady pounding of millet reached me, and for a moment I thought we had returned to the caravan.

I heard children's voices, the call of a woman. To my left I spied a mud hut, then another, and finally a granary formed of matted grasses. A procession built around us. The two men in front shouted to make way, but our progress slowed. Fifty curious heads appeared above me, their glances quickly gone as our momentum carried us on to the next group of onlookers.

I couldn't know that I was being delivered to white women—nuns at that. When at last I was placed on cement in front of a hut, I couldn't believe the firmness of the structure. The procession had abandoned us—doubtless in fear, for the Africans always fear the whites—and it was left to the men to explain my provenance. The last thing I remember before becoming unconscious was a white woman bending near, her face clouded by concern for my welfare, her eyes unmistakably blue.

WHAT
THE GRASS
SAID

1941 · 1942

MY NAME IS SISTER MARIE DUCHAMP and I set forth this document to record the brief contact I had with a man known as Father Fraujas. That he was a saint, I have no doubt. That he performed miracles, I state as a witness. That he performed other sins, perhaps quite heinous ones, during the Second World War in Europe, I cannot comment about with certainty. His destiny led him to an isolated outpost in the African bush, where his ability to cure the sick by virtue of his miraculous powers was never known to the larger world. It is the purpose of this record to establish the history of a man I believe a saint. Whatever verdict is reached concerning his life or the merits of his Beatification, I claim this as a true record of a man who resides with God Our Father in the Heaven He has promised.

I knew Loebus—I will call him that, although he is better known as Fraujas for reasons I will explain later—for a very brief period, though he existed on the edge of my consciousness until his death. He took my virginity, which I gave willingly. I have made peace with the carnal side of my nature and I hold nothing against him for having encouraged its expression. He was a man recently quit of the war. I was a young woman more than prepared to grant him favors. Our union was not a surprise. Indeed, looking back, it would have been a surprise if we had remained apart.

The beginning of my relationship with Loebus was innocent. At that time the White Sisters had just moved into the Tenado region. I had joined them seven months earlier after having served as a novice in a small village near the Alsace. What I did, how I gained my appointment to that outpost, is of little interest now. Why I petitioned to be stationed in such a desolate place is of more importance. Certainly some of it may be explained by saying I was a romantic; that the romance of being a nun, in particular a White

Sister, was a powerful inducement. Add to that an impoverished home life, a stern father, a mother too weak-willed to be of value to any of her six children, and an almost theatrical inclination to rites and ritual, and you will have some glimpse of me at the age of twenty-two.

I also had, even at that age, a fairly keen sense of how things worked. I knew how to approach the local bishop; I manipulated the hierarchies of the Church, as well as I could in my relatively obscure position, until I was granted permission to leave, given a traveling allowance, and placed on a boat departing from Le Havre. Had I not been so capable at arranging things in my favor, it's probable my impulse to join the White Sisters would have diminished, and I would have lived my life in a small parish not far from Strasbourg. Circumstances combined as they often do, however, and I received my wish without fully understanding the implications of the gift.

I was the youngest member of the order. The other nuns were older, settled in their work and habits, devoted to God in a way that I only attained much later. The Mother Superior, a stern but generous nun who was called Belle Mère by all of us, was a tireless woman who believed our mission in Africa should be especially devoted to native women. Childrearing, and all its complications, was her chief concern. She schooled us in nutrition, midwifery, and sterilization. We were to be Sisters of Works. Faith, she told us, was massaged into existence by laboring hands.

On the day I met Frederich Loebus, I was at work in the birthing room. My duty at that time was to clean and maintain the delivery room: wash the instruments in boiling water, change the sheets and boil them, scrub the floor and walls. The White Fathers had built this room as a storage vault for their well-digging equipment, but Belle Mère had appropriated it for our use. It was constructed of plain cement block which had been repeatedly whitewashed, the paint soaking into the porous materials until the walls became smooth. Nevertheless, the paint eventually dried and flaked in the severe heat, and it was the sound of lizards dancing across these dry chips that I will always associate with my early experiences in that chamber.

My work was extremely demanding. In the way of young nuns, I was pleased by such difficult labor, a fact that Belle Mère well understood. Shall I admit that I had the usual impulse toward martyrdom? Can I write this without mentioning that I had a hunger—a hunger unlike any I have known before or since—for self-mortification? For the sake of truth, and the effect such claims might have on my belief that Loebus was a saint, I admit freely that I wore a hair garment, one fashioned by my own fingers, beneath my habit. I wore a strip of cloth across my breasts to flatten them and to hide my nipples. The coarsest garments, the heaviest skirts, the poorest sandals—these things pleased me immensely. My first Christmas present from Belle Mère was a rude wooden rosary, one so ugly that she foresaw what beauty I would find in it.

I was boiling water for the sheets and surgery tools when Loebus was brought to the porch. Four African men carried him on a crude litter. Loebus was very sick. His body was covered with sweat and I suspected fever at once. The Africans were plainly hunters or poachers, because they placed Loebus's body on the porch, then disappeared, refusing to answer my questions poorly phrased in the More language.

I wasn't alone with Loebus; two African girls worked with me. I turned to one, a young girl given the Christian name of Immaculata, and told her to get Belle Mère. Then I knelt beside Loebus and tried to assess his condition.

Probably malaria. His temperature was high; his color was poor. His shirt was washed with sweat; the front of his trousers seemed coated with urine. I told the second girl, Jude, to bring me a bucket of water and a washcloth.

Before she returned, Belle Mère appeared. As I have said, she was an extremely forceful woman. She was large, which was unusual for anyone living in the tropics, and her full skirts had a maternal knack of knicking against doorways or brushing against chair legs. Her spectacles were rimless. They were also extremely well polished, so that any glance from her was thrown out through one's own reflection.

"Who is he?" she asked, bending next to him. Her hands went over his body, checking him with greater efficiency than I had done. She checked for broken bones or any limbs that didn't seem properly positioned. When she was satisfied it was only fever, she reached behind him for his wallet. She found nothing.

"He was brought by some African hunters, Belle Mère," I said.

"Did they say where they had found him?"

"No, Belle Mère."

"Probably frightened of the authorities. All right then," she said, struggling to her feet. "We'll carry him."

With our hands linked under him, we carried him to a second cement hut. These huts were generally reserved for the women who needed to "lie-in," but occasionally they served as hospital rooms for the sick or dying. They were warm and reasonably clean.

We placed him on a bed made of sticks. A sheet covered the wooden struts, but there was no mattress. As soon as he was settled, Belle Mère began to undress him. She sent the African girls off for a bucket of water and alcohol, then told me to help her remove his clothes.

I did as I was told. I unlaced and removed his boots. I stripped off his socks. It was not coincidence that I restricted myself to the remote parts of his body. I was a virgin. More than that, I was in love with my own purity. Purity was my obsession. Though I professed obedience and humility, it was my tremendous pride in my own goodness that I loved.

Belle Mère was aware of this. No doubt she had seen it before in other girls my age, and she knew how to break it. She called me to help take off his pants, leaving for me the embarrassing job of unhooking his belt and unzipping his fly. She did this with the utmost indifference, pretending interest in the alcohol that Novice Jude now brought to her.

For a moment I paused. I had never touched a man below his

belt. I had never actually seen an adult man's penis. "Hurry, girl," Belle Mère said, as she began washing his forehead with a washcloth, but her words only made me more reluctant to begin.

"It's just flesh," Belle Mère said when she detected my hesitation. "All the sick are children—think of it that way."

"Yes, Belle Mère."

I undid his belt, unzipped his fly. With the help of the two novices, I stripped down his pants and wrestled them over his legs. Then, attempting to preserve my purity by making my mind as cold and analytical as possible, I pulled his underwear over his feet.

Belle Mère, her hand still moving the washcloth across his forehead, nodded at the bucket of water.

"Clean him," she told me. "Give his clothes to Novice Immaculata to burn."

I knew what Belle Mère was doing. Temptation, of course, is at the root of training. How do we know ourselves without knowing what tempts us? She reached in her bucket and handed me a washcloth. I took it and began to clean Loebus's body.

I felt nothing at first. This was flesh, nothing more. I cleaned harshly, rubbing hard over his pale body. Dirt came free in muddy swipes, and I rinsed my cloth in the bucket frequently. I gained the impression, cleaning him, that he had undergone severe physical hardship. The soles of his feet were badly blistered; his hands were torn and covered with nettles.

In time, naturally, my hands grew accustomed to his skin and I began to feel the pleasure of it. The details of that afternoon were sensuous: the heat, the dripping water, the soft glide of the washcloth across his body, his ribs defined, his hips swelling into his penis. His thighs were muscled; his buttocks taut and hard from walking.

I understand now, so many years later, that I was part of the sensuousness. I was a twenty-two-year-old girl, a virgin in mind and body. What color were my cheeks? My hands working over his beautiful body—where did my eyes rest? Did I lose consciousness for periods of time, as I seem to remember? Or did I pretend efficiency throughout, acting as transparently as I have seen young girls act in my own presence since that time?

As soon as I finished, Belle Mère had me hold his head while she gave him quinine. Then, placing a light sheet over him, we left him to rest. On the doorstep Immaculata showed Belle Mère the only thing she had found in his pockets. It was a copy of *The Odyssey* translated to German.

WE WORKED THE REST of the day. I finished cleaning the delivery room with Immaculata and Jude. It was extremely hot. Afterward, we rested beneath the shade of a hedge and fanned ourselves with heavy palm leaves. Flies swarmed everywhere, glinting and sliding through the air like warm sparks of coal. No wind moved at all.

The heat added to the sexual awareness I had experienced, however briefly, with the German. Of course I didn't call it that at the time, and would have been shocked to have thought it of myself. Nevertheless, touching his skin had made me familiar with my own loneliness and the isolation of my body. I was conscious of my arm socket moving smoothly, sweat turning it slick; the hair shirt I wore grew matted with my perspiration. One breast slipped out of the wrapping I wore across my chest and remained pressed against the front of my gown.

I took the girls to the front porch of our living quarters and forced them to scrub the floor. I worked beside them, trying to escape the senses of my own body through exhaustion. I was short-tempered; nothing was done correctly. I scolded them several times, but was hardest on myself. I allowed my knuckles to grate against the dense cinder blocks as I scrubbed, taking pleasure in each bark of flesh that was stripped back. I doused my hands in water that was almost boiling, nearly scalding my wrists and hands in the process. Pain I knew; this other, more pleasurable sensation, I feared.

At dinner that night there was great speculation about the stranger. We were four at table: Belle Mère, myself, Sister Catherine, and Sister Bernard. Jude and Immaculata stayed with the sick while we ate, then we relieved them. Our meals, quite simple, consisted of bread and fruit and light tea. Occasionally, when one of the priests came to stay, we had fresh game. Otherwise we rationed meat, preferring to keep the chickens alive for the eggs they provided. Our goats gave milk, which we reserved for the infants.

"He must be a soldier," Sister Bernard said at some point after the blessing. She was a tight, rather prudish woman, easily the most scholarly among us.

"Why would he be down here?" Belle Mère asked. "Wasn't the fighting in Algeria? That's all the way on the northern side of the Sahara."

"He might have made a run for it," Sister Catherine said. Sister Catherine was a bumbling, kindly woman who never got anything quite straight. Her hair peeked out from under her habit; her rosary often slipped about her waist, giving her the appearance of having a tail.

"Run across the Sahara?" Sister Bernard asked her. Sister Catherine exasperated her. "Is that what you're saying?"

"There are caravans, aren't there?" asked Sister Catherine. "Don't they still bring salt up from Mopti?"

"It's more likely that he put in at Dakar and came overland," Belle Mère said. "We don't even know he's German, do we?"

"He's German, all right," Sister Catherine said. "I'd bet a great deal of money that he's escaped from somewhere and staggered around in the bush for weeks."

Belle Mère suggested that the young man was actually a pilot.

This, she said, would answer the question of how he had come here. But Sister Bernard contradicted her.

"Where would he have been flying to?" she asked. "Don't you see? There's no airport here, no military installations."

"Should we report him to the French Commandant?" Sister Catherine asked. "If he is a German soldier . . . I mean, it would be our duty, wouldn't it?"

"Yes, he could be spying on us," Sister Bernard said, then laughed when she saw Sister Catherine had taken her seriously. "Really, Catherine, what could he find of interest here?"

We went to vespers after dinner. Our chapel was constructed of wood and earthen bricks. It was situated on a small rise which allowed the air to find us. On the front wall there was a crucifix; the roof was made of thatch. The pews consisted of mud benches, which grew up from the dirt floor like mushrooms. Lanterns provided the only light.

Belle Mère led us in the recitation of the rosary. We prayed for an hour. Afterward, it was time for bed. However, Belle Mère told me as we left the chapel that I should accompany her to check the young soldier.

When we entered Loebus's room, Novice Jude rose from a chair in the corner and bowed to Belle Mère. She touched Jude's shoulder and asked how the man was resting.

"Good, Belle Mère," Jude said. "He is still asleep."

"And the fever?" Belle Mère asked, leaning across the bed to check the man's temperature. "Has it rolled back at all?"

"I don't think so, Belle Mère."

Belle Mère sent Novice Jude to dinner, then called me over to the bed and asked me what I thought. I had some limited nursing experience from my childhood in the Alsace, so it wasn't unusual for Belle Mère to ask me about treatment. She handed me a damp washcloth. While I sponged his forehead and neck, she asked what could we do about the man's dehydration? How could we lower the temperature?

"We might wet down a sheet and place it under him," I said. "It might help with the fever."

"Yes, probably so. I'll get the fresh sheets. Keep sponging him."

For the first time I was left alone with him. I washed him slowly, bathing his neck and shoulders. The sound of my washcloth dipping into the bucket of water seemed loud to me. Everything was still except the moths hitting against the lantern. A lizard hung from the roof above us. Flies landed on him. When they jumped away, their legs left tiny indentations in the sheen of moisture I applied to his skin.

I allowed myself to inspect him. I saw his slender body disappearing into the sheet, the cartilage over his ribs a small ladder connecting with his hips. His arms were muscular; his shoulders were thick knobs on the ends of his clavicle.

But it was his face that captured my attention. Looking at him, I realized I didn't know the color of his eyes. Blue, I imagined. Blue with perhaps a fleck of gold or green. It was a romantic assumption, but it seemed true nevertheless. His cheeks were nearly covered by a rough beard, which only served to make him more handsome. His brow was wide and his nose angular, his mouth full.

Belle Mère returned a short time later. She pretended to be in a hurry. It was late, she said, and she needed her rest. I wouldn't mind, would I, if she left me to stay with him through the night? She couldn't ask it of the African girls since they were too young. I could sleep on a small cot she would help me arrange.

She said all this in a matter-of-fact manner. The request wasn't unusual. Even in my short time in Africa I had stayed various nights with women having difficulty delivering a baby. I knew, however, as did Belle Mère, that this was a different request.

I helped her roll the German from side to side as we placed the sheet beneath him. His skin responded with goose flesh. We placed a second damp sheet on top of him which outlined the contours of his body. I noted it. Belle Mère noted it, but said nothing.

Finally we placed a mosquito net over the bed. Then Belle Mère helped me make up my own cot. This was a simple wooden pallet we dragged in from outside. I placed a sheet on it and we hung a mosquito net from the roof. It would not be comfortable, but it would do.

"You should be all right like that," Belle Mère said. "I doubt he will wake, but it's better if someone is here in case he does."

"Yes, Belle Mère."

"Do you think he's handsome?" she asked.

Her glasses caught the lantern light and turned silver for a moment.

"I hadn't looked."

"Are you going to lie to me, Sister Marie? Haven't you noticed anything about him? His muscles? His handsome nose? He makes me want to jump in there beside him."

She laughed when she said this. She laughed loudly, and it was only after she had gone on for a few seconds that I realized she was laughing at me. She laughed even harder when I shook my head in disapproval.

"Oh, don't pretend you're shocked or haven't thought of it yourself," she went on. "He's a very handsome man. That's the truth. What you're pretending is not a truth."

"Yes, he's handsome," I admitted.

"And are you having thoughts about him? Answer honestly now."

"Yes, Belle Mère."

"Well, that's good, isn't it? Reading the Bible as a woman, well, I've always wondered what Jesus felt about Mary Magdalene. Do you think they had carnal relations?"

"No, Belle Mère," I answered. Such an interpretation had never occurred to me.

"I've always thought they did, though the Bible isn't clear on the matter. I suppose it's a subject for the scholars, but a study of human behavior would find it a hard conclusion to resist."

"I wouldn't know, Belle Mère."

She looked at me and smiled. She shook her head slightly, then blessed me and left. When she was gone, I knelt and said a rosary, though I was distracted. My eyes kept wanting to glance at Loebus, and I had to start over several times. Each time I began with renewed concentration, then gradually lost my place.

Finally, after I had struggled through the entire chain, I prepared for bed. I went to the small porch outside the hut and washed my face and hands in the basin kept there. I brushed my teeth with a type of chewing stick the Africans used. For some time I stood and let the water cool me. The night was warm, the sky clear. It was quiet in the compound. Everyone was asleep, or at least closed within her cell.

I shut and latched the door when I returned to Loebus. I removed my veil and placed it on a chair near my pallet. Then, turning my back to the German, I loosened my gown and allowed some air to find my chest and legs. It was an enormous relief. I fanned the gown over and over, billowing it out so I could breathe freely. My skin smelled warm.

Eventually I stepped to the foot of his bed and stared through the mosquito net at him. I intended nothing by it; I simply looked in on him. His sleep was solid and his breathing appeared regular. Already the color in his cheeks had improved.

How long I stood there, I cannot say. What went through my mind is impossible to recollect. Looking at him, studying his form, I could barely breathe. His flesh pulled at me. His lips, full and wet from where I had dabbed them, were impossible to resist. Skin, flesh, warmth, the heat, insects—they combined to make me dizzy. My own virginity and the secretiveness of what I was about to do made me almost stumble against the foot of the bed.

I took off my habit. I looked a thousand times at the door behind me, expecting any moment Belle Mère to appear. I placed my habit on the cot without ceremony, yet with a sensation that what I was doing wasn't quite real. Walking quietly on my bare feet, I took the rosary from the belt of my habit and turned Christ's face against the bed covers.

Then, carefully, I removed the mosquito net, pulled down the sheet that covered him, and climbed on the bed beside him. I didn't put my weight on him at first. I remained just to one side, my skin nervous, my eyes fixed on his face. I told myself that he could not possibly wake.

It wasn't easy to move on top of him while keeping most of my weight on my own arms. Our knees touched first. Then my toe touched the side of his foot and I nearly slipped and fell directly on top of him. I caught myself in time, however, and I allowed a little more of my body to rest on his. Our thighs came together, then merged along their length. Our stomachs clamped together, skin on skin. Then, for the first time in my life, I felt my pubic hair against a man's pubic hair, his penis against my vagina. I slid my hands along his arms, then finally ended with my hands in his, my lips pressed against his lips.

I lay on him for five, perhaps ten minutes, then stood. I was mechanical about restoring his rest. I pulled the sheet up around him and replaced the mosquito net. With quick, efficient movement I dressed and went to my cot. I stared at the cement wall until I fell asleep.

IT WAS FIVE O'CLOCK in the morning when Belle Mère relieved me at the young man's bedside. I was awake and prepared for the day. In the pale light I searched her face for signs of suspicion, but she seemed preoccupied. Someone had been stealing from the kitchen accounts—she suspected Armand, our cook—and she wanted to get to the bottom of it. She told Novice Jude, who trailed her into the room, to bathe the soldier and sit with him through the morning.

After a few general questions about his fever I was dismissed and told to retreat to my cell for prayer and contemplation. I went at once.

The bed frame in my cell was constructed of sticks lashed together by gut. As soon as I closed the door behind me, I removed two rods from the frame. I placed one on the floor in front of the crucifix on the wall; I held the other in my palm. Using my free hand, I unbuttoned the back of my habit and pulled it away from my shoulders. I also lifted the cloth covering my breasts, and similarly forced up the hair shirt I wore beneath everything.

Then I knelt on the stick at my feet. I knelt carefully so that the roundness of the stick hit exactly onto my kneecaps. The pain was sharp but cleansing. I slumped in order to increase the pressure on the stick. Sweat instantly started on my forehead. I rocked back and forth, jamming the stick deeper into my knees. My ankles began to go numb. The sensation passed into my toes and finally my heels.

As I recited the Lord's Prayer, I struck myself with the second stick across my back. It didn't cut, but it did raise large red welts. I hit myself harder, whipping until my arm grew tired. Then, still anxious to cleanse myself, I switched hands and repeatedly struck my back again. Throughout it all I recited prayers.

I hardly thought of the young German. I intended to confess my sin in regard to him when the priests visited. Instead, I thought of Christ, His pain on the cross, His suffering. I leaned forward, increasing the pressure on my knees, and placed my forehead against the rough cinder-block wall. A few flecks fell to the floor as I felt my skin pitting on the harsh surface of the stone. This was the stone of Christ's tomb; here it was rolled back, and I was witness to it. I pressed harder and harder into the wall, the pain in my knees excruciating, the welts on my back stinging, my forehead aching with tension and pressure.

"Christ save me, Christ my husband," I murmured. I thought of Saint Therese and wished passionately for my own martyrdom. I called to the Virgin to allow me to die in grace, in the full service of the Lord. I whispered that I wished to die in agony.

Finally I rolled off the stick. This brought about the highest, and most satisfactory, level of pain. Blood, cut off by my weight, suddenly surged into my lower legs. My head grew light and I lay facedown on the cement floor, prostrating myself before Christ and Mary. My toes and heels, formerly numb, now received circulation. They burned. I followed the pain as it crept down my legs, swelling and increasing as it went.

Often I passed out at this moment, but this time I remained conscious as the pain slowly receded. As young as I was, my circulation returned quickly. My head cleared. In a short time, I stood and rearranged my habit.

I checked the position of the sticks twice when I finished. Belle Mère did not approve of self-flagellation or any extreme method of worship, and she constantly looked for evidence of such behavior. Lacking a mirror, I went out to the walkway connecting our cells and glanced at myself in the reflection of a bucket of water. My face was clean. The welts and scars on my back were safely covered by the habit.

After breakfast I spent the morning instructing African women on the looms. The looms were set up on a wide porch around our central building. It was a lovely place to sit. Even in the hottest season air reached us and continued to move around the corners of the building. The sounds of the looms were constant and calming.

I instructed three women. In return, they taught me More, the dominant language of the area. The blankets they wove were sent back to our mission in Brest. The sisters there took the blankets around European markets and sold them for a considerable profit. It was fair business for the African women, and excellent business for the mission. It didn't strike me odd at the time—though it has since—that the Catholic Church gained by their labors. To my thinking then, the African women were privileged to learn about Christ.

I was indifferent toward two of the women. They came to the porch only for the milk and other gifts of food we often handed out. They weren't impolite; they were simply unimpressed by anything I did or said.

Perhaps I should have concentrated my efforts on them. But as a young woman convinced of my own salvation, I was anxious for a convert. The most likely candidate was a woman named Muna.

Muna was intelligent. She had an intuitive grasp of the world—why it worked, what motivated the people who passed through her life. She was tall and well-formed, with exquisite posture forged by carrying heavy burdens on her head since childhood. At the time I knew her she was perhaps thirty years old.

The condition of her marriage, and its spiritual implications, vexed me inordinately. She was the first African I had truly come to know. As a result, she served as my teacher not only in the local language, but in the local customs as well. Through the course of our association, I learned she was a second wife. Naturally this was an abomination to me, and I told her that directly. My reaction, however, caused her only delight. Didn't I realize, she often asked, that many of the women here were second wives? Didn't a man take a second wife in my country? If not, how was the work divided? How could the man be sure he would have heirs to care for him in his dotage?

This was the common line of our conversations. Fortunately for my state of mind at the time, I was able to obscure some of what she told me by blaming it on my inability to understand the language. My intolerance was vast; my zeal to convert, extraordinarily firm. I believed what I wanted to believe from her accounts, and weighted my own observations and advice with greater credibility than they could possibly have possessed when judged from her position.

On this day the conversation centered around the young Nassarra. The women were curious to hear about him, but Muna had information she was anxious to tell.

"My uncle was on the train with him from Dakar to Bamako," she told me as we went over the design of her blanket. She was a gifted and imaginative artist, whose designs were always more intricate than any of the other women's. "He jumped from the train before it entered Bamako. The military police were after him."

"Do you know this for a fact?" I asked.

"That is what my uncle said."

"What was your uncle doing on the train?"

"He is a merchant," Muna said.

"What did the police want with the Nassarra?"

Muna shrugged. The police didn't need a reason, her shrug suggested.

"How do you know he's the same man?" I asked.

"The grass talks, Nassarra."

"How long ago did he jump from the train?"

"Two months or more."

"Do you know what he has been doing since then?"

"Hiding, Nassarra."

A few minutes later Sister Catherine appeared with the noon meal. The women left their looms and formed a loose line in front of the small table from which Sister Catherine served dehydrated milk and beans. Before she allowed any of them to eat, she made them kneel and recite the Lord's Prayer.

During siesta I rested in my cell. I felt confused. Was it my duty to inform Belle Mère of what Muna had told me? Was the young man dangerous?

In the end it didn't matter. Sister Bernard met me on the porch after siesta and told me the young man had regained consciousness.

"He's an Austrian named Loebus," she said, her pronunciation of his nationality conveying her disdain. "He only speaks broken French. He's frightened we'll summon the authorities."

"How did he come here?"

"He walked, apparently. He traveled with the Tuareg and

learned to live in the desert. But the water and heat finally got to
him."

"What will Belle Mère do with him?"

"I don't know. She's with him now."

Sister Bernard had no pity for him. Of us all, her feeling toward
the German occupation was strongest. Her brother had been killed
in Paris, hung as a spy and an informer. This was a fact she often
brought into conversation whenever it turned to political matters.
It served to make the war her war, the deaths her deaths.

Sister Catherine came for me later in the day. Because I had
been raised in the Alsace and spoke some German, she wanted me
to interview the young man. The conversation, she made me understand, had gone past the man's command of French.

Belle Mère looked up as I entered the room where Loebus was
confined. He was propped up in bed.

"How good is your German?" Belle Mère inquired. "Either
he doesn't know how to say anything else, or he's hiding something."

"My German is more of a trade language. I never learned to
speak it formally."

"Try it anyway. Here, pull up a chair."

I sat beside her. Although I found it difficult to look directly
at him, I did notice that his eyes were blue. They were bright blue,
the type of eyes that seemed to project as well as receive light. He
was very thin and still extremely weak, but he appeared to take
heart when I spoke to him in his own language.

"*Guten Tag*," I said, and followed this with other pleasantries.
With each statement that passed between us he seemed more comfortable. I wanted to warn him not to speak too freely simply
because I phrased some questions in German. He was so obviously
pleased to hear someone speak his tongue, however, that he seemed
prepared to answer any question.

At Belle Mère's command, I went over everything he had said
to her and in this way I gathered his story. He had indeed come
to Africa on a boat from Marseilles. Yes, he had participated in

the war, but he didn't wish to say in what capacity. He had joined a party of Tuaregs. He had been a Nazi, yes. Everyone had been a Nazi. He was done with that and only wished to be left alone.

Belle Mère nodded when I translated this information. She had gathered the same thing herself. She told me to ask him why he was afraid to contact the authorities. Was he a war criminal?

He didn't answer. Instead, he asked a question that I'm sure surprised Belle Mère as it surprised me.

"When does a priest come here?" he asked. "I wish to confess. I am a Catholic."

Belle Mère straightened in her chair, then answered that a priest was due in a few days. She told him to rest and signaled to me that we should leave him alone.

On our walk back to the main house she called over Armand's brother. He was a young man named Kouliba, who was always ready to perform any job we gave him. She told him to run to the Prefect's office and explain that an Austrian man had appeared at the mission. She said to tell him the man's name was Loebus and he appeared to be a young soldier. She said she would wait for his advice.

I KNEW IT WOULD TAKE over a week for Kouliba to make the journey and return to us with the Prefect's response. The Prefect's office was in Koudougou, thirty kilometers away. Even if the Prefect sent an envoy, or came himself, Loebus was safe for a little while longer.

Because of my ability to speak some German, I was called on to sit with Loebus more frequently than any of the other sisters. Belle Mère didn't request it of me, but it was clear by inference

that if I could gain his confidence and find out more about him, it
might be useful. Whether she placed me there to face my own
temptations, I can't say.

When I recall that week, I think of heat. It was well over a
hundred degrees each day. The heat was so great that it might have
been harmful to Loebus if we confined him to his small hut. Every
day at ten I pulled the cot—the cot I slept on that first night—out
beneath a shea tree, then held Loebus's arm while he walked to it.
The shade the tree provided wasn't dense, but at least the wind
moved freely over him.

I sat beside him, often with a breviary open on my lap, and
studied him through sideways glances. He was no older than I. His
skin was clear and fresh; his eyes were beautiful. In the languid
heat I watched the flesh of his arm, the sweat beginning on his
brow, his blue veins faintly outlined on his temple. Often I found
myself staring at the way the sun touched the hairs on his forearm,
or the line of his jaw as it cut across the angle of his neck. Dazed,
I watched sometimes for minutes the movements of his hand as he
explained something, his hand dancing and absorbing my entire
concentration.

He didn't talk about the war, or his journey to Africa. Any
question I asked about his background was turned gently aside.
Instead, he was intent on discovering what he could about our part
of Africa. Since I was new here and felt the romance of my own
position, I tended to be more forthcoming than was my habit.
Besides, he had a knack of getting others to speak while he listened.
It wasn't with me alone that he did this. I saw him ask a leading
question of Sister Catherine or Belle Mère, then sit quietly as the
information was provided. I had the notion that he was planning
his escape, or at least the next leg of his journey.

On the third day I sat with him, a strange event occurred. It
was midday, very hot and still. Women slept on the porch, the
looms quiet. I had been about to go to my cell, giving him the
chance to rest, but I stopped when he leaned forward and looked
carefully around him.

His expression was one of keen curiosity, as if he could hear and detect the world about him more sharply than I. He was extremely intent; his eyes seemed almost unfocused. His head cocked to one side and remained in that position for what seemed a long time.

"Are you all right?" I asked, but he didn't answer. The intensity of his expression kept me suspended between a number of thoughts: that he was going mad, that he had always been mad and had simply covered the symptoms while receiving our medical treatment. I wondered if I should call Belle Mère. I looked around for help, or at least a second witness, but no one was near.

Then he raised his hand in what I can only describe as a spastic manner. His right wrist bent; his body folded forward. Small drops of spittle flecked his lips.

The silence was absolutely solid. I looked around again, conscious of the veil on my habit scratching against the yoke of my gown. At any moment I expected him to laugh. This was all a joke, he would say. But his posture became more gnarled; his hands vibrated from the tension in his arms.

It took a moment longer before I discovered the animals watching us. A chicken stood on one leg just at the corner of shade thrown by the porch; a mourning dove perched on the roof of Loebus's hut; a dog lay quietly panting beneath the edge of the porch where the women slept. All of them were turned to face us. All of them were intent on Loebus's slightest movement.

I had the distinct impression that the animals were communicating with him. It was too fantastic to be true, but it was happening right in front of me. The dog continued looking at him; the rooster didn't make even the slightest alteration in its stance; the mourning dove remained stationary on its branch.

Loebus said nothing, yet I felt his soul—I have no other word for it—reach out to these animals. In that instant I believed what he attempted was possible.

As quickly as it had come, the moment passed. Loebus sat back against the pillows. The animals didn't move away, but neither did they show evidence of any intelligence. The sun, I remember, was very hot on my veil.

THE NEXT DAY WAS SUNDAY. Together with the other sisters, I prepared to make the journey to Lati where the White Fathers were stationed. A runner had been sent ahead, telling the priests we were coming for mass. On alternating Sundays we went to Lati; on the next mass day a priest came to us.

I stood in the rear donkey cart with Sister Bernard. A young African man named Dominique prodded the donkey forward. We followed a game path widened by traffic over the years. Much of it had been reclaimed by bush grass. It was difficult to see an obstacle until we were directly on top of it. The ride was jerky and rough.

Lati was beautiful at that season. The agricultural year had been a good one; millet was high. Children ran after the carts shouting, *"Nassarra Paga,"* which meant "White Women." They didn't understand our habits and our life of celibacy. Few of the Africans did. But our coming to the village meant we would hand out candy and other treats after mass.

The mission was situated to the east of the village. Since we had inherited the White Fathers' mission in Tenado, their own quarters were new. Using African building materials, the fathers had constructed a compound of huts. They had also pieced together a church from rough timber. It was a masterwork of tropical architecture. It had a solid roof to keep out the sun and rain, but the sides had been left open so that wind could keep the celebrants cool. The church had been consecrated to St. Michael the Archangel.

The priests waited for us at the church. On this Sunday all three were present. Father John, who was the nominal head of the mission, was a kindly man who must have been nearly sixty. His hair was gray and this made him appear very old to me. He was thin—all the priests were thin—and wore a pair of spectacles that always seemed to be in disrepair. On one visit the left lens would be missing; on the next, the ear piece would be broken and mended by tape.

Father Thaddeus was a scholar. His job at the mission was to catalog the African dialects and prepare the way for the first translations of the New Testament into phonetic More. He was a solitary man, who spent long hours in his cell. He was also a naturalist, an entomologist well-regarded in academic circles. He recorded the insect life in Africa, pressing samples between heavy pages with Latin titles beneath each specimen. His correspondence with other entomologists around the world was voluminous. He possessed honorary degrees from several European universities. His work in bringing our Lord's gospel to the Africans was weak at best. But the Church, I understood from the sisters, encouraged his scholarly endeavors, and he answered in only the most tenuous way to Father John.

Father Fraujas, whose name Loebus would one day possess, was perhaps thirty. He was vain—vain about his personal appearance, and vain about his power over the Africans. I don't know why he was in Africa, because he didn't like the people. He saw them as ignorant and filthy. He enjoyed recounting his latest discovery concerning their backward customs or hateful behavior toward one another. He was an avid hunter; he camped and followed migrating herds for weeks at a time. He hunted in the name of bringing meat to the mission—something we sorely needed—but it was impossible to separate his trips from a desire to kill and an attraction to arms and blood. He struck me always as a man first, a priest second.

Besides the priests, a small party of villagers had assembled to hear mass. These villagers were easily distinguished from the rest of the population because they wore cast-off clothing from European gift boxes—nothing matching, nothing suitable. A man in a top hat; a child wearing a man's vest as his only covering. Had it not been for the poverty surrounding them, and their own pride in their appearance, they would have been comical. We greeted them in the African fashion, shaking hands with each person in turn.

Father John said mass. He was sincere in his devotion and the mass held obvious meaning for him. He also seemed to welcome the quick responses he could count on from us, which must have been an improvement over the stumbling masses he held with the Africans. His sermon was on the connection of all people with the Lord. His words were translated by a young man named Joshua, who was one of the first converts he had made. It was an uplifting, if clumsy scene, with Father John turning after each sentence and pausing to give Joshua time to paraphrase his meaning. Occasionally the African women trilled at something they admired, and then we were required to wait in silence while this passed.

I did not receive the Eucharist; I was conscious of my sin with Loebus. I remained kneeling in my place as the others went forward. I said a rosary and kept my eyes on the dirt floor.

After mass, a meal was set out on the wide tables beneath the thatched porch. The priests stood by the baskets and marveled at what Belle Mère had prepared. She was an excellent baker and managed to make delicious pastries even from the rough millet flour available in the bush.

The Africans didn't sit with us. Some of the parishioners acted as servants and we saw no incongruity in this. We were colonialists, and despite the fact that we were there to bring them the word of the Lord, charity did not extend to having them as dinner partners.

We had hardly started to eat when Father John broached the subject of Loebus.

"We've heard you have a young man staying with you," he said. "Is it true he's a German?"

"An Austrian," Belle Mère said.

"German, Austrian—they're all the same, aren't they?" Father John said. "Did he fight in the war?"

"He will only admit he participated in the war, but he won't say how," Sister Bernard said. "He's hiding something."

"What?" Father Fraujas asked.

"If we knew that, then he wouldn't be hiding anything, would he?" Sister Bernard answered, sipping tea. "I don't trust him."

"Oh, he's a boy," Sister Catherine said, waving her hand to dismiss us all. "It was a war. People were swept into it. You can't hold him responsible for it."

"In any case, he wants to confess. If one of you could follow us back, he would appreciate it," Belle Mère said.

"I'm interested in what you said a moment ago, Sister Catherine," Father Thaddeus said. "You don't think people can resist entering into such things?"

"As war?" Sister Catherine said, apparently surprised that anyone would consider the possibility. "He is a young man. No doubt there were parades, a great deal of flag waving, fancy uniforms—I don't think it's fair to imagine him any more enlightened than anyone else who participated. Besides, we don't really know anything about him."

"A rumor exists in the bush that he is a magic man," Father Fraujas said. "I met a small caravan on one of my hunts and the men said the man has powers."

"What kind of powers?" I had to ask.

"Small things. He can make a fire burn in different ways. They weren't very clear about it. Most of it is rumor, of course. They found him living in a tree. He had hollowed out an old baobab by burning it slowly. He had a camp there and lived close to the earth—that was their expression. No water for miles around him."

"Sounds like a hermit," Father Thaddeus said.

"But where would he have found water?" Father John asked.

"There might be ways," Father Thaddeus told us. "He could

have drunk blood, or maybe he knew of certain gourds that contained enough liquid to satisfy him. Water is a relative concept. There is always water, otherwise things couldn't grow, and even in the bush plants find moisture. Quantity is perhaps what they were discussing."

"Did you notify the Prefect?" Father John asked Belle Mère.

"I thought it best."

"Probably so. Even for his own good, we can't let him wander around. My guess is he's mentally off. Why would anyone come here and live as a hermit unless he's a little unbalanced?"

As we made plans for our departure, Father John proposed to hear our confessions. I went after Belle Mère and Sister Catherine. Father John sat behind a makeshift confessional designed from bed sheets and a wooden frame.

I knelt on the ground in front of him and whispered through the white fabric. His silhouette was clearly defined by the sun. His profile was turned to me and he seemed to look out on the open bush as he listened. We went through the opening stages rapidly. His responses were automatic. Finally, bowing, I told him of my act with Loebus.

"Were you aware of how grievous this sin might be?" he asked quietly.

"Yes, Father."

"And you proceeded anyway?"

"Yes, Father."

"This is a mortal sin. Do you know that?"

"I thought so, Father."

"I will give you nothing for your penance, Sister. I have no doubt you have already punished yourself enough. Also, the penance that is most harsh is the one that we cannot complete. I want you to remember this sin—it is a sin against your vows as well as a sin against our Lord."

"I understand, Father."

He absolved me of my sin, his hand a dark shadow raised against the sun.

FATHER FRAUJAS RETURNED with us to hear Loebus's confession. He rode a horse he had acquired from a village chief for his own use. It was typical of him to own a horse rather than a more humble donkey; equally typical that he wore a pair of trousers beneath his cassock in order not to be reminded he was a priest.

Halfway back to Tenado, we saw a dust cloud rise to the south. The land in that direction consisted of flat plains. Fraujas, whose eyesight was excellent, said that the Prefect and his guard were riding to intercept us.

Serge Joly, the Prefect, rode at the head of the group. He was a short man, whose left leg had been crippled in an accident during the war. Like Fraujas, he was a sportsman who took his official duties lightly. The only African resistance his group encountered in the region was feeble, poorly armed, and easily defeated. He treated the Africans fairly and only conscripted them to build roads that were absolutely essential.

His guard was composed of five ragtag French soldiers. The men were inseparable in their slovenliness. They were heavily armed, with guns strapped to the sides of their mounts. They also affected swords and high black boots. Their uniforms were covered with dust and sweat. Yokes of stains from large gulps of water and hasty baths ringed their necks.

"Hello, Sisters. Hello, Reverend Mother," the Prefect said when his party caught up. "It's good to see you all looking so well."

"Prefect, we didn't expect to see you," Fraujas called, spurring his horse to ride beside the Prefect's. "Did you come for our young Austrian? Is the man dangerous?"

"Oh, no, it was time I toured this area anyway. Is he still with you, Reverend Mother?"

"Yes, Prefect."

"Did he come overland all this way from Bamako?" the Prefect asked with apparent admiration.

"Dakar seems more likely," Belle Mère answered.

"We'll take him back for questioning, although it would be a greater punishment to leave him where he is. Has he said what he's doing here?"

"No," Sister Bernard volunteered. "I'm certain he's hiding from something."

"Well, he's picked his spot, hasn't he?"

Perhaps it was only their military bearing, or the inescapable fact that they were men, but the group brought tension with them. I glanced back at Belle Mère and noted she stared straight ahead. I wondered if she now regretted calling the authorities. Loebus seemed harmless, and the weight of the men's presence was too large for such an insignificant matter. It also occurred to me—as it no doubt did to Belle Mère—that Loebus would be made to walk beside their horses all the way back to Koudougou. It was not out of the question that he would be beaten. He was an Austrian in a French territory; there would be no sympathy for him.

The sun was beginning to set as we entered Tenado. A few of the village children ran to our carts and shouted for candy. I was in the process of climbing from the cart when I saw Loebus appear from his hut. The Prefect turned to his guard and told them to place Loebus under arrest. It wasn't an emphatic command. Obviously, Loebus couldn't escape five soldiers on horseback, nor did he carry a weapon.

Before the men carried out the order, however, a surprising thing occurred. Loebus began limping very rapidly toward the church. He carried a stone in one hand and an object I couldn't make out in the other. He glanced back and forth at the men, limping more profoundly, his speed increasing as the men nudged their horses to move.

He arrived at the church before the men had time to reach him. Standing at his full height, pain evident on his face, he held the stone high above his head. I thought at first he meant to throw the stone at the soldiers. Apparently one of the guardsmen thought the same thing, because he drew his sword and held it up. "Don't," the soldier yelled, but Loebus did not take notice. Turning to the mud wall of the church, he held up the second object in his hand and placed it against the wall.

With one blow from the rock, he sank the object into the wall. I saw that it was a large carpenter's nail, bent to form a hook at the end. It wasn't much longer than a pencil. He drove it up to the hilt, then faced the guard.

"Sanctuary!" he screamed.

He placed his finger through the ring of the nail and slumped to the ground. His finger remained suspended in the nail above him; his voice was broken by emotion and fatigue and pain.

"Sanctuary," he called again.

He began to sob. The children who begged for candy a moment before, suddenly stopped. The soldiers reigned in their horses. Our donkey, the one who had pulled us all day, flicked its ears and stepped once sideways.

I stared at Loebus, as we all did. Then, a moment afterward, my attention was drawn to Belle Mère. She who had called the authorities in the first place, suddenly ran toward Loebus. She was a stout woman who never moved hastily if she could avoid it, but she ran now across the packed dirt road. Her rosary jingled. Her habit flipped up in back. Her sandals tapped against her heels.

"Leave him alone," she called, nearly getting knocked back by one of the guardsman's horses which shied at her steps. "Leave him. Sanctuary is granted."

It was absurd and somehow sublime. The soldiers turned and looked at the Prefect. The Prefect glanced at Father Fraujas. Loebus remained at the base of the church wall. Belle Mère knelt beside him. She tried to take him in her arms, but his finger remained pinned in the nail and his weight rested against the wall.

She whispered something to Loebus, but from where I stood I couldn't hear. He seemed to listen, but said nothing. His sobs were deep and painful. His cheek took up mud from the wall.

None of the men moved closer. They looked back and forth between the Prefect and Belle Mère. Should they go forward? Should they pull him away from the wall? They would follow orders; otherwise, they had no interest.

The Prefect slowly dismounted. Father Fraujas did the same and walked beside him through the guard. The Prefect spoke first.

"I understand your feelings," he said to Belle Mère. "The man is obviously not well. I wasn't aware of his condition."

"He has sanctuary in this church," Belle Mère said, not even looking at the Prefect.

"Sanctuary is a religious term. I'm afraid he is a prisoner of the state, Reverend Mother."

"As long as he remains with the church, he is protected," she answered. "He has anchored himself to the wall."

"Well, that's a point of view. Father Fraujas? Does the Church still grant sanctuary to criminals?"

"No, I don't believe so," said Father Fraujas.

"There, you see?" The Prefect raised his hands and opened his palms as if to show us he was not a devious man. "Your own priest agrees with me. We can't grant sanctuary to every criminal who drives a nail in the wall, can we? You can see that wouldn't be reasonable."

"He has sanctuary."

"Reverend Mother, I'm afraid I can't permit it."

"He's harmed no one."

"How do you know?" he said. "This is out of your realm."

"Just the opposite, Prefect—this has been removed from your realm."

"You're being sentimental now. I respect your religious feelings—I can't tell you how I admire what you've done here. But this man, really Reverend Mother—it would be unsafe to leave him here. You're women as well as nuns."

"He has asked for sanctuary and he has received it," Belle Mère said, turning for the first time to face the Prefect. "I couldn't remove it if I wanted to. This is a compact with our Heavenly Father."

"Oh, now . . . ," the Prefect began, but Father Fraujas interrupted him.

"We must release this man to the Prefect, Reverend Mother. I insist. I'm not sure sanctuary was ever a concept the Church took seriously. We can ask Father Thaddeus later. I'm as impressed by this man's devotion as you are—and by your own courage in taking up his position—but this is a political question, not a religious one."

"You have no charges against him," Sister Catherine said, coming through the guard. "You, Father Fraujas, should be taking his confession, not arguing to pry him from the wall of the church."

This was gross insubordination. Father Fraujas, however, treated it as only a manifestation of feminine emotionalism. He shook his head and glanced at the Prefect. It would cure itself, his expression seemed to imply. He looked back at Sister Catherine, clearly marking her for further conversation at the appropriate time.

The Prefect remained standing quietly a moment longer, then told two of his guardsmen to tie up the horses for the night. He instructed the other three to make their beds around Loebus. No one spoke as the men pulled their bed rolls from the horses. The guards' presence was ominous; the patience implied in ringing Loebus was unsettling.

"You've forced me to this," the Prefect said to Belle Mère. "My orders to these men will be to knock any food or water you attempt to bring to this man onto the ground. There will be a guard around him until his finger slips from the anchor. Sooner or later, it will happen. I ask you to think about what will be the most merciful course of action. I won't accept responsibility for his death if you persist in this."

"That's inhuman," Sister Catherine said.

"Until his finger slips from the anchor," the Prefect repeated.

BELLE MÈRE SAT UP with Loebus throughout the night. At dawn
when I brought coffee, I found she had driven a second nail into
the wall, this one lower down to allow Loebus to sit more comfortably. She did not say if the guards had tried to stop her.

In the soft light Loebus appeared very weak. His hair was
disheveled. His face was streaked with mud; his white robe was
covered with dirt and the front seemed stained by urine. His eyes
were wary, his glances nervous and filled with distrust.

"He asked for you during the night, Sister Marie," Belle Mère
said quietly, her glasses rimmed with pale moons of steam from
the coffee. "He wanted to speak to you in German. See if he
understands what the Prefect has ordered."

I spoke to Loebus, but he didn't seem to understand. He shook
his head, then nodded in random sequence. I explained the conditions of his sanctuary; I explained that we wouldn't be allowed
to help him; I offered that it might be easier in the end if he were
to leave the wall of the church now, before his fever returned in
full force.

None of this appeared to make an impression on him. His
only reaction was to place his cheek more firmly against the wall
of the church. He seemed reluctant to break any contact whatsoever
with the mud bricks. Moving to his left, he kept his right palm
against the church. Settling more comfortably onto his haunches,
he kept his knee pressed to the wall.

As I finished speaking, the guards began to wake. Loebus
followed each movement with great attention. He looked back and
forth between Belle Mère and myself repeatedly. He reminded me
of the legends of mad men living alone in the woods, perhaps raised
by animals. The attention he directed toward the guards was more
than human. It was sharp and pointed, almost lupine in its intensity.

Before I could explain anything else to Loebus, the guards
interrupted us. In a ridiculous show of power, they made Belle

Mère and me move away from Loebus. One of them inscribed a half circle around him with the point of his sword.

"Stay that far away from him," the guard said. "If you get closer, we'll pull him away from the wall."

"Are you a Catholic?" Belle Mère asked. The man said nothing.

"If you are a Catholic," Belle Mère went on, "you should know that you are drawing a ring around your own soul."

"I'm following orders," the soldier replied.

"I warn you, be careful how you treat this."

The soldier waited while we stepped behind the line. A few minutes later the Prefect appeared. He looked refreshed. He had shaved and apparently already taken his breakfast. He made a point of stopping in the center of the small courtyard and examining the day. He looked east at the sunrise. He closed his eyes and let the light hit him for a moment. With his eyes still shut he patted his pockets and found a cigarette. The message in these preparations was evident: It was a new day, matters were more clear now, he was prepared to take his time.

"Good morning," he said when he finally stood in front of us. "Is the gentleman feeling any better?"

"No, Prefect," Belle Mère answered.

"I'm sorry. He should be in bed, not out here. The sun will be on him in an hour or so. It could go badly for him."

"I'm sure the sun won't do him any good."

"Would you allow me to speak to him?" the Prefect asked, though of course we couldn't prevent it.

Belle Mère nodded. The Prefect came forward and held out his pack of cigarettes to Loebus. Loebus only shrank farther against the wall. The Prefect placed the cigarettes back in his pocket. He squatted next to Loebus and tried to find the young man's eyes with his own. Loebus, however, couldn't hold his gaze still.

"Your name is Frederich Loebus?" the Prefect asked. "And you are Austrian? Do you mind if I call you Frederich?"

Loebus said nothing.

"I want you to realize that you cannot hold out very long. It is my duty to prevent these sisters from feeding you or bringing you water. Who wins by all this? If you come with me to Koudougou, I promise you decent treatment. We can telegraph Abijan and find out a little more about you. If there's no report on you, if you have nothing to hide, I'll release you immediately. That's fair, isn't it?"

I couldn't tell if Loebus understood. The Prefect turned and asked me to translate what he had offered. I did as I was told. My words made no impression. If anything, they seemed to push Loebus more firmly against the wall.

Yet when I finished, Loebus finally broke his silence. He spoke directly to me. His words came slowly.

"Tell the Prefect that God grants me sanctuary. Tell him that he has no power to grant me sanctuary."

I told the Prefect what Loebus had said. Hearing it, he grinned. It was an ironic grin, one which signified that Loebus would regret his decision. As the Prefect stood, the sun cleared the church, delineating the first harsh shadows on the sandy earth.

"Tell him that perhaps God intended his sanctuary to be with me. I've made him an offer. Tell him one of the soldiers will ask every hour to see which offer he chooses—God's, or mine."

The Prefect then turned to Belle Mère.

"Reverend Mother," he started, "I wonder if you have considered that this man might have crimes against him? Have you given enough weight to that possibility?"

"I realize the possibility exists."

"It seems to me he wouldn't request sanctuary unless he has something to hide. Perhaps it's something quite heinous. In theory, would it matter to you what his crimes might be?"

"His crimes have nothing to do with his sanctuary."

"Don't they? Suppose you discovered he had killed children, or innocent women? Would you feel the same way?"

"Yes."

"No second thoughts? No reservations? Anyone may claim sanctuary, is that how you see it?"

"Yes."

"I will seek a ruling on this from Bishop Claude in Ouagadougou. Father Fraujas suggested the Church has never truly granted sanctuary. It's a popular myth. Do you see how impractical it would be? Men could commit any crime whatsoever, then run to the Church and throw themselves on its mercy. The result of your system would be chaos."

"What is the result of your way?"

"That answer is beneath you, Reverend Mother. Of course our system is imperfect, but you must have consequences for actions. Without consequence, where would we be?"

"You don't know that this man has done anything, so the argument is pointless."

"I know that he's afraid of some consequence. From that I can reason backward."

"Not only the guilty are punished."

"But you see, he is punishing himself. I don't think you've taken that into account. Perhaps he's unable to reason, or perhaps he sees this as his own penance. The sun will kill him in a day or two. Self-destruction is a mortal sin. He's making a choice."

He left shortly after this on a hunting excursion with Father Fraujas; the guardsmen remained. Sister Catherine relieved Belle Mère, who went with me to the porch where the first village women arrived for their work on the looms. Belle Mère didn't tell the African women what had occurred, though it was clear they had heard. Throughout the morning they made excuses to leave their work for a look at the Nassarra.

I worked all morning with the women, but it was impossible to concentrate. I was relieved when Belle Mère appeared later in the day and asked me to go with her.

"I need you to help me convince the young man that I was mistaken," she said as we crossed the courtyard toward the church. "We cannot allow this to go on any longer."

"Are you sure, Belle Mère?"

"I've prayed over it. It will serve no one to continue. We are encouraging him out of our own interests."

"It was his choice."

Belle Mère looked at me quickly, then shook her head. Her glasses blinked silver.

"You approach the Lord with a romantic heart," she said. "I'm not sure if such a heart will injure you in the long run or prove your salvation. But be careful of letting it blind you to reality. The Prefect was right—I was unfair to allow it to go on this far."

"I don't think Loebus will stop."

"I'm counting on you for that."

I was disappointed in Belle Mère. To betray Loebus at this point in his passion was to betray something in all of us.

When we turned the corner of the church, however, I no longer felt sure of myself. Sister Catherine was sitting on a small stool, her rosary strung across her lap. She had pushed as close as possible to the line drawn in the dirt in the futile hope that her shadow would eventually lend some comfort to the prisoner. Her face was red. Her hands were red. The armpits of her habit were wet with perspiration.

But it was Loebus who captured my complete attention. He had melted against the wall. Yet to say "melt" is to imply water, and there was nothing liquid about him. His finger hung by the first joint on the nail, but this was the hand and arm of a man drowning in heat. His essence was gone. It had been lifted from him, evaporated into the air. His eyes were swollen almost closed. His mouth was open. He breathed in short pants, his forehead tucked under his extended arm in an attempt to find shade. I couldn't be sure, but I thought his tongue had begun to swell inside his mouth. His lips were singed by harsh red ulcers.

Belle Mère attempted to go to him at once, no doubt to pull

his finger from the wall. The guard nearly missed stepping in front of her.

"I'm sorry, Reverend Mother," he said.

"I'm going to take his finger from the wall," Belle Mère said.

"I can't let you go beyond the line. Those are my orders."

"Don't be a fool. You've made your point."

"I can only let you near him if the Prefect commands it."

"You can see for yourself that the man is almost dead. Let me by."

For a moment I thought Belle Mère was going to try and push her way past. The guard seemed to think this as well, because he braced his legs, prepared to accept the weight of her thrust. But it never came; Belle Mère stepped back. Sister Catherine came to stand beside us.

"He's unconscious," Sister Catherine said, her hands hidden in the loose sleeves of her habit. "He hasn't spoken in over an hour."

Looking at the guard, Belle Mère said, "If we approach with water, he can't prevent us all from getting past. Are you prepared to strike us?"

"No, Reverend Mother, I don't want to strike you, but I'll do what I have to."

The sun was everywhere. I could not imagine its cumulative effect on Loebus's skin and eyes. The sun brought confusion. It was impossible to conceive of any plan in such harsh light. Even the lizards basking in the warmth appeared stunned with the heaviness of the heat. The air smelled of grass reaching toward its kindling point.

Belle Mère did nothing for what seemed a long time. No doubt she checked through her choices and found each one lacking. We would have to wait for the Prefect to return. This thought, and her own loss of authority, apparently paralyzed her.

"I will fast beside him," she said finally.

"Belle Mère—" Sister Catherine began, but Belle Mère cut her off.

"No, it's the only way. I'll endure what he endures, and the Prefect can decide what he wants to do."

"I would like to fast with you," I said.

"No," Belle Mère said, "this is my responsibility. Sister Marie, you think too highly of sacrifice. I am doing this only because there is nothing else left to be done. I'm too old to love sacrifice the way you do."

Saying this, she walked around the half circle until she was able to place her hand against the wall of the church. She knelt carefully. The guard bent to speak with her, but she wouldn't look at him.

Before the guard could speak, Loebus slowly swung his head from beneath his arm. His eyes opened, but I had the notion that he saw us from a great distance. His senses needed time to clear, and for a full minute he simply watched Belle Mère without saying anything.

Then, licking his lips, he tried to speak. He managed nothing more than a small croak, then again tried to lick his lips. Belle Mère faced him, her hand still on the wall. He closed his eyes, as if resigned to speaking with her, though she, through her good intentions, would only cause him more pain. He squinted against the sunlight, his eyelids fluttering.

"Outside of Vienna," he said in broken French, his voice barely audible, "I executed two men and a woman. I shot them with a rifle. This is my penance, Reverend Mother. Please don't add to my guilt by trying to share it."

He said nothing else. His head slowly rolled down to the cover of his arm, his eyes closing in pain.

Belle Mère bowed her head and said a short prayer. Then, slowly, she stood and dusted the dirt from her knees. She did not comment about his confession, but told Sister Catherine to stay with him as long as she was able to stand the sunlight. When the sun became too much, she said, Sister Catherine was to call one of us to take her place.

A RUNNER FROM THE PREFECT arrived at dusk to report the Prefect had shot a buffalo on its evening drink. Father Fraujas and the Prefect had decided to remain with the carcass to keep off any scavengers and to oversee the butchering. Could a donkey cart be sent? It was the Prefect's wish that the buffalo be brought to the mission at night in order to avoid the sunlight that so quickly spoiled meat. The runner also added that wood should be gathered so that the meat could be smoked and cured the next day. The buffalo was prime, the runner said.

Sister Catherine and I stood beside Belle Mère as she received this information. We had just finished with vespers. She thanked the runner and sent him to the kitchen for a meal. Then, turning to me, she asked that I purchase the wood. She gave me two or three names among the villagers who had often done similar service for her. I was permitted to double the price if they provided the wood by sunrise.

Belle Mère left with Sister Catherine to arrange for a donkey cart. I went to Muna's compound and arranged to buy wood. Afterward, I went to my room and read the Bible until I fell asleep. Sister Bernard woke me for my shift at four a.m. As I dressed she told me he had begun to hallucinate. Occasionally he spoke to the air. He had been fitful for the last hour. She expected him to break at dawn, if not before.

When I was ready, I followed her across the courtyard. Sister Bernard swung a lantern in front of her to watch for snakes or scorpions. The light wasn't strong, but I made out the sleeping forms of two guards. They slept with their mosquito nets rolled haphazardly over their faces. Their sleeping seemed an aggressive act. The guard on duty had apparently drifted away for a few minutes.

Before we went much further, Loebus muttered something unintelligible. The sound went on and on, stopping only at short intervals when he seemed to have expended his breath. It was difficult to determine whether he spoke French or German.

Sister Bernard raised her lantern at the sound and I saw Loebus. I had never seen a human in such a state. His skin was horribly raw. It had been scorched by the sun and now had blistered in terrible sores. His face was covered with dirt that still held the webbed pattern of afternoon sweat. His tongue and mouth were fattened by swelling. The words he spoke were strangled by dryness and the blubbery flap of his heavy lips.

He was completely still for strange intervals of time, then suddenly became agitated. It wasn't possible to tell what triggered these fits of movement, though it appeared he answered questions he put to himself.

"We will have to take him from the wall if he doesn't give in soon," Sister Bernard said. "He won't be able to stand another day."

"It looks like his fever has returned."

"Do you feel pity for him?" asked Sister Bernard suddenly. She lowered the lantern and placed it at our feet.

"Yes, don't you?"

"In my heart? I don't know. I feel anger toward him. I forgive him as a man, but not as a soldier. I can't forget he executed three human beings. Have you considered we might have an obligation to deny forgiveness?" she asked.

"I don't think in those ways, Sister Bernard."

"It's better you don't. My mind is too active. It always has been. My first Reverend Mother told me that it was my greatest obstacle in becoming a nun."

She looked at Loebus a long time. Before she finally gathered her things, she made a strange remark.

"I wanted him to pray for me," she whispered. "He is closer to God than I will ever be."

"That isn't true."

"You know it as well as I do. Belle Mère knows it," she said, picking up her things. "Good night, Sister. The sun will be up soon."

Sister Bernard left. I saw the guard pass by, walking slowly, a cigarette in his mouth. I sat on the wooden stool Sister Bernard had used. If Loebus knew I was nearby, he made no sign of recognition.

It wasn't much later when I heard the Prefect's hunting party return. The approach awakened the sleeping guards. They jumped up and ran off to meet the Prefect; the remaining guard assumed a position near Loebus.

The Prefect came directly to the church, Father Fraujas riding alongside him.

"He's still at it?" the Prefect asked when he dismounted.

"Yes, Prefect," I answered.

"The poor man," the Prefect said, handing his horse's reins to a guard. "Father Fraujas, have you seen him? Look at this sad example. I predicted as much, didn't I? Such a waste, really."

Father Fraujas came and stood beside the Prefect.

"This can't go on another day," he said, calmly appraising Loebus. "I had no idea it would get this bad so quickly."

"You have to admire his stubbornness."

"It isn't stubbornness," I said.

"No? What is it then, Sister Marie?" the Prefect asked.

"It is devotion to Our Savior."

"Is it? Does your Savior require such sacrifices?"

"At times, yes, He does."

"Sister Marie," Father Fraujas said, "the Lord does not require this man's life. To pretend He does is a subtle form of blasphemy. We can't presume to know the Lord's intentions."

Before I could answer, the guard stepped forward and reported that Loebus had confessed to killing three people. This information seemed to make little additional impression on the Prefect. He grunted and shook his head, as if the last piece of the puzzle now fit together.

"Father Fraujas, do I have your permission to remove this man from the wall?" he asked.

"Yes, this has gone on long enough."

"Father," I said, "he is doing this as penance."

"Don't be ridiculous, Sister Marie," Father Fraujas said. "Do you want the man to die?"

At a sign from the Prefect the guard stepped forward and tried to wake Loebus. He touched his arm, then slapped him lightly on the cheek. Loebus did not respond. The guard brushed back Loebus's hair and attempted to make the prisoner open his eyes.

"Wake up, now," he said, "come on."

It was futile; his body did not react. Several times the guard tried unsuccessfully to bring Loebus awake. Finally, Father Fraujas stepped forward and offered to help carry Loebus to a recovery hut. He picked up Loebus's feet while the guard took his arms. When they lifted, his body was completely limp.

His hand, however, did not come free from the wall. It remained anchored, his finger apparently cramped and solid around the nail. An absurd moment followed where Father Fraujas and the guard strained to pull him away, Loebus bowing between them.

They tried this twice before Father Fraujas bothered to look at the finger. He put down Loebus's legs, bent close to examine the wall, then shook his head.

"He's hammered the nail through his finger," Father Fraujas said. He spoke in a flat voice, showing no emotion whatsoever. "It looks infected."

"Can you work it free from the wall?" the Prefect asked.

I turned my back. I heard Father Fraujas pull and slip, then pull again. A piece of mud brick fell to the ground. Loebus groaned softly in pain.

"Really . . ." Father Fraujas exclaimed, but the word carried as much derision as sympathy. It implied annoyance that Loebus put them to so much trouble.

The Prefect had the good manners not to speak. I turned in time to see Loebus carried to the same hut he had occupied before the Prefect's arrival. His hand dangled at his side, his finger still skewered by the nail. It was only later, when he was returned to the hut with a guard posted at the doorway, that it occurred to me that he might have had help. It was Belle Mère who had lowered the nail.

SISTER CATHERINE AND I tended to Loebus. We bathed him, rubbed his skin with alcohol, tried to feed him liquids. He vomited once, though his weakness made it difficult for him to accomplish even that. Afterward, however, he was able to hold down a cup of water.

Our last treatment was to remove the nail from his finger. It was a gruesome job. The flesh had scabbed around the metal, making it difficult to withdraw. Sister Catherine held his hand between her knees, then pulled in a sudden movement. The hand jolted; the fingers spread in pain, then collapsed. The nail came out, reopening the wound as it did so. Sister Catherine said the blood that accompanied the extraction was a good sign. We washed his finger in more alcohol, then bandaged it carefully.

"I think he'll survive," Sister Catherine said. "I don't understand why he should, but I think he will."

I helped Sister Catherine carry a chair into the room, then left. Near the porch, the Prefect and Father Fraujas supervised the preparation of the buffalo, which had arrived at last. Armand, our cook, worked with a young apprentice, cutting the carcass into quarters, then slicing long strips of beef for drying. As each strip came free, he hung it from a line strung between two of the porch posts. Flies swarmed everywhere. A pair of vultures had taken up a position in one of the larger trees at the edge of the courtyard.

"How is the prisoner?" the Prefect asked as I walked toward the door.

"I'm not sure. He's very sick."

"Do you think he requires Extreme Unction?" Father Fraujas asked.

"That's for you to determine, Father," I said as calmly as I could, trying to continue on my way.

"Sister, you blame me, don't you?" the Prefect asked. He smiled around a cigarette. "Speak freely. I want to know your opinion."

"You seem indifferent to his suffering, Prefect. I can't judge what else you might think."

"This young man wanted to suffer. Don't you think that's true?"

"I don't know what to think about any of this," I said.

"I hope you won't hold it against me, Sister. Believe me when I say that if I hadn't afforded him the chance to suffer, he would have found another way. I was an instrument, that's all. Christ needed his Pontius Pilate. We blame Pilate unjustly. Pilate was a fulcrum for Christ—a magnificent fulcrum. At least I've always believed so."

"Maybe it's a little early for such discussions," Father Fraujas interceded. "For me it is, at any rate. Sister, were you going somewhere?"

I nodded, went inside to the common room, and sat on the first available chair. Behind me, I heard the whack of Armand's machete as he hacked at the carcass. A headache started in my temples and began to pulse. I covered my eyes and put my head on the table. I placed my cheek on the wood surface, stealing its coolness.

Sister Bernard found me a little later. I'm not sure if I dozed, but suddenly she was there, sitting next to me. She had apparently just risen from bed, because the edge of her veil was damp, her face freshly washed.

"Are you all right, Sister?" she asked.

"I felt weak. I'm better now."

"You should go to bed. This has thrown our schedules off."

"Where is Belle Mère? I haven't seen her," I said.

"In her cell. I just spoke with her. She's praying over Loebus. She nailed his finger to the wall."

"Are you sure?" I asked.

"She told me she did it. He asked her several times, and finally she gave in. The guard was asleep. It has upset her a great deal."

"I can't imagine her doing such a thing."

Sister Bernard looked around; she bent closer and lowered her voice.

"I have something to confide in you. I want to tell you because I think you'll believe me. Do you remember when I came to wake you last night?" she asked.

I nodded. A pressure suddenly built in me. I did not wish to hear what she had to say.

"I woke you because I couldn't stand to be alone. I wasn't tired. In fact, when I returned to my cell I couldn't sleep. I have seen something, Sister, that made me question my senses."

Again Sister Bernard looked around the room.

"Late last night a halo surrounded Loebus," Sister Bernard whispered. "Yes, a halo—I see your look. I didn't believe it myself at first. I blamed it on being tired. I even put it to a test. I looked away three or four times, then looked back. The halo didn't disappear."

"Are you sure, Sister?"

"I'm not sure if I believe it myself. It wasn't as I had always imagined a halo to be. It was a thin shield of light that covered his arm, and it was brightest where his hand was anchored to the church wall. It wasn't at all as it's pictured in religious paintings. I thought of it as the Lord's sight resting on this poor man's hand."

"Could it have been the lantern light?"

"No. I checked that. I even doused the light. The halo remained."

"Are you saying he is a saint?" I asked softly, deliberately giving her an opportunity to retract what she had said.

"I don't know what he might be. I choose to think of it as the attention of our Lord. His sacrifice received the attention of the Lord."

"Did you confess this to Belle Mère?" I asked after a moment of silence.

"Yes. I told her only just now."

"And what did she say?"

"She told me a story in return. She said that when Loebus asked her to place the nail through his finger, his request was irresistible. That was her word. She said she knew the guards wouldn't wake. She said when she struck the nail with a rock that the sound was loud—and yet the sound was also contained. And Loebus made no cry of pain. No one woke."

Sister Bernard pulled slowly back, as if her testimony had drained her. My first impulse was to tell her my own story: that Loebus had somehow communicated with the animals a week before. But I did not. I was filled with immense light and excitement. I had waited for such a moment all my life—but was it reasonable to believe it?

"Does Belle Mère intend to tell Father Fraujas?" I asked.

"No, of course not. He wouldn't believe us. He'd ridicule the whole idea."

"Do you believe what you've told me, Sister? Tell me exactly what you think."

"I'm afraid to believe it," Sister Bernard said. She closed her eyes, as if trying to understand her thinking, then said, "I feel as if we have always believed in picture books . . . do you understand? I've never been asked to believe in something that occurred in front of me. And it is . . . seeing something like this, it undermines us in some way, doesn't it? If you believe in something and it appears . . . well, then it is no longer a question of faith. It's simply there. Because of that, I fear what I've seen."

"Fear it for what it does to you?"

"For what it does to my faith."

I told Sister Bernard I needed to speak with Belle Mère—that I had another story about Loebus to contribute. Sister Bernard squeezed my hand, then led me to Belle Mère's cell.

We knocked; Belle Mère called for us to enter. She knelt at a *prie dieu* that was cut diagonally by sunlight. Kneeling, she looked old and tired. Sister Bernard surprised me by going forward and kissing Belle Mère's hand. Belle Mère touched the back of Sister Bernard's head. Watching them, I understood how long they had prayed for such an occurrence. Sister Bernard began to weep, not uncontrollably, but with a passion I hadn't guessed she possessed.

"Close the door, Sister Marie," Belle Mère said.

Without prompting, I told Belle Mère what had transpired concerning Loebus and the animals. She questioned me in detail about the actual events. Had I seen any evidence of a halo? What was my feeling during the period that I witnessed this? Was it one of grace?

I answered each question without embellishing anything. Belle Mère took pains to get the precise movement of the story. Twice she caught me in minor discrepancies and made me repeat pertinent sections.

Afterward she stood, pushing to her feet with some difficulty. Her habit hung loosely on her limbs. Her breathing, even after such a minor exertion, was labored.

"I'll tell Sister Catherine what both of you have told me," she said. "We will repeat this to no one else."

"Yes, Belle Mère," we answered almost simultaneously.

"You may think me a coward, but I intend to do nothing about this. The Prefect will take him or leave him here. It's a choice I can't make. It's beyond my power to help the young man."

"But Belle Mère, what if he is what we believe him to be?" Sister Bernard asked.

"And what is that?" Belle Mère asked calmly. "Can any of us say what he is exactly? If he is a man blessed with the presence of our Lord, then it is out of our hands in any case. We must watch and wait. Our Lord has never come as . . . as directly to me. How can we judge what to do?"

"If he is taken, I want to go with him to Koudougou to make sure he is treated humanely," Sister Bernard said.

"To help him carry his cross?" asked Belle Mère.

"I have waited a lifetime for something like this. You know my struggles, Belle Mère. I've never had your faith," Sister Bernard answered.

Belle Mère embraced Sister Bernard, then surprised me by embracing me as well. We stood for a moment in silence; afterward we went to prepare lunch for the village women.

BELLE MÈRE KEPT US fully occupied for the rest of the day to discourage idle talking. Near evening we were collected on the porch to leave for vespers when the Prefect paid us a visit. He carried a cigarette in one hand; in the other, a severed horse tail, an affectation many of the soldiers in West Africa took on during their service. He employed the horse tail like a riding crop, slashing it around his neck to chase away insects.

"Good evening, Sisters," he said. "I came to thank you for your hospitality. I'm afraid I must leave tomorrow morning. Duty in Koudougou—clerical matters really, but I should be going."

"Will you take the young Austrian?" Belle Mère asked.

"Yes. We have no choice in the matter. He's admitted to executing three innocent people."

"How will you transport him?"

"I'm afraid he'll have to walk."

"He'll die."

The Prefect shrugged. "It's the normal procedure. I can't ask my men to give up their mounts. He's a prisoner . . . keep that in mind."

"Why are you doing this, Prefect? I really can't understand your behavior in this matter."

"Reverend Mother, your attachment and charity toward this man is commendable. Believe it or not, I also feel some regard for him. But I am a civil authority. I'm responsible for keeping order in this territory. As I said, I have no choice. I promise you I'll give him adequate food and water. I'll allow him to rest at prescribed intervals. I'll do what I can for him."

"Have you told Father Fraujas?"

"He knows I'm leaving," the Prefect said simply.

"And he doesn't oppose the idea? He hasn't asked you to delay at least until the young man has recovered his strength?"

"Like me, he is sympathetic toward the boy, but he also understands the need for law and discipline. Charity toward one individual means injustice in a hundred other instances. We aren't the Church, Reverend Mother."

Belle Mère took up another tack.

"Will you permit us to give him a donkey for the journey? At least let us do that. We can send a boy to bring it back," she said.

"How is it that donkeys and the Church are always ready to help one another?" the Prefect said, then laughed. "Yes, all right, if you will arrange to bring the donkey back, I'll make an exception."

"Thank you, Prefect," she said, then asked Sister Bernard to see about arranging for the animal.

"We were on our way to vespers, Prefect. I hope you will excuse us," Belle Mère said.

The Prefect bowed and stepped aside. We walked to the church a different group than we had been five minutes before. Father Fraujas waited for us at the entrance. He was freshly washed and shaved and his simple cassock had been laundered. His rosary and crucifix had been rubbed with oil. They were black and shiny against the pale cloth of his robe.

"Hello, Sisters," he said as we approached. "I thought I might lead you in prayer this evening."

"Have you heard the young man's confession, Father?" Belle Mère asked.

"Not yet, Reverend Mother."

"With due respect, I think your time would be better spent with him."

She didn't wait for his response. Indeed, we all filed past him without speaking. It was a shallow victory, but one we all needed.

When we had finished our prayers and started back, Belle Mère took my arm and pulled me to one side.

"I would like to speak to the young man before he is taken from us. Will you come with me and help translate?"

"Of course, Belle Mère."

Loebus was propped against several pillows when we entered. He was reading from his book, *The Odyssey*. The mosquito net was in place between us, making it difficult to examine his features. Nevertheless, I saw the sores on his flesh had healed with remarkable speed. His recuperative powers were extremely strong.

A guard sat in the room, smoking a cigarette. Belle Mère asked politely if he would leave us alone for a moment. The guard hesitated, apparently weighing his orders, then shrugged and stood. To his credit, he placed the chair beside the bed for Belle Mère's use. He walked out the door and stood beyond earshot. Belle Mère sat in the chair by the bed.

"Have you been getting enough rest?" she asked in French, then turned to me for the translation. Before I spoke, Loebus raised his hand and answered in his rough French.

"Yes, enough, Mother."

"And you feel . . . somewhat better?"

"Yes, thank you."

"Has the Prefect been in to speak with you?"

"About tomorrow? Yes, Father Fraujas informed me we will leave in the morning. Yes, I know about it. He heard my confession."

"I'm worried you will perish on the journey. I feel I'm responsible for your predicament."

Loebus did not understand the word *perish*, and when he asked me for the translation I couldn't come up with the word. I circumvented the phrase, saying "to become sick again," and eventually Loebus understood.

"Don't worry," he said. "I have done what I have had to do. I feel better inside."

I would like to ask you a question . . ." Belle Mère started, then stopped. "It isn't easy for me. I'm not sure you'll understand my purpose in asking."

Loebus smiled at her, then at me. He closed the book he had held propped on his stomach and set it beside him.

"I wonder if you have ever felt the Lord favored you in any way?" Belle Mère asked finally.

"Favored? In what way?"

"That he touched your life . . . I am not making myself clear. Help me, Marie."

I could not think of the appropriate way to pose the question, but Loebus saved me. He told us an odd story about going out in the fishing boats with the people of Batie. The story didn't convince me. Such an occurrence might have been caused by a variation in temperature or current. Yet the story apparently held meaning for him. He seemed to hold it in his mind as evidence he had been altered since his arrival in Africa. Several times he said he wasn't the same as he had been in Austria, but the phrasing, and my inadequate grasp of German, made the essence of the story vague. He went on to mention his long journey in the desert where he had stumbled in fever until he entered a sort of rapture. He had been changed, but how, and for what purpose, remained unclear. It seemed his words were an attempt to understand the events himself.

He drank from a cup of water. Belle Mère leaned closer to the mosquito net.

"What you have described, if it is true, could be a miracle," she whispered.

"I don't claim it to be."

I didn't believe any of it. The story seemed juvenile; for the first time I wondered if we were mistaken about him. Belle Mère, however, seemed to approve of the account. She asked no more questions. Instead, she took up a pitcher of water and went to the end of the bed. Pulling the mosquito net back, she poured water into her hands and began to wash his feet. Loebus, embarrassed, drew back his legs. I took a step toward Belle Mère, intending to stop her.

"Please allow me to do this," she said to both of us. "It's an act of humility, and by performing it I ask that you forgive me."

"There is no need," Loebus said.

"For my own peace of mind," she answered.

Belle Mère held out her hands. Slowly, Loebus extended his feet to her. He turned his eyes away and stared at the wall beside him. I couldn't look. I glanced at the guard to see if he watched, because this didn't seem honest. Loebus wasn't a saint; he was not even particularly holy.

When she finished, Belle Mère kissed each foot on the arch, then tucked the mosquito net back in place. She waited for me to take the pitcher and replace it by his bed. That done, she nodded for us to leave.

"You don't approve," she said as we approached the porch.

"He isn't a saint."

"But if he is, I kissed his flesh. If he isn't, then he will leave for Koudougou with clean feet. Ask yourself what I risked, and what I may have gained."

BEFORE SUNRISE, Loebus escaped. Shouts brought me awake. At first I didn't understand what had occurred. The shouts were distant, coming from Loebus's hut, but they increased in urgency as I dressed.

As soon as I opened my cell door, the Prefect's voice became the dominant note. He was loudly berating a guard, only stopping to issue further orders. By the time I reached Loebus's hut, Sister Bernard was already there. Sister Catherine appeared a moment later, reporting that Belle Mère was on the way.

We did not ask the men about Loebus's escape, but by listening carefully we pieced together the information. The escape itself had not been particularly daring. The guard had dozed off; Loebus, apparently staying awake for such a moment, had slipped out of the hut and disappeared into the bush. No, the guard didn't know how long he had slept; no, he had heard nothing; no, the animals were all accounted for. Loebus was on foot.

By the time the Prefect had gathered the necessary information, Belle Mère appeared. Father Fraujas came from his own quarters at the same time.

"How long ago?" Belle Mère asked when she heard all the details.

The Prefect shrugged.

"There's nowhere he can go," Father Fraujas said. "Even if the Africans hide him, he'll turn up after a time. In his condition . . ."

"In his condition he escaped," the Prefect said, then turned to Belle Mère. "You see what I've caused? I have myself to blame."

The Prefect did not wait for her response. He looked at the sky; it was rapidly becoming lighter. He called his men and ordered three of them to circle the mission and look for footprints leaving the village. Naturally it was futile, since there were any number of paths in and out of the village, but it was a start. He told the other two guards to pack the horses.

The Prefect himself went to inspect the hut where Loebus had been housed, Father Fraujas tagging after him. Together they examined the doorway, using a lantern close to the ground. I noted that they took care not to obscure the tracks around the doorway. They stood on either side of the door, moving the lantern down and forward to see the footprints.

"There are no tracks leading out," the Prefect said after a time. "None in bare feet in any case."

"That's impossible," Fraujas said.

The Prefect stepped inside the hut and lifted the lantern as if expecting to see Loebus clinging to the roof. He looked under the bed. A moment later he again stepped outside. He blew out the lantern and walked slowly around the hut. He made one circuit, then returned to the doorway and positioned himself so that his shadow wouldn't block the morning light. He crouched and examined the soil carefully once more. Fraujas made a show of crouching beside him.

"Either he obscured his footprints somehow, or he found a pair of shoes and walked backward away from the hut," the Prefect finally concluded. "It doesn't matter, but it is curious. Reverend Mother, did you give him shoes as well as a donkey for the journey?"

"No, Prefect. I intended to give him a pair of sandals this morning."

"Are you sure?"

"Yes."

"You'll forgive me if I ask the guard?"

"Of course."

The Prefect stood. He called quickly to the guard who had permitted the escape, posed the question about the shoes, then dismissed him. Loebus was without shoes. The Prefect nodded to Belle Mère.

"I'm afraid the birds will find him. This isn't Europe, remember. Lions, hyenas, jackals. He'll attract their attention by noon," the Prefect said.

"It's certain he won't go north," Father Fraujas said. "The desert would be suicide. He'll probably move south."

"If he's smart, he'll follow water," the Prefect said. "He'll go southeast, just as the animals do."

"If you're so sure he'll die, why not let him be?" Sister Bernard asked.

"Oh, it's a game now. He has provoked me," the Prefect said. "Besides, it's my responsibility."

The guards he had sent away returned. Each one, as he came from his respective point of the compass, raised his hands to indicate he had uncovered no sign. In answer to the Prefect's question, one commented that there were too many prints leading off into the bush. It was impossible to pick out Loebus's. His initial escape, at least, was clean.

A number of Africans had gathered, hanging back to keep away from the Prefect, yet close enough to watch the events. The Prefect went to them and asked if any of them had seen the white man, Loebus. The Africans stared at him. Two women I knew from the looms shook their heads as if they couldn't understand his French.

"Help me, Fraujas," the Prefect said. "Tell them I offer a reward. Tell them they can have one hundred francs if they give me the necessary information."

Fraujas translated the offer. His More was excellent. When he mentioned the one hundred francs the women became more attentive. It was an enormous sum in such a small village. Nevertheless, they did not speak when Father Fraujas finished.

In a quick motion, Father Fraujas slapped the woman nearest him. The action was so sudden, the sound of his hand snapping against the woman's mouth so loud, that at first I didn't understand what had happened. Before anyone moved, Fraujas slapped her again. This slap, if anything, was even more cruel. She had bent under the first one, coiling, so the second time Fraujas was obliged to punch down at her. It was calculated; it was sadistic. It demonstrated his frustration and pettiness so clearly that it was as painful to watch him as it was to see the woman go to one knee. His face quivered. I could hardly look at him.

Slowly, he became aware of us watching. With difficulty he suppressed his impulse to strike her again. The violence of his attitude and posture slowly subsided. He turned and smiled at the Prefect, asking for him to sanction this mistreatment, but the Prefect only shook his head.

"Really, this is what they understand," Fraujas said. "They're children. I've been through this before."

"If you say so, Father," the Prefect said. "But I don't think we will get anywhere that way. It's possible they didn't see him leave."

"They know something, I promise," Father Fraujas said, stepping back and adjusting his cassock.

The Africans gradually drifted off. The woman who had been struck limped away, as if normal footsteps would be too jarring on her injury. She didn't look back.

"One thing is certain," the Prefect said, "he won't have traveled very far. He'll hide during the daylight hours. There isn't enough cover for him to continue walking. I doubt he would risk going into one of the villages. He wouldn't know whom to trust."

I sensed that for the first time, he doubted what he said. Obviously, they had no way to determine which way Loebus had gone. If they ruled out the north—though he could travel some distance in that direction without being in true desert—that still left miles of countryside. Loebus could climb into a thicket of acacia and make himself virtually invisible. It would be a simple trick to obscure his tracks. An hour's hike over a patch of rock would do it. He wouldn't have to be particularly skilled in such things to pull it off.

All of these thoughts no doubt occurred to the Prefect. He called the four guards together and instructed them to each ride in a specific direction. They were to ride until noon, then return. He mounted his own horse and rode with them to the edge of the village. We followed. The Prefect then turned his horse, said something to the other men, and one guard dismounted.

The guard drew a machete from a side brace on his horse and

began hacking at a stand of bamboo. In no time he felled a large stalk which he then split lengthwise. Bisected this way, the stalk yielded two long halves, hollow as rain gutters. He turned the stalks and again splintered them lengthwise until the original stalk was now in quarters. Each strip was long and green. They smelled of coconut.

Working smoothly, the guard shortened each rod to two or three meters, then sharpened the individual ends into tapered points. Chopping and rolling the rods in order to strike the proper angle, he eventually fashioned four lightweight lances.

He handed them to the other guards, then got back on his horse. The men trotted off in their predetermined directions. I watched one man stop at a thicket perhaps fifty meters away and stab vigorously with his lance. He maneuvered his horse around the thicket so that he stabbed from every direction. Finally he leaned across his horse and stared into the depths of the bush. Satisfied, he moved on.

On each horizon this same scene was reenacted. Watching them methodically inspect each thicket, I didn't give Loebus much chance. He couldn't be far; the guards would root him out like a boar.

Before we dispersed for morning chapel, the Prefect asked our permission to search our cells and common grounds. He apologized even as he asked, and he assured us that he did not suspect us in any way. But it was possible, wasn't it, that he had hidden somewhere in one of the buildings? A corner, a shelf, a neglected closet? He asked us to postpone our chapel until he had the opportunity to search the church.

Belle Mère agreed, though not with any pleasure. The Prefect thanked her, then rode off about seventy meters into the bush. From there, sitting high in his saddle, he inspected the roofs of our buildings. Many were thatched. Only the common building was roofed with tin. But the Prefect rode in a circle around the entire village before he returned, evidently satisfied that Loebus had not climbed out of view.

"THEY WON'T CATCH the Nassarra," Muna said.

She was working at the loom in late afternoon. I sat beside her, helping her finish her blanket. It was cool and pleasant on the porch. The guards had passed by only a few minutes before and the dust from their horses still hung in the air. They hadn't seen Loebus.

"Why won't they find him?" I asked.

"He is *nyanga* . . . a witch man."

"Do you know where he is?"

"He is not out there," she said, pointing with her chin toward the bush.

"Have you seen him?"

"I haven't seen him. He has probably made himself invisible by now. Maybe he has turned himself into an animal."

"Do you believe he can do such things?" I asked.

"Have these guards caught him?"

Sister Catherine stopped by to tell me an African woman had come in from the bush to give birth. Sister Bernard was with her now, but would I look in sometime during the next half hour?

It was then, as I watched Sister Catherine leave, that I suddenly figured out where Loebus was hidden—the fireplace where the buffalo had been smoked and dried. It was near the center of the courtyard, in plain view. I knew the fire had been built in a fair-sized depression, thereby keeping the smoke dense and the coals protected from wind. The depression was large enough to contain a man. Burrowing down, he might have covered himself with ash. The few charred logs remaining would hide his bulk, or at least obscure the outline of his body. The odor of ashes and meat drippings would hide his scent from the neighborhood dogs.

It was an ingenious place to hide, the better for being so close. He risked little. If he was discovered, he had expended no energy. From where he lay, he could hear the Prefect's instructions. He would know when to rise or when to remain hidden. He could conceivably escape for a time, then return to his hiding place to await the Prefect's final departure. Unless one of the guards or the Prefect knew the fire had been built in a depression, they wouldn't bother to look closely at it. It was tantamount to being hidden beneath water. The ashes were a surface; it would require imagination to believe someone rested beneath it.

Of course I couldn't know if I was correct. And yet continuing to stare, I sensed he was there. It was more than logic that directed me. Just as we may enter a room and know by instinct that we are not alone, I knew that Loebus lay beneath the ashes. Looking up from the tangle of charred logs, his face covered with ash, he waited.

I delayed for a half hour before I finally stood and told Muna we would finish the blanket tomorrow. The expectant mother needed me, I said. She nodded and tucked the blanket away under the overhanging porch. I said good-bye and started to walk across the courtyard to the delivery room.

As I approached the fireplace, the sense that he was hidden beneath the ashes increased. His presence couldn't have been more distinct if I had heard his heart. When I was within a meter or two of the fireplace, I pretended to drop something from my habit: a pin, a bead, a button. I bent to the ground, dug in the dust for a moment. When I straightened, I saw him.

He was a ghost. His skin was gray; his face and the stubble of his beard were flecked with white ashes. His hair had long since taken on the coloration of the ashes, so that it seemed to weave, like roots, into the pile beneath. His head appeared a stone; not a stone, a stump, something living that forced its way into the world. His eyes stared straight up into the sky. The faint outline of his body was clear, though it would have been easy to miss if I hadn't been looking for it. It too was covered with ash, and across his waist he had pulled three of the charred logs.

I wasn't certain he was alive. His body resembled the lid of an elaborate sarcophagus, the type where the body flows into the eventual lines of the coffin. His eyes did not move; they exhibited no intelligence.

"I'll help you," I said.

I spoke softly, but I didn't whisper. Any secretiveness would only be more conspicuous. I couldn't risk pausing too long near the fireplace, but I was alone in the courtyard. No one was near. I glanced back at the porch and saw that Muna had left.

"Bring food to your cell," he answered, his voice barely audible.

I prayed for an hour after I returned to my cell that evening. I knelt on the floor and stared at the crucifix hanging from the wall. The lantern light lent just the smallest shade of animation to Christ's features.

Eventually I stopped, doused the lantern, and lay quietly on the bed. I listened for the guards. Several times I imagined footsteps approaching. Each time, however, the sound faded and was replaced by the drone of insects. I slept finally. When I woke, I knew Loebus was near. If he wasn't already at the door, I sensed his approach. Perhaps it was only the pure silence that accompanied his visit; perhaps he found it possible to send his thoughts ahead. I sat up in bed and was ready for the first knock.

It came shortly afterward. A soft knock, a tap with the edge of his knuckle. My cell was entirely dark, but I had positioned everything carefully and I gathered the fruit I had taken from the kitchen onto my lap before he knocked again. I crossed the room quickly, then reconsidered. It might not be Loebus at all. It could be the guard, or even the Prefect himself. I moved back to the bed and tucked the fruit under the top cover. A third knock. I crossed the room again and opened the door.

Loebus stood in the doorway. Without a word he stepped inside. He touched my shoulder in the darkness.

"Don't worry," he whispered. "No one saw me. They're all asleep."

It was too dark to see him distinctly. I smelled sweat and ashes. We stood for what felt like a long time in the darkness. Loebus did not move. I was paralyzed.

"In the morning sweep out my tracks," he said finally. "Did you bring any food?"

"Just fruit."

"May I have it?"

I went to the bed, got the fruit, and returned to the doorway. I couldn't see him, and for two or three heartbeats I believed he had gone. But then his hand touched mine. It groped first on my forearm, then, like a blind man's hand, worked its way down. Suddenly we both held the fruit and I pulled back, too quickly I knew, but I couldn't tolerate the frantic touch of our hands.

"You should go," I said. "They think you're still nearby."

"Yes," he answered, but began to eat the fruit. A slight groan escaped his lips as he ate. I had forgotten how sick he had been. He was starved and probably terribly thirsty. I listened to him consume the fruit, his hands working to peel back the banana skin while his mouth still ate a mango.

"Is that the cross you pray to?" he whispered when he slowed his eating.

How had he seen it? I turned my head to where I knew the cross to be and *I* couldn't see it. Not even an outline cast by its darker wood was visible.

I got the water pitcher I kept by my bed and brought him a glass. He knew what I had done and his hands found mine immediately. He drank three glasses with deep swallows.

It was time for him to leave, but he made no move to go. I placed the glass beside my bed, drying my hands as I returned to the center of the room. I knew, of course, what would happen next, though I tried to deny my own knowledge. I wanted him there, next to me. The force of this understanding was frightening.

"I have nowhere to go," he said.

"You have to go."

He put his arms around me. He was clumsy. He tried to kiss me, but I pushed my face against his chest.

Imagine if you can that you have never felt another human being press close. Skin, hair, the smell of his neck, the force of his lower body, his thigh flat against my thigh, his hand spread on my back. Darkness and his breath, tinged by the fruit he had just consumed, his chest moving, his blood and arms becoming warmer. My own reaction, always hinted at but never realized. Slowly I lifted my arms and placed them around his back. I trembled. Yes, I trembled partially from the heat of my body, but also from the comprehension that I could not close this part of my mind ever again. I could not forget this.

We stayed a long time in this position. It was hot and sweat glided over my body. He moved his hands down to my waist, tucking me closer, and at last I turned my face to kiss him.

My mind was not free of my vows. I was not deluded. Indeed, my senses had never been more focused. I touched his neck and arms. I touched his chest over and over. Each caress he returned, gently, patiently. Without really moving apart, we went to my cot and lay down on it. I listened to the noise this created, but it was negligible. I held him close, feeling his weight on top of me. Everything was darkness and motion, cinched sometimes by complete stillness.

Loebus entered me and held me tightly. We did not move for long intervals, only holding each other, sometimes kissing. Eventually he shivered and then it was finished. Afterward, he lay beside me.

"Where will you go?" I asked.

"I don't know. To the river. From there probably south."

I waited a moment before asking him the next question.

"When the Reverend Mother asked if the Lord had ever showed you special attention, what did you mean by your answer?"

"I can't explain it."

"But there are other things?"

"No, not really."

I wanted to ask more questions, but Loebus fell asleep and I couldn't bring myself to wake him. I stayed awake listening for the guards. When the night became less dark, I woke him and told him it was time to leave.

He dressed quickly. I stayed in bed and covered myself. He sat beside me when he finished. He touched my forehead, then my cheek. Finally he bent down and kissed me. Without another word, he left the room.

I remained in bed until the first sunlight pushed into the courtyard beyond my window. A bird called faintly. Another joined it, lacing closed the last hum of the insects. I listened for a time, trying to pick up a trace of Loebus's departure, though I suspected he was some distance away by now. When the sun became bright enough to see by, I went to the water bucket. I bathed, then poured the remaining water over my head. I stood in the dull rays of sunlight until I felt my hair beginning to dry.

I dressed, then went out onto the porch. I looked for the guard but saw no sign of him. No one was awake; it was barely dawn. A dog trotted past, oblivious of me. From one of the cells, I heard a sister cough.

I circled the mission house, the grass damp from dew as it reached up over my sandals. As I walked, I recited a Hail Mary. The words were mechanical, just as I expected them to be. When I finished, I found myself standing in front of the woodpile. The pile was divided into two equal parts. The first section, to my left, was composed of green wood, probably gathered by Muna's husband in order to smoke the buffalo. The second pile was made up of old brambles and rotted logs. I bent to the green wood and selected a long, thin pole. I carried it to the second pile and held it in front of me. The scent of the pole's bark was calming.

I turned logs over carefully, using the pole as a lever. I pried each log up until I could see under it. Beetles scurried away, and once a mouse shot off into the bush. I did nothing haphazardly. I knew there could be snakes, possibly cobras, and for them I kept the pole tightly in hand. Once the logs were loose, I maneuvered them into a rough stack. These, I had already decided, I would tell Belle Mère I arranged to bring to the kitchen for the morning meal.

On the fourth or fifth log, I found what I was looking for. It was a scorpion, perhaps four inches long, and perfectly black. As soon as it was uncovered, it raised its pincers and arched its tail—smoothly, like a finger straightening with infinite patience to point out a direction. It held its ground, its body armored, its vision dulled by the bright light.

I pinned it to the ground with the end of the pole, though its stinger repeatedly struck the green wood. Holding it in place, I bent and timed its rhythm. When it flexed upward, administering another sting to the pole, I grasped its tail just below the stinger.

I let the pole drop. The claws, now entirely free, groped wildly in front of it. Once its claws actually fastened to the flesh of my palm and I almost panicked and dropped it altogether. Nevertheless, I held its tail between my first two fingers. The tail was vile; the skin, if it can be called that, felt like the beads of a rosary.

I stepped back from the woodpile and knelt. I began the Act of Contrition, though I was dazed and had difficulty recalling the words. Slowly, with great concentration, I pressed my hands together around the scorpion. For an instant, there was nothing. I felt the scorpion scrambling between my palms, perhaps trying to right itself in order to deliver its venom. I prayed intensely, suspecting somehow in the next moment I would have a judgment from God.

The first sting stopped my prayer. The venom burned up my left arm, bringing such remarkable heat to that limb that I felt my eyes flicker. I nearly screamed. The venom moved in my blood, climbing my arm with each pulse. If it reaches my heart or brain, I thought, I will die. But gradually—it must have taken only seconds—I felt the poison settle in my armpit. It swelled in my lymph gland there, then began pushing into my chest cavity.

As I fell I threw the scorpion away, back toward the woodpile. The poison spread down my left side, searing the inside of my flesh. My head began to convulse—the pain so sharp I couldn't see the ground though I was only inches away from it. I pressed my forehead into the dirt, hoping somehow to muffle the pain that increased with each breath. It continued to climb, tentatively exploring each new limb until it found its way clear. The poison pushed me across the ground and I tore at the spot on my palm where I feared the stinger remained lodged.

It was only later, when I examined my hand closely, that I discovered I had been stung in the exact center of my palm. I took this as a sign of God's forgiveness.

"WHY WERE YOU collecting wood so early in the morning?"

"I couldn't sleep, Belle Mère."

"Armand usually gets the wood . . . I don't understand what you were doing there. When I first saw you, I thought you were dead, Sister Marie."

"I'm sorry. I only meant to help."

"How did the scorpion sting you?"

"I reached out to pull a log toward me, and apparently it was on the wood. I never saw the scorpion. I fell back and that's the last I remember."

"You're lucky to be alive."

"As God wishes."

"God doesn't wish our destinies, Sister Marie," Belle Mère said, straightening in her chair as if she needed to gain the correct posture for what she wanted to say. "God isn't a judge in a horse show, watching us jump hurdles. He doesn't wish our suffering. He wishes us to be healthy and of use in this life."

"Yes, Belle Mère."

"There is something else I want to speak to you about. When we removed your habit we found welts on your back. Do you have an explanation?"

"No, Belle Mère, unless my mattress is infested."

"I'm afraid I find that a little difficult to believe. They must be extremely aggressive insects. We will have Father Thaddeus over to do an investigation. Perhaps he could do an entire field study on your mattress alone. I think I would prefer to sleep on glass."

"I've grown accustomed to it."

Belle Mère snorted. She sat in the afternoon sunlight, her glasses picking up the light and dropping it anywhere she glanced. She looked tired. She pressed her hands together in her lap and bent forward.

"When I was your age," she now said with obvious reluctance, "I wore a girdle of thorns around my waist. You look surprised. You probably think I'm too old to have had feelings like yours ... passion for the Lord, or whatever it is you think you have discovered just for yourself."

"No, Belle Mère, I didn't think that."

"I wore the girdle only when I found it difficult to concentrate on my love of the Lord. I wrapped a bandage around my waist so the blood wouldn't soak through my habit. My Reverend Mother never suspected my secret—we love secrets, I know that—and the thorns had the desired effect of turning my attention to the Lord. Of course, I was conscious of the parallel with the crown of thorns given to Christ ... more than conscious really, since I wore mine in direct emulation. What eventually frightened me was that I began to look forward to the suffering. If we look forward to our pain, is it still suffering?"

"I'm not sure, Belle Mère."

"Yes you are. You know exactly what I'm talking about. You also have your opinion about it, and you may even find my peering—is that the word?—into your devotion to Christ offensive. No, don't say anything. I discovered, however, that my girdle of thorns was actually an act of pride. Pride is a sin. Pride, when it is masked by false acts of humility, is a harmful sin because it mocks Christ's true suffering. Do you see that, Sister Marie?"

"Yes, Belle Mère."

"Nothing can hide the heart from our Lord," she said, standing and preparing to go. "Pray with your heart, Sister. In the end, it is a much greater challenge."

Sister Catherine came in carrying a tray of food as soon as Belle Mère left.

"So you're feeling better?" she asked, coming close to kiss my cheek. "We were very worried. Did you know Father John came to give you Extreme Unction?"

"What day is this?" I asked.

"The third day since you were stung. Thursday."

"Have the guards left?"

"Yes, they left the morning you were stung. Of course, you couldn't know what's happened, could you? Here, eat this," she said, offering me a piece of mango.

While I ate, Sister Catherine told me what occurred in the three days I had been unconscious. Loebus, she said, stole a horse early in the morning on the day I was stung. He accomplished this with remarkable stealth, not even waking the men who slept nearby. The remaining horses made no sound—the guards were quite sure of this. He had apparently walked the horse off toward the south before mounting it. There were tracks of human feet—without shoes, fortunately for Belle Mère—and then there were only the tracks of the horse's hooves. Not once afterward did they find a human track. She heard this from Father Fraujas, who had returned to tell them all what had transpired. As inconceivable as it seemed, Loebus either never dismounted, or left the horse's back in some clever manner. Perhaps he swung onto a branch, and then descended to move on in a different direction while the horse continued to lead them off. All of this was theory. Loebus hadn't again been sighted.

Other tracks had joined the path formed by Loebus's horse. There had been at least five riders, possibly more. These riders took up Loebus's direction three miles before the river. Each one, after accompanying Loebus's horse for a mile, road off in a different direction. Only one continued to the river, and at that point the

Prefect couldn't be sure it was still Loebus. It was an ingenious trick, since it divided the Prefect's guard. Each man had to follow a track and each had the same experience: The tracks led him in a large circle, then rejoined the clustered tracks where the horses had first come together. How then had five horses shrunk to one? That was the puzzle they couldn't solve.

A mile from the river, when all of them were reunited and following the sole track, the Prefect and his men encountered a monkey dancing directly in their path. At least this was their thought when they saw it. When they moved closer they realized the monkey wasn't alive. It had been artfully arranged on five small saplings planted in the ground, which provided just enough tension to keep the animal upright. One pole had been driven through each paw; the fifth pole was skewered through the flesh on the animal's neck. The result was that the monkey moved in any breeze, its paws flapping madly, its legs running two feet from the ground.

At any movement from the monkey, the horses shied as if from a snake. Two men had to be left behind to hold the horses' reins, and even with the men beside them, the horses continued to throw their heads and try to break free.

One of the guards declared that the monkey was a gris-gris fetish. He had seen similar things before. The monkey had been left to warn them off the trail. It would bring bad luck to whoever passed it; it could bring death to the members of the party. The guard said that when he had patrolled with native soldiers, the Africans wouldn't proceed after striking such a sign.

By this time the men were tired—tired from their day of riding and tired of their search for Loebus. Loebus wasn't important, after all. Whatever he had done had occurred on another continent, at a different time. They began to grumble among themselves—not openly, of course, but an air of discontent had settled on them. They followed the Prefect's orders lethargically. One rode north to scout the river in that direction; another was sent south to check the shoreline there. A third was ordered to ford the river and to search for tracks on that side. All of them—and Father Fraujas was quite clear on this point—believed they had underestimated Loebus. He was clever beyond their measure. They didn't expect to catch him.

After riding all afternoon, the guards returned without anything to report. Loebus had vanished. Fraujas believed he had taken up with a tribe of Tuareg who were known for their accomplishments in the open bush. In any case, it didn't seem likely they could proceed with any real hope, so they decided to camp near the river and wait until morning.

At sunset a troop of baboons came to the river to drink. As the sun continued to set, the baboons took to the trees along the river. Some of them climbed into trees almost directly above the campsite. Among the leaves, they went about setting up their evening nests. They found wide branches and notches for the night. The apes settled with their faces peering down at the men. Their eyes caught light, and the men couldn't look up without being stared at in return.

In the last light, after dinner, the Prefect took out a rifle and walked under the trees. One of the guards saw what he planned and even gathered the courage to say something. But the Prefect was frustrated after letting Loebus get away, so he fired into the tree, striking a well-formed male squarely in the chest.

The baboon dropped to the earth, dead. The sound of the shot, and the heavy thud of the baboon, awakened the other apes. Suddenly the trees began to swing and shake. The baboons screeched and screamed and moved down the trunks. Even the mothers, some with babies clinging to their stomachs, dropped to the ground and circled the dead male.

None of the men moved. The Prefect, although visibly rattled, raised his gun again. He fired into the center of the group. Another baboon screamed, but didn't fall. He ran back, wounded, just as the others charged.

The charge was a bluff. The Prefect fired and wounded another male. The baboons scattered to the trees, but they did not become silent. They were more excited than ever, and they continued to swing in the trees, their sound almost intolerable. More than one guard claimed the baboons seemed to be communicating.

So there the men stood, the light gone now, the apes shrieking in the trees above them. The Prefect finally lowered his rifle and returned to the campfire. He laughed and made jokes about what he had done. When the other men mentioned that the apes' screams were unsettling, the Prefect fired another shot into the air in order to make the baboons screech even louder. This time the men were able only to see the glinting eyes and the fury of the trees as the animals bounded from branch to branch. Occasionally the men were pelted by small sticks and leaves.

The guard who had talked to the Prefect earlier suggested they relocate the camp. The Prefect said he would not allow them to move. He would kill every animal if necessary. He wouldn't hear of his men being chased off by a troop of baboons.

The atmosphere of the camp was tense and somewhat unearthly. The baboons continued their racket long past any reasonable limit. Sleep under such conditions was impossible. The Prefect himself slid down against a log, pretending to ignore the baboons, but even he couldn't carry out the charade. The men, despite their nervousness, took special pleasure whenever a twig or branch struck the Prefect. The irony of the bombardment, and the absurdity of seeing the Prefect casually brushing off the debris, was undermined by the possibility that it might provoke him to more rifle fire.

The sound of the apes gradually diminished. It wasn't, however, a healthy silence. Now only a few branches moved, as if the baboons were being deliberately stealthy. It didn't occur to any of the men that the apes were finally settling down for sleep. The men sensed they were being lulled into coming off their guard. The new silence made them even more edgy—without making them more prepared—than they had been previously. Bushes innocent a moment before suddenly appeared to conceal an ape. A natural movement in the trees, signaling a breeze, now became a baboon running along a limb.

Combined with this, Fraujas also reported a distinct impression of timelessness. Had the fire not continued to consume wood, they might have had no reckoning of any temporal movement. Their only thought—this they concurred about later—was that morning was distant. Long periods passed between one sound and another. How long ago had the log snapped in the fire? When had the last wind ruffled the leaves?

It was soon apparent that their supply of wood, which on any other night would have been more than adequate, couldn't hold the men through the night. Someone would have to go for wood, or they would be obliged to sit in darkness.

All of this, Sister Catherine told me, was pieced together after the fact. At the time the men didn't know what the others thought. Yet each of them later testified to the same feelings: a sense of how ludicrous he had become lingering by the fire, matched by an overwhelming desire to stay exactly where he was. Each one was also aware that the Prefect observed them closely. At his whim he could send them out for wood or let the fire die.

A conversation followed. Though she couldn't report exactly what was said, Sister Catherine maintained that the Prefect, when he spoke, sounded slightly drunk. The men were at a loss. He couldn't have been drunk. None of them had consumed any alcohol. But the Prefect's voice was heavy and slow, and carried with it a belligerent tone suggesting someone not in control of his faculties.

The Prefect said, "You are actually afraid, aren't you?"

No one spoke.

"You are all cowards. What about you, Fraujas? Is this black magic stronger than your own? Will you sit there and allow the fire to go out?"

"Perhaps we should all go for wood," Fraujas answered.

"I'll get the wood," the Prefect said, climbing to his feet.

Suddenly the trees above them grew even more silent. The Prefect seemed to notice this as well, because he grabbed his rifle and carried it with him into the darkness. One of the guards rose to his feet, as if to follow, but then sat down again. All of them turned to watch the point where the Prefect had disappeared. They heard nothing. At any moment they expected a rifle report, or at least the noise of the Prefect gathering wood, but nothing came.

Father Fraujas called out. His voice was tentative at first. He didn't want to antagonize the Prefect, but he also felt that something should be done. Indeed, he had begun to wonder if the Prefect hadn't somehow become unhinged. But there was no light and there was no real direction to follow, since the Prefect had made no sound from the moment of his departure. None of the men relished the idea of going out into the darkness, with the baboons prepared to drop on them from any branch. If the Prefect had answered, or even called for help, it would have been a different matter. The silence continued, however, and Fraujas admitted he had to summon his courage to break it.

After a considerable period had passed, one of the guards attempted to rally the men. He stood and told them they must make a search. It was inhuman to allow the Prefect to stumble about on his own. Clearly something had happened. The Prefect might have returned with ten armloads of wood by this time.

It was the lack of wood, Fraujas contended later, that forced them from the fire. Though they each began speaking about the need to find the Prefect, he was quite certain none of them would have moved if the wood had been abundant. But what choice did they have? The wood was going, and really, they couldn't abandon the Prefect.

They called repeatedly as they moved into the darkness. All of them carried rifles. They didn't spread out or make any pretense of combing the river's edge. Their eyes passed up and down the bole of each tree. They stopped at any overhanging branch and inspected it carefully before proceeding.

The first substantial thing any of them actually saw was that the wounded ape had been dragged away. They were certain about this detail. They found flecks of blood on the dirt. Near it, leading to several wide trees, were marks made by an animal being dragged.

Could that be? They tried to check their bearings, but it was dark. Who could say that the animal had been shot exactly here? Or there? But then, of course, there could be no other explanation for the blood. Fraujas asked if any of them had ever seen such a thing before. The men didn't answer, but the uneasiness, if possible, grew even more pronounced.

They moved farther into the cover of the trees, now and then looking back to keep sight of the fire, which had subsided to mere coals. Maybe twenty or thirty meters stood between the last suggestion of light and pure darkness.

Twenty paces further into the shadows, they found the Prefect. He stood completely still, looking into the darkness. They began to move toward him, when they were stopped by a remarkable sight. Circled about the Prefect, just on the edge of vision, was the entire troop of baboons. They made no sound. Each one, however, held a branch of wood. The pieces of wood were proportionate to the size of the animal: a large male with a moderately large branch; an adolescent with a twig. The ground beneath the trees had been scrupulously cleaned.

"If you move toward them, they run back," the Prefect said.

"Are they waiting for the fire to go out?" Fraujas asked.

"I don't know."

The Prefect took a step to demonstrate. The animals disappeared without a noise. It was possible to sense them just out of eyesight, but they were uncanny in their ability to judge the situation. Whenever the Prefect raised his rifle—which he proceeded to do, more out of wonder than anger—the baboons again faded into the darkness.

It was at this point that one of the guards realized the baboons had flanked them and were now raiding the campsite. The animals crept in and walked off with anything close at hand. A guard shouted. The baboons in the camp disappeared at once.

A mutiny occurred at this juncture. The guards, without consulting the Prefect, loaded the horses and tied up their bundles. It was exceedingly dark and the work was clumsy. The baboons lingered just at the edge of the campsite, inspecting every move. The horses were again unnerved, bucking and kicking, eager to flee if given the opportunity.

Slowly the guards assembled the scattered goods. Now and then there was a moment of surprise when they determined that something was missing. The baboons had been indiscriminate in their theft: a shoe, a tin cup, a coil of rope, a dusty handkerchief. Other things, doubtless, would prove missing the next day. For the time being, the men concentrated on loading the horses.

When all was prepared, they led the horses directly away from the river. Fewer trees grew in the open plain, and the men hoped this would prevent the baboons from following. The tactic worked. They rode off for several kilometers and waited in the open countryside for daylight. With the first sunlight, they returned to find the baboon troop had moved on. Everything that had been stolen remained suspended in the trees bordering the river. The dead males were also there, propped in the nests the troop had made the evening before.

"Was it gris-gris?" I asked Sister Catherine when she finished.

"The Prefect agreed to give up the search for Loebus," she said.

"But how do they account for it?"

"I don't know. No one knows. Father Fraujas rode with them until the sun was completely up, then returned here. During the ride the men compared their different accounts. The Prefect tried to pretend that nothing out of the ordinary had occurred."

I wanted to ask other questions, but Sister Catherine wouldn't hear of it. I had been awake too long; she should have waited until I was stronger. She filled my water pitcher and left a few pieces of fruit to eat should I wake and find myself hungry.

When she left I pushed myself from my bed and knelt on the floor. I was unsteady, but my need to pray was almost instinctual. I said a rosary, then spent the rest of my strength searching the room for any sign of Loebus's visit. In the darkness I looked for some trace of him. But the skins from the fruit he had eaten were gone. The ashes he had inadvertently carried to my door had long ago been swept away.

WHILE I RECOVERED, the season began to change, and I thought frequently of Loebus. I listened attentively for news that he was still in the vicinity. When the reports didn't come after two or three weeks, I felt a mixture of relief and anguish: relief that I wouldn't be tested once more; anguish that I wouldn't see him again.

I imagined him making his way to one of the port cities in the south. Abidjan, perhaps. Accra was more likely, however, since it was still under British rule. From there he would board a ship and continue on his way to South America.

Perhaps my powers of observation were sharper due to my leisure, or the sense that I was returning to life, but it was during this period that I also realized Belle Mère was ill. Her clothes didn't fit her; where before she had been robust, her breast full against the yoke of her habit, now I noticed a distinct sag. She used her rosary to cinch her waist, leaving the material on either side of it puckered.

She was easily fatigued. In a matter of weeks she lost the vitality I had always associated with her. The movements of her hands grew deliberate; her steps became hesitant. Nevertheless, she conceded nothing to her illness, and no one spoke of her decline. A nun's possible approach to the Lord is a private matter. This was especially true of Belle Mère.

Eventually a crisis came. I recall the night because it coincided with the arrival of the harmattan, the long, steady wind that blows down from the Sahara throughout the rainy season. At dusk the Africans set their fields on fire. This was an annual rite, one they performed when they could be certain of the wind's direction. It was done to clear the stubble from the fields and to create a bed of ash that served as fertilizer.

Together with the other sisters, I went into the fields after vespers on the night appointed by the village elders. Belle Mère walked with us. The fields had been hacked at during harvest, and small clods of dirt lay everywhere. Our habits often snagged on the rough stubble, and this proved especially troublesome to Belle Mère. More than once I saw her pulled nearly off her feet by the sudden catch of her skirt.

We met the party as it moved out from the village. A line of young men carrying drums and rattles walked at the front of the group. The drums were held beneath the men's arms to that they could be squeezed, thus changing the pitch of the drums as they reverberated. A second group of men wore costumes made of feathers, with tall African masks hiding their features. The feathers were gaudy, almost luminescent.

Coming behind them was a third group consisting of women and children. The women trilled, their voices undulating with the rhythm of their walking. The children were dogged by still another group of men—mostly adolescent boys—who dodged in and out of the crowd, screaming and moaning like lost souls. The young men were painted white, the African mourning color, and they appeared to represent the dying season. Perhaps they represented the village ancestors—I can't say with any certainty. But the children feared them in the way children can fear a known threat, so that each rush by the painted young men sent the children screaming back to their mothers in a combination of terror and joy.

It was a wonderful spectacle. The color, the sound, the deepening night—it was powerful. They approached from a small valley at the back of the village, moving slowly up a gentle incline. When they saw us, their noise increased. The costumed men danced forward. The harvest was finished. The cold season, which meant death to many of the weak and old, lay before them.

"How long do you think they've done this?" Belle Mère asked of no one in particular.

"How long?" Sister Bernard repeated.

"When I see them like this, I wonder what we're doing here," Belle Mère said.

Before anyone could respond, the group swarmed over us. We walked among them to the top of the rise. The *chef de village*, Ki-Zerbo, stepped forward with a flaming torch. The top of the hill was bordered by stacks of old millet stalks, well dried by a day or two in full sunlight. The chief held the torch high for what seemed a long time. The feathered devils danced forward and made strange passes at the light. The drummers beat out rhythms with even greater force. The white-painted boys ran into the open fields, then returned with great speed, pretending, it seemed, to flee whatever evil lingered in the darkness beyond.

At last the chief stepped forward and pressed the torch against the dried stalks. The flame needed no prodding. At once it roared up, sending sparks high into the sky. Almost in answer the wind pushed the flame farther into the fields. The entire circle of stacked millet caught. In an instant we were ringed by fire.

I was so absorbed in this spectacle that at first I didn't notice Sister Bernard moving past me in a great hurry. I saw her veil trailing behind her, but I didn't think what it could mean. Turning, I saw Belle Mère lying prone on the ground.

When I arrived at Sister Bernard's side, she already had her arm under Belle Mère's head. Belle Mère was faintly conscious, though she didn't seem to know where she was. Her breathing was shallow. Her hand at her side groped weakly for the crucifix attached to her rosary.

"You should not have come . . . it's too warm," Sister Bernard said. "Hold on, we'll have you down the hill in no time."

I began to cry; I couldn't control myself. Then Sister Catherine approached with a group of men. I stayed by Belle Mère's side, afraid to move. I reached forward and pressed the crucifix into her palm. For a moment her hand worked over it, as if testing to see if this was indeed her crucifix.

"Sister Marie," Sister Bernard said to me, her voice only a little more controlled than I felt myself to be. "You can't do anything here. Run down to the mission and prepare her bed—make sure everything is in order. Hurry. Get water . . . hurry."

"I want to stay."

"No, go at once. Hurry. You'll help that way."

The Africans had become quiet. When I looked around, I was dazed by the light of the fires. I didn't know which direction to take. I moved toward the brightest part of the fire and at last saw the dim shape of the mission house below me. I cut off at an angle, escaping the flames, and bellied underneath the crest of the hill.

What I did when I reached the mission house, I can hardly recall. I remember calling to Armand that Belle Mère was ill. He appeared in a tattered pair of shorts; he had been asleep.

"Nassarra Paga?" he asked, calling her by the name the Africans used when addressing her.

"Yes, help me now. Bring water. We must change the bed."

We had barely finished when the men carrying Belle Mère arrived. After placing her on the bed, two of the men dropped to their knees. They refused to move until Belle Mère touched each man on the shoulder. Armand came forward as well and knelt at her feet. He leaned across the bed and pressed his face in the hem of her habit.

"Armand, she needs to rest now," Sister Bernard said, but he wouldn't move. He cried into her gown until Belle Mère spoke to him.

"Go now, Armand," she said, her voice scarcely audible.

Armand left, taking the other men with him. Sister Bernard came forward and undressed Belle Mère. Then Belle Mère coughed and Sister Bernard held a cloth to her mouth. When she removed it the cloth was pocked with blood. I was stunned by this, but equally shocked that Sister Bernard showed no surprise at the blood. Obviously, they had been through this before.

"How long have you known?" I whispered.

"Shhh, not now," Sister Bernard said. "I'll sit with her. Keep the grounds quiet if you can. Sister Catherine, please send for Father John."

Sister Catherine took my arm gently in hers and led me from the room. We closed the door just as Armand came down the hallway with a straw mat under his arm. He rolled the mat out on the floor, then lay down on it without ceremony. His head rested near the door.

FATHER JOHN ARRIVED late that night.

"Is she resting?" he asked when we greeted him by the mission house.

"Yes, Father," Sister Bernard said, "but she's very weak."

"Do you have any idea what it might be?"

"Not really, Father. She's coughing blood and running a fever. She moves in and out of consciousness."

"Can she be transported?" he asked, evidently calculating the chances of getting her to the capital, Ouagadougou. From there she might be taken by rail to Abijan.

"I don't think so," Sister Bernard answered. "If she recovers some of her strength, perhaps. It's difficult to say right now."

"She showed no sign of this before?"

"She has been weak for some time. You know how she is, though, Father. She would rather be here, regardless of her health."

Father John tilted his head, appeared to absorb this last information, then sent Armand out to the donkey for his wicker saddlebag. When Armand returned, Father John took out a small chalice, a vial of wine, and his surplice. This was remarkably ornate, doubtless a gift at his ordination. It was badly stained, however, the lace embroidery tinted bone-yellow. It looked like a fine table-cloth left forgotten for a season on a summer porch.

Father John intended to perform the Viataticum, which meant Belle Mère was near death. He sent Sister Catherine to the kitchen for bread, which he broke into small morsels and placed on a golden plate. Then he nodded and asked us to lead him to her cell.

The door was open. A breeze passed through the room, car-rying the scent of the burning fields. Father John advanced to the *prie dieu,* genuflected, then stepped to the bed. In that instant he wasn't a priest, but rather an old friend. His body sagged; one of the morsels of bread threatened to slide from the plate. He stood for a moment and looked down at Belle Mère. They were the same age, give or take a year.

"Reverend Mother," he said finally, in a voice he reserved for the mass, "your work is over. It is time for you to rest."

She didn't hear him. I am quite sure of that. Her face was white; her hair was white; the flesh on the bridge of her nose, where her glasses had always held their position, was bright red. The delicate white of her scalp shone through her hair. The features of her face were pulled tight over the underlying bone structure. A skeleton fought to shake free beneath her skin.

He asked us to leave. He would hear her confession. I hadn't thought of this, but of course it was the proper procedure. He would hear her confession, absolve her of her sins even if she couldn't speak, then grant her Extreme Unction.

We stood outside for a short time until Father John called us back. He performed a beautiful, simple Mass. We knelt to receive the Host. Father John turned to Belle Mère and placed a sliver of crust between her lips. Her lips made no move to reject or claim it. Seeing this, Father John reached forward and crushed the bread, then rubbed the paste across the inside of her lips.

"The Body of Christ," he said in Latin.

"Amen," we answered.

"Let her rest now," Father John concluded after giving us each a Eucharist.

Before we left the room we saw Belle Mère swallow. Whether this was an act of will, or a mere reflex, I cannot say. Sister Bernard told us to go and rest. She didn't feel at all sleepy.

Outside in the common room, Armand brought tea to Sister Catherine and me. We sat at the large table. It was growing lighter. The smoke from the burning fields had now turned dense and cold. Birds began calling; a rooster crowed. Father John joined us a little later.

"I'm not much of an expert on these things," he said, "but it looks to me like tuberculosis. Maybe a small stroke as well. I would have said so at once, but I thought tuberculosis was a long, disabling disease."

"Perhaps the heat and dryness kept it under control," Sister Catherine said.

"Even if we succeeded in getting her to Abijan, there would be a long ocean voyage," Father John said. "This might be the best climate she could have. Perhaps she's only gone this long because of the dry air. She would have to go to the mountains if she returned to France."

"Sister Bernard might know more. She has been with the Mother Superior since their school days," said Sister Catherine.

"I'll talk to her. I should tell you both that I'm placing Sister Bernard in charge. She's the senior member of your order. Let's all hope that it is a temporary arrangement, but it's important the Reverend Mother's work go on. Sister Catherine, I hope you understand the appointment."

"Certainly, Father. I had always expected it."

Father John covered a yawn, then stood.

"I'll show you to your room, Father," I said.

He carried his wicker saddlebag as we walked across the courtyard. I led him to the chamber the Prefect had used. When I pulled open the door I was surprised that it was now light enough outside to see the interior of the room. I went to the far wall and opened the shutters. When I turned around, Father John was seated on the edge of the small cot.

"Are you in need of confession, Sister Marie?" he asked. He appeared tired, not from this night alone, but from years of asking such questions.

"Yes, Father, how did you know?"

"We are always in need of confession," he sighed. "The scorpion sting was suspicious, I'm afraid. Belle Mère spoke to me. She found several pieces of fruit in your cell and a number of footprints. Don't be embarrassed—she told no one but me. Besides, you have already confessed, Sister Marie. When I gave you the sacrament of Extreme Unction, I also absolved you of your sins. Will you sin in this way again?"

"No, Father."

"Then God has possession of your sin. Don't wrestle it away from Him."

"Thank you, Father."

"Now let me sleep. Go and sin no more. That is what we always say and what we can never do. If I can understand that, certainly God can too."

I remember this period as inseparable from smoke. The burning fields continued to smolder, and when the wind shifted, our mission was left with the stale scent of burning grass and millet. A few trees caught fire and their trunks pulsed with bright orange scales that reverted to gray when the wind forgot them. Father John told us that dragons lived inside the trees, and it wasn't difficult to believe him.

Belle Mère's condition did not improve. She continued to cough and bring up blood. Sister Bernard admitted to Father John that Belle Mère had contracted tuberculosis years before. There had been an incident in France; a trip to a sanatorium; consultations with doctors. Her condition had been a constant fact of her life. She had hidden her illness from the Church authorities, prayed for recovery, and to a remarkable degree had been free of the symptoms during her time in Africa. It had only been recently, at the beginning of the rains, that the disease had returned.

During Belle Mère's second week of illness, the Provision Master from Ouagadougou arrived. The Provision Master, our regional bookkeeper, was a young priest named Father Bartholomew. He was a short man, no taller than I, who was soft and somewhat effeminate. He reminded me of the dairy; I associated him with cream and butter and milk warm from an udder. Seeing him in the harsh sunlight of the bush, one thought of him not burning, but going sour.

Father Bartholomew rode in advance of a fair-sized caravan of perhaps twenty African men, each leading a packhorse loaded with goods. Naturally the caravan was attended by Africans from miles around who had heard, through one means or another, that Father Bartholomew was in the district. It was understood that he brought payment for the blankets the women sent to our sisters in France. It was also understood that wherever he arrived soon became the site of a vigorous market, accompanied by a great deal of drinking and gambling.

"Sisters," he said when we met, "I've brought everything you requested."

"Hello, Father Bartholomew," Sister Catherine said. "You know Sister Marie, don't you?"

"Yes, we met in Ouagadougou when she first arrived. This life seems to agree with you, Sister."

He shook our hands. I couldn't erase the sensation that he didn't grip my hand, but weighed it.

"Now, what is this I've heard?" he asked, turning to walk with us to the porch. "The Reverend Mother is ill?"

"Yes, Father," said Sister Catherine. "It appears to be tuberculosis."

"How sad. How very sad."

Father John was waiting on the porch for us. He shook Father Bartholomew's hand and slapped him softly on the back. Armand appeared a moment later with a tray of cool tea.

"I saw Fraujas as we cut up from the Black Volta," Father Bartholomew said after we had passed through the pleasantries. "He was shooting up the countryside."

"He loves to hunt," Father John said.

"He told me the Prefect was out this way. A curious story, isn't it?"

"Very curious."

"I suppose you know there are rumors about this Austrian fellow? The Africans say he is over by Arly, camped right next to the game preserve. A local *chef de village* has taken a shine to him. They're building him a house. He's gained a reputation as a magic man, or some such nonsense. They say he can disappear if he likes and there is no point in looking for him. Until I spoke with Fraujas, I wasn't sure the man really existed."

I was stunned by this report. Loebus was alive; he was near.

It turned out Father Bartholomew had little of substance to relate. Loebus was a rumor. The Africans had once again spoken of him as a man who lived "close to the earth," which was a euphemism, I knew, for a man of spiritual power. Father Bartholomew mentioned, however, that a portion of Loebus's power apparently stemmed from his ability in taxidermy. He created lifelike models of any animal the Africans brought him. No, Father Bartholomew hadn't seen any of these models, in response to Sister Catherine. No, he didn't know any of the methods Loebus employed, but he suggested that the stuffed animals were coveted for their magical powers.

"So, he has a way to make a living," Father Bartholomew concluded. "He must be clever, at the very least. I would like to meet him."

"What sort of magical powers do these models bring?" Sister Catherine asked.

"Oh, I don't know, really," Father Bartholomew said, evidently finding Loebus's ability to make a living in the bush the most remarkable thing about him. "It's a primitive conceit that by consuming a creature one gains a portion of its nature. You know how it is. Women aren't allowed to eat the flesh of a carnivore, for example, because it will make them intractable. Men don't eat the flesh of an animal they are about to hunt, because that will make the hunters too sympathetic to the animal's plight. Lion meat before a battle—that sort of thing."

At this point the conversation turned to the supplies Father Bartholomew brought with him; payment for the blankets; the well-drilling team that was supposed to arrive at the end of the next month.

"Tomorrow, if I can get everything finished here, we can ride to your mission. Would that be satisfactory?" Father Bartholomew asked Father John.

"Happy to have you," Father John replied.

"Now, if you think it a good time, I'd like to look in on the Reverend Mother. Is Sister Bernard with her?"

"Yes," Sister Catherine said. "She'll be glad to see you."

"As far as the books go—should I sit down with Sister Bernard?" Father Bartholomew asked Father John, rising. "It won't take long, but I'm sure the villagers will be impatient."

"Why don't you sit down with Sister Marie as well," Father John suggested. "She has a head for figures, and perhaps she would like to assume the responsibility. Would you mind, Sister Marie?"

"Of course not, Father."

I glanced at Sister Catherine. If she felt any injustice at being excluded, she showed no sign of it. It was common knowledge that she was easily confused by business matters, not because she lacked the intelligence to understand them, but because she found them uninteresting. Nevertheless, I felt a slight glow of ambition. It was a terrible thing to admit in such circumstances, yet I could not fight down my pride in being selected. Belle Mère might not regain her health. Sister Bernard would remain with Belle Mère, even if it meant being sent home to France. In that event, Sister Catherine would be elevated to the position of Reverend Mother, but I knew, as Father John certainly understood as well, that it would be a titular position only. The daily business of running the mission would fall to me. I was suited for it, more so than Sister Catherine, whose true gift rested with the children and animals surrounding the mission. She was the better nun; I, potentially, the better administrator.

I didn't like this understanding of myself, nor did I arrive at it all at once. When Father Bartholomew returned for his session with the ledger, I sat beside Sister Bernard and listened intently. The figures, the careful balancing of shipments and payments, appealed to me more strongly than I could have anticipated. I had a talent for such work—I saw that at once. And when Sister Bernard, confused about several entries, threw up her hands and told Father Bartholomew she would like to turn over the bookkeeping to me, I didn't grasp at the offer, nor did I contradict her. I found in my nature a cool center that was untouched by emotion. Ambition, yes, but also the feeling of being finally matched to a task.

THAT NIGHT AS I SAT with Belle Mère, Armand appeared at the door.

"Sister Marie," he whispered, "can I speak with you?"

He stepped into the room without creating any sound. He wore no sandals. His forearms were still wet from the evening dishes.

He seemed reluctant to begin. He looked at Belle Mère, as if afraid she would wake and hear him. Finally he came beside my chair and squatted, his comfort immediate as only an African's can be in such a position. Oddly, he circled his hands in a funnel around his mouth, as if his words must be guided to me.

"I've come to you because the others wouldn't understand," he began.

"Understand what?"

"There is someone here to see you."

"Who is it?"

He wouldn't say within Belle Mère's hearing. He lifted one hand from his mouth and pointed to the hallway.

I stood. He went to the door and stepped into the hallway, then stopped. The hallway was entirely dark. I squeezed between him and the door frame and immediately sensed that a person, deliberately keeping to the blackest portions of the hallway, lingered at the farthest end of the passage. Armand whispered that I should go ahead.

I took a few steps forward. My eyes adjusted slowly. It was, I saw, an African, though I could tell little else. The figure's movement was slow and uncertain. A foot scraped on the rough tile, then another dragged and echoed the sound.

"Who is it?" I asked, trying to give my voice authority.

"Nassarra?"

It was a woman's voice.

I stepped closer, halving the distance between us. It was an old woman. Her movement was restricted because she wasn't sure of her surroundings. She kept one hand against the wall as if to steady herself. She pressed her other hand to her chest in the African style of greeting. With effort she executed a small curtsy, though her limbs were not supple enough to give this action much definition. That done, she waited, moving neither forward nor back.

Armand brushed past me then. He took her arm and led her the few remaining steps between us. He said something to her, apparently repeating some instruction he had rehearsed with her beforehand, but this seemed lost on the woman. She attempted another curtsy, this one no more successful, then stood wavering in front of me.

Her body was emaciated. Her breasts were flat weights against her chest. She smelled of grease and perspiration. Her eyes glowed with cataracts, glassy tissues that turned the white part of the eyes an ivory color. I couldn't tell if she saw me or responded only to my voice.

"This woman was cured by Nassarra Loebus," Armand told me, then muttered something to the woman. She nodded and brushed her free hand over her eyes. She repeated the gesture twice.

"Where was this?" I asked.

"Near Arly," Armand told me, looking again at the woman for confirmation.

"How did he cure her?"

"He is *nyanga,* a witch man . . . he touched his hand to her eyes. She was blind. Now she can see," Armand said. "She lives in Lati. She traveled to see him. Everyone knows he can cure the sick. He is *nyanga.* She was cured."

"Why did you bring her to me, Armand? What do you want?"

"She has a message from Nassarra Loebus. He heard of the Reverend Mother's illness. He sent her to tell you he is coming here," he said.

"Armand . . ." I began, then realized I didn't know what I wanted to say. "Take her away now. Thank her for coming. Tell her I'll find her if I need to speak with her again. Ask her to tell you everything she knows about Nassarra Loebus."

He spoke to the woman. She nodded again, but this time dug in a small fold of her pagna. I didn't see at first what she held, but she extended it to me and I took it.

It was a small rodent, no more than four or five centimeters long, perfectly preserved on a wooden stand. It looked like a weasel, its back arched, its teeth bared. One paw was raised to fend off an attacker. It possessed no eyes, though this only seemed to give it a more crude and powerful energy.

The woman backed down the hallway. Armand accompanied her to the kitchen. I heard his voice once more, the door close softly, and finally the rapid sound of his steps returning.

"What did she say?" I asked.

"The animal was sent by Nassarra Loebus. He told the woman to give it to you," Armand said.

"Armand, Loebus is only a man. We can't bring him here to cure Belle Mère."

"He is more than a man," Armand answered.

"I want you to take this animal and return it to the woman. Tell her I appreciate her offer, but we have our own magic."

"She won't accept it from me. She didn't give it to me. Besides, Nassarra Loebus sent it."

"Will its magic be destroyed if you give it back?"

"She won't accept it from me."

"All right, I'll return it to her tomorrow. Keep it for me in a safe place. If the other sisters hear of this, they might not be so lenient."

"Let me put it under Nassarra Paga's bed, Sister."

"She believes in Christ as her Savior."

"Maybe Christ needs help."

"That's blasphemous, Armand. Don't be disrespectful."

But he didn't move away, and I didn't give him the animal. What harm would it cause to put the animal beneath her bed? Besides, I was fairly certain Armand would contrive to get it in Belle Mère's room somehow.

I took it to Belle Mère's room and slid it under the bed. Armand remained in the doorway as I put the fetish in place. When I stood, he clicked his tongue against his teeth.

"Now tell me what you know about Loebus," I said, leading him back to the hallway. "Don't leave anything out."

"I told you—he is *nyanga*."

"He is a magic man?"

"Yes, Nassarra."

"What are his powers?"

Armand shrugged as if to indicate that Loebus's powers could not be so easily defined.

"Has he cured the sick?" I asked, trying to keep my voice calm.

"Yes, Nassarra. People follow him everywhere."

"Was the woman you just brought here really blind?"

"Before she went to Loebus, yes, Nassarra."

"Her eyes are still covered."

"But every day she sees better. I've known her all my life."

"When will he be here?"

"I don't know, Nassarra. You cannot predict how a *nyanga* will move."

"Does he use African magic or nassarra magic?"

"I have only heard stories . . ."

"What kind of stories?"

"He can live underwater."

"How does he live there?"

"He takes the breath from animals."

I stopped. What could it mean? I had heard other stories of *nyanga,* mostly fantastic and easily dismissed, but never one to rival this. I had no grounds to refute it, nor was I able to imagine how such a story began. I couldn't even think of a question that would help me move in the proper direction. I took another tack instead.

"Why does he make these animals?" I asked.

"They bring power."

"For him? Or for the person who asks for one?"

"For the person he gives it to. He takes dead animals and makes them live."

"Not really live."

"At night they do. He uses them to hear plots against him. If there is a spell on someone, he can send an animal to hear why it has been placed on the person," said Armand.

"Is that his claim?"

"He does not claim anything. That is why he is powerful."

I was getting nowhere with him. Armand's answers seemed wild, yet it occurred to me that what we are prepared to believe we will find a way to believe. The mission's stories of Christ's miracles must have sounded no less fantastic to him.

I asked him to tell no one else what he had told me. I also

asked that he tell me at once if he heard of Loebus's approach to the village. He agreed to both requests. After that I thanked him and let him go. He disappeared down the hallway without a noise.

FATHER JOHN and Father Bartholomew left the next day. Father John gave instructions to send for him if Belle Mère's condition worsened. Father Bartholomew took our last-minute requests before mounting his horse, promising he would bring what he could when he returned near the end of the year, some six months distant. They rode off with a large wedge of African followers trailing behind the packhorses.

Two weeks passed with no sign of Loebus. During that time my importance to the mission increased dramatically. Financial questions were referred to me: Were there funds for a new donkey cart? How much should we pay for wood? What was a reasonable price for yarn delivered from Koudougou? I found Belle Mère had let our supply arrangements stand too long without review. In many instances she hadn't bargained for prime prices. Tactfully, I called in the local merchants who provided us with goods and asked them to do better. It became evident to me that we frequently received "nassarra" prices which were well above the established rates. I was able to reduce our overhead while still maintaining the even flow of goods and services. My command of the local language improved. I kept track of the payroll, the feed expenses, even the expenditure for wax candles in the chapel. I was given a set of keys and a tin box that served as our vault.

The same period also brought swarms of blister beetles released by the late rains and cooler nights. The beetles were long and green, with an iridescence one normally associates with common flies. The beetles were notorious in that part of Africa. They flew

to light and often landed on our arms or faces, where, sensing only
an insect, we brushed quickly and thereby crushed the beetle. The
beetle in turn released acid, drawing a burning red welt from the
exposed skin. The welt did not always disappear; occasionally it remained as a scar. As a result, we were obliged to inspect each insect
that landed on our skin before we pushed it away. Mosquitoes
took advantage of this delay, enhancing the possibility of malaria.

Loebus appeared at the end of the third week as the tide of
beetles receded. He came at night. It was eleven o'clock, perhaps
later. I had been visiting with a patient and was on my way to my
cell when Loebus stepped onto the edge of the courtyard. He didn't
take a position in my path, nor did he approach. He remained to
one side, his figure obscured by a fan of shadows thrown by two
kapok trees.

He said nothing to identify himself. As I took several steps
toward him my mind played with the possibility that it wasn't
Loebus at all, but simply a man from the nearby village. But as I
moved closer I saw the reason for my confusion.

Loebus was dressed in native clothing. His shirt was made of
coarsely spun wool; his shorts were of the roughest khaki. His right
bicep was circled by an arm bracelet of feathers and cowrie shells,
a fetish I had seen other men wear. He wore no shoes. His posture,
even his manner of standing, was entirely African. His face had been
darkened by sunlight; his muscles had taken on a new firmness.
He was graceful—patient in the African manner that Europeans
can rarely duplicate—as he waited for the rim of my lantern light
to reveal his features. He had rid himself of his essence as a European.

His eyes had been burned clear. His illness was gone, and in
its place was a remarkable vitality. His eyes gathered in too much;
they were wary, not unlike an animal's. He was attuned to the air
around us, the sounds of the night, even the hiss of the lantern. I
felt that by raising my voice I might send him back into the bush.

When the light from my lantern finally touched his legs, he
stepped back into the shadows. He did this, I realized, not from
fear, but from a new inclination to darkness.

"I'm glad you escaped," I said.

"Are you glad I returned?"

"Yes, I wanted you to return."

I lowered the lantern so that it would not throw light toward him. The courtyard was empty. It was late, too late for anyone to be awake. I knew he had waited for such an hour, perhaps watching from the bush until he could approach.

"I've come to see the Reverend Mother," he said.

"To cure her?"

"To look at her."

"But you've cured people in the bush? Is that what you are saying?"

He ignored the question, then said, "Armand is waiting."

"For you?"

"He'll let me in the kitchen. No one needs to know I visited."

I listened to the sounds around me, almost hoping for Sister Catherine or Bernard to appear. But that was unlikely. Sister Catherine was in bed; Sister Bernard, when I saw her last, had been reading in her cell.

I led him around the mission house toward the back door. I opened it expecting to see Armand, but he wasn't there. Loebus entered behind me and closed the door. The kitchen seemed too small for him; his bare feet made no sound whatsoever. He had learned to move silently.

"You're sure no one else knows you're here?" I whispered, turning to look at him.

He shook his head without appearing to give the question any thought. He looked slowly around the room, as if finding himself enclosed in solid walls was a sensation he had forgotten. Watching him, I was reminded of fantastic stories about young children being raised by wolves. Ridiculous, perhaps, but he possessed something wild and essential—something he didn't even suspect about himself until he was confronted with the room.

Armand came into the kitchen, a lantern in his right hand. He paused for a moment to look at me. When I said nothing, he bowed stiffly from the waist, and Loebus, to my surprise, accepted the deference as his right.

"Does she know I'm here?" Loebus asked him.

"No, Nassarra, she is unconscious."

"Is she still coughing blood?"

"Yes, Nassarra, but not as much as before."

Loebus followed Armand through the kitchen and entered the dark hallway leading to Belle Mère's room. I went after them. I walked on the toes of my sandals in order to be quiet, but still created more noise than either of them.

At the doorway to Belle Mère's room Armand stepped back and allowed us to pass. He then entered and placed his lantern on the floor. The light, thrown at an angle from below, enlarged our shadows on the ceiling and walls to immense proportions. We couldn't move without giants of darkness performing our actions in a slow dance.

I waited for Loebus to move to the bed, but he remained stationary, his eyes directed just to the left of Belle Mère's head. He listened, his head cocked slightly. Armand squatted next to the door, an amulet of shells and small leather pouches held loosely in his hands. The pouches doubtless contained magical powders, purchased from a shaman. I felt a moment's frustration that Armand, our most solid convert, had reverted to paganism so easily.

When I turned back to Leobus, he stood next to the bed. He had accomplished this without disturbing the shadows above him or scraping the floor. No change in light caught my eye.

At the same time the air changed. The breeze from the window suddenly ceased. A moth hit against the chimney of my lantern and flew off to the roof. My own breathing grew labored and for an instant I felt faint. Armand began a chant—a murmur really—that was, to my ears, like the sound of blood moving through a vein.

Loebus experienced his first spasm at this moment. His left hand, the hand closest to me, folded back against his wrist. It arched painfully backward. I expected a tendon to pop, a bone to break, but the hand continued to bend until it lay nearly flat against his wrist. I looked at his face for a sign of pain, but Loebus's head was now bent more severely to one side, as if the sound he had listened for was pulling him almost off his feet.

Then a muscle in his left thigh began to tremble and cramp— heavy, thick convulsions of a muscle tricked to rolling underneath the skin.

Loebus leaned across the bed. He had difficulty forcing his limbs to move. Twice he nearly lost his balance and fell on top of Belle Mère. His deformed hand was of no use to him. It remained clutched at his side, withered, while he pulled himself onto the bed with his right arm.

At last he lay directly on top of Belle Mère. The bed depressed, a spring giving off a short bray as it accepted the new weight. Beneath him, Belle Mère's shoulders became hunched by the density of his body. Her mouth opened to take in more air; a tiny fleck of orange peel on her top lip picked up the light and settled a minute shadow on her cheek.

Loebus turned her head to him and kissed her. His kiss was not chaste. I almost spoke and told him to stop, but his body grew more flaccid as the kiss continued. The wrist, spasming rapidly, slowly uncoiled. The cramping muscle in his thigh subsided. The length of his frame took on the contours of Belle Mère's body. He appeared, grotesquely, to contain no bone or cartilage.

I took a step forward, thinking this was sacrilege, but stopped as Loebus looked at me. His expression was confused; it was also exhausted. Noticing his spastic wrist and hand for the first time, he pressed it against his leg and stilled the spasms. He lifted the hand two or three times from his thigh only to see the tremors return. Finally the hand calmed and he trusted it sufficiently to move it away from his leg.

"Was it horrible to watch?" he whispered, slowly crawling back from Belle Mère's body.

I shook my head.

"You look ashamed. Is it so replusive then?" he asked.

"Is she cured?"

"I don't know," he said.

He remained on his knees at the end of the bed. He rubbed his thigh absently with his left hand. A black bruise had fixed itself under his skin. It seemed to expand as he massaged it.

"You kissed her. I almost stopped you."

"I'm sorry if I offended you."

"Are you all right?" I asked. His hand was still cramped. He held it awkwardly in front of him like a man recently bandaged.

Armand interrupted us. Someone was coming, he whispered. Loebus stepped free of the bed and crossed to the window. He sat on the sill and swung his legs out, then dropped quietly onto the ground below. I wanted to ask him when he would return, but there wasn't time. Already someone approached down the hallway. The steps were hurried.

Armand pulled a chair close to Belle Mère's bed and sat. He pointed rapidly at the *prie dieu,* signaling for me to kneel there. I knelt, crossing myself, just as Sister Bernard pushed open the door.

She stopped, her hand on the door handle, her chest panting. She looked carefully at us both. Before she could speak, Armand stood and offered her his place. He was convincing.

"You're here," Sister Bernard said, somewhat dazed.

"What's wrong, Sister?" I asked.

"I heard her calling to me. Belle Mère's voice . . . it was like a dream, but it was . . . I thought she was in my cell."

"She's right here, Sister," I said.

Sister Bernard moved to the bed and placed her hand on Belle Mère's forehead. I said three Hail Marys at the *prie dieu,* then excused myself. I learned the next day from Armand that Sister Bernard slept in Belle Mère's cell the remainder of the night. He had helped her close the window because the wind, she said, was too strong and constant.

It rained on the day Belle Mère regained consciousness. Since rain came so infrequently to the mission, it was our habit to turn any storm into a brief holiday. Sister Catherine requested tea from

Armand, while we arranged a table on the porch. Sister Bernard produced a linen tablecloth, which we pinned to the legs of the table. I set out three chairs, turning each to face the southern landscape. From there we could watch the storm in comfort. By the time the first drops began to fall, we were forced to light a lantern in order to see clearly.

The rain was beautiful. It banged against the tin roof of our mission, making it nearly impossible to hear each other speak. The gutters began to run, then to gush. A family of African children— two boys and a girl, all less than ten—came to the corner of our house and bathed in the spouts of water falling from our roof. They removed their clothes and washed with laundry soap, their bodies extraordinarily handsome.

As I watched them, Belle Mère came up from the depth of her illness. I don't know how I sensed it, but I felt her presence slowly return to the house. I didn't mark it at first, or at least I didn't give the sensation any credence. I continued to stare at the rain, to take an occasional sip of tea, while the thought of her entered my mind. She didn't call out or speak to me—nothing as dramatic as that. Yet I gradually realized an element of our household had been missing, and now it had come back. I was slowly convinced that if I went to her I would find her awake, waiting for me.

I didn't go immediately. I looked at Sister Catherine, then at Sister Bernard, but they showed no sign of anything unusual passing through their thoughts. Sister Catherine was in a near doze, her cup of tea tilting dangerously on her lap. Sister Bernard stared straight ahead, her expression peaceful and reflective.

Eventually I excused myself, promising to return in a moment. When I reached Belle Mère's room I didn't look at her bed. Instead, my eyes went immediately to the open window. Mud was scattered over the window sill; more mud, human footprints, climbing in and out, marked the floor. When I turned to look at Belle Mère, her eyes were watching me.

"He was here," she said weakly.

I could not speak. I moved to her bed and knelt beside it. I

began to cry and leaned forward until my forehead touched the
edge of her blanket. I felt Belle Mère reach a hand toward me, but
she lacked the strength to carry it to my shoulder.

"Clean the room before the others come," she whispered.

I nodded and pushed myself to my feet. I used one of her cloths
to clean away all traces of Loebus's visit. The sheet of Belle Mère's
bed was also stained with mud. I changed it quickly, appalled at
the emaciated state of her body beneath the top sheet.

"Did you allow him to come here?" she asked when I finished.

"Yes, Belle Mère," I answered, my eyes down.

"He found me. I don't know where I was . . . but he was
suddenly beside me. He carried light."

We exchanged a look. I don't know what she thought—what
she made of all that had happened concerning Loebus—but she
attempted to say something to me with that look. The look said
that Loebus was a saint—or, if not a saint, at least proof . . . proof
of something divine, something the natural world could not define.
I didn't doubt for an instant that Belle Mère was cured. The atmosphere of the room was lighter; the tone and color of her skin
was richer. If death possesses a color or sound or scent, Loebus
had removed them.

YEARS HAVE PASSED since I last saw Loebus. He came to be
called Fraujas when the real Father Fraujas was killed by a jealous
husband—killed by his own rifle while he was on top of a village
woman in a remote district of the French Territory—and the confusion of identity was never tested by the authorities. We began,
first in jest, then in seriousness, to call Loebus Fraujas so that he
might be left in peace. "Fraujas is at it again," we would say on

hearing a story of Loebus. "Fraujas has become a great bush doctor."

Before she returned with Sister Bernard to France, Belle Mère suggested we adopt this name for Loebus. It was one of her last acts as the Mother Superior. By doing so, she offered him the protection of the Church. It was the sanctuary she had been unable to grant him while he stayed with us, though I am uncertain Loebus ever knew he was called Fraujas.

The Prefect left and was replaced by other French officers until Upper Volta took its independence. The educated Africans who then became prefects and government officials had little interest in Loebus. He was old by this time, and well-established, and it made no difference to them if he was called Loebus or Fraujas or if he existed at all. The officials were concerned with their own rush of nationalism, and it is doubtful they even thought of the white man lost in their midst.

Belle Mère died in 1961, of old age and the vestiges of the illness that forced her from Africa. Sister Bernard wrote from France to give me the news. Belle Mère's rosary was given to a female relative taking orders, but she bequeathed to me the statue of the Virgin that had adorned her *prie dieu*. I placed the statue in my room and have been comforted by it often. I don't believe it's a coincidence that that particular statue portrayed the Virgin pinning a viper to the ground with her foot. Belle Mère was reminding me of temptation.

Sister Bernard still lives in France, quite old and somewhat lonely. Sister Catherine died of fever in 1959 and is buried in the small cemetery behind the mission. She was the Reverend Mother before me.

My last conversation with Loebus was held shortly after Belle Mère's recovery. For a week he sent food to our mission, gifts of antelope and wild pigs. The gifts were left each night on the front doorstep of the mission house and were invariably discovered by Armand early in the morning. I can't say what the others thought of these gifts of food, but I knew very well they were gifts of parting.

Loebus sent for me the last night I ever saw him. It was my choice to go to him or remain. Armand came to my door at midnight and stood uneasily while I asked him what he wanted.

"Nassarra Loebus sent me," he said.

"For what purpose, Armand?"

"He is waiting."

"Where?"

Armand waved his hand. To the south. To the bush. His expression gave me to understand that I was wasting time by my questions. I then dressed quickly, never pausing to consider what I was doing.

We circled the mission, keeping to the rear of the sleeping quarters so that our passing would not distrub Sisters Bernard or Catherine. We passed the woodpile where I had found the scorpion, then entered onto a small path I hadn't known existed. It led us directly west, toward the priests' mission in Lati.

We entered a wide, grassy field which I eventually recognized from our Sunday trips to mass with the priests. My orientation was skewed, however, and I stopped for a moment to get my bearings. To my left, the south, I saw the plain across which the Prefect had approached. I could pick out no landmarks, nor could I see the cart path we usually followed, though I knew it had to be less than two hundred meters from where we stood. The terrain failed to take shape for me. I had never seen it before in darkness.

Armand drew a wooden flute from his shirt and played a few notes. Two or three flutes answered, each from a direction that seemed to change whenever I turned to hear it more clearly.

The sound was haunting. Each flute, without changing pitch or key, seemed to take up the tone of Armand's flute and carry it out into the grasses.

"It isn't much farther," said Armand.

"Are they friends?" I asked, referring to the other flute players.

"They're Loebus's men," he answered.

After another fifteen minutes I heard something move in the grass to the right of the path. Armand didn't stop, even though the grass continued to part in a wake of noise just out of our vision. Someone trotted beside the path, using his arms to push aside the tall rushes. A second runner began on our left, his progress strangely in time with the movement on the right.

At last we entered a small clearing freshly cut from the surrounding grass. At the rear of the clearing was a baobab, its skin pale white in the moonlight. Though a single hut was situated at the other end of the space, my eyes remained on the baobab. It was, I knew, a fetish tree. People hung fetishes on it in hope of having prayers answered, favors granted, curses set in motion. I had never seen one before. I was surprised by its power—there is no other word for it—and its ability to dominate its setting. I could not distinguish the individual fetishes, but seeing the black silhouettes dangling from the branches gave the tree a macabre vitality that seemed to affect the air. Hope trees, the African called them. Viper trees.

The men appeared next. Five of them stepped out from the grass surrounding the clearing, each wearing an ornate mask carved of wood and elaborately painted. The masks were fashioned to look like animal heads—a zebra, a gazelle, a gaping fish, a lion, and an elephant. The eye sockets and mouth holes were deeply gouged so that the resulting expressions were ones of wonder or amazement.

Once they entered the clearing, the men did not move. They stood in a rough circle, staring at me. I looked to see if I might identify any of them, but they were nearly naked, their bodies uniformly muscled by the harsh conditions of their lives. It was impossible to say if they were young or old; impossible to say if they were men of my acquaintance or strangers from a different village.

"Do not be frightened, Nassarra," Armand whispered, his eyes to the ground.

Without any sign that I could detect, the men began to retreat into the bushes, stepping backward without turning, an attempt, I realized, to prevent me from seeing the backs of their masks.

Then Loebus stepped out of the hut. He was, if possible, more purely African than before. He wore a white robe and leather sandals. His face was kind, tremendously kind, and his hair and beard had recently been cut. He was a different man from the one I had met two months earlier.

"Thank you for coming," he said.

I nodded. I looked about me, but the men had disappeared altogether.

"Are you leaving?" I asked finally.

"This area, yes," he said in French. "I'm not leaving Africa."

"Belle Mère is improved."

"God's mercy."

The insects were loud. The night was clear. A fire burned inside his hut, its flame low.

"Is there anything you need?" I asked.

"Maybe in the future. You have all been kind to me. You most of all."

"It was our duty," I said, though it wasn't what was in my mind.

I didn't know what he wanted, nor did I know what was in my own heart. I felt, perhaps, that he saw in me something he was giving up. A woman, yes, but also a life he had known and forfeited.

Nothing was left to be said. I turned and walked through the clearing and entered the path. Armand was crouched to wait, smoking a cigarette. He jumped up at my approach and started walking immediately. He didn't meet my eyes; I said nothing to him.

We were only a short distance away from the clearing when the flutes began once more. Their sound was constant now. The men ran on each side of the path, the grass pushing in great swirls before them. The exertion of running didn't seem to lessen the breath they devoted to the flutes. One after another ran forward of our progress and leaped for a moment in the grass. The sky above them was brilliant with stars, and it was possible to see them clearly. One after another they leaped above the grasses: zebra, elephant, lion, gazelle, their masks magnificent in the moonlight.

GRIS-GRIS

1977

THE SUMMER OF 1977 was hot in West Africa. By nine o'clock most days the temperature reached one hundred degrees. I drank in the morning, slept, then drank through the afternoons and into the evening. I seldom became drunk. I drank to keep cool; I drank out of boredom.

I was bored because my job as a hydrologist for a Catholic relief agency was on hold through the dry season. It was on hold for obvious reasons—there was no water, the local population was engaged in planting millet, and the monies pumped in by various relief organizations, mine included, were coming gradually to a halt. There had been a tremendous influx of money after the 1975 droughts, but now West Africa was no longer in the news. As Simmons, my immediate supervisor, said on one of his rare visits to my outpost: "The Halloween kids aren't carrying cans anymore. Not for West Africa, anyway."

It isn't surprising, then, that I happened to be in the Tenado Bar when four villagers brought in the priest. It was a big event in the village. A stranger, a white man no less, appearing as he did out of the bush. Even I felt my interest sparked. What made it all the more intriguing was that he was about to die—anyone who looked at him could tell that.

After they settled him in one of the back rooms, Hamaria, the bar owner, came to me.

"He is dying, Nassarra Hawley. In America, they don't die like this, do they?" he asked, shaking his head. "No one to mourn him. No friends. It's terrible, isn't it?"

I nodded. I knew what Hamaria was after. He wanted me to bring out my truck and carry the body over to the Prefect's, so the Prefect, an African named Suliman, would be able to verify that the priest had died of natural causes. Hamaria was anxious for the villagers to be rid of the responsibility. He didn't want any talk of gris-gris or bad magic to begin.

"Is he really dying?" I asked, stalling, though I didn't quite know why.

"Yes. He has been saying he wants to talk to a white man. He told me to bring one if there were any nearby."

"I don't want to talk to him. I'll carry his body over if he dies. How's that?"

Hamaria put his hand on my shoulder to thank me, then went off, back into the small mud rooms I never entered when I was in the bar. They were his family rooms, or whore rooms, or rooms where people could sleep off their drunkenness.

I stayed at my table and watched Fatama dance. She had an old portable stereo and she danced for me for the price of a few batteries. She was young and pretty. Her face had been scarred ritualistically in childhood to make her somehow more beautiful. I liked to watch her and I paid for the batteries often.

She put on a record by Bob Marley and danced, her feet never raising above the shuffle she made. She dragged her sandals and waved her arms at her sides. I watched and drank and tried to ignore Hamaria when he came back. He stood beside me for a few minutes, pretending to clean glasses. He waited until Fatama changed records, then spoke.

"He wants to confess," Hamaria said.

"I know he does. I knew that when you said he was looking for a white man."

"Will you do it?"

"I'm not a priest."

"He wouldn't know."

"I don't want to, Hamaria. Bring him out and let him see Fatama dance. How would that be?"

"Nassarra, please."

Hamaria was a Catholic and I knew he wouldn't leave me alone until I went inside and saw the man. I stood and felt the beer go directly to my head. I shuffled over and danced a little with

Fatama. Slowly, she took a cigarette and a book of matches out of my shirt pocket and lit the cigarette herself.

"Nassarra, please," Hamaria said again.

"How can I go in like a priest? *He's* a priest, for God's sake."

"We can give you his collar."

"He'll still know."

"He's very weak and he's begun to imagine. He won't know."

"He'll know words . . . Latin. I can't do that."

"Please."

I paused and Hamaria used the time to signal to a small boy named Peter who squatted against the back wall. Peter ran off and returned a few minutes later with the priest's collar. He held it out to Hamaria, but Hamaria wouldn't touch it.

"Give it to Nassarra," Hamaria told the boy.

I took it. Fatama started to laugh. I went back to my table, lit a cigarette, and tried to think of a way out of this.

"It's a sin," I finally told Hamaria. "You know that."

"He will forgive himself. You only have to listen."

I put my cigarette on the edge of the bar and tried the collar around my neck. It fit well enough and I buttoned my shirt around it. Fatama came by, turned me by the shoulder, then laughed. Peter snapped his fingers several times in a rapid motion that could mean pleasure, or humor, or pain.

"Would you like a missal?" asked Hamaria.

"No."

"I'll give you one in case you need it. I know the pages."

"I won't need it. I'm just going to listen. I don't know any blessing."

"But perhaps he will and you'll have to read along."

"Hamaria, I thought you said he was delirious."

"He is."

"Then I won't need the missal."

"Only in case." He reached behind the bar and handed me a small black book.

Catherine, Hamaria's wife, came to the doorway leading to

the back rooms and said something rapidly to Hamaria. She spoke in More and I didn't catch all of it, but I heard repeatedly the word *nassarra*. The "nassarra" was me and she wanted me inside. The priest's breathing, I understood, had changed.

"Nassarra Hawley . . . ," Hamaria said as his wife started back, but I cut him off by nodding and coming around the bar.

"I'm just going to listen," I said.

"That should be enough."

I followed him down a small, mud-brick passage, through two tiny rooms, then past a woman cooking chicken and millet beer in a room without a roof. Hamaria turned frequently to make sure I was still with him.

A few chickens moved in the thatched roof as we ducked through the last door. Inside, three women sat near the priest, fanning smoke at his body. None of them wore tops and their breasts were flat and lined from feeding children.

"Nassarra," they said, and stopped fanning long enough to put their fingers against their chests. It was a sign of respect and I returned it.

"How is he?" Hamaria asked them.

"Dying," one of the women said. She sat closest to the priest.

"It's too hot in here," I said. "He needs air."

"This is better," Hamaria said.

It was not worth arguing about. Catherine appeared with a small milking stool and put it near the priest's head.

"Did he bring in any identification?" I asked.

"No," Hamaria said.

"None at all?"

"No."

"Have you checked his pockets?"

"We wanted you to do that."

I sat down next to the priest. At first glance I thought he was dead. His breathing was shallow and uncertain. His skin looked white, pure white, and I saw where the women had washed his forehead and left dust stripes near his temples.

"Can you ask them to stop fanning? Maybe they should go," I said.

Hamaria said something and they stopped. Catherine said something else and the women stood and left. Hamaria and Catherine followed them out. Hamaria said he would be just outside the door if I needed anything.

I did nothing at first. I looked at the man carefully, thinking he would give me some clue to his background. But there was nothing. He wore a white robe and leather sandals; the robe looked terribly old. A rosary and a crucifix girdled his waist but these, in contrast to the robe, appeared quite new. He looked to be about sixty years old, perhaps older. He had a poorly groomed beard on his chin, but it didn't grow up to his sideburns. His hair was gray and thin and long.

I leaned forward on my stool, searching his robe for pockets. It took me some time to find any opening at all, and when I did there was only an airmail envelope with some figures written on the back. The envelope had no address. When I reached in his pocket again, I found a heel of bread and a tire patching kit—that was all. I put them at his feet and was about to check his other side more closely when he suddenly spoke.

"Bless me, Father, for I have sinned," he whispered in French. The strength of his voice surprised me.

"Bless me," he said again.

"For these sins and all the sins of your past," I said, thinking to put him at peace, gradually remembering the ritual, but he interrupted me.

"Forgive me . . ." he said, then gave off a long, quiet moan. His hand reached out and his fingers closed lightly on my forearm. I bent closer to hear him.

Then, suddenly, his head raised slightly and his lips actually touched my ear. I felt such unexpected revulsion at his touch, such fear, that I pulled away and almost lost my balance on the stool.

"I'm not a priest," I whispered.

"Protect me," he said.

"Protect you from what?"

"Protect me."

He said this clearly. I couldn't have mistaken it. And then in the darkness, in the lantern light, his face grew pointed and evil and his tongue, mining deeper and deeper for his guilt, slid back and forth in his mouth. I pulled back and waited for the illusion to pass, but instead it only became more intense until I imagined his body writhing ever so smoothly on the straw mat. A chicken clucked and a donkey brayed, and it was only these sounds that slowly broke his final illusion. I watched it slowly fall away from him, the evil I had sensed in him even more clever in taking cover beneath his skin.

"I'm not a priest. I have no power to forgive you," I said. I felt the missal in my hand and raised it. I couldn't believe I was doing so, but I placed it between the priest and myself and held it there.

Then he was gone. I sensed this as I stood. I called to Hamaria, who returned with the women. They sat down around the priest and began fanning again.

"Are you all right, Nassarra?" Hamaria asked me, walking back to the bar. "Did he believe you were a priest?"

"I don't know."

"Did he confess?"

"Yes."

"Then he will go to heaven."

Back in the bar, Fatama slept in a chair. I woke her and asked her to dance, but she said she was too tired. Peter brought me more beer and I sent him to the store for batteries. We put on Bob Marley and played both sides of the record. Once, in the silence while we changed sides, I heard the women trilling their tongues, calling through the village of the priest's death. They brought his body around and put it in the back of my truck. I told them to cover it with a tarp and they did. Peter stood guard to keep the dogs off, but he stayed near the light, a slingshot and a pile of stones set out on the floor.

I WOKE IN THE MORNING with Fatama beside me. Her bare breasts pressed against my ribs and her hand, curled in sleep, made a small fist against the mosquito net. Mosquitoes had bitten it through the net, their bites raising a pink welt of flesh over her knuckles and fingers. She scratched it once in her sleep while I watched her, then woke.

She said nothing. She pulled up the net and stepped out. She crossed to my stock room, the room where I kept my tools and cement for irrigation projects, and scooped a calabash of water from one of the cisterns. She brought the water back and washed in the light of one window, her young body black and smooth, the water forming veins of reflection and light down the length of her torso and thighs.

When she finished, she went into the kitchen and put water on for coffee.

"Is the body still out there?" I asked her, sitting up and sliding into my sandals.

"The tarp is still on."

"I was worried the dogs would get to it."

"Peter watched it."

"All night?"

"Probably. Hamaria probably made him."

She put on the kettle, then changed the water in the calabash. She went back in the kitchen while I washed. When I finished, she brought me cigarettes and coffee. I went out to check on the body. Already the temperature was up around one hundred.

Peter sat against the back tire of my truck. He was covered with dust and looked exhausted. He dozed, his head loose on his neck, but jumped up when my boot touched the ground near him.

"Did you stay here all night?" I asked him.

"Yes, Nassarra."

"Did anyone come to look?"

"No."

"Did the dogs give you trouble?"

"No, Nasarra. Only dreams and demons."

"What dreams?"

"Magic dreams. The priest has gris-gris," Peter said, then crossed himself.

I stood looking at the boy for a moment. I knew about gris-gris. I had heard too many stories not to be aware of its existence, but it was rare that an African admitted to sensing it.

"What kind of gris-gris?" I asked him.

"White man's. And others. Hamaria said he is maribou. The priest makes miracles."

"What kind of miracles?"

"All kinds. Last night I saw the dogs come and sit in a ring around the truck. They listened and the body talked to them."

"How did it talk to them?"

"It rolled back and forth. I heard it and I moved away. The dogs talked back to him."

"I didn't hear anything."

"They came and put their feet up on the truck and talked to him over the edge. They talked quietly."

"And didn't you stop them?"

Peter shook his head. His expression showed me my question was ridiculous. This was gris-gris.

"Well, thank you," I said, giving him a few francs. "Thank you for standing guard."

"Nassarra," he said, touching his chest with the same hand that held the money. Then he left.

I smelled the priest now. I pulled out a large handkerchief from my pants pocket, tied it over my mouth and nose, then climbed in the cab of the truck. The engine started on the second turn and I backed out of the compound.

I took the Po road toward the Prefect's office. It wasn't far, only eight or nine kilometers, and I knew the road well. I drove carefully, aware of the body at all times, and avoided potholes and ruts from run-off whenever possible. Each time I slowed the truck

his scent came to me, rolling forward from the flatbed, lifting with
the dust and heat until I had to breathe through my mouth in short
pulls.

Near Boromo I noticed the dogs. At first it was only one—a
brown bush dog, its body lean and muscled, its nose flat and level
with the ground. It was not uncommon to have dogs chase the
truck, but it was the intensity with which it pursued that made me
take notice. Glancing at it, watching it leap bushes and deadfalls
in its path, I became aware of its eyes staring not at me but at the
flatbed. It ran in silence except for the desperate click of its nails
on the laterite soil.

It was soon joined by a second dog. This one was black, almost
pure black, and it swept in from my right, leaping a small patch
of bush thorns as it took the trail. The sight of it, the suddenness
of its appearance, made me involuntarily jam down on the accel-
erator. The truck rammed over a deep rut in the road and I looked
quickly behind me to see the tarp bend and nearly rip from the
metal studs that held it secure. For an instant I saw the outline of
the priest's body surge against the soft tarp, the contours of its
form, for the barest flicker, exceptionally clear. It was like the bulge
of a trampoline seen from underneath.

And for the second time I felt something evil and disturbing
attached to the priest. I remembered the touch of his lips against
my ear. What had he wanted to say in that last moment? What
did he fear? Whatever it was, it still remained with the body; I felt
it as surely as I smelled his flesh turning.

Two more dogs joined the first two, but this seemed to distract
the entire pack. They fell back, stopping on stiff front legs, their
tongues pink against the brown dirt. Dust obscured my last vision
of them.

It took me longer than usual to reach Boulsa. I turned left up
the circular driveway connecting the Prefect's office to the Po road.
The building, which remained from the days of French coloniza-
tion, was in a state of disrepair. White paint, chipped and burned
pale by the sun, held only here and there on the wall. A tin roof

was patched with straw and banko. Three elephant skulls stood in front of the veranda, the bone pure white. On either side of the main building were the military compounds, brown huts which provided housing for the guards and their wives.

I parked the truck near the front door. A senior guard, Ourbri, came out and stood in the shade. He carried a machine gun at his side and wore camouflage fatigues. He made a casual salute when he saw me, then came down the stairs.

"Nassarra," he said. "We haven't seen you in some time."

"How are you, Ourbri?"

We shook hands. His hand was strong and had thick calluses on his fingers and palms. He wore a new red beret, which made his face look handsome.

"What do you have back there?" he asked, pointing at the flatbed. The smell had reached him.

"A body."

"I'll get the Prefect," he said.

He walked back up the stairs, and a moment later the Prefect stepped onto the porch. He was a short man, with a wide face and hips. His hands and feet turned out as if he was herding something forward at all times.

He wore sandals and white khaki pants, a large, flowing boo-boo shirt on top, and thick sunglasses. He often used the sunglasses for effect, but now, as he stopped on the top step, he took them off to show me his eyes. His expression was open and ready to take any direction I wished to give. He would be excited, concerned, or annoyed depending on my news, but primarily he wished to show his willingness to hear what I had to say.

"Ourbri says you have a body?" the Prefect asked. "Are you serious?"

"A priest died last night in Tenado."

"There is no priest in Tenado. Was he from the mission?"

"No. Or at least I don't think so. He came from the north."

"May I see? Perhaps I'll recognize him."

The Prefect snapped his fingers at Ourbri, who jumped ahead

of him and went to the back of the truck. He unbuttoned the tarp and pulled it away. Even from where we stood on the step, I smelled the rot leap into the air.

"How long has he been dead?" the Prefect asked, starting down the steps.

"Just last night."

"He must have been sick before. He shouldn't be so bad already."

I didn't want to look at the priest again, but I saw no way to avoid it. I went with the Prefect and stood next to the truck. The Prefect looked at the priest for a moment, then motioned for Ourbri to pull the tarp back farther.

I looked in at the priest myself, but now there was nothing to see but a dead man. His face was slack and slightly swollen; there was nothing exceptional about it. Flat in the bed of the truck, full sun on him, he merely looked like an old man.

"I don't know him. Do you, Ourbri?"

"No. I thought I did, but no, I don't know him."

"And they said he was from the north?" the Prefect asked me.

"That's what they said. A driver found him coming overland from Mopti or Bamako. I didn't hear it all."

The Prefect turned to Ourbri. "Call the Catholic mission in Ouahabou on the shortwave and tell them we have one of their priests," he said. "Tell them they better hurry in this heat. Then get Diallo to help you take the body into the shade in back. Keep someone near it to fend off the dogs."

WE DRANK UNTIL Father Joseph showed up at noon. The heat kept us fairly sober, but I noticed the Prefect wobbled as he stood to greet the priest.

Father Joseph was a tall, thin man with a gray beard and curly hair. His face was sharp and anxious. He had the deep-set eyes of the aesthete, the man who is solitary even in company. He was French or Belgian, I never knew which, and he spoke More with natural fluency. He liked the Africans, yet he held toward them a paternal tolerance beyond what his role as priest might demand. Even now, as he accepted a glass of warm scotch from the Prefect, he had about him the air of a parent visiting the first apartment of a newly married couple.

"Are there any priests missing?" the Prefect asked once he had filled our glasses and moved back around the desk.

"There was a priest," Father Joseph answered, "named Fraujas who disappeared some years back from up around Dori. He wasn't liked and a rumor came down from the north that he had been killed. It was some bad business of gris-gris. A great deal of superstition about it, as I recall. Not too long afterward they found the body."

"I remember the case," the Prefect said, but whether he really did, or whether he was simply encouraging Father Joseph, I couldn't tell.

"Poachers," Father Joseph continued. "They had been down in Arly shooting ivory and the priest had somehow heard about the ivory being sold out on the desert. It was confusing, I can tell you. You know we've all been told to turn our back on that kind of thing. What would life be like here if we enforced every rule handed to us? It's food after all, isn't it?"

"Of course," I said.

"When the mission first came here, we hunted for our food. We're in no position to turn back on it."

"Was it proven that the poachers did it?" I asked.

"No, just suspected. The authorities found the body in a termite mound. Of course, most of its flesh was gone. They never would have found it except part of the mound cracked open in a storm. He was in there, tucked in the fetal position, and the termites had used him. He was part of the mound, if you see my meaning. The insects had used him as earth."

"Did they check dental records?" I asked.

"Not to my knowledge. I think they determined it was a white man, that was all."

"Didn't the mission follow up on it?"

"No. There were many rumors about him. We let the matter drop."

An uncomfortable silence followed. The Prefect rose to pour more scotch, but Father Joseph stood and put his glass on the desk.

"I really should be getting him back if he's ours. It's been a hot morning," said Father Joseph.

"He's out back," the Prefect said.

We went out the front, past the bald elephant heads, then circled the house.

"Ourbri," the Prefect called when we reached the back. "Ourbri!"

Ourbri was gone. A small girl stood next to the body, a slingshot hanging like a necklace around her neck. She was naked.

"Where is Ourbri?" asked the Prefect.

The girl pointed to the mud compound beside the Prefect's office.

"Go and get him," the Prefect said, angry now.

The little girl ran off, the slingshot thrown onto her back to keep it out of the way.

Ourbri appeared a moment later. He had been eating. He wiped his hands on his pants as he ran. He stopped and saluted the Prefect.

"I told you to stay with him," the Prefect said. "Take the tarp down. Do it now."

Ourbri pulled the tarp away slowly. A burst of flies moved into the air.

"I don't recognize him," Father Joseph said.

He dug in his pocket and pulled out a small black and white photo. He held the photo next to the man's face and compared it.

"It looks something like him," the Prefect said.

"We need a razor," Father Joseph said.

Ourbri was sent. He returned with cool water and a straight razor. The Prefect told Ourbri to shave the dead priest, but Father Joseph took over instead.

"Let me," he said.

I felt dizzy watching him and moved into the shade. A few children appeared but a wave by Ourbri dispersed them.

Shaving the dead priest took some time. Ourbri was sent for another basin of water. When Father Joseph had half the dead priest's face cleaned, he again held up the picture.

"What do you think?" he asked us.

"It's him," the Prefect said.

"It's difficult to say. The picture must be thirty years old," I told him.

Father Joseph handed the razor to Ourbri and indicated for him to continue shaving the dead priest. Father Joseph lifted the rosary from the corpse's waist and carried it into the sun. He looked for quite a while at the back. The reflection ran up and down the wall of the house.

"It's from our mission," Father Joseph said eventually.

"Then it's Father Fraujas," said the Prefect.

"Either that or someone who's taken his cassock."

"Why bother?" I asked.

"Who knows? I only know the man's been gone nearly ten years. What brought him back here now?"

"He came to die," the Prefect said. "Perhaps he came to find other men like himself."

"But he had lived without Europeans for such a long time . . . it doesn't make sense."

Father Joseph returned to the corpse. Ourbri worked awkwardly on the dead priest. The beard came off bit by bit, leaving the skin beneath white. The priest's smell was now so strong it was difficult to be near him.

I'm not sure what made Father Joseph toss back the dead

priest's cossack, but he did it with such assurance that I suspected afterward he knew what he would find. He stepped back immediately when the body was exposed. Ourbri dropped the razor in the basin and ran five steps away. Even the Prefect recoiled.

Father Joseph lifted his own cross, held it in front of him, and prayed. I heard something of the Hail Mary as I stepped past him to see. I regretted it as soon as I did so, because the sight of the priest's body sickened me.

Small tracks of skin, slivers, had been removed from every surface of his body. The cuts hadn't scabbed. They had been taken from the corpse sometime after he had died. The red hue of the cuts against the pale skin seemed a deliberate pattern. The cuts covered his legs, his chest, his hips and ribs. A knife had whittled them, lifting fine diamonds of skin away from the matted tissue beneath.

I backed away, repulsed by the serpentine quality the cuts gave the corpse. The cuts might have been scales.

Father Joseph rescued us. His initial fear gone, he became remarkably clinical. He tilted the dead priest's head and examined it.

"They cut his hair and his nails," he said, looking at the back of the corpse's head, then lifted the dead hands.

"For gris-gris?" I asked.

"Of course. Did you look at the body last night?"

"I didn't examine it closely."

"Were there any bloodstains on the cassock?"

"Not that I noticed."

"There probably weren't. Even now the blood hasn't soaked into the cloth."

"That means they did it last night?" I asked.

"Probably. Did you have a guard?"

"A little boy."

"Anything could have scared him off."

Father Joseph looked at Ourbri, who hadn't come closer.

"I don't suppose you'd like to finish shaving him?" he asked.

"He will if I order it," said the Prefect.

"No, don't do that. He'd never forgive either of us. I'll finish, then take him back to the mission. I want the Mother Superior to see him."

AFTER LEAVING THE PREFECT I went to the Tenado Bar and found Hamaria inside, cleaning the counter. A new shipment of Sovabra beer and Youki soda had arrived, and was now stacked against the far wall. No one else was in the bar. Fatama's record player, which was normally stationed near the back, was gone.

"Good evening," I said to Hamaria.

He smiled and handed me a beer from a calabash. The beer wasn't cold, but at least it was cooler than the air. I sat at the bar and let him open it.

"Where's Fatama?" I asked.

"I don't know. She hasn't been in all day."

"Did you hear about the priest?"

"What about him?"

"His skin had been cut away. Someone had taken small diamonds of flesh from different parts of his body."

Hamaria ignored me. He bent over an invoice and checked off something about his beverage shipment. At that moment Peter came in carrying beef brochettes he had grilled outside. Hamaria looked at him, and I knew they had anticipated my coming to them with questions. Hamaria's look told the boy that now was the time for which he had been prepared.

Before I could go on, Hamaria put a tin plate and a soiled napkin in front of me.

"Here, child. Give the man some food."

Peter placed the brochettes on the plate. He didn't stay to be paid; he went out again quickly. Hamaria gave me a small pinch of salt wrapped in a corner of an old paper bag.

"His skin was cut last night in my yard," I said, drinking more beer.

"No, Nassarra. He must have had an accident. I talked to the driver who brought him in. The priest fell from a bicycle."

"Hamaria, tell the truth."

"It is the truth."

"The boy said the dogs came to speak to the body last night," I said. "He says the priest had strong gris-gris."

"Boys always imagine things."

"His skin was cut. It wasn't an accident."

"I've told you what I know."

"Hamaria, I listened to his confession as a favor to you. I forgave him things and now I find out he was a witch man. Did you know?"

"He was a priest. That's all I knew."

"He was more than a priest. I felt it myself. I felt he was something more."

"He was just an old man," Hamaria said.

"Why would they want his skin if he was just an old man?"

"No one wanted his skin."

"They wanted his skin for something. I've seen Fatama take my hair when she's finished cutting it. I know things are taken. Hamaria, don't pretend things don't occur."

Hamaria shrugged and looked away. He fanned a horse tail at the flies that moved along the bar. I asked for another beer. While he pulled it out of a calabash, Fatama came in carrying her record player. She greeted us, then put on a Jimmy Cliff record and danced slowly, her sandals scuffing the floor. She took a wedge of kola nut out of her pagna and bit off a corner.

The music echoed in the bare bar. Peter came to stand in the doorway and watch. I thought about calling him over, but decided against it.

I drank the second beer, then ordered another. I sent Peter for more batteries. Fatama danced, sweat shining on her forehead and cheeks. I watched her, trying to forget the priest, already worried my dreams would bring him back to me.

Fatama and I had sex under the mosquito net, but it was fast and sharp and violent. Afterward, she turned away from me and fell asleep instantly. Her ability to fall asleep so quickly always astonished me, but this night it was even more immediate than usual. I stayed close to her and listened to her breathing. In the windows I saw the light of the moon and heard a diesel truck pass on the Po road.

I dozed eventually and then woke to hear her shivering. She was often cold in the middle of the night and I offered my arm, but she shook fiercely and didn't respond.

"Fata," I said softly, "wake up."

But she didn't wake. Her body vibrated and caused the wooden slats under the mattress to creak. It sounded like a ship in wind and I tried to hold her and make her still.

She was quiet after a time. I grabbed my flashlight from the bedside table and shone it on her. I worried about fever, perhaps malaria, but she looked calm now and slept with no expression on her features. I touched her forehead, her cheek, and found them cool.

In the morning she was up before me. She washed from a bucket near the kitchen. Perhaps she didn't think I watched her because she was freer with her body than usual. She stood in the sunlight, naked, and turned quietly, letting the sun dry her. She looked beautiful and I wanted her back in bed. But when I spoke her name softly, she grabbed for her pagna and disappeared into the kitchen. A few minutes later I smelled coffee and bread warming.

I got up, washed, shaved, then went outside to watch morning come. Pentards flocked in a flamboyant tree outside the compound. An old sow rooted in the abandoned garden and I lobbed a stone at it. She snorted and jugged off a few paces, then returned cautiously to the same spot.

Fatama brought me coffee and bread. She didn't say much, but neither did she go back inside as she normally did. She stayed by the door, her pagna loosely tucked across her stomach, an old pair of sweat socks I had given her over her hands for gloves.

"I thought you had a fever last night," I said, drinking some of the coffee. "You shivered for a good half hour."

"Nassarra," she said, "they are fishing your dreams."

It was odd to hear her call me Nassarra. It put a distance between us that was not commonly there. I tried to catch her eye, but she looked away.

"What do you mean?"

"They're luring your soul."

"Who is?"

"I don't know."

"Is it the same people who took the flesh from the priest?"

"I don't know."

I understood she wouldn't tell me. I lit a cigarette and drank more coffee.

"How do they lure my soul away?" I asked eventually.

"They use bait. They make your soul wander."

"With what?"

"With whatever your soul wants. Then, when it's free of your body, they trap it."

"How do you know they're doing this to me?"

"They touched my dreams last night. That's why I shivered."

"You shivered because you were cold."

She clicked her tongue and nodded. I knew it signified she wouldn't speak to me again on the subject until I was more open to hear it. She rubbed the sweat socks over her arms and went back inside.

She was gone ten or fifteen minutes and I smoked two cigarettes waiting for her. When she came back out, she was prepared to go. She wore a hooded sweatshirt I had given her.

"See, you are cold," I told her.

"Don't ask any more questions. Leave it alone. You shouldn't have gone in to talk to the priest."

"To hear his confession?"

She nodded.

"Why do they want me?"

"I don't know why. Don't ask any more questions."

She left soon afterward. I was still out there when Ourbri drove up to the compound gate. I saw his red beret before anything else. He clapped his hands to announce himself and I waved him in.

"Coffee?" I asked as we shook hands.

"No, no thank you."

"A cigarette?"

"Yes, if you're having one."

Ourbri seemed nervous. He struck a match two or three times before he managed to light his cigarette. Finally he leaned back in his chair and crossed his legs.

"What brings you to Tenado?" I asked him.

"The Prefect sent me. It concerns the priest."

"Father Joseph?"

"No, Father Fraujas. The dead priest."

"Did they decide if he was Father Fraujas?"

"Yes, he was. A few scars matched. They checked his dental records."

"Do they know where he was for ten years?"

"No, not yet."

Ourbri smoked awkwardly. His seat was in the sun and sweat had started around his hatband. I pushed my chair over a little to let him into the shade, but he shook his head and smiled.

"You said the Prefect sent you?" I said.

"He sent me to ask you to help. We need your truck. Someone's stolen the body."

"The priest's body?"

"Yes. They dug it up last night. There was a guard—the Prefect suspected something like this could happen—but the guard heard nothing."

"How are we supposed to find it now? It could be anywhere."

"The Prefect said the mission is upset and he said to tell you he would consider it a favor."

This meant, of course, that I couldn't refuse. I nodded. This was a form we would have to follow. We would not find the body. That was out of the question. We would drive through the bush, perhaps stop and ask some questions, but that would be all.

I drove Father Joseph down the Po road, then took a branch up toward Lati. The Lati road was gutted and pocked by run-off. At times the road disappeared entirely and we were left in the center of quiet fields, our truck the only noise for kilometers.

It was exceedingly hot. It was too hot to talk; Father Joseph said little. I wanted to ask him questions, but held off. I couldn't tell if he possessed any feeling for Father Fraujas. Did he regret the priest's fate? Did he feel the man had been persecuted at the end? On one hand I felt Father Joseph followed the form of things only to satisfy his Mother Superior, who had been furious about her small cemetery being disturbed. On the other hand, part of me suspected Father Joseph might be able to track the body. His knowledge of the area was extensive. He knew villagers throughout the countryside and he carried the combined weight of a white man and a priest.

He had brought a shotgun with him which he kept on the door, the tip of the barrel extending into the air beyond the truck. Once or twice he aimed at random trees or bushes, leaning forward in his seat and bringing the sight of the shotgun to his eye. He squinted at the object and followed it carefully as we passed. He didn't ask me to slow or stop. When we finally moved beyond the object, he swung the gun down and put it back in place.

We came to the village of Lati. Dogs met us at the border of the village, and then some young boys appeared and waved. They wore slingshots around their necks and carried throwing sticks clipped onto their shoulders.

"Don't stop," said Father Joseph. "I don't want to talk to them today."

"All right."

"Tell the Mother Superior when we get back that we had a long chat with the villagers. Do that, would you? I don't know what she expects. Does she think they'll have the damn body sitting out for a picnic?"

"Do you have any idea who stole it?"

"It's gris-gris. They'd eat us if they thought they could get away with it. There's a tribe just to the south of here, not the Dioula but the Busansi, I think, who used to eat the center of a man's forehead. They'd eat his forehead and his eyebrow so that they could look their enemies in the eyes without fear."

I pulled the truck off the road and turned it. We headed back toward the mission.

"A girl in Tenado says they're fishing my dreams," I told him.

"Be careful then."

"What's it all about?"

Father Joseph lined up another shot and followed until we were past. Then he put the gun down and looked at me. He smiled and shook his head. For the first time since I had met him, he seemed genuinely friendly. He was relieved that I didn't insist on going into Lati.

"They'll steal something . . . a picture or hair or a book you read. Then they'll use it and say spells over it and try to conjure your soul away. Then want to make your soul yearn for something. They do it all the time to each other. They believe the soul can leave through the nose or mouth. It's the whole idea we have of saying God bless you when you sneeze. If they start fishing your dreams, you're supposed to tie up your chin so your mouth won't open when you sleep. Plug your nose too. Then they can't get you."

"Do you believe all this?"

"Don't you?" he asked.

"No, I don't think so."

"It doesn't matter if you do or not. They believe it, so that's the important thing."

"Why me, though?"

"I don't know. They believe if they eat something of an enemy, they gain the man's soul. Perhaps they think you took the soul of Fraujas. If they have your soul, then they have two. A double cheeseburger."

He looked at me, smacked my thigh, then laughed.

"You see? I have been to America. Isn't that what it is? Double cheeseburger? My theory is that Fraujas became mixed up in some sort of cult or rituals. Maybe he joined with a maribou or a witch man. Then, near the end, he tried to make a run for it and he ended up with you. Be careful if they want you. It can be dangerous."

"I had nothing to do with him, though."

"You heard his confession, didn't you?"

I slowed the truck when he said this and looked at him. But he had picked up the rifle once more, and this time he raised his left hand and signaled for me to slow down.

The blast of the shotgun stunned me. I thought I had been prepared for it, but I jerked my hands on the wheel and stepped on the brake. Father Joseph jammed back against the seat and whistled. The next moment he climbed out of the truck, his cassock tucked between his legs.

I put the parking brake on and followed him. He ran across an open field, zig-zagging slightly to avoid thorns and acacia clumps.

When I caught up to him he was bent over a bush antelope. The animal was small and fawn-colored. Blood soaked into the ground next to its head, and I saw where the shotgun spray had ripped a hole in the animal's neck.

"You have to get them clean to keep the adrenaline from making the meat tough," said Father Joseph.

"How did you see him at that distance?"

"They're always in here. I usually bring a gun over to Lati. This is the sweetest meat you'll ever eat."

He brought out a knife from under his cassock and slit the antelope's throat, then quickly field-dressed the carcass. After cleaning the knife blade on the shank of a bush, he lifted the antelope by its hind legs and began to bleed it. He stuck the knife blade through the tendons of the back legs, just by the forelocks, and finally wedged the knife into the crotch of a kapok tree. The antelope continued to bleed slowly.

"It will just take a second. We'll get our cook, François, to clean it back at the mission. Wait until you taste it. They boil it soft, then roast it. It tastes almost like a bird. You'll have to stay. The Mother Superior will want to speak with you anyway. She's very upset about Fraujas."

"Did she know him well?"

"Fairly well. He sometimes came to stay with the mission here—that was years ago, of course."

I waited for him to go on, but he turned back to the antelope and swung it from side to side. Then he massaged the limbs with his hands, running the last free blood down to the open throat. When he was satisfied the antelope was properly bled, he freed the knife blade from the crotch of the tree. I helped him put the antelope in the flatbed.

We drove back to the mission. Father Joseph called out the truck window when we pulled into the small garden behind the mission compound. François appeared instantly, a white apron over his bare chest and legs.

"Antelope," Father Joseph said, climbing out and pointing at the back. "We got it near Lati. Finish cleaning it, will you? This nassarra has never eaten any."

While François pulled the antelope out of the flatbed, Father Joseph took me around the small garden that formed the back yard. The garden was beautiful and lush. One wall was taken up

by mango trees, the fruit bright orange and pendulous. A large
gazebo covered by bougainvillea stood in the center of the garden.
The rest of the garden was lavishly planted with mums and violets
and petunias. But the other flowers served only as a backdrop for
a wall of roses, all deeply embedded in manure, which grew beside
the south wall.

"Magnificent smell here, isn't it?" Father Joseph said, stopping
next to the roses.

"Yes, it's wonderful."

"The Africans hate it, of course, hate having so many plants
near their houses. They worry about snakes, and they're right.
We've had our share slip into the house."

"But it's worth it in the long run. Do you have a well?"

"A deep one. It's never gone dry so far. There's enough even
for the plants."

Father Joseph put his hand on the small of my back and
escorted me to the house. He took out two beers from a calabash
of water in the corner of the kitchen and gave me one. He clinked
my bottle with his.

"Come here," he said to me after he took a sip, "you should
watch him skin it."

We went out onto the porch and watched François work. He
had already removed the skin. Flies swarmed over the hide and ribs.
François had to flick his hand continually to keep his eyes free.

"What will you do with those horns, François?" Father Joseph
asked, touching my shoulder to indicate the response would interest
me.

"What, Nassarra?" François said, not looking up.

"With the horns."

"Whatever you want me to do."

"I think you should grind them up into a powder, don't you?
They'll make you very fertile."

François said nothing. Father Joseph looked at me and smiled.
I felt faint watching the skin come free. I concentrated on smelling
the flowers.

DINNER WAS DULL. The Mother Superior, a dry, tired old nun named Marie, permitted little conversation about Fraujas except to receive reports about our search.

I waited anxiously until she had excused herself from the table and I was left alone with the priests. Besides Father Joseph there were two others. One, Father William, smoked incessantly. His fingers were yellow and the skin around his lips appeared translucent. He seemed made of glass, or perhaps the clear plastic of a cigar holder. His countenance, his movements, reminded me of smoke.

The other priest, Father Claude, was a short, nervous man, possessing little appetite. The heat bothered him and he stood often and went to the window, his hand touching the screen, his fingers flicking at the moths collected there. Sitting, he was in motion, and even during conversations he hummed curiously to himself as if underlining the words of the other speakers.

They relaxed, however, when the Mother Superior left. Father Joseph brought out cigars and cigarettes, and Father William offered brandy. We moved our chairs closer to the double screen doors at the end of the room waiting for the evening wind to begin.

"They've had him by now," Father Claude said, lighting a cigar. "There wasn't much point in looking for him to begin with, but by now he's gone."

"Reminds you what this country's like," said Father William.

"We eat the body of Christ every day," Father Joseph said. "That's nothing but cannibalism. We're only shocked when it's done without our own kind of rituals."

"You can't really connect the two," Father Claude said. "That's even too simple for you, Joseph."

"I could argue it," Father Joseph said. "You could argue it yourselves if you wanted to."

"Did the Mother Superior say anything about Father Fraujas's past?" I asked. "Did she know him well?"

"She said something about him being difficult to discipline, but she says that about so many people it's hard to know what it means," Father Joseph said. "She said he was one of those priests who begins to see his mission here as an anthropological adventure. He also liked to hunt."

"He was also caught sleeping with an African girl, to tell the truth," Father Claude said, standing up quickly and touching the screen. "It's not the first time it's happened, God knows."

"Wouldn't he have been drummed out?" I asked, not knowing how else to phrase it.

Father William, smoking a Gauloise, made a buzzing sound between his lips. It was a typical French sound, a dismissal of prudery or a lack of worldliness.

"The Catholic Church loves a fornicator," he said. "It always has."

"But there would be official channels and perhaps some protests. You have to grant that," Father Claude said from his spot by the double doors.

"Where the hell was he going to be sent by way of punishment?" Father William laughed. "Can you imagine a more hellish spot than this one?"

"Or out on the Benin border. That's where he ended up, you know," Father Joseph said. "Out by W National Park. He hunted along the Pendjari. It's boggy country, but the game's still good. They have lion and elephant and buffalo. That's where he spent his time even though he was supposed to be up in Dori."

"Well, it isn't really cannibalism anyway, is it?" said Father William. "I mean, it's not as if they want to make him into so many sandwiches."

"Just as bad," Claude said. "They want his essence, don't they? Isn't that what has everyone so unnerved?"

"What exactly would they do with the body?" I asked.

Father Claude smiled and tapped the screen once more, shaking free a few moths. He looked at Father William. Father William moved in his chair, then spoke.

"They could do a number of things. They might take the rest of his flesh and dry it, then grind it into powder. I'm not sure what they would use it for—perhaps as a boost to potency, or fertility, or simply as a fetish to help them gain money. Some of their gris-gris is used to tell the future. They believe a great deal in traveling spirits, spirits that can leave the body of one man, hover into the darkness, then return at daylight."

"African vampires," Father Joseph said, though it was impossible to tell if he was joking.

"You see," Father Claude said, "we don't know exactly what they might do with the body. We don't know much about gris-gris at all. It works in the way that voodoo or any primitive religion works. It seeks to alter the natural forces on one person's behalf. That's religion, after all, isn't it? Charms and chants against our fate."

"That's heresy, of course," Father William said.

"Of course."

"But there is the idea of possession in it as well," Father Joseph said. "That's the dangerous element. We've all seen men and women who believe themselves taken by a larger spirit. Father Fraujas may have been taken because he had what the Africans call a great life—great in the sense of size and dimension, you understand. A great life carries its own force."

I made my excuses a while later and Father Joseph walked me out to my truck. It was a dark night and hot.

"I don't know how to say this without alarming you," he said. "I suppose I just want to tell you it is a serious business if they're after you."

"Who are they?"

"Witch men, shamans, witch doctors—whatever you wish to call them. They take themselves very seriously."

"I'll be careful."

"Good," he said, and slapped the door of my truck. "Good night."

I drove home on the Po road. It was too dark to go quickly.

Bats flew through the light from my headlamps, cutting insects out of the darkness. Once a hare darted across my path and disappeared into the brush. I braked and went carefully along the gutted road.

Near Boromo I saw the first white figure running parallel to the truck, perhaps thirty yards off the road to the right. It was not a white man, but an African coated with white dust or lime. He ran silently, alone, sprinting full out. I knew the Africans painted their bodies white at funerals, and the sight of this man made me suddenly sit up straight behind the wheel. I watched him intently, but he took no notice of me. He ran as the dogs had run a few nights before.

I watched him until he disappeared, veering off into the bush. I expected to see another runner take up his place, perhaps in relay, but the road and its borders remained empty. It occurred to me that he might want me to follow. Perhaps he showed me where the body had been taken. Or perhaps he had nothing at all to do with the death of the priest. It was probable he ran to inform relatives that one of their kinsmen had died.

It made no difference. I had no intention of getting out of the truck. I drove into Tenado and stopped at Hamaria's bar. The lights were out and a quick glance told me Fatama wasn't there. Only Peter was at his post, cooking the last of his beef brochettes.

I climbed out and asked him where Fatama had gone.

"I don't know, Nassarra."

"Are you sure?"

He nodded and clicked his tongue. I squatted beside him. He kept his eyes on the fire.

"Tell me, Peter, did the dogs really come to the truck that night?" I asked.

He didn't answer. He turned the brochettes over the fire. It was pointless to ask him anything else.

I began to get back into my truck, but stopped at the sight of a black fetish necklace dangling from the door on the driver's side. It was a black leather square with a single cowrie shell embossed in the top casing. It was gris-gris and I knew Father Joseph had placed it there.

I pulled it off the door and tied it around my throat. I felt no effect. When I looked back at Peter, he nodded his head once more and clicked.

Ourbri came early the next morning. I saw him glance quickly at the fetish I wore around my neck, but he didn't mention it. We sat in the shade, side by side, watching women pass. They carried wood piled high on their heads, calling their greetings over the wall, sometimes stopping to genuflect in respect.

"Did they have any luck finding the body?" I asked after I had given him a cigarette. "Was there any trace?"

"None."

"We went to Lati," I told him, feeling it my duty to protect Father Joseph, "but the villagers were very cautious."

Ourbri clicked his tongue.

"The Prefect has put out a reward for the body," he said. "The body will come back."

"Wouldn't it be just as well to let it go?"

"No, the law was broken."

"You won't get it, of course. The body will remain hidden."

"Perhaps, but people always need money. The Prefect has gone to see the Mother Superior to find out if she will match the reward. If that happens, then it will be almost irresistible."

"But gris-gris is working against it. Anyone who reports the body will be taking his life into his hands, won't he?" I asked, baiting Ourbri.

"Gris-gris is nonsense."

"You think so?"

"Of course," he said. "Once when I was a little boy a scorpion dancer came to my village. He put the head of a live scorpion in his mouth and he danced in a trance around the fire. Look as you might, you couldn't see his feet move. Perhaps his toes pulled him, or some vibration. Or perhaps, when we all looked at his mouth, ready to see the scorpion sting him, his feet shuffled in the dirt. It was an illusion."

"Why didn't the scorpion sting him?"

"Who knows? I think he squeezed it just enough with his teeth so that some impulse went down the insect's body, and the scorpion flattened. But the people were convinced he was a magic man and they ran forward and put money on his head. They licked the money so it would stick on the scorpion dancer's forehead and sometimes he flung his sweat at them. If his sweat touched you, scorpions never bothered you again."

"A man painted white ran beside my truck last night," I said. Ourbri nodded.

"That's it. That's it exactly. That's why I'm here. The Prefect asked me to come and explain how some of our people might behave."

"What did it mean?"

"The man running beside the truck? Nothing. Nothing to you, at any rate. An old man died near Boromo and runners were sent out to let his kinsmen know. At night, to keep spirits away, he painted himself white."

"That's all?"

Ourbri nodded, then stood to go. I walked him to his truck. He saluted me before climbing in, and I saw his eyes move again to the fetish around my neck.

"Did someone give you that?" Ourbri asked, raising his chin to indicate the fetish.

"Yes."

"It's foolishness."

"I thought I would just wear it for a time."

"Do what you like, but if you wear it you become part of it, do you see? Nassarra are protected from this. If you wear it, you admit it could have some influence on you."

"I think I'll wear it anyway."

Ourbri climbed back in his truck. I waved him off, not quite

sure what the purpose of his visit had been. Perhaps he had come
to warn me of unusual behavior, but his impatience with stories
of gris-gris made me suspect otherwise. I had the impression he
had come on official orders from the Prefect and that the conversation had been dictated to him beforehand.

NEAR TEN, I climbed in my truck and drove to Hamaria's bar
searching for Fatama. The sun was hot, but there were clouds to
the south. The clouds were black and heavy, and if I squinted I
saw squalls of rain approaching as if across the sea.

Hamaria was not there. His wife, Catherine, stood behind the
bar, idly waving a horse tail at flies. Peter played on a tuna can
which he had fashioned into a finger piano. He plucked individual
pieces of metal and they resonated in the hollow shell of the can.

"Good morning," I said to Catherine, and shook her hand.
She touched her fingers to her chest and genuflected as African
women always did. Yet with her it was only a gesture. She was
not at all submissive.

"A beer?" she asked.

"Yes, please. Where is Hamaria?"

"Gone to Koudougou to do his ordering," she said, getting
the beer from the canary. She held the beer out to me and let me
feel if it was cold enough. I nodded and she opened it.

"Have you seen Fatama?" I asked.

"No. Haven't you?"

"Was she in last night?"

Catherine looked quickly at Peter, then shook her head. She
didn't say anything else. Her posture made it evident she wasn't
willing to discuss things with me.

Awhile later a 404 Peugeot pulled in and the Mother Superior stepped out. She hurried into the bar, moving remarkably well for an older woman, her driver barely beating her to the door in order to open it.

"*Ne Zabre*," she said in More to Catherine. "*Wena con biego,* God give you tomorrow."

"*Ne Zabre*," Catherine answered, and went around the bar to shake the Mother Superior's hand.

"Good afternoon," the Mother Superior said, turning to me. "I've run into you quite a bit in the last few days, haven't I?"

"It's been my pleasure," I said.

"Well, I hope you don't take pleasure in the death of one of our priests?"

She said this with such a tranquil expression that it was impossible to tell if she was joking. She smiled, then went over to Peter and tried to play his finger piano.

There was something about the presence of the Mother Superior, the building pressure from the storm, that seemed to take air out of the room. I wanted it to rain. I wanted a breeze to start, but instead we simply heard thunder. The Mother Superior eventually ordered orange soda for herself and her driver, then took a table by the door where she could watch the advance of the storm. She sat alone. Once she started at a tag of thunder, and I noted with interest that she was not as old as I had thought the night before. Her skin was somewhat the worse for years in the tropics, but her eyes contained a large kindness, a willingness to be of service. However, there was a certain hunger to her eyes as well. She glanced rapidly in many directions, taking things in, and I realized, watching her, that her kindness could very easily be calculated. She possessed an element of theater that priests and nuns sometimes have. She was aware of making an impression while making it, so that nothing seemed entirely genuine about her.

She called for me to join her a little later. Without knowing why, I was reluctant to do so, but I saw no way out.

"Now tell me, it was here, wasn't it, that Fraujas expired?" she asked when I sat. "In the back rooms?"

"Yes."

"So sad to die that way. It's always a pity for a priest to die without confession."

She said this with her eyes on the storm, but I thought I perceived a glimmer of humor in her expression. Did she know about my charade as a priest? Father Joseph had known, and if he had found out, then certainly the Mother Superior would know as well.

I decided to tell her the truth.

"I was with him when he died. I'm afraid I pretended to be a priest so that he would die feeling at peace."

"And did he?"

"No, he was weak but excited. He asked me to protect him."

The wind came in stronger gusts. The Mother Superior's veil blew back and a glass rolled somewhere on the surface of a table. Peter played more quietly on the finger piano.

"This rain will pass quickly," the Mother Superior said, "but at least the day will be that much cooler. Would you say he was afraid?"

"Yes, I think so."

"Of death, or something in life?"

"Of something in life."

"Of gris-gris?"

"I couldn't be sure," I said.

She took a sip of soda and leaned forward to see the sky beyond the doorway.

"Would you say he knew he was going to die?" she asked.

"Again, I couldn't be sure."

"I've always been told a man about to die lets go of this life very easily. You've heard I knew Fraujas? I knew him when he first came to Africa. We were both very young."

"So Father Fraujas was here?"

"Here in Tenado, yes, for a time. But he was a man who didn't like discipline of any kind. He didn't care for even the few regulations the mission had in order to make things run more smoothly. He asked permission to go off by himself and we granted it."

"He went to Dori?"

"Yes, but he spent most of his time hunting near the border of Benin. That's really what he was, you see. He didn't have the priestly temperament. He was a wolf, not a shepherd. That's a cliché by now, isn't it, but most men can be divided into those two categories. He was a carnivore."

The rain began. Wind came up out of the south carrying with it the scent of rice and palm oil and mud. Catherine opened a door on the other side of the bar and we gained a fine cross breeze. I ordered another beer and asked the Mother Superior if she would drink a second soda, but she refused.

"Why do you think his body was taken?" I asked. "What do you think he was running from?"

"Running from?"

"Yes. Why come here after spending so long in the bush?"

"I don't know. Maybe he wished to die with his own kind. Maybe he wanted to confess out of worry for his immortal soul. You're not a Catholic, are you?"

"I was."

"Then perhaps you believe in the soul?"

"I'm not sure."

"I never know whether such doubt is wise or cowardly. In any case, Fraujas might very well have believed in his soul. If he did, he would have wanted to come back for confession and Extreme Unction. Whatever he became, he was a priest for twenty years."

"I still don't understand why they took his body," I said.

"I don't either. I don't really understand the Africans even after spending a good part of my life here. They do it among themselves, as you know, so why not a priest?"

She took a large breath of the fresh air and continued. "I don't mean to equate the two in any respect, but saintly relics were used in the Middle Ages for the same purpose. People believed the relics contained power and they built their cathedrals around them. It's still possible to see entire corpses, long since past any real resemblance to a human form, beneath altars in some of the finest cathedrals in the world."

"Why do they want me, then?" I asked.

"Do they want you?"

"Several people have told me to be cautious."

"Who?" she asked.

"I'd rather not say."

"To be cautious of what exactly?"

"Of gris-gris. Of my soul, I think you would say."

The Mother Superior said nothing, but once again I felt the smallest doubt in her sincerity. Her eyes moved too quickly while her body took on a practiced calm. It reminded me of Ourbri and the feeling that he had been sticking close to a script of some sort.

"Possession? Is that what you're saying?" she asked.

"Yes."

"It's possible they believe Fraujas somehow passed his soul on to you. I'll go that far. I know the Africans believe that the great land priests in their villages try to send their souls into other creatures when they sense they are dying. They slaughter a chief's dogs, for example, when he dies. It's an interesting theory."

The rain let up enough to allow the Mother Superior to call her driver and prepare to leave. I said good-bye, insisted on paying for her drinks, then watched her out the door. She was gone a moment later, her truck splashing through large puddles as it made its way out to Po. I knew she had come deliberately to speak to me. She knew something about Fraujas that I didn't know, but I doubted she would ever tell me.

FATHER JOSEPH CAME BY in his truck three days later with a report that Fraujas's cassock had been found. He was going to see it and asked if I wanted to go along.

We drove to Boromo, where I had seen the naked runner. The road was excellent for two or three kilometers outside of Tenado, but then we came to rutted cart tracks and had to follow the path slowly. Occasionally I had to climb out and go down on my hands and knees to see if the truck would bottom on a particularly bad rut.

"I saw the Mother Superior a few days ago," I said when we had reached the flat approach to Boromo.

"Did you? Where was she?"

"In Hamaria's bar."

"She came to see you?"

"I think so, but I don't know why. I wanted to ask her if she had matched the Prefect's reward for the body."

"She did. She won't let this go. She doesn't like you, you know?"

"I didn't know."

He looked over and grinned.

"You're not offended?" he asked.

"Why should I be? I don't think she really knows me."

"Of course she doesn't, but she says she doesn't trust you. She didn't take your dressing up like a priest lightly."

"It was for a good cause."

"The Mother Superior doesn't believe in circumstantial morality. Things are right or wrong. She has a very comfortable outlook on the world. It doesn't allow much waffling."

"And I was wrong to wear a collar?"

"To her, yes. Perhaps if she thought you had taken it more seriously, I think that's it, then she wouldn't be as cross with you. She thinks you probably wore the collar with a good dose of mockery."

"I did," I said.

"See? The Mother Superior was right all along."

We reached the outskirts of Boromo. To the north, perhaps two hundred yards off the road, we saw a large group of people standing around a kapok tree. When they saw us they began to yell, and the smaller children, mostly boys, ran across the field waving their throwing sticks and pointing behind them at the white cassock I now saw spread out and crucified on the tree.

"They haven't even taken it down," Father Joseph said, turning off the ignition. We got out and walked to meet the children and villagers.

A few old women, mostly toothless with bright orange gums from chewing kola, went down on their knees and touched their foreheads to the ground. The younger women made a loud trilling sound with their tongues. This was the sound that accompanied births and deaths, and it was odd to hear it now, plain and clear in the bright sunlight.

"They won't touch it," Father Joseph said, nodding at the cassock. "It would stay there until it rotted if it were up to them."

We entered the crowd, shaking hands, nodding and greeting everyone. Only after a few minutes did I actually get to inspect the cassock. I knew at first glance it was Fraujas's. The cloth had been baked in sunlight until the faint marks of his cuts had worked through the fibers. Pale pink triangles were linked in even scales running the better part of his body. One of the pockets had been turned out like a white ear from the slim cheek of the material.

But the arms gathered my full attention. They were pulled back in the form of crucifixion, wide and even, the forward thrust of the breast supplied by the branches behind the cassock. The bottom hem had been tied down so that the legs might also be spread-eagled. This was not the slim, almost elegant body of Christ I was accustomed to seeing, but a man being tortured in final agony.

I looked at the cassock so closely that I didn't realize the people had suddenly become quiet. They were obviously frightened by the cassock; the crowd became thinner as we moved closer to the tree.

"What do you think?" I asked Father Joseph.

"I have no idea," he said. "It was done with thought, that's certain."

"Is it a message?"

"What else could it be? I'd like William to look at this. He has more experience in these things than any of us."

"Should we leave it up?"

"No. They'll think we're afraid. If possible, I think it's best to make light of it."

Father Joseph stepped forward and tugged at the hem of the cassock. The entire tree bent slightly, and the cloth started to tear free. He pulled harder and the cloth ripped with a loud sound, the villagers moving back as the material fell. They didn't want to be touched by any portion of the cassock, and a few boys actually ran well into the field beyond the tree to avoid it.

I didn't want to touch it myself. My revulsion was more than can be explained by calling the cloth a shroud. To go close to it called for conscious persuasion, the type of concentration one must muster before jumping off a high cliff or platform into water. As I moved, I was aware of the different parts of my body I called on, so that I couldn't reach out to help Father Joseph fold the cassock without thinking, now my hands are touching the material, now my thigh has brushed it, now my forearm.

"I've never seen anything like this before," Father Joseph said, shaken, I think, as much by the reaction of the Africans as by the cassock itself.

We folded the cassock like a flag between us, walking closer and bending the cloth into a rough triangular shape. With each fold the Africans moved in, some of them going near the tree to see if anything else was visible.

"The Mother Superior will bury this until she has something else," Father Joseph said when we had the cassock folded. I was grateful that he held the cloth under his arm.

Out of a sense of protocol, and perhaps to cover himself with the Mother Superior, Father Joseph repeated the offer of a reward.

The villagers listened, raising their voices when the amount was mentioned, then turning to talk quickly to one another. No, no one had seen anything, one of the older men told us. No, they had no idea how the cassock had come to be in the tree. Yes, they would tell us if they knew anything at all.

The conversation was predictable; I hardly listened. Instead, I circled the tree, examining it from every angle while Father Joseph shook hands in preparation of leaving.

"Did you see anything?" Father Joseph asked me back in the truck.

"No. It seemed empty."

"Do you know I once visited a village where a baobab on the edge of town had been designated as a fetish tree. They had hung all sorts of magic from the tree—pieces of cloth, bicycle spokes, little sacks of pulverized bone. There was a maribou there who dominated half the tree. A great land priest. People went to him and asked for prayers and favors, that sort of thing, and the priest used his half of the tree as a bulletin board. I know it sounds odd, but it's true. Anyway, whenever he hung something from the tree he also found a viper and hung it beside the fetish. He took a sharp thorn from an acacia bush and pierced the snake through the tail, perhaps five or six centimeters from where the body actually ended. He tied this thorn to the baobab branch in such a way that most of the snake's body was free, yet the tail was securely anchored. The snake died eventually, of course, but for a time it was an excellent guardian of whatever magic he had put in the tree. Anyone who was unsuspecting would be bitten, because the snake normally entwined itself over the branch, making it virtually invisible."

"But when the snake died, whoever wanted to could take the fetish down," I said.

"By then it had granted whatever favor or power it had been designed to give. Besides, the snakes were eventually picked apart by birds. They hung limp in the trees, still attached by the thorn through their remaining cartilage until a wind shook them free. But sometimes the wind didn't shake them hard enough and on the priest's half of the tree there would be ten or fifteen skeletons of poisonous snakes all hanging like tinsel. It was powerful, I promise you."

Father Joseph looked strangely at me. "Are you telling me this to frighten me?"

"Not at all," he said, his voice conciliatory. "I thought you were interested in gris-gris."

"I'm not necessarily interested in gris-gris. I'm not even sure it exists."

"But, if it exists," he said, "imagine how much more complex the world becomes. If one thing exists outside the natural world, then anything might exist. That's the thought that intrigues me."

"Of course it intrigues you, you're a priest."

Father Joseph shrugged and asked me to get out to watch the truck pass over a severe rut. I squatted next to the truck and waved him on slowly. When I climbed back in, we let the topic go.

IT WAS THE NIGHT after we had taken down the cassock that I began to feel them fish my dreams. It was very subtle; at first I didn't believe it had actually happened. I woke in the middle of the night to feel a tremendous longing to be somewhere—I didn't know where—and an impatience to be moving to it at that moment. It was strong, remarkably strong, and it stayed with me even after I was fully awake. It took considerable effort to remain in bed. My impulse was to be up and gone.

When I put my head down again I saw a mountain and wild animals, African animals, moving through the brush. I couldn't call it a dream. I was awake, staring straight up at my mosquito net. The house was dark and I heard an occasional bat fly through the rooms, always in the same pattern, its wings ever so lightly touching the tin siding that had been lashed down as a roof.

In the morning I woke slowly, feeling almost drugged; I found it exceedingly difficult to get out of bed. I thought of malaria, or perhaps some other type of fever, and I took a thermometer and held it under my tongue for the prescribed time. My temperature was normal, but I couldn't shake the tremendous lethargy I felt. Oddly, however, the lethargy was combined with an astonishing restlessness. It grew throughout the morning, climbing in me and holding me until I finally forced myself to step out of the house and face the bright sun.

What I experienced, I told myself, was merely the effect of isolation on any spirit. Too much thinking, too much self-reflection, too much self-analysis. The gris-gris had entered my thoughts now, and with little else to distract me, I had woven it into the threads of my daily life without being aware of doing so. Chess could do the same thing. So could roulette, or black jack—any game that demanded concentration could gradually cause the player to become preoccupied with it. As a boy, when I had played chess a great deal, I went to sleep dreaming of bishops angling across the board, or knights forking a rook and king. My preoccupation with gris-gris was nothing more, I concluded. It would pass if I could give my mind another theme to work.

But that wasn't easy. There was no radio, no television, no phone or amusement of any kind. I might read, but reading called for concentration. I was afraid reading would trigger another round of thoughts. I didn't want to be inward; I wanted something outward, a run, a game, something to get me out of myself.

Fortunately, Ourbri arrived to distract me. He came in the late afternoon as the day turned unbearably hot. He drove his pickup, and in the back, shackled to the spare tire, was a young boy about fifteen years old. The boy looked miserable. He was gaunt; his shorts and shirt were badly tattered. He had obviously been beaten by Ourbri, because each time Ourbri leaned against the flatbed the boy flinched. When I inspected the boy more closely, I saw large purple welts on his arms and shoulders.

"What did he do?" I asked after I had greeted Ourbri.

"He was caught stealing in the Boromo market. I'm taking him into Koudougou."

"What will they do with him?"

"They'll grind him into pieces, won't they?" he said and flicked his hand at the boy. "He won't last long."

I had often seen Africans behave with calm cruelty toward someone in their power, and I wasn't particularly shocked by it now. Once, more than a year ago, I had seen a thief stoned to death in a large marketplace. Children and women had thrown stones along with the men. They had thrown stones long after the boy had crumpled on the ground.

"I stopped because the Prefect wanted me to tell you we've discovered Fraujas's body. An informer confessed everything."

"Where was it?" I asked.

"It was being sold out in a small village—out by Lati, where you went with Father Joseph that day. The body was kept underground and sold in bits and pieces. We found what was left."

"Sold for gris-gris?"

Ourbri nodded. "This makes an educated man like me, an African functionaire, appear ridiculous. My people embarrass me with their superstitions."

"Has the mission been informed?"

"Someone was sent. The Prefect wanted you to know, and since I was coming past, I thought I would stop."

"Will they exhume the body for burial?" I asked.

"I don't know," Ourbri said. "That depends on the Mother Superior."

"Are you sure it's him?"

"Yes. I don't want to go into details—it's not very pleasant—but yes, it's him."

Ourbri left a few minutes later. He pulled away, the boy

hunched in his awkward squat, his arm shackled so closely to the tire that he couldn't begin to straighten.

I drank more than I normally did that night. I didn't want to see Fraujas's body. I wanted nothing to do with bringing his body up from the ground. It was enough to imagine what the heat and earth had done to it. Nevertheless, I knew I would go.

The next morning I drove out the Po road, following the same trail I had taken with Father Joseph on our trip to look for the body. A large group of children chased me as I entered the clearing around Lati. They were more animated than usual. This was clearly a day out of the ordinary. They sprinted to get ahead of the truck, shouting "Nassarra, Nassarra," and jumped and leaped to show off for me. They ran toward a group of trucks parked in the shade of a baobab tree. I recognized the Prefect's truck, and a truck belonging to the mission. Beside the trucks was a row of mopeds.

"Where are the others?" I asked the children after I parked and climbed out.

One boy pointed. Another jumped and began to trot in the direction I should take. I followed him.

I smelled the body before I had rounded the corner of the village. I nearly turned back. The smell was of death, but it was something else as well. It smelled of the dampness under a rock, or the cold stench of a cellar recently flooded. It sickened me, and yet it was familiar. A second smell, more shrill, was also present. This was the scent of some chemical, probably lime. It didn't cover the stench of the body entirely; it underlined the odor somehow, making it at once both more palatable and lurid.

The group—the Prefect and Ourbri, Fathers Joseph, William, and Claude, as well as two African chiefs I didn't recognize—stood near a small copse of acacia trees on a slight incline above the village. They formed a half circle and examined something at their feet. An African man of about fifty had been staked out on the ground. He moaned as I approached, but no one seemed to notice. Instead, they concentrated on the object. I didn't have to see it to know it was Fraujas's body.

I didn't look directly at the body for some time. When I glanced at it, I saw a blanket had been draped over the corpse. The contours of the blanket fell in gruesome depressions which clearly marked the separation between the legs, an arm extended, the head and neck tilted to one side. The smell was overwhelming. Lime had been sprinkled across the blanket and over much of the grave area; the sandals of the entire group were powdered white. Tracks circled the grave and led off in various directions, gradually disappearing as if formed of snow. Heat touched everything; flies collected in masses until the Prefect motioned for Ourbri to flick them away.

"Well, he's come up at last," Father William said. The conversation, I realized, resumed along the track it had followed before my arrival. "It was only a matter of time. A reward like that . . ."

"Does the Mother Superior know?" I asked.

"Yes," William said.

"Do you want to see the body, Nassarra?" Ourbri asked me.

"No, it isn't necessary."

"You would be amazed at its condition," Claude said. "They treated the skin with arsenic to keep the insects off. They preserved it. It almost looks as though they smoked it."

"I'm ashamed of my people," the Prefect said.

The two chiefs agreed with the Prefect. It was scandalous. They would talk to their people about it. Such superstition wasn't healthy.

They made these speeches out of deference to us. Father Joseph, I noticed, nodded but didn't look at them. Only the Prefect took the remarks seriously. To have the chiefs volunteer to intercede with the villages removed considerable responsibility from him. Otherwise he would be obliged to hold town meetings and bluster and threaten the villagers. To have the chiefs take care of such things was infinitely better.

"Who is the man on the ground?" I asked.

"One of your *nyanga*. A magic man," Father Joseph said. "He haunted this hill—at least that's what the villagers believed. He engineered the theft of the body."

"Was he selling it?" I asked.

"Yes, but he must have had help."

"What powers did he say the body possessed?"

"The normal things," said Father Joseph. "Virility, long life, magical cures. This was very powerful gris-gris. I've never heard of such prices. The teeth, they said, could be rolled to tell the future—it was supposed to be infallible."

"We should decide what to do with the body," Father William said. "In this heat it will go even if they have cured it somehow."

"We can post a guard at this grave," the Prefect said. "I can leave Ourbri here to see to it that the body is not disturbed again."

"For how long?" Father Claude asked. "A week? A month? Someone will dig it up for the bones."

"We should bring it to the mission," Father Joseph said. "The Mother Superior would want it that way."

There was nothing for it but to lift the body into Father Joseph's truck. The Prefect ordered Ourbri to bring a group of villagers to do the work, but the priests stopped him and said they would do it. It was a disgusting operation. First Father Joseph backed his truck into position. Then, slowly, the body was lifted so that a second blanket could be placed beneath it. I didn't look to see what condition the body was in, but the priests cursed repeatedly and their tempers grew short. When the body was squarely on the blanket, they asked Ourbri and me to take the middle positions, and at the count of three we lifted.

The blanket sagged. The body was light, but it seemed like an egg of liquid in the wool of the blanket. We shuffled to the flatbed and slowly slid the body into position. Each movement caused the odor of the body to be released; lime puffed up at every shift of position.

Father Claude closed the back gate on the truck. Father Joseph climbed into the flatbed and bound the blanket more securely around the body. It would be bounced about, he explained. He didn't know how it would hold together.

When the body was secured, we went to where the African man lay. He was about fifty years old, average size, but extremely well proportioned. His face was cut with ritual scars which ran horizontally on his cheeks, giving to his features an expression of constant surprise. His hands were tied behind his back; his ankles were tightly bound, and a third piece of rawhide connected the two. He couldn't move at all, and the entire left side of his body was coated with lime.

Ourbri kicked him; the man tried to inch away. He didn't look fearful. He was uncomfortable, obviously, but his movements were shrewd. He groveled as well as he could, but it was an extremely practical thing to do, tactical beyond Ourbri's understanding. Ourbri kicked him again.

"What do you want me to do with him?" Ourbri asked the Prefect.

"He'll have to be brought to Koudougou."

"Have we asked him everything we need to know?" Father William inquired. "We won't have the chance again."

"He won't tell us who helped him," Father Joseph said.

I looked closely at the man. He hadn't been beaten. This surprised me, especially since Ourbri had a sadistic streak. It was possible Ourbri was frightened of the man. Furthermore, it was probable even the Prefect preferred to treat him humanely because he couldn't be sure of his power.

But this didn't shock me as much as what happened next. Imperceptibly at first, I saw, in full daylight, the man take on the reptilian features that I had seen in Fraujas. It didn't happen for more than an instant; no one else saw it, I was certain. Yet it was there, the same sense of evil I had first witnessed in Fraujas. It might almost have been a shadow cast by a cloud crossing the sun, so fast did it occur. I couldn't even swear that it had happened. It was there, then gone. The *nyanga* looked at me and communicated nothing.

I recovered by forcing myself into the conversation with the priests, who were all agreed now that nothing else could be done with the *nyanga*. He should be sent to prison in Koudougou. Ourbri would take him immediately.

The priests left, driving carefully to keep the body from jostling. I walked with the Prefect to our trucks. Ourbri ran ahead and drove his truck back for the *nyanga*.

"It's a terrible thing, isn't it?" the Prefect said to me as we walked. "We won't progress in this country until we do away with these old ways."

"You no longer believe in gris-gris?" I asked.

"As a psychological force, yes. As a spiritual power, no. I was educated in France, and one day, in Notre Dame, I saw a woman with a twisted back lighting candles. It's the same thing, isn't it?"

"Sometimes the twisted backs are cured."

"Not by magic, surely. By belief perhaps. That woman had great belief. It caused her pain even to lift up the long taper and light the candle."

"Maybe she wasn't wishing for a straight back," I suggested.

"Maybe not. But if I was in her position, it's what I would wish for," the Prefect finished.

I WAS INVITED for the interment a day later. The body could wait no longer. Even as I arrived, François, the cook, still worked in the grave. A small boy helped him; together they had succeeded in deepening the original hole to a respectable depth. The soil was heavily laced with laterite. It had been difficult digging, I was sure, and it was an accomplishment to have it done in a day.

I found Father Joseph sitting alone on the back porch.

"I'll be happy when the body's gone," he told me as I sat beside him. "The dogs howled all last night."

"I didn't smell him when I pulled up."

"He's covered in lime and they've put him in a wooden casket. A carpent up in Boromo knew how to put one together. He was a carpenter in France during World War Two, of all things. It's beautifully done—almost airtight."

"Was there a coffin last time?"

"No, the body was just wrapped in a sheet. It's the usual practice. This carpenter up in Boromo has done a few for us in the past, but to tell the truth, I thought he had died. The Mother Superior found him."

Father Claude came out to say the Mother Superior was ready. Evidently the Prefect had arrived at the front of the mission and had been inside for the last five minutes. Was the grave finished? Was it arranged properly, with some sort of tarp over the loose earth?

Father Joseph and I went to inspect the work while Claude went back inside to say it would just be a few more minutes. François stopped digging at our approach. He was in a good five feet, up to his chest, and one glance was enough to know the soil beneath was increasingly blocked with laterite. He knocked the blade of the shovel against it to show us the sparks created by any attempt to dig. This was as deep as he could go.

"Tell the boy to bring a blanket," Father Joseph instructed. "Is the cement ready?"

"Yes, Nassarra," François said.

François climbed out, propping the shovel against the side of the grave and using it as a ladder. He put a loose white shirt on over his sweaty chest. Flecks of dirt remained on his face and arms, but he didn't seem to mind. When the boy returned with an old blanket, he stretched the cloth over the dirt and pinned it in place with four heavy stones.

After the dirt was secured, François freshened the mixed cement in an old wheelbarrow. The boy brought water and added it on François's command. When the cement reached the proper consistency, François entered the grave once more. He stood on one side of the hole and poured out the buckets handed him by the boy. Deftly, he created a rough floor, perhaps two or three inches thick.

"The Mother Superior insisted on the cement," Father Joseph said.

"Did the body actually resist decomposition?"

"It appears so. You know, Claude believes they treated it with poison, but it's hard to say."

The boy was sent to tell the group inside that we were ready. A few moments later the Prefect came out, holding the door for the Mother Superior. Fathers Claude and William followed.

The entire group waited on the porch until the casket was brought around the house. Ourbri and three other guards carried the casket on their shoulders. They marched in step, their posture excellent, their eyes straight forward. Their rigidity and military bearing seemed out of place, yet I realized this was in some way compensation for the Mother Superior. The Prefect was showing what respect he could.

The group on the porch fell in behind the casket as it passed. At a command by Ourbri, the guards raised their hands to the coffin and slowly lowered it into the grave.

Ourbri and the guards moved away and stood at attention. Fathers Claude and William came to stand by Father Joseph. The Prefect remained with the Mother Superior. He held a handkerchief in his hand which he frequently applied to his forehead. I was across from them.

Father William said the final blessing. It was a short ceremony. He sprinkled the coffin with holy water, made the sign of the cross, and in Latin intoned the phrase, "From dust to dust." We all said amen.

I watched the Mother Superior closely throughout the ceremony. She showed no emotion. She was cordial when the ceremony ended.

"We will cover the casket in cement, and that way nothing

can get at it," she assured the Prefect. "As kind as you are to offer it, there is no need of a guard."

"But really—" he began.

"There's no need. We can see the grave from the back of the mission. Our help comes and goes, and one of us is almost always back here because of the garden. It would be impossible for a man to dig up the body now unless he had several days."

"Well, yes, that's true," the Prefect conceded.

We stayed while the cement was poured over the coffin. It was as if each of us wished to witness the final act of Fraujas's entombment. Starting at the foot of the grave, François worked the cement carefully along the length of the hole. To speed the work and to stretch the cement he wedged rocks against the walls of the pit.

When the lid of the coffin was covered, the Mother Superior gave him a plain wooden cross to place in the damp mortar. François was forced to lie on his belly and stretch across the grave, but he managed to get the cross properly positioned.

At three o'clock I left and drove back to Tenado. I felt tired but also relieved. I stopped at Hamaria's and drank two beers. Hamaria avoided conversation with me, but I didn't care. I watched him sweep the floor of the bar with a damp clump of millet stalks.

Afterward I went home and found Fatama waiting for me. I didn't believe it was her at first. Her hair had streaks of white in it; her eyes looked cold and dull. Her pagna was ripped and torn in places.

As I approached she moved to avoid me. She placed a chair between us. I walked slowly toward her. A string of cartilage strained in quick flashes along her neck.

"I need money to go to Ghana," was all she said by way of greeting.

"Will you sit down?" I said, trying to make my voice soothing.

She shook her head as if I were trying to lure her closer. She was terrified of me. Her movements rested just on the edge of panic. Had I made any sudden motion, I was certain she would run. I consciously made my voice even softer.

"What happened to you?" I asked.

"The *nyanga* came for my soul."

"Are they still after you?"

"No, they're after you," she said.

"Was Fraujas a *nyanga?*"

"The most powerful," she said. "You should never have listened to his confession."

She nodded and clicked her tongue as if someone not present had spoken to her. The tick stretched her neck muscles again.

"What will you do in Ghana?" I asked.

"I'll dance for men."

I took money out of my wallet and gave it to her. She wouldn't take it from my hand. I placed it on the table. It was a small fortune for her, but she didn't even count it. She put it between her breasts, then moved in a slow circle away from me. She kept her face turned to me. She seemed frightened to turn her back.

"I'm not a *nyanga,*" I said.

"You have Fraujas's soul."

"He's buried now. He's gone."

"Are you sure that was his body?" she asked, still backing away.

"Of course."

"Did you look at it?"

"No. The others did."

She smiled, then walked out of the compound. I listened to her go off, her sandals flapping against her feet.

I DROVE TO KOUDOUGOU in the morning. I needed money and supplies. It was only thirty kilometers from Tenado and I arrived when the sun was just gaining heat. The streets were brown and dusty. To the west, visible from the main avenue, was a large balfon where villagers and prisoners mined mud for bricks. The balfon was empty except for a few donkeys that waded in the water, now and then drinking and rolling in the sandy shore.

I ate breakfast at an outside stand created from an old door propped between two empty oil drums. I had several mangoes and dark coffee. Afterward I sat in the sun and smoke cigarettes. I thought of Fatama but couldn't come to any conclusion about what she had said. I hadn't meant to put her in danger. Although I didn't give much credence to her warning, I didn't doubt she believed in the *nyanga*'s power. I decided to go see the prisoner accused of selling parts of Fraujas's corpse. I didn't quite know what I would say to him, but it seemed possible I could scare him and any others in his group into leaving Fatama alone.

The Gendarmerie was an old colonial building, erected when the French were still in power. Bougainvillea grew over the entire south wall. A tall flagpole stood near the front door, but something had happened to the pulleys which raised and lowered the flag. As a result the flag was tied directly to the pole and hung limply against the metal.

There were two men standing guard when I climbed the steps to the wide porch. The porch must have been an excellent place to sit at one time, but now the paint was chipped from the walls and roof. Lizards passing over the curled paint made a sound like a deer stepping on leaves. There were no normal chairs or tables. Boxes were positioned in different places so that a wall or pillar might form a backrest. A deck of cards was spread out on a plank of lumber balanced between the outer wall of the porch and a windowsill.

The guards attempted to greet me officially, but they couldn't quite pull it off. One man was very young and appeared extremely tentative. The other man, a sergeant, was wide and gruff, apparently uneasy with protocol. He was flustered by my appearance and stood too long in salute.

"Welcome, Nassarra," he told me. "How can we help you?"

"I wanted to find out if I could see a prisoner."

"Which one?"

"A man brought here a day or two ago from Tenado."

"Yes, Nassarra, a young boy and an older man. The man was from Lati."

"Yes, that's the one."

"He is no longer here."

"Where is he?"

"He escaped."

I looked closely at the man. I knew very well the cruelty of the African police and I didn't believe for a moment that anyone could escape them. If he was gone, they had let him escape. The guard didn't allow himself any expression.

"Is the boy still here? The thief from Boromo?" I asked.

"Yes, Nassarra. Do you want to see him?"

"Please."

"He is being chained for today's work. Will you come around back?"

Behind the house, twenty or thirty men stood in the early sunlight. All of them were malnourished; all of them carried the scars of multiple beatings. Each wore a shackle around his right leg. In many instances the shackle had rubbed against the man's ankle until a wound opened permanently. These wounds, in turn, were infected, so that many of the men's legs were actually swollen around the band of the shackle. Looking closely, it was difficult to see where the ankle gave way to metal.

The men were being prepared for a day mining mud. A guard was in the process of stringing a heavy chain down the line. He handed each man the end of the chain, and the prisoner strung it through his own shackle, then handed it back to the guard. The prisoners didn't hesitate. The guard carried a whip with him, which he constantly tapped against his leg.

The boy I searched for was near the end of the line. The sergeant called him over before he was chained in with the other men. He was thinner now and he had obviously suffered frequent beatings. A cut was open over his right eye, wide enough to reveal a suggestion of the bone beneath. Flies moved to it whenever the boy rested his arms at his sides.

"This Nassarra wants to speak with you," the guard said.

The boy nodded and said nothing.

"I'd like to speak to him privately," I told the guard. "Would you let us walk over to the edge of the clearing?"

The sergeant considered, then agreed. He told the boy not to think of escaping. If he attempted to flee he would be caught and killed.

The boy waited for me to move. I walked in front of him to the edge of the clearing and waited until he joined me. He wasn't easy to be near. He smelled badly and his wound was definitely infected. Combined with this was a tremendous sense of lassitude. He was a prisoner and he could look forward to working until he died.

"I want to ask you about the other prisoner," I said when we stopped. "The man who was brought from Lati."

"He's gone," the boy said.

"How did he escape?"

The boy shrugged.

"Did they let him go?" I asked. "I know he was *nyanga*."

The boy looked at me closely, then said, "They couldn't keep him."

"Why not?"

"Because he was *nyanga*. He was too strong for them. They would have had to keep him off the ground."

"What do you mean?"

"If he could touch the ground, then he had his powers. They would have had to keep him suspended in the air."

"Did he threaten them with gris-gris?"

"I don't know."

"Did he spend the night, or did he get away immediately?"

"The first night, Nassarra."

"Did they go after him?"

The boy smiled. You didn't pursue *nyanga,* I understood. I waited for him to go on, but he was quiet. The subject was closed as far as he was concerned.

Back at the chain gang, he was linked in at the rear. Another guard passed down the line and handed out dabas, small hand hoes which the prisoners needed to make the bricks. Every other man was given a tool. The boy didn't receive one.

I walked with the sergeant to the front of the house. He was more calm with me now that he had seen my reason for coming. I wasn't there for the government, nor was I a religious representative come to argue for humane treatment. The sergeant had classified me and he no longer worried what I thought of his work. I tried to take advantage of this. I waited until the right moment, then asked a question as casually as I could.

"How did the man from Lati escape?" I asked as we stood at my truck.

"We don't know. He was locked up in the night, but he wasn't there in the morning."

"Did any others escape?"

"No, Nassarra, just him."

"It doesn't seem possible, does it?"

"The guard on duty has been reprimanded," the sergeant said.

"Does the Prefect know?"

"Yes, Nassarra."

"The prisoner was a *nyanga,* wasn't he?"

"A *nyanga?*" the sergeant asked, but he was transparent.

"A witch man."

"I don't know, Nassarra. Is that what you believe?"

I thanked him and left. I drove back toward Tenado, taking a short detour to the Prefect's office. Ourbri was on the front porch, half dozing in the afternoon heat. The scent of bougainvillea was everywhere. The white elephant skulls in front of the building gleamed in the sunlight.

"Nassarra," Ourbri said, coming awake at the sound of the truck. "It's good to see you."

"Is the Prefect in?" I asked, climbing the stairs.

"Yes, but he's quite busy."

"I wanted to ask him about the man who escaped."

"Escaped?" Ourbri asked, looking genuinely surprised.

"The man who sold fetishes."

"He didn't escape. We've had no report of it."

"I was just in Koudougou and the sergeant there told me the man was gone."

Ourbri asked me to wait. He went inside and returned a few minutes later. The Prefect would see me.

The Prefect had the tired, pale look of an alcoholic. Slightly annoyed, he rose to meet me. The business of the priest had gone on too long and had become a burden. Now I was here again asking for information, and I sensed his reluctance to go into detail.

"I came to ask you about the man from Lati, the one accused of selling fetishes," I told him after he had asked me to sit.

The Prefect drew a pad of paper toward him. He looked down at the paper and appeared to study it.

"I think perhaps he was moved on to Ouagadougou," he said at last. "I don't have the orders here, but the prison isn't my responsibility."

"The sergeant at the prison said he escaped."

"Maybe the sergeant wasn't on duty when the man was removed. That's possible, isn't it?"

"He said the man escaped the very first night he was locked up."

"I'm sure he was transferred to Ouagadougou."

The Prefect said this in a tight voice. It was his final word on the subject. I thought to bring up the testimony of the young boy, then realized I might be sentencing the boy to a beating by doing so. I dropped the idea and went on to the next.

"Did you find any of the fetishes?"

"No, the Mother Superior asked that I forget the matter. I think it's time we all did."

"I'm not sure I can."

"Well," the Prefect said, waving a hand over the paper on his desk, "that's up to you. From my standpoint the affair is finished. I'm not sure what you are after, Mr. Hawley. You were involved to a very small degree. You brought the body to our attention and we appreciate that. But you were also present when the body was finally interred. I don't see what else remains to be done."

"Did you inspect the body?"

"Yes, of course."

"And you're certain it was Fraujas?"

"Certainly. Who else should it be?"

"There is a rumor that it wasn't Fraujas's body."

The Prefect stood. I knew I had gone too far. He came around his desk and held out his hand.

"The body is buried and the entire affair is finished. The Mother Superior is satisfied. Father Joseph inspected the body. You seem to be searching for straws, Mr. Hawley. Now, if you'll forgive me."

I shook his hand and left. I couldn't antagonize him and hope to accomplish any work in the region. Besides, I didn't really know why I had come, his answers were so predictable.

MY LIFE REGAINED its rhythm. I picked up temporary work supervising the repair of a dam in Tenkodougou, a small village to the east of Tenado. Occasionally I went to Hamaria's bar, though I wasn't made to feel welcome.

I heard nothing of Fatama. I assumed she had departed for Ghana. I asked Hamaria once, but he shrugged and said she hadn't been in touch with him since she stopped coming to the bar. We didn't go into why she had left.

Father Joseph came by about three weeks after the burial. He came early in the morning, his truck filled with supplies. He often traveled for days in the bush, and it wasn't surprising to see him prepared with a mattress, lamps, food, and cigarettes.

"You've caused me quite an evening," he told me as he came into the compound.

I went to get him coffee while he sat in a wooden chair. He inched it over to the left to place it more squarely in the shade. He didn't explain his first remark at once, but concentrated on lighting a cigarette and making himself comfortable.

"How did I cause you a difficult evening?" I asked when I returned with the coffee.

"The Prefect came to dinner and went on about you," Father Joseph said. "You've made your mark, I promise. The truth is, he'd like to send you home. He's annoyed with you, but he had the Mother Superior nearly convinced it was for your own welfare."

"Annoyed about what?" I asked, sitting.

"He said you asked if we had inspected the body. Isn't that true?"

"Fatama told me it wasn't Fraujas's body."

He blew a long wedge of smoke straight up into the air. I drank some coffee and waited for him to go on. He rubbed his eyes, then threw away his cigarette.

"This is what happened," he said. "A woman came to the mission looking for you. She wouldn't be satisfied with anyone else. She thought you lived with us. She started yelling at everyone in sight. Claude tried to reason with her, then William, and finally the Mother Superior heard the commotion and came to see what was wrong. The woman had a very sick baby on her back and she wouldn't let anyone near it. I honestly thought the child was dead.

There was absolutely no sign of life, nothing at all. Normally the African women are the most pragmatic people on earth, but not this one. The Mother Superior offered to give the baby medicine, but the woman screamed that she wanted to speak with you. You are the inheritor of Fraujas's miraculous powers, you see. That is the rumor in the bush."

"That's ridiculous."

"Not to the Africans," Father Joseph said, unable to cover his impatience with me. "You don't seem to get this, do you? They believe in gris-gris as strongly as I believe in Christ. To make matters worse, the Mother Superior thinks you're encouraging the rumors. I think you've been mixed up in things you really don't understand."

"Well, was it Fraujas's body we buried?" I asked in defense.

"Yes, of course."

"Are you certain?"

Father Joseph looked at me and smiled.

"I couldn't tell a thing," he admitted.

"So it might not have been Fraujas's body?"

"I think it was, but I couldn't swear to it. I thought it was better to have the whole matter ended."

We were obviously at a standstill. Father Joseph switched to another topic.

"Why in the world did you go to the Prefect about the escape?" he asked.

"I visited the prison at Koudougou. The guard there said the *nyanga* had escaped from a locked room in the middle of the night. I think they let him go. I went to the Prefect to see what he knew."

"And what did the Prefect say?"

"That the man was transferred to Ouagadougou. He became angry at my questions."

"You should have known the Prefect would answer according to official channels. For all of his sophistication, he believes in gris-gris as much as the most ignorant villager. Get that through your head once and for all."

He waited a little while before continuing. I lit a cigarette and finished my coffee.

"I'm going to Gambaga. It's a two days' ride. I thought you might want to go for your own peace of mind. I want to determine for myself if Fraujas performed miracles. I doubt that even more now that they've come looking to you for cures . . . forgive me, but whatever Fraujas might have been, I don't think you're a saint. Don't come along if you don't want to. This is something the mission probably should have looked into long ago, as soon as he turned up in Gambaga. The Mother Superior never seemed very interested, though. I never understood that."

There really was no decision to be made. I packed quickly. Father Joseph's only demand was that I bring iodine tablets with which to treat my drinking water. He was low.

We climbed in the truck by mid-afternoon. I wasn't surprised to find Father Joseph's shotgun angled across the passenger's seat. He pulled the gun toward him and kept it leaning against his thigh.

We passed through Koudougou by four, then entered rougher territory to the east. By five we spotted the earliest traces of the Black Volta. The water was down. We pased through several large cattle herds driven by Fulanis. The Fulanis followed the river in its slow bend to the west and north. They moved just ahead of the rainy season, allowing it to catch them and bring new grass.

When the sun began to fade, Father Joseph looked for a place to camp. He was fussy. He wanted clear access to the river, trees for protection against the wind, level ground, and no rotted wood about.

We finally stopped in a fairly sheltered meadow near the river. Wide trees obstructed our view of the water, but at least the camp-site was cool. I left him to the unloading and went to collect wood.

"Ready for a drink?" he asked when I returned. "I brought a bottle of scotch. It almost kills the taste of the iodine in the water."

"I'd love one."

While he fixed my drink, I found some dry grass and started

the fire. Father Joseph lifted down two camp stools and placed them next to the fire. He sat and lit a cigarette.

"What if you could perform a miracle? Have you thought of that?" he asked when I sat down.

"I can't perform a miracle."

"I don't think you can either, but make the leap. Suppose you could. Suppose Fraujas passed along some power to you. What would you do if you found out you could cure the sick?"

"I never considered it. What would you do?" I asked.

"I don't know. That's what interests me about Fraujas. Imagine if he found out he had some miraculous powers—it doesn't matter if he brought them to Africa or acquired them here. What could he have done? If he had gone back to France or Belgium or wherever he was from, what would it have accomplished? The Catholic Church would have investigated him, people would have come from around the world, a thousand scientists would have offered up logical explanations . . . the same old exercises in rational thinking. He would have been placed in the position of defending himself, and maybe he would have been forced to try and explain his gift, though perhaps he didn't understand it himself. He might have been assassinated as a heretic."

"So it makes sense to you that he stayed in a small outpost?" I asked.

"Absolutely. No radio, no TV, no mass communication. Just word of mouth and people's faith. I think the faith element would have something to do with it. I'm not sure if the West can believe in something wholeheartedly any longer. I think it's almost impossible."

"You haven't answered what you would do."

"I can't say. It's all conjecture, isn't it? If I had the power to perform miracles?" he asked. "Perhaps I would have done what he's supposed to have done. Whatever I decided to do, I would have been very secretive about it, but then of course, if you were too secretive you couldn't reach many people. Fraujas's way was very clever. It accomplished quite a lot without turning the whole thing into a magic show."

"You think whatever Fraujas might have done was some sort of magic?"

"What's the difference between magic and religion? I'm not asking that question just to bait you. God knows I've asked it of myself enough. In old Russia the priests sometimes kept magic jewels that could make one chaste, or help a warrior in battle. No one felt the need to separate magic and religion until fairly recently. Both try to sway the . . . what should we call them? The indifferent elements. Let's not try to bend the rules and call Fraujas a saint any longer, because the term is mixed up with piety and prayer. Maybe he was an accomplished sorcerer."

"That seems more likely," I said. "A shaman, but a more powerful shaman."

"He was still a conduit for supernatural intervention—if any of this is true, which I make no claim about right now. That's the thought that excites me."

In the morning we broke camp quickly. We drove southeast, keeping the Black Volta to our right. By late afternoon we entered the environs of Gambaga. The land grew more green. The heat pressed on us, but now it was a dark, tropical warmth, accompanied by the scent of vegetation. The air became thicker and more difficult to breathe. For a good portion of the final approach I was forced to walk ahead of the truck and guide Father Joseph around the hummocks and soft soil which threatened to bog the tires.

When we finally gained firm ground, I climbed back inside. A few thatch roofs were now visible through the trees.

The village was located on the Pendjari River with dark green hills for a backdrop. The huts were built from mud brick with traditional straw-thatched roofs, but they appeared well-kept and neat, their tiny courtyards swept with hand whisks of millet and grass. Between the huts I saw patches of the river. The typical dryness of most villages, the feeling that the village was on the edge of drought and profound hunger, wasn't present. Even as we approached I saw racks of drying fish and heard the strained cries of numerous goats.

We stopped the truck a hundred meters from the village. We climbed out, knowing protocol demanded we wait for the *chef de village* to come out and greet us. I sat on the hood of the truck and lit a cigarette while Father Joseph checked how our provisions had weathered the bumpy ride over the hummocks. A few boys appeared from the surrounding forest and watched us. They liked the click of my lighter and I flicked it several more times. Each time the boys elbowed one another and made high, astonished sounds which carried through the group. I made my cigarette disappear behind my hand, pretended to take it from my ear, then showed them, abracadabra, the cigarette once more. They began to push each other in excitement, jostling one another forward.

The chief arrived surrounded by a retinue of elders. He was old, perhaps seventy, and he walked with difficulty, leaning at all times on two boys on either side of him. He wore a loose shirt, one with no sleeves or collar, and a pair of army shorts. On his feet he wore sandals cut from truck tires. His name was Sido.

"Welcome to the village," he said to us. "The village is yours."

We shook hands all around. They had heard of Father Joseph; they made no mention of me. Afterward, we followed the chief into the hive of mud-brick huts. My initial impression had been correct. The village was extremely light and airy, with a slight breeze blowing constantly off the river. I knew we couldn't be more than ten or twelve degrees off the equator, but the temperature wasn't unbearable.

We walked toward the river in single file, Father Joseph just ahead of me. The Pendjari itself, when we finally struck it, was typical of many African rivers. It was muddy and wide, with a current just fast enough to keep the water rippling. The banks were scarred by large quarries where mud had been taken up for bricks.

Even now, several young men treaded straw into the mud and water, tramping it into a mortar that would be cut into bricks and left to dry in the sun.

Eventually we came to the southern edge of the village. I was so intent on the river that at first I didn't see the large cement building located perhaps fifty feet from shore, under two large trees. It was Fraujas's house, I was sure. Father Joseph apparently shared my opinion, because he turned to me and nodded.

The building was extremely attractive by African standards. It was bright white and appeared to be freshly washed. A tin roof, a wide porch around the entire house. The porch was covered by thatch so that it was possible to sit in the shade and watch the boats come in from the river. Throughout the day, I imagined, there would be a steady breeze.

As we moved closer, I became aware that the building was empty. The metal door appeared bolted. The windows, which should have been open to let in the air, were shuttered closed. Lizards moved on the walls, occasionally climbing up to the tin roof to soak in the reflected heat, and I had a sense that they had grown accustomed to using the house without interference from any inhabitant. Their movements were as intricate and as sullen as the growth of a vine.

At the house, Father Joseph did a curious thing. He drew from the arm of his cassock a small vial of holy water and circled the house, chanting a prayer in Latin. He flicked water on the porch and made an elaborate show of purifying the residence.

It seemed a silly, slightly offensive thing to do, but the reaction of the Africans was worth it. A few, the women in the background, a child or two near the front of the milling group, knelt and watched respectfully. Sido called for a small sitting stool and propped himself up to wait until it was finished.

Father Joseph then came toward me, and without warning flicked a silver rope of water across me. I recoiled, but Father Joseph shook his head just a fraction of an inch and handed the vial to me.

"Bless me with the holy water," he said.

"I'm not a priest."

"It doesn't matter, not right now. Bless me with holy water."

I took the vial and did as he had done. I flicked a few dots of water on him while he crossed himself. That finished, he took the vial back and calmly returned it to his sleeve.

AFTER THE SHORT BLESSING, we stood in front of the house in an uncomfortable circle until chairs and millet beer were brought by village women. We kept our eyes on the river while it was done. It would have been impolite to have noticed the work. As a result, Father Joseph and I acted surprised and pleased when the chief and several of the elders asked us to sit.

"You must be tired," Sido said. "Have you come far?"

"From Tenado," I said, sitting down.

A few of the men clicked their tongues. A younger man, perhaps fifty, passed additional calabashes of millet beer around. We drank for a time before food was brought. After eating an excellent meal of chicken sauce and saga bowl, I passed around cigarettes while Father Joseph, in fluent More, politely inquired about the crops and rain. The men smoked with the cigarettes between their thumbs, cupping their palms in a funnel around the length of the cigarette.

The subject of Fraujas did not come up. The conversation grew tedious. By eight o'clock I had had enough. I was annoyed with Father Joseph and the secrecy surrounding Fraujas. Without consulting him or even looking in his direction, I leaned close to the man who had poured our beer and said, "If you don't mind . . ."

Father Joseph glanced at me and shook his head. Did he believe he was getting closer to a truth about Fraujas? Was it a warning? I didn't care; he was taking too many pains. I was exhausted and ready for sleep.

"You must be fatigued," Sido said. Then, turning to the other men he told them I was tired from my day's travel and needed to sleep.

This announcement caused a strong reaction; it appeared to be the one statement they had waited for all evening. The men who had been drinking a moment before suddenly stood, all thoughts of drink forgotten. Sido instructed the women to make my place ready. Father Joseph also stood.

"We have bedding with us," I told Sido. "If you can just show us back to our truck."

"No, not at all," Sido said.

"It's easy for us," I said.

I wanted to sleep in the truck. I had spent other nights in African huts and had always found them hot and stale. I preferred to be outside in the air, free to wake and move about. I suggested this again to Sido.

"There are animals here," he said softly. "It's not safe to sleep outside at night."

"Don't worry about us. We're old hands at it," I said.

I looked to Father Joseph for help, but he had stepped close to the porch steps and seemed intent on watching the river.

I became aware of the entire circle of men watching me—me, not Father Joseph. Sido also seemed aware of this, and he looked at the ground in front of me, the weight of village opinion resting squarely with him.

Seeing his position and not knowing what it was Father Joseph hoped to convey to me, I reversed myself.

"We don't want to inconvenience anyone," I said.

This statement, when translated by various men throughout the group, was received with relief. No inconvenience to anyone, I was told. Their village was open to us.

I was resigned at this point to sleeping in a stuffy mud-brick hut. I was disappointed since the night promised to be exquisite, the breeze cool and constant, the sound of water peaceful. I waited to be led away, but the women appeared and removed the tables and chairs. Several girls began sweeping away any debris that had collected during our feast. Sido and another man conferred, then called a young boy over and whispered something to him. The boy ran off and returned almost at once, a key clasped in his hand.

"Please," Sido said to me, holding his arm forward in the manner of hosts everywhere asking a guest to step inside.

For the first time I realized they wanted us to sleep in Fraujas's large cement house. I looked at Father Joseph; he refused to meet my eye. Sleeping in the house didn't seem such a bad turn of events, however. Certainly it would be fresher than a hot African hut, and it would give us a chance to examine the interior. But the sense of abandonment was strong around the house. I couldn't help feeling the villagers wanted me in the house as a replacement for Fraujas. Father Joseph, turning back to watch me, nodded his head as if he too had accepted the outcome.

I took the key from Sido, turned the lock, and pushed into a dark room. Someone handed me a lantern which I lifted, then heard people push forward to peer inside with me. A ring of men stood outside the door, waiting. They did not cross the threshold.

The room reminded me of a cell in the mission home. It was spartan and clean, with few ornaments. The walls were painted white and lined with mounted animal heads. Even if the animals hadn't been there, I would have known it for Fraujas's room. Something about the room held his essence.

"Father Fraujas was a hunter," I said absently.

"Yes, Nassarra," answered someone.

The strangest feeling entered me. I had the impression that the men behind me waited for certain responses. I was almost positive the house hadn't been opened in some time, possibly not since Fraujas's death.

Father Joseph took over the formalities of saying good night. He shook hands with the men, then gently closed the door. He didn't speak to me. While he adjusted the lantern, I went around the room and opened the windows. Immediately a breeze came through the house, cooling it and making it feel less oppressive. The sense of Fraujas's presence was slightly dispersed by the wind.

"Well, they got you inside," Father Joseph finally said.

"You think that was their intention?" I asked.

"It was obvious from the first minute we arrived. You are to inherit his kingdom. Didn't you know?"

"THIS IS EXCELLENT taxidermy," Father Joseph said. "If Fraujas did it himself, he knew what he was doing. I wonder where he found the eyes?"

It was late. The village was quiet except for the sound of the river moving smoothly against the shore. After a few more minutes of examining the animals, he waved me closer and held his lantern to the wall. He had discovered a black border running beneath the animals' heads. The border followed the molding throughout the room, framing doorways and windows, lining the molding near the floor. I had mistaken it for a decorative stripe, but he now pointed out that the line wasn't solid at all. The border contained a hundred panels apparently drawn by Fraujas, drawn, moreover, with fierce precision.

It was a tapestry, everything rendered in pen and ink, black against white. Each panel was an entire work in itself. A few panels I recognized immediately: Pandora opening the box, the evil spirits escaping to plague the world; Perseus holding the Medusa's head; the Minotaur in the Labyrinth. But there were other panels, ones which called up only a vague association to my mind, all equally well done.

Gradually, among the classical scenes, I began to recognize depictions of Africa. Fraujas's transition from one to the other, the gradual blurring of line, the appearance of an African lizard behind Zeus, or the presence of a mud hut in the background of a portrait of Hercules, was extremely subtle. Looking at these panels, I couldn't determine for myself whether Fraujas had been aware of his vision changing. Had he known Africa was slowly permeating his drawings? Had he permitted it? Encouraged it?

"Fraujas had a strong command of the Bible," Father Joseph said, lifting the lantern to follow the panels. "It seems to be mixed with classical figures. Did you notice that he appears in many of the panels? Come here and look at this one."

I knelt next to Joseph and examined the panel. It was the New Testament story of Christ's journey to the Temple where he had been questioned by the temple's scholars. Christ, at only twelve or thirteen, had astounded the rabbi with his knowledge of Talmudic law.

Fraujas appeared as one of the marveling rabbi. He wore a long gown and his hands were thrown out in amazement. The left side of his forehead was obscured by Christ's halo, which was represented by a wide ring touched by fire. Nonetheless, Fraujas's face was unmistakable. His mouth was open, his eyes wide. His legs, just evident beneath the gown, flexed to push him up from his seat.

"He appears in a number of these panels," Father Joseph said. "Not all, but quite a few. It's a fascinating record."

Moving slowly along the wall, I saw him appear in any number of panels. Never did he appear as a primary figure. His face was generally used to represent an observer witnessing some miracle or torment. Occasionally he appeared as a fat burgher, his face distorted to support the weight added to it. Once, on a panel depicting the Day of Judgment, his face was affixed to a skeleton rising from a tomb.

"It seems to be some sort of life history woven in with stories from the Bible and Greek mythology," Father Joseph said. "I don't doubt that he has a few souls imprisoned here as well."

"African souls?"

Father Joseph nodded, then grunted as he stood. He continued his search. Underneath a dresser he found a cache of books. He pulled them out one by one and examined them by lantern light, sitting calmly at Fraujas's desk. The titles seemed to make little sense. Or rather, I couldn't see any aspect to connect them together, nor did there seem to be any reason Fraujas would have kept them hidden beneath the dresser.

The Iliad and *The Odyssey* were among them, both in German translations. In addition, there were several other books on mythology. Pendow's *Tales of Magic Trees* and Olivetti's *The Soul of the Land Beneath* and a book by a man named Park, whose volume was called the definitive work on *Religion Among the Aborigines*— all of these were new to me and all were written in German.

There was also a King James Bible, in English. Wedged into the pages of the Bible were several pamphlets. One was on sleight of hand, by a man named Professor Ivan. The book was replete with illustrative drawings, showing fingers swallowing coins, cards disappearing up sleeves. Beneath each illustration was an alphabetized set of instructions, in a foreign language I did not know.

Another pamphlet was on the Tarot and the final one was entitled "The Knights of Malta."

"The source of his drawing?" Father Joseph asked me. "Mysticism, religion . . . he had an appetite for this sort of thing, it seems."

Father Joseph had barely finished speaking when we heard the first cry. It was a human cry. I was shocked by the noise, but Father Joseph listened intently, as if he had expected something like this to happen all along.

The cry continued with hardly a moment for the person to collect his breath. Several times I heard African phrases. A man said,

"*Badika, badika, pousse badika.* Thank you, thank you, many thanks." And another man responded by saying, "Quiet, you aren't an infant." But the screams grew wilder as they came closer.

"It sounds like a man," I said.

"No, it's a goat," Father Joseph replied. "Listen closely."

It did indeed sound like a goat, although I was certain that was not the case. I stepped to the window and looked out. A small crowd of men stood near the water's edge, trying to lift a single man from a canoe. It was the man inside the canoe who screamed continually. He couldn't quiet himself, and each attempt on the group's part to lift him to the beach resulted in the man's renewed screams and vicious kicks. Several times the men pointed to Fraujas's house, trying to explain something to the man in the canoe, but the man seemed terrified, or beyond reason.

"They're bringing someone," I said.

"Who is it?"

"I don't know. I can't see from here."

I opened the door and stepped out. Father Joseph came and stood next to me just as one man broke away from the crowd and ran toward us. I couldn't see him well in the darkness, but he appeared to be around thirty years old. He wore several fetishes around his neck. He began speaking before he reached us. We couldn't calm him sufficiently to get the story straight at first. Gradually, however, through Father Joseph's questioning, we pieced together the course of events.

A *nyanga* had placed a curse on the man in the canoe. We couldn't determine why the curse had been cast in the first place, but it didn't matter. The *nyanga* had stolen a goat and broken the goat's two front legs. He had tortured the animal and had actually broken the legs so severely that he was able to bind the goat's legs above the animal's neck. The legs were tethered straight up, like a man shackled to a wall with heavy metal cuffs. The goat was in the canoe with the man. This, of course, explained why we had heard the bleating.

The goat had been left at the owner's hut with a curse: If the man raised his hands above his head at any time while the goat still lived, he would die when the goat died.

The man in the canoe, who was named Ouedraogo, hadn't taken the curse lightly. He had gone directly to bed, but not before tying a rope from one wrist to the other, then passing the rope between his legs. It was impossible afterward, for him to raise his hands above his head.

But something had gone wrong. The *nyanga* had managed to cut the rope without Ouedraogo knowing—through more magic, we were made to understand—and the *nyanga* had been in a tree when Ouedraogo went outside to relieve himself. The *nyanga* had thrown a snake at Ouedraogo, who naturally lifted his hands to protect himself. The snake was nothing, just an illusion, but Ouedraogo realized the curse had worked and he fell to the ground and screamed. He hadn't stopped since that time.

Father Joseph and I followed the man down to the canoe. The cries grew louder. Ouedraogo thrashed madly in the canoe, his legs striking the gunwales repeatedly.

"Get him out of there," Father Joseph said.

The men stepped forward, but they didn't grab for Ouedraogo. I was about to instruct them to simply lift the canoe when Father Joseph bent over Ouedraogo and grabbed his head between his hands.

The effect of this small action was to make Ouedraogo enter into a trance. His body went limp; his cries ceased. He didn't close his eyes, however. He lay on the bottom of the canoe, his legs bleeding from where they had struck the gunwales, his arms still above his head. He chanted something under his breath, repeating it so that his lips moved as if reciting a rosary. The chant was no louder than a whisper.

On Father Joseph's command, the men lifted Ouedraogo and carried him to the front porch. I stayed behind for a moment with the goat. The goat was a sad spectacle. Its breathing was labored; it no longer had the strength to bleat with any force.

By this time a few villagers had come to witness the events. I told two men nearby to find a goat resembling the one in the canoe. I told them I would pay, promising to double the price if they found one immediately. The men nodded, but didn't move off. They wouldn't become involved with a *nyanga*. The curse was placed on the man and the goat, and to work to remove it would put them in jeopardy.

I lifted the goat from the canoe myself. Its back legs rowed softly, too weak to make any attempt at escape. Its wide eyes—its human eyes—stared at me without blinking. I carried it to the front porch. The men who had carried Ouedraogo to the porch made room for me.

"Maybe we should keep the goat away from this man," Father Joseph said.

"I'll carry it inside."

"Do you think it would take water?"

"I don't think so," I said.

I placed the goat in the center of the floor inside the house. It didn't move except to pant. I tried to think of some way to make it comfortable. It should have been killed, of course, but that was impossible under the circumstances.

When I returned to the porch, I saw Father Joseph had ordered Ouedraogo to be placed on a straw mat on the cement floor. Two men squatted on either side of him. Father Joseph stood at Ouedraogo's feet, instructing the men.

"I'm going to tell them to bring his arms down by force," said Father Joseph. "His pectoral muscles are cutting off his breath. He'll suffocate."

"You're sure it won't kill him?"

"He's in trouble either way. Do you have another idea?"

"No, not really."

Father Joseph reached forward and took Ouedraogo's head between his hands. He looked for a long time into the African's eyes. Ouedraogo didn't seem to see him, though his lips continued to move, chanting whatever it was he chanted.

"On my count," Father Joseph said to the men.

The men nodded, but they didn't look confident. I went to help the man on the left. Father Joseph spoke very deliberately. He continued to hold Ouedraogo's head.

"One . . . two . . . three."

At first I didn't exert much force. How could a man hope to resist the efforts of three men pushing at his arms? But he did so with ease. Our pushing only skidded the body across the cement in a grotesque mockery. Father Joseph had to step back, nearly falling in the process, though he never let go of Ouedraogo's head.

Without any count, we pushed again. I pushed with all my strength. Ouedraogo slid again, but only until he came in contact with one of the pillars supporting the porch roof. His feet pressed against the wooden beam and at least we had a purchase. I pushed once more, and this time Ouedraogo's legs gave way. They slipped, or perhaps merely crumpled, but whatever leverage we had was gone. Father Joseph sat on Ouedraogo's chest, pinning him to the ground, but even this wasn't enough. His arms remained raised above his head.

Father Joseph stood and instructed the men to again place Ouedraogo on the mat. Then he sat on the railing overlooking the river, and said nothing for a time.

"I can't help wondering what Fraujas could have done with this man," Father Joseph finally said.

"No more than we're doing, probably."

"Didn't you feel how clumsy we were? I'll always remember him skidding across the porch. It was absurd."

I told him to rest for a few minutes while I went inside to get the bottle of scotch. He drank a large swallow directly from the neck. I followed. The Africans remained squatting in their positions near the straw mat.

"How was the goat?" Father Joseph asked.

"I don't think it will live much past the morning."

"The cure for this sort of thing—this possession—is to lift the man off the ground and wrap him in cloth. Plug his nose, his ears . . . feed him through a straw. Keep him in a hammock to break all connection with the earth. The land priests draw their power from the earth. That's the local cure, anyway. The curse lifts if it doesn't kill you."

"Have you ever seen it done?" I asked.

"No, but it was done to Fatama. That's what the grass says."

He looked at me. Before I could ask anything, the goat died. It kicked once, shuddered, then ceased to breathe.

We didn't move, nor did we speak. We remained where we were until the cries began. Women trilled their tongues. The trill rose and fell, sweeping in new voices constantly, the sound running across the village. A man is dead, a man is dead, a man is dead.

Father Joseph sat beside Fraujas's desk and looked at me. I couldn't believe what I had just seen, but no other explanation fit the evidence. The goat had died; the man had died in the same instant. The *nyanga*'s prediction had been exact, his curse fatal.

"Ouedraogo couldn't have known," I said. "He couldn't possibly see the goat from his position on the porch. The curse might have had a psychological explanation, but this . . ."

"I intend to find the *nyanga*," said Father Joseph after a moment or two.

"What good will it do?" I asked.

"Perhaps it will do you more good than me," Father Joseph said softly. "The man was brought to you."

FATHER JOSEPH TRIED to get additional information about the *nyanga* who had placed the curse. He learned it was a man named Mazi from the village of Orodara, which was located on the open savannah. The village was famous for its hunting. Safaris sometimes rested there, taking on provisions for the second leg of their journey. There was an outpost where some Western goods could be purchased. It was an irregular supply post, but it was the only one in the area.

By sunrise, Ouedraogo's body had been loaded into the canoe. The goat was also taken. I found it difficult to look at either creature. Ouedraogo's arms had at last sunk beneath his shoulders and now were limp under the blanket. The goat already collected the morning swarms of flies.

We started for Orodara by first full light. After we forded the river the land began to open. We followed a game path which was not wide or well-marked. Acacia trees lined the horizon, their tops pale wedges which seemed translucent in the increasing sun. The hazy spread of the trees might have been clouds or mountaintops. Everywhere the land gave up moisture and heat, so that the air around us quavered with refracted light. Crickets and grasshoppers sprayed against the truck, at times flicking away in a wide burr of noise, at other times splattering on the windshield in white explosions.

We stopped at noon for food and refueling.

"What do you intend to do with this Mazi?" I asked him as we settled in the shade of a shea tree and ate bread and some dried strips of beef.

"Nothing, really. I want to see him and maybe talk to him."

"Will you report him to the authorities?"

"Of course not. They won't do anything. And really, what could they prove?"

We reached Orodara by nightfall. It was a frontier town, built against the backdrop of a large balfon. We passed over an earthen dam to enter the village. The houses were well-built, with quite a few constructed of concrete. We drove down the center street, which was lined with karite trees to provide shade during the day.

We parked near the Safari Hotel and Bar. This was a fairly well-maintained establishment on the outskirts of town. Metal tables were set out on a gravel terrace beneath two or three Roman torches. A large flamboyant tree stood at the southern corner of the courtyard. The leaves of the tree were heavy. Lizards used the tree for a refuge, coming down it to steal crumbs from the tables, then darting back up its thick bark.

The outside terrace was fairly crowded. Several tables were taken up by Africans, local functionaires dressed in boo-boos and Muslim caps. A German hunting party, consisting of ten men, sat at the far side of the terrace. They had pulled three or four tables together and now sat around it drinking. They were loud and obviously drunk.

Father Joseph and I took a table at the opposite end of the terrace. We ordered beer and chicken with roasted onions.

"Wherever they go, the Germans are like that," Father Joseph said to me as he lit a cigarette. "They are obnoxious people . . . self-centered and arrogant. Nazism shouldn't surprise anyone who has ever shared a vacation spot with a German."

"Have you had trouble with them before?"

"Oh, nothing too terrible. They're just rude."

After dinner we went inside to get rooms for the night. The hotel was constructed of plain cement. It may have served as a French colonial residence at one time. The lobby was lighted by two kerosene lanterns; the floor was covered by several skins— zebra, giraffe, lion. The skins were worn by hard use and barely retained their distinctive patterns. Several prize heads hung from the wall, all of them badly moth-eaten.

The rooms were reasonably clean, each with a tiny terrace. It was possible to sleep and still have some sort of breeze coming off the balfon and plains. We took adjoining rooms and sent down for our baggage.

Once we were installed, we agreed to go back downstairs for a nightcap. In the courtyard, the Germans played some sort of drinking game. They tossed peanuts the entire length of the table, cheering when a peanut came close to going into a glass. Several times they whooped and looked about them, as if anyone watching them would naturally share in their amusement.

"It's the food they eat," Father Joseph said after we ordered a drink. "The sausage and beer and cabbage. They're babied by their mothers until they're quite old. The Germans are a detestable race."

"Are you speaking from experience?"

"The experience of most Frenchmen my age. I was too young to really know what it was like—the Occupation, I'm speaking of now. But I've always remembered a small detail that took place in my school. The German officer who was in charge of the district demanded that the children's choir sing German Christmas carols. Even as children we knew we weren't getting anything for Christmas. No one really minded that. But the songs held a certain nostalgic healing power—you know how Christmas carols can be. The German officer heard that we sang our little songs in French, and he demanded, on pain of whipping, that the children sing in German. That to me was the perfect example of the German mind. I'm sure the German officer demanded it because he genuinely believed German was the more beautiful language, or the purer sound—some nonsense. Can you imagine being in a war and worrying about the Christmas songs of your conquered countries? Only the Germans could do it with such thoroughness."

"And you sang in German?"

"Of course. We sang at the officer's mess. Several of the men stopped us to correct our pronunciation. Some of them sang along and called out requests. They gave us candy afterward."

Just then a small boy appeared by our table. He was ten years old and very thin. His eyes were sharp and restless. He carried an owl on his right hand, two old wool socks serving as a gauntlet. The owl was small. I couldn't tell if it was fully grown. Its eyes were wide and green-colored. Large tufts of feathers circled its face, and when the slightest breeze came it lifted the facial feathers and made them flutter. The boy had a strap of rawhide wrapped around the bird's right talon and his own wrist, anchoring the bird in place.

"Two hundred francs," the boy said.

"No thanks," I said.

"Where did you get that owl?" asked Father Joseph.

"With a slingshot."

"Can it fly?"

"Yes, Nassarra," the boy answered.

He goosed the bird slightly by shaking his hand. The bird threw out its wings for balance and strained against the rawhide talon. It faltered once it reached the limit of the rawhide and almost failed to regain its position on the boy's hand.

He also carried a wicker basket, which he lifted onto the table, straining under its weight. The basket had a strange smell. It wasn't an unpleasant smell exactly. It was a gamey scent, one which I felt I vaguely recognized. The boy lifted the lid an inch and tilted the basket to us.

Inside was a python, curled in huge coils. The snake made a move to get out, but the boy quickly lowered the lid and fitted a small stick into a wicker latch.

"Where is the snake from?" I asked.

The boy waved to indicate the bush behind him.

"Five hundred francs," he said.

"How did you catch it?" Father Joseph asked.

The boy's story was ordinary. The snake had snuck into his family's chicken coop and swallowed a rooster. Because of the resulting bulge in the snake's gut, it couldn't escape. The boy had captured the snake in the morning. It had been as simple as loading a length of chain into a carton.

I asked to see the snake again. It wasn't enormous, as pythons go, but it was large nevertheless. The most remarkable thing about it was its girth. It was, I guessed, eight to ten inches round at its center. It was no longer, the boy said, than a man standing.

Father Joseph talked to the boy for a moment in More. The boy repeated the prices, lowering them a bit, then moved to the German table.

The Germans ignored him at first. They spoke in broken

French and the boy pretended not to understand them. He put down the wicker basket and moved around the table, just on the edge of light, letting the men glimpse the owl.

The peanut game soon finished, and the men turned their attention to the boy. I knew they weren't particularly interested in the owl or the boy, but they needed a new diversion. Several of the men called to the boy, asking to see the owl. He brought the owl past them one by one, not staying with any of them for long. He was working them, I realized. He was leading up to the sale of the python, which would seem more a marvel in contrast to the owl.

Eventually he placed the owl carefully on the back of one of the chairs. He wrapped the rawhide talon around the top strut of the chairback, and let the owl sit quietly while he fetched the python.

"*Was ist das?*" a few of the men asked with genuine interest.

But the boy delayed his presentation. He was quite good. He slowly lifted the basket onto the table, inching it forward while the Germans made room for it. They cleared bottles and dirty plates, calling repeatedly for the waiters to come and take things away. A number stood and came to see what was inside the basket.

The boy lifted the lid for each German in turn, never allowing any of them to get a clear look. The light on the terrace wasn't good to begin with, and the boy had shrewdly placed the basket in such a way that each time he lifted the lid, shadows covered most of the snake. It was natural for the Germans to want the snake out. I wanted the same thing myself.

The Germans began to argue among themselves. I couldn't understand them, although I picked up a word or two. They discussed price. Did they want to chip in one hundred francs apiece? Could the boy skin it? Could they have anything made from the skin if they got it home? Was it illegal to import a snake skin?

The conclusion was obvious. It cost them almost nothing to buy the snake from the boy. After a great deal of consultation, they finally laughed and shouted for the boy to remove the snake from the basket. The boy told them the snake couldn't easily be restrained once it was free of the basket, but they insisted.

We ordered more drinks while the Germans pooled their money and tried to figure a way to remove the snake. Several times they lifted the lid to peer inside, then quickly slammed it shut as the snake made a move to escape. The boy, after folding the money away in his shorts, tried to help them.

In the end the lid of the basket was removed and the snake began to climb out. Two or three of the men jumped back instantly, but one man, a large, heavy man who had obviously been drinking a great deal, stabbed his hand toward the snake and grabbed it behind the head. His comrades yelled and sent up a cheer, but the man was not prepared for the snake's next move. In long sweeping waves, the snake frothed out of the basket, reaching with its immense coils for a purchase on the man's body.

"*Gott in Himmel*," the man said and tried to laugh.

But he was in a peculiar position. He couldn't let go of the snake's head without risking being bitten. He couldn't continue to hold the snake or it would wrap around him. A few of his friends stepped forward and tried to pry the snake away. It wasn't easy. The python moved with tremendous constrictions. It was thick— thicker than I had imagined. Its weight was sufficient to pull the man off balance; this, combined with the men yanking from different directions, almost toppled the man twice.

Nevertheless, the man was not in danger. His comrades could eventually organize themselves and pull the snake away. But they were drunk and enjoying the spectacle of their friend struggling with the snake.

Then the man's face changed. I saw it clearly, though I'm certain his friends didn't. The man's face began to cloud with fear. His expression changed almost imperceptibly at first, but gradually it took on deeper concern. He was roped by the snake. It continued to move around him, settling slowly in huge folds around his neck and arms. The snake didn't seem to possess a head or tail; it merely moved in viscous folds.

The man's first yell retained some humor. But his breath was now being affected; his steps were uneven. One of the snake's coils went around his neck and he slapped at it with his free hand. He yanked at the snake, trying to get it away from his neck, but the python was relentless. Again it wrapped around him in waves, this time finding a better position. It pinned the man's left arm to his chest.

The German shouted louder. He was genuinely frightened now. He attempted to keep it under control, but it was only a matter of time before he broke. Some of his comrades saw this as well, because they stepped forward and tugged at the bottom portion of the snake. But again it wasn't easy. The python was enormously strong and its entire body now had a purchase on the man.

"Get him off, get him off!" the man yelled.

The boy tried to direct them, but they wouldn't listen to him. I looked at Father Joseph. He shook his head and continued to watch.

The man moved slowly from one comrade to the next, telling each to pull the snake off. There was still time to pull it away, or, failing that, time to kill it. But the men had decided to let him struggle. It was a joke, and they conspired to let it go on a little longer. One of them shouted about remembering the time the man had done thus and so. Another shouted that he would take care of the man's wife. A third asked if he could have the man's automobile.

The man nearly fell. He called for help repeatedly and finally two of his friends grabbed the snake's tail and began to unloop it. They walked backward, letting the snake droop between them and the victim. The snake gradually let go. The man, sensing his freedom, did an odd pirouette, spinning the length of the last coil, then stepping free. He threw the head of the snake violently at the ground and staggered to a chair. His shirt was stained in sashes of perspiration.

The python's fate was sealed. Two men approached with knives. Two more held the snake. The men with knives captured the head, sawed the snake's throat in half, then danced away as the python began a final series of coils. Blood spurted. A nervous tremor passed down its length, then it died.

We watched as the boy went forward and bargained for three hundred francs to skin the snake. He would have the skin by morning, he told the Germans. He would treat it with magic so that it would bring them luck.

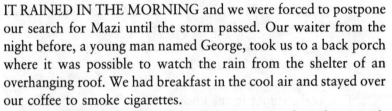

IT RAINED IN THE MORNING and we were forced to postpone our search for Mazi until the storm passed. Our waiter from the night before, a young man named George, took us to a back porch where it was possible to watch the rain from the shelter of an overhanging roof. We had breakfast in the cool air and stayed over our coffee to smoke cigarettes.

We remained on the porch until noon. I read; Father Joseph did some paperwork. Near noon he excused himself for a nap. The sun came out after he went upstairs and soon the land began to dry. George came by and asked me if I needed anything. He was about to go off to his siesta. I told him no and continued to sit and watch the sunlight.

Mazi found me during the hours of siesta. I had the notion that George had passed him the message that I was alone, but I had no way of proving it. No doubt Mazi had heard of our entrance into the village. It was ridiculous, I realized, to believe we would have the drop on him. He lived in the village and had hundreds of ways to follow our progress through the area. His appearance on the porch was entirely natural.

He sat at a table a few feet away from me. He was a short, brutish-looking man, perhaps fifty-five years old. His brow ridge was excessively thick. He wore clothes typical of a Moslem. A white boo-boo was draped over his body, but I was conscious of the heaviness of his muscles beneath the cloth. White shoes covered his feet—cheap plastic shoes worn at the soles. Around his neck was a collection of amulets and fetishes. They swayed with the slightest motion of his head. Their effect was somewhat hypnotic.

After looking at me for some time, he spoke.

"Good afternoon, Nassarra Hawley," he said. "I am Mazi. Were you looking for me, Nassarra?"

"We were going to come see you," I said.

"I came to see you instead."

"I'm glad you did."

For a moment neither of us spoke. I was uneasy with Mazi's presence. The effect of his personality was one of density. His body seemed more dense than any human I had ever met. His look, his movements, even his deep voice—everything implied weight.

"Fraujas was a very powerful man. Do you believe you have inherited his power?" Mazi asked.

"I don't know."

"That is the rumor in the bush."

"I don't want his power."

"You don't? I don't believe you."

Suddenly he stepped between me and the sun. He cut off the light. He stood for fifteen or twenty seconds, staring at me. It should have been ridiculous, but his bearing, his strength of personality, forced me to take him seriously. I tried to return his stare, but his eyes were much stronger than mine. He dominated me.

I almost got up from my chair when Mazi shifted his position and the sunlight struck me full force. It blinded me for an instant. I put my hand to my eyes to shade them. When I was able to see again, Mazi leaned toward me and slowly opened his mouth.

He had somehow passed a spider onto his tongue. He opened his mouth in a funnel and the spider began to crawl out. It was a cheap trick, but I couldn't deny its macabre power. He worked it well. The spider emerged slowly, as if reluctant to leave the cavity of his mouth, its legs weaving in the air before it advanced. I couldn't imagine allowing the spider to touch my skin, much less my mouth.

The spider continued its exit. It was a hideous, terrible sight. Mazi closed his eyes and apparently concentrated on issuing the spider.

I wanted to make some comment to undermine the strange quality of the moment, but I couldn't think of anything to say. Mazi raised his hand and allowed the spider to crawl onto his palm. The spider remained for a moment on his open hand, then turned and started back into his mouth.

The spider's behavior confused me. I couldn't know for certain how Mazi had arranged the details of the first portion of the trick. I supposed he had slipped the spider into his mouth, probably taking it from his pocket when the sun had blinded me. But now the spider turned, checked the air with its front legs, then slowly moved toward his open mouth. I watched to see if Mazi inhaled, but he did nothing. He opened his mouth tentatively at first, almost as if forced to summon strength in order to allow the spider to return. The spider appeared to live in his mouth. Or perhaps the spider had climbed from much deeper inside the man, moving slowly up his chest and throat, appearing in the sunlight to startle me.

I don't know how long it took to finally enter Mazi's mouth completely. At one point Mazi lowered his hand. It was not until that instant that I realized the spider now rested entirely in his mouth. It hung there, a dark black shape still moving its legs, until Mazi closed his mouth.

Mazi said nothing; he did nothing. He looked at me, his arms at his side. Then he walked back through the hotel. He passed two or three young waiters, and each time the waiters moved deferentially away. One waiter even went so far as to make the sign of the cross when Mazi was well by. Another genuflected and backed away, his reverse movement not ceasing until Mazi at last pushed out the door.

I sat down and lit a cigarette. Never in my life had I felt more shaken. It wasn't much later that George appeared to say that Mazi had sent me something. He was nearly overcome with fright. Very deliberately, he handed me a dead rooster.

Surprisingly, I did not recoil from the sight.

I took the rooster and placed it on the table in front of me. Its head had been twisted backward, its neck broken. Its eyes had been scooped out, the bare sockets left empty. An incision had been made in its chest cavity, but the cavity itself was swelled to at least twice its normal size. The chest bulged grotesquely. Something— or things—had been stuffed inside it, pushing the skin out in queer, tumorous shapes. The chest had been roughly stitched closed with twine, the breasts pulled almost to the point of ripping.

I tried to make my mind clinical. This was, after all, only a dead rooster. I had killed hundreds myself during my stay in Africa. I was conscious of George standing behind my chair. No doubt there were others watching from the windows of the hotel. They would report to Mazi; all of them would remember how I reacted.

At last I reached forward and turned the rooster directly toward me. Slowly, I pulled the cavity open. It took me only an instant to recognize the contents. I found at least ten items that had been stolen from me over the last month. I hadn't noticed them missing, but here they were: a scrap of paper with my handwriting, a razor blade, a few locks of hair probably taken by Fatama. All of the items were covered with blood; all were bound into a fetish. Some of the items had been charred by fire. Some had been worked into wax, since there was evidence they had been placed in the fire to melt, thereby diminishing me. At the very core of the fetish was a bright silver object, which I recognized even before I saw it clearly. It was the crucifix from Fraujas's rosary, buried once, and now resurrected.

MAZI RETURNED TO PLACE his final curse on me later that night. I sat with Father Joseph on the terrace at the time. The bar was virtually empty. The air was clear and warm. The moisture from the earlier rain had worked countless insects up from the earth, breeding them in small puddles across the savannah, and now they launched themselves at the torches which were placed around the courtyard. Their bodies made a constant crackling sound as they hit the flames. Occasionally a larger insect flew through the heat, emerging as a glinting cinder as it fell to the gravel.

The wind changed; the air grew still. I'm not sure if Father Joseph noticed the sudden quiet, but I detected it at once. I sat up in my chair and looked out at the savannah, but there was nothing to see. There was only grass and wind and a few trees that moved in the darkness above us. I looked around the bar and realized no one had come out, no one else shared the terrace. This couldn't have been coincidence; the emptiness seemed too exact. No waiter came to our table; none of the boys who generally circulated with cigarettes appeared.

Only slowly did I become aware of a figure moving near us, perhaps sixty meters beyond the border of light. I knew immediately it was Mazi. I knew his shape; I knew his movement in the manner of animals knowing a predator. Although it was impossible, I smelled him in the open air. He was after me; he came for me.

Father Joseph stood. To my astonishment, he picked up a knife that had been left after dinner and held it in front of him. He turned back and forth, quartering the darkness, but it was evident to me he didn't sense Mazi in the way I did. He turned to face a moving bush when I knew the bush was innocent.

I heard a footfall far off to my left, but I didn't turn to face it. Mazi was now fifty meters away, moving just on the edge of my vision. Parts of him came clear to me. I saw he wore a costume. His face was covered by a hideous mask and he wore a cloak fabricated from animal skins. The cloak was topped by an animal head—a wolf, a lion, I couldn't see the details of it. The cape gave his body a second movement, a shadow movement, which made him flow in the darkness.

"What do you want?" Father Joseph called into the darkness, but I grabbed his arm and shook my head. I pulled him back away from the nearest lantern. Light worked against us, I knew, and I looked for a way to douse the lanterns. I went around the courtyard and covered each light with the lids chained to the lantern poles. The sound of the flames licking was suddenly gone, and now the night was changed into a solid block of black quiet.

Mazi had moved a remarkable distance in my short lapse of attention. This was a lesson, but one I could do nothing about. Straining to see, I discovered that he carried something at his side. It was a sack, bell-shaped, which he repeatedly swung near the ground. He paused each time he swung the sack, then moved on, effortlessly covering ground.

He moved in a clockwise direction. He swung the sack several times, but it wasn't a continuous thing. He moved twenty paces, swung the sack, then moved twenty more. He spoke something, but I couldn't distinguish individual words. I didn't like the steadiness of his voice or the methodical way he used the sack.

I moved toward him at last, trying to make my steps light on the ground. I was no match for him in the darkness; my sounds were comparatively loud. Father Joseph, following behind me, couldn't walk at all silently. It was no use to quiet him, however. Mazi had watched us from the moment we began walking in his direction and any pretense about sneaking toward him was ridiculous. He let us come nearer, though I sensed in him a warning, not unlike the unconscious posture a dog takes before it bites. He would permit us to approach only to a certain distance. Then he would halt us.

The walk into the open plain was terrifying. I knew that my mind was the only true protection. If he succeeded in daunting me, if I showed him fright or the slightest indecision, it meant his magic had power over me.

Mazi emerged out of the darkness as I approached. Light didn't find him—quite the contrary. His blackness and pure shape became more visible. The features of the mask became clear. I saw the hood of his cape was made from a hyena's head. Rounded ears, the thick muzzle, the spotted skin—all of this I saw by whatever glimmer my eyes found. The mask itself was unnerving. It was carved from dark wood, yet the features were twisted and grotesquely large. A straw beard covered the chin; in the circle of its mouth, I could just make out Mazi's own mouth speaking his incantation. The lips moved over and over, rowing out words that barely carried beyond the mask.

I stopped when I was fifteen meters away and watched Mazi with fear but also with fascination. The sack he carried was not a sack at all; it was the body of a white goat whose head had been hacked away. Jagged folds of skin extended beyond the neck joint and sometimes swept the ground. The back legs had been trussed, forming a handle by which Mazi swung the goat. On each tilt and shake of the body, a small sop of blood dripped down onto the soil.

"He's circling the hotel with blood," Father Joseph whispered. "There are some others working over that way. Do you see them?"

"*Nyanga*," I said, though I didn't bother to look.

"We should find some light."

"What good would it do?" I asked.

Eventually I turned to see the other *nyanga*. Father Joseph was correct. Three more *nyanga* worked behind us, all of them swinging decapitated goats.

I watched for some time before I approached Mazi.

"What do you want?" I asked, trying to keep my voice calm. He was still ten meters away. He didn't stop moving and circling with the goat.

"If you cross the circle you will die," he said.

I took a few steps forward, thinking I should cross the circle immediately, but Father Joseph grabbed me. He actually put his arms around my chest and restrained me. I let him do it. The truth was, I didn't want to test the line. I smelled the blood; I saw its black moisture in the dirt. I struggled only slightly against Father Joseph's arms.

A second *nyanga* joined Mazi. His approach had been absolutely silent. Together they completed the circle. They tossed the goats inside its perimeter. Far away, from various points along the circle, I heard similar sounds. I turned and saw three different *nyanga* discarding goats. No one moved inside the circle, or dared cross it even with his hands.

Then they backed away—Mazi, the second *nyanga*, all of them down the line. They didn't turn their backs. They retreated into the darkness and I was struck by the perfect theatricality of this gesture. The effect, like the trick with the spider, was haunting.

"I should cross it now," I said to Father Joseph when they were gone. The weakness of my voice surprised me. I could barely speak.

"Wait and think," he cautioned.

"It will only grow stronger."

"Don't say that. Don't say that it will grow at all. If you say that, you admit its existence."

"Why shouldn't I cross it now, then? If it doesn't exist, why shouldn't I test it now?"

"Just wait until we can think."

But of course it was too late. We followed the circle, knowing we had already admitted its power. Dogs were on the goats. We passed them at a safe distance, but they snarled anyway. One of them, a large brown bitch, tried to drag the carcass away from the others. Two other dogs pulled in the opposite direction. The carcass hung suspended between them.

We circled the eastern corner of the hotel, then around behind, back where we had spent the morning. At any point I could have stepped across the line. I could have tested it. Yet each moment that I stayed inside the line increased its effect. It was this realization that made me stop and put my hands on my knees. I couldn't catch my breath.

"Are you all right?" Father Joseph asked.

"I feel light-headed."

"Sit down. Put your head between your knees."

"I'm all right."

"No, sit down."

He forced me to sit. He placed his hand on my neck and gently bent me forward. I put my head down and felt better. I felt hungry suddenly. It was not a typical hunger, not one born of appetite, but rather an emptiness in my stomach and chest. The physical sensation increased until it became a nausea. I turned to one side and retched, Father Joseph's hands still on my shoulders.

"What does he want from me?" I asked.

"I don't know. Let's get you inside."

As I rose I came close to surging over the line. It would have been a simple thing to do. One lunge and I would have crossed it, my chest out like a sprinter. The line held the same attraction for me that I sometimes felt approaching a cliff or the ledge of a high building. It wasn't that I wanted to die; it was only knowing I could jump that appealed to me.

"We don't have to do anything right now," Father Joseph said. "Let's go back inside and think this over."

"He's won," I said.

"Not at all."

Father Joseph put his arm around my waist and led me back. George was stationed on the porch again, lighting the torches. He didn't meet my eyes; no one, not the cigarette boys or the few African guests, met my look. Behind us, I heard the dogs stripping a carcass clean.

I HARDLY SLEPT. Father Joseph gave me a tranquilizer from the medicine kit he kept in the truck. It didn't work; I was too anxious to consider sleep. Father Joseph mentioned confession; I questioned him about an exorcism. Yet it was all, in some way, an attempt to forestall the real impact of the curse: We did not discuss the possibility of my death.

Near ten o'clock Father Joseph left to look for Mazi. I was left alone. I pulled a chair close to the tiny terrace that led off my room and watched the animals finishing the last of the goats. It was a raw sight, though it wasn't without its own fascination. The animals proceeded in an ecological rhythm: carnivore, scavenger, and at last insects.

A little later I heard the Germans leaving. George had explained that they planned to spend the night in the bush. The following day they would push through to Ouagadougou and their chartered plane back to Germany. In a day, Africa would be a memory to them.

The hotel staff hung near, waiting for tips and last dashes of money. Occasionally I saw a German slip something to one of the waiters, invariably slapping him on the shoulder as he did so. It was then that a plan occurred to me.

I stepped into my sandals and hurried downstairs. The Germans were already in their trucks. A few of them had tied handkerchiefs over their noses and mouths to protect them from the road dust.

"Wait a moment!" I yelled in French, struggling to find the German phrase.

"*Halten Sie! Halt!*" one of the men shouted to the driver.

I explained my request. At first they only laughed. Why should they sell me a camera? What would they do for the remainder of the trip? How could they trade the West African francs for German marks?

But there must have been something in my expression to make

them take me seriously. I offered them double the price of the camera, then triple. I explained, as well as I could, that I required the type of camera that instantly developed the photograph; I could use no other.

This narrowed the bargaining down to three individuals. One man was in the front truck; the other two rested on benches in the back of the third truck. As soon as I took the cash from my wallet, they began shouting to one another.

A long conversation followed, then all three shook their heads. I didn't give up. I asked who among them spoke French. One of them asked if I wasn't American. Did I speak English? I told him yes, and he leaned across the others, speaking with great deliberateness.

"What do you want?" he asked.

"I need a camera that develops the pictures automatically."

"Yes, but what do you want?" he asked again, unaware he had added no new meaning to his question.

"I will pay triple its worth."

"*Ja,*" the man said, then turned back and explained our conversation to the others.

I have no notion of how the switch to English accomplished anything more than my broken German, but one of the men finally relented. But they wouldn't give me additional film, regardless of how I phrased the plea. It was impossible to buy in West Africa, and they couldn't give me any without depleting their own supply. Seven shots were left on the present roll.

I carried the camera upstairs and waited impatiently for Father Joseph. He returned around three o'clock. He was excited to tell me what he had seen. I was equally excited, but let him go first.

"He's a scribe," Father Joseph said, sitting beside the open terrace door and pouring himself a drink. "I visited his house. There were ten or fifteen people lined up outside. At first I thought it was this healing business again, but then I asked some of the people in line what they waited for, and they answered that Mazi wrote letters for them to relatives around West Africa. Most of the people in the line were old. Their children had gone off to Abijan or Dakar—the bright city lights, you know. Mazi writes letters and the children feel guilty and eventually send their parents some money."

"Did you see him?"

"Yes. He sat behind a plain wooden table. A chair was set up to one side of the table so that the people could sit and tell him what to write. He was very quick about composing the letters."

"And he probably steals them blind."

"Yes, of course," Father Joseph said, nodding. "He asks for more money in the letters. Then, when the envelopes return, he opens the letters, removes some of the money, and gives the rest to their parents. Maybe he tells them some letters never arrive. Besides getting their money, he gets their information without leaving his house. It's clever employment for a _nyanga_."

"What did he say when you approached him?"

Father Joseph considered a moment before replying. He brushed a cigarette ash from his cassock. The motion of his hand made his rosary swing and beat softly against the wooden chair.

"He was very good," he said finally. "He showed no surprise at all. He stood and shook my hand and asked if I came to have a letter written. It was a joke and we both knew it, but it somehow prevented us from going into the curse. It wasn't a subject I could just leap into."

"So how did you leave it?"

Father Joseph shrugged. "No particular way. He knew why I had come. We passed the time of day for a few minutes, then I left. It's a step, that's all."

I showed him the camera. Initially, he didn't get the implication. But then, when I reminded him of Fraujas's practice of drawing sketches of African figures, he anticipated me.

"So you want to take his picture, is that it?" he asked. "It might work. It's an idea, anyway."

He took the camera and went off. I went downstairs and found George. He was preparing tables for the evening meal and at first pretended to be too occupied to help me. He continued wiping the tables as I talked to him.

"George," I said after he had ignored several questions, "I could easily place a curse on you. Stand up and talk to me."

I spoke without thinking, but the effect on George was startling. He grabbed a fetish that hung around his neck and didn't let go of it while I spoke to him. I told him to find the things I needed and bring them to me quickly. He nodded repeatedly, and when he saw I was finished speaking, he ran off, slamming the screen door on his way through the lobby.

I returned to my room and waited for George. In a short while he knocked on my door and entered with a small basket packed with the items I had requested. He put the basket on the bed, anxious to be away from me.

I dismissed him, then checked the contents of the basket. A pigeon was trussed up and lay in the center of the basket. It was an ordinary pigeon, although its markings were rather beautiful. It had a white saddle across its gray back. I placed it on the bed.

The rest of the contents I had chosen randomly: an ear of corn; a piece of cloth; a white stone, not unlike smokey quartz. I arranged each item on the bed around the pigeon. When I finished, I carried the pigeon to the terrace and killed it.

I made a show of killing the pigeon, aware the waiters below would report my actions to Mazi. I broke the neck in half, prying it apart until it split. It was an ugly business, but a certain authority entered me. I tied a piece of twine to its two legs and began to swing the pigeon in a circle.

This had the desired effect. The split in the neck of the pigeon allowed a spray of blood to sporadically spray down on the terrace. A few diners—there weren't many—stood and moved away, looking up at me with their napkins to their mouths. Several exclaimed with surprise, but none told me to stop.

I didn't dare swing the pigeon too hard for fear the feet would snap off. As I made the last few circles, letting the pigeon appear to tire, I recited what I could remember of the "Jabberwocky." I felt ridiculous, but the tone of the poem, the careful rhythm and rhyme, were as much like a spell as anything I could recall.

Whatever my feeling about the ritual, it made an impression on the Africans below me. They stood in stunned amazement, watching everything I did. I grabbed the pigeon and made an incision down through its thorax. The internal organs were still warm. I dished them out over the terrace, scattering them as a man broadcasts seeds. The Africans moved back even farther. Finally, I spread my arms wide and backed inside.

Sitting on my bed, I spread the pigeon's breast wide and filled it with the cloth and five kernels of corn; I wedged the rock up toward the pigeon's neck, expanding its gorge as if it were puffed out in a mating dance.

Afterward, I waited for Father Joseph. He returned soon, his cassock damp with sweat. He had two photos. The first was a frontal shot of Mazi, who stared at the camera and the flash in complete wonder. It wasn't, I was sure, that he hadn't seen a camera before. It was only that he had been taken off-guard.

The second photograph was useless. It showed Mazi ducking under the table, his hand up to shield his face. The picture wasn't particularly clear.

"He ran after that," Father Joseph said, washing his face and hands in a bucket of water. "He seemed frightened."

Father Joseph watched as I took the frontal photo and attached it to the pigeon. I snapped off what remained of the pigeon's neck and head and placed it inside the breast of the bird. Then, carefully bending the picture, I pinned it to the blank breast of the pigeon, so that it looked in some hideous way like its head.

Father Joseph nodded his approval. I was about to close the breast when he had another idea. He left for about five minutes, and when he returned he had a pale ghekko lizard cupped in his palms.

Careful to keep the lizard trapped, he pulled back the pigeon breast far enough to slip the lizard inside. There was little room, but he quickly clamped the flaps shut. We slipped three rubber bands around the bird, pinching it entirely closed. The lizard, trapped inside, thrashed about enough to make the breast heave slightly, almost as if the headless bird breathed.

"It's blasphemous as hell, what I'm doing," Father Joseph said, then grinned.

I called George. He didn't raise his eyes at all. I held out the bird to him, but before I passed it over, he fell on the ground in front of me and pleaded not to make him carry it to Mazi. I felt pity for him, caught as he was between us, but I didn't think it wise to appear soft at this point. I told him to stand and take the bird. He stood, held out his hands, then made a startled cry as he sensed the lizard moving inside the bird.

"I'll make you a fetish to protect you from Mazi," I told him. "Now hurry and carry this to him."

"What do you want me to say, Nassarra?"

"Nothing. Just give it to him."

He walked rapidly, like a man carrying a hot kettle of water. I went to the terrace and watched him hurry up the street. Everyone he passed stepped backward.

IN THE DARKNESS, Mazi came again. I heard no sound; no disturbance woke me. It was as if Mazi had entered my dreams, pulling me to consciousness.

Rationally, I knew he must have climbed the building, gaining the balcony from the lattice of bougainvillea that grew across the front of the hotel, but I couldn't quiet the notion that he flew.

He wore the cloak he had worn the night before. The hyena head, worn like the rear cowl of a cape, gave him added stature. But it was the carved mask that mesmerized me. It was hideous in its heavy features, its hollow eyes and mouth. Looking into its eyes, I saw nothing—no pupils, no iris.

I waited for him to move. I drew my legs up, prepared to kick at him if he approached. The mosquito net hung between us, heightening the feeling that I was trapped. I had no weapon close at hand. I wanted the camera, but Father Joseph had taken it to his room.

I can't say how long he stood there. Slowly, I lifted the edge of the mosquito net and placed one foot on the floor. My toes touched, then my heel, and finally the arch of my sole. The smallest details were remarkably clear to me. Always I kept my eyes on him.

We didn't speak. I continued moving, gradually freeing myself from the mosquito net. My clumsiness annoyed me; the awkwardness of the motion, first sitting forward, then lifting the net over my head—all of it took too much of my attention. At last, however, I stood, my hand reaching out to steady myself on the net.

It was at that moment, with my attention slightly shifted, that Mazi stepped back over the porch railing. He did this with tremendous grace. One leg lifted, then the next. His eyes didn't leave mine. How he could have been sure of his footing, how he moved with such knowledge of the balcony, I didn't know. He made no threatening gestures.

Then he was gone. He dropped straight down from the ledge of the balcony, his hands out at his sides. He looked exactly like a man taking a step off the edge of a swimming pool. He made no waving motions with his arms to maintain his balance; he didn't look down. He didn't grab at anything. Most startling of all, I didn't hear him land.

I was quite sure of that. I listened attentively. A moment passed, then two, before I realized I listened to hear him hit the ground. The fall could have been easily survived, but it would have been impossible to perform it without sound.

I ran to the window, placed my hands on the balcony railing, and looked over.

The courtyard below was empty. This fact alone paralyzed me temporarily. Eventually I leaned farther out and looked both ways. To my left I saw the flamboyant tree; to the right the courtyard gave way to the road, then to the balfon on the outskirts of the village. The courtyard was made of loose gravel. Nothing could have landed on it from such a drop, then run across it, without creating a great deal of noise.

Pulling back, I noticed a pigeon resting on the cement floor of the balcony, its wings trussed, its legs held by twine. It was alive. Its chest moved rapidly, probably from fear, but it was undoubtedly alive. It was the pigeon I had sent Mazi. The saddle of white across its back was too distinctive to be mistaken for any other. I bent and picked it up, my breathing short and uneven.

The pigeon pecked softly at my hand. Its body quivered. Several times it tried to raise its wings, but they were tied by the same rubber bands we had used to hold the open chest cavity together. Clamping the bird to my chest, I used my free hand to inspect its body. The feathers on its breast were dense, but I fanned them back, looking for any scar or mark along the flesh. I expected to see nothing, but found a long red line, a scar, which seemed to have been mended without the use of stitches or gut.

I went to Father Joseph's door and knocked softly. His voice came through the door, but it was tentative and worried.

"Who's there?" he asked, and I knew from the sound of his voice that he spoke to the door which communicated to the hallway. When I knocked again, he realized it was me.

As soon as he opened the door, he saw the pigeon. For a moment he remained in the doorway. Finally he reached for the bird and began inspecting it.

"Was he here?" Father Joseph asked, turning on lights.

"Yes, on the balcony."

He looked old, standing in the dim light, morning just beginning outside the window. His hair was tousled; his eyes looked red and troubled. His hands, however, were tremendously gentle with the bird. He turned it back and forth, examining it from every angle. The pigeon's feathers captured what there was of light, glowing gray-pearl, then purple, then back to gray.

Father Joseph shook his head, then asked for my penknife. I gave it to him and he carried the pigeon to the balcony. I sat on the edge of the bed. A moment later he made a long incision in the bird's breast.

He stood and held the bird on the flat platform of the railing. The pigeon struggled for longer than I thought possible. It made a high, cawing sound which was, I suppose, only air escaping in a final rush from its lungs. Father Joseph kept it pinned to the top of the railing, his fingers turning red. Once he lifted his hand, but the pigeon continued to kick and he quickly pressed on the bird again.

At last the bird ceased moving. Father Joseph cut the twine that secured its legs. Then, deftly, he separated the breast. The cartilage yawned and cracked. Father Joseph placed the knife on the railing and used his thumbs to pull the breast completely apart.

He bent close to the bird. I didn't stand or move any nearer. I thought to tell him that Mazi had flown, or at least had dropped from the balcony without sound, but I could not form the words.

"Come here," he said.

"What is it?"

"I want you to see something."

I walked to the balcony. His fingers dug in the pigeon's breast. The bird moved back and forth, its legs flapping limply, its wings held away from its body as if to cool itself.

He picked one small white stone from the bird's craw. It wasn't entirely white, however. It was doused in blood and it wasn't until Father Joseph wiped it against the bird's feathers that I realized exactly what it was.

"Does this look like the stone?" he asked, setting it out on the railing.

"I think so."

"Do you remember anything particular about it?"

"No, not really."

"Of course it proves nothing," he said. "He may have fed it to the bird. It would have accomplished the same thing."

"I can't tell if it's the stone or not."

"He's very good, though, isn't he?" Father Joseph said with genuine admiration, shaking his head softly. "He's thorough and he's good. The pigeon would have been enough, but this . . ."

He finished with the pigeon; he found nothing else of interest. The intestines were clogged with millet. I returned to the room, found a pack of cigarettes, and brought them out to Father Joseph.

We had a drink out on the porch and smoked a few cigarettes. Father Joseph tossed the pigeon out on the courtyard and we waited for the dogs to find it. Eventually they came, their paws anxious on the gravel.

Father Joseph spoke finally, his voice careful.

"I'd like to hear your confession. It's probably a sin to ask a man for his confession, but I don't care. Will you do it?"

"I couldn't do that to you."

"Do what? Are you worried you'll pass on the curse to me? Maybe you would give me the ability to perform miracles—had you thought of that?" he asked, looking at me gently.

"It had occurred to me."

"It's a decision, isn't it? Maybe you've been touched by a saint. You might give up something extraordinary."

He looked at me and put his arm around me. I realized that I had become very fond of him. But to confess?

The most powerful feeling was my reluctance to give up Fraujas's soul. It was that exact phrase that repeated over and over in my mind: I could not release his soul. Whatever magic it possessed was mine. If I had indeed been touched by a saint, how could I allow this to pass from me?

I stalled. Eventually, however, I was too exhausted to resist. It no longer seemed to matter. If he wanted me to confess, I would. A tremendous lassitude entered me. Father Joseph's intentions were honorable—I saw that. I nodded to him and he began the sacrament.

I was astonished at how words and phrases came back to me. I felt, for lack of a better phrase, to be speaking in tongues. Before a thought could be digested, my tongue pronounced the word. All of it was translated immediately into French. I didn't think at all in English.

Father Joseph gave the appropriate responses, his rosary in hand. I didn't notice at first how hard he gripped it. His fingers completely covered the crucifix. But his hand trembled. His entire body shook slightly and I couldn't escape the impression that my confession was entering him forcibly.

"Are you all right?" I asked.

"Yes, go ahead," he said, his voice husky and distant.

When I stopped, Father Joseph granted me absolution. He appeared very weak. His hand continued to clutch his rosary, while his other arm supported him on the railing.

"Are you all right?" I asked again.

"I'm fine," he said. "I think we should leave today."

"I agree."

"I'm going back to my room and pack. We should go while it's still cool."

He left. A short time later I heard him praying. He spoke quietly, but I had no doubt it was the drone of his rosary. I had never heard him pray before.

BY NINE IN THE MORNING it was a hundred degrees. We spread cotton shirts across the upholstery of the truck to protect our legs from the heat. The buttons turned into hot pinpoints, and we had to shift on the seats before we could sit comfortably.

Father Joseph started the engine. The sound of the engine

turning over brought home to me what we were about to do. We had purposely avoided speaking of the circle as we packed. Now, however, with the engine pushing more heat up through the floor, I couldn't think of anything else.

"Are you ready?" Father Joseph asked.

I nodded. He shifted into gear and we began moving.

"There he is. There's Mazi," Father Joseph said.

"Where?" I asked.

Father Joseph pointed across the front of the truck, off to our right. I followed his finger, but I saw nothing. I glanced quickly at Father Joseph. He still watched to his right, staring at something in the bright sunlight. I looked again in the direction he indicated; I didn't see anything.

Before I could speak, we arrived at the line. Father Joseph didn't stop the truck, nor did he slow down. "Now," Father Joseph said in a whisper. "Now," he said again, as if to be sure that we had passed over the line.

I felt nothing strange. My pulse was steady, my stomach quiet. I had the merest headache, but that, I suspected, was from tension.

I turned to tell Father Joseph, then saw he could barely sit up straight behind the wheel. I reached for his shoulder but he knocked away my hand.

"We have to get out of the village," he said.

His skin had turned blank white. His eyes barely remained open. Twice, while I watched him, his hands slipped from the steering wheel.

"Turn around," I said. "We should turn around."

"I'll be all right."

"No you won't. Turn around."

But he continued driving out of town. We passed over the earthen bridge that stretched across the balfon. There was an instant of intense light from the reflection of sunlight on water, then we were in the open bush, alone for the first time in several days.

"Take the wheel," Father Joseph said, stopping the truck.

He made no attempt to get out. As I ran around to his side,

he inched over into the passenger's seat. As soon as he was there, he retched out the window, his entire body convulsing.

"Keep going," he said.

I drove. I drove fast at first, thinking somehow that distance would protect us. We weren't more than five or six kilometers from the village when I heard a change enter his breathing. His chest barely moved. The air that passed up his throat stuttered on its way out. A liquid gurgle entered the pattern, and several times he tried weakly to cough up phlegm. His eyes closed. When I called his name, he didn't respond.

I took his hand and gradually slowed the truck. He panted in the heat. I sat for a moment trying to think what to do. Flies buzzed. A few birds dipped across the open plain, their colors exceedingly bright.

There was only one thing to do and I went about it quickly. I drove another hundred yards until we came to a likely place, then stopped. As soon as I turned the truck off, I jumped out and untied the ropes securing the luggage. Once I had freed several lengths, I hurried to the small copse of trees off the road and began fabricating a hammock.

It was, of course, the cure Father Joseph had talked about himself. It was the cure Fatama received before she left for Ghana. I knew it was essential to break Father Joseph's connection with the earth. Mazi drew his power from the land; to escape him meant it was necessary to leave the ground altogether.

I tested the ropes to make sure they would hold his weight, then went to the truck for Father Joseph. At first glance I feared he was dead. But his breathing still continued, shallow though it was, and he even coughed softly as I pulled him from the front seat.

I picked him up in a fireman's carry. He wasn't heavy. I nearly stumbled on the road bed as I climbed down to the hammock. Small stones skidded under my feet and I had to caution myself to take things slowly. Three lizards ran up the trees, their yellow necks bright against the pale bark.

I removed his clothes when I had him near the hammock. He was too weak to help me and this took some time. I had to support his weight while I wrestled his cassock slowly over his head. Finally I removed his underwear and placed him completely naked on the webs of ropes.

As soon as he was safely suspended, I ripped his clothes apart. I ripped his cassock into long strips. In a short while I had a pile of white bandages. I placed them over his body, but they wouldn't remain in position. I went to the truck, removed a large five-gallon jug of water, and poured the water into a trough near the side of the road. The dirt turned instantly to mud. Dropping to my knees, I took the strips and caked them in the soft soil, rolling them until they were well-covered. I tucked each bandage into a round coil so that they would be easier to wrap around his body.

With the damp bandages, I constructed a cast around Father Joseph. I lay the bandages on very carefully. Beginning at his crown, I moved down his body slowly. I did his back first, then stretched the bandages around to his front. I left no gap except at his mouth. I covered his eyes and ears; I covered his stomach and chest, returning to the mud several times to make the bandages more pliable. I smoothed the bandages onto his skin, hoping the mud would cake on his chest hair and hold the bandages close. I wanted no air to enter. I wanted Mazi to have no access.

As soon as the bandages were applied, they began to dry in the sunlight. They stayed together, held in place more perfectly than I could have imagined. I bent to his lips and felt breath on my ear.

I brought more water and applied it throughout the afternoon. I fashioned a straw from a piece of dried grass. I unloaded our baggage and formed a small ring around us. It was probable, I realized, that animals would be attracted to the scent of his body. I carried Father Joseph's shotgun to the ring of baggage and kept it propped near me.

By nightfall, Father Joseph's breathing was regular. I gave him warm soup through a straw, but it was a messy business.

When it became completely dark, I placed the shotgun across my lap and stood guard. There were no wood for fire. I didn't sleep. The stars came out above me. I heard Father Joseph urinate and, a little later, I heard a pack of dogs draw near. I shouted and threw a rock at them and eventually they disappeared.

I waited, of course, for Mazi. I promised myself that I would shoot him if he came near. I would murder him without the slightest hesitation. Several times during the night I actually placed the gun to my shoulder, thinking I heard him. Each time it turned out to be just an animal, or the wind brushing against a bush.

It was completely dark, the very center of the night, when Father Joseph spoke. His voice was little more than a whisper, but it was distinct. I moved closer. His voice came from deep in his body.

"Water," he said.

I gave it to him, sliding the drops down the dry grass. My eyes continued to search around the campsite. I was still looking around me when I heard Father Joseph begin his confession—at least I believed it was his confession. I backed away before I could be certain. His voice was too soft to carry more than a foot, and I moved to the farthest edge of the campsite so that I wouldn't hear him. Perhaps, after all, it wasn't his confession. Perhaps it was only his subconscious speaking mumbled words. I couldn't tell and I had no desire to find out. I stood guard and watched until it was morning, then fed him breakfast and went to sleep.